allergic

Megan Wagner Lloyd
and Michelle Mee Nutter

An Imprint of
📖 SCHOLASTIC

For Lucy
M. W. L.

For Ethan
M. M. N.

Library of Congress Control Number: 2019957352

ISBN 978-1-338-56891-2 (hardcover)
ISBN 978-1-338-56890-5 (paperback)

10 9 8 7 6 5 4 3 2 1   21 22 23 24 25

Printed in the U.S.A.   40
First edition, March 2021

Color flatting by Veda Kasireddy and Madison Coyne

Edited by Cassandra Pelham Fulton
Creative Director: Phil Falco
Publisher: David Saylor

Chapter One

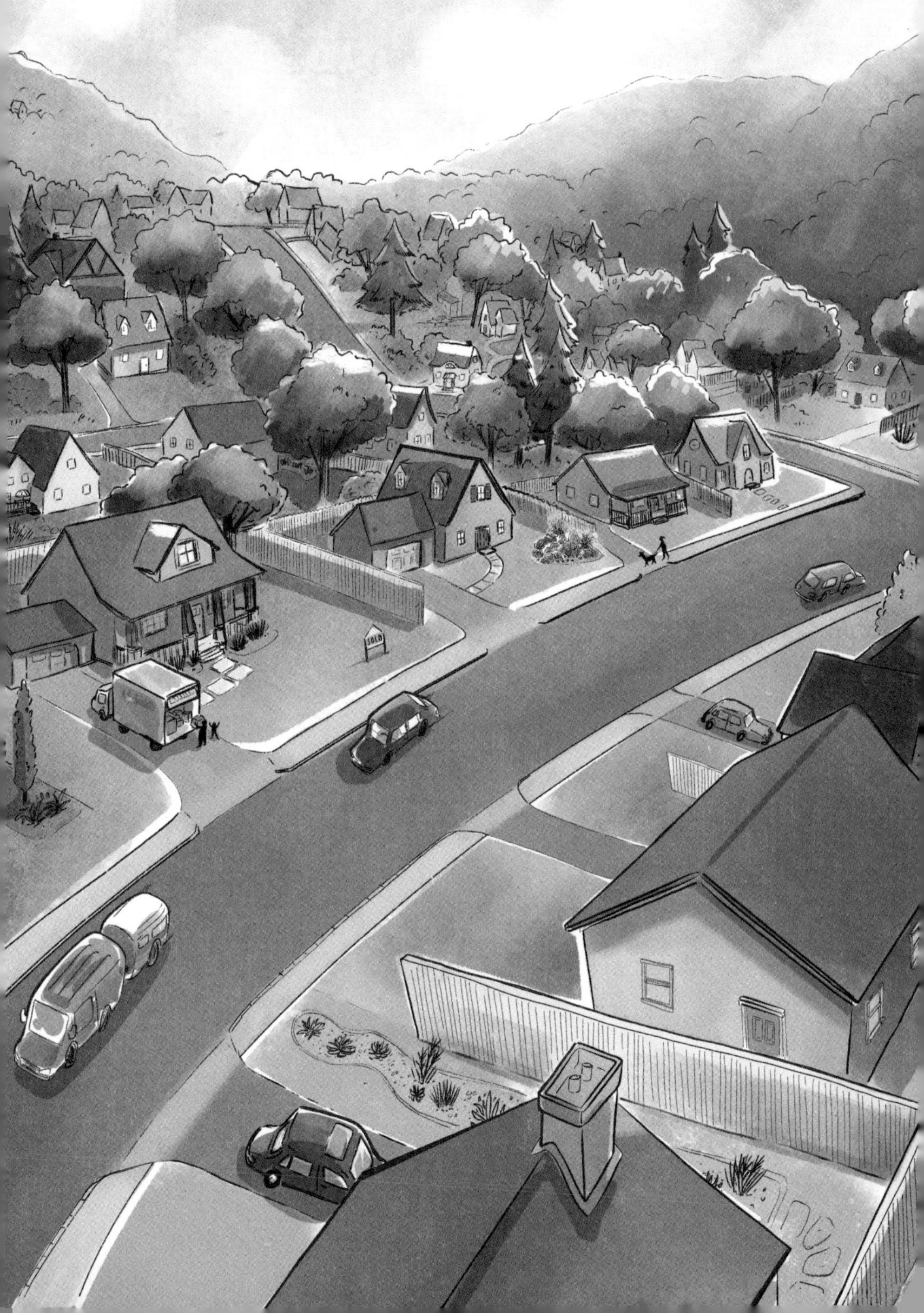
SOLD

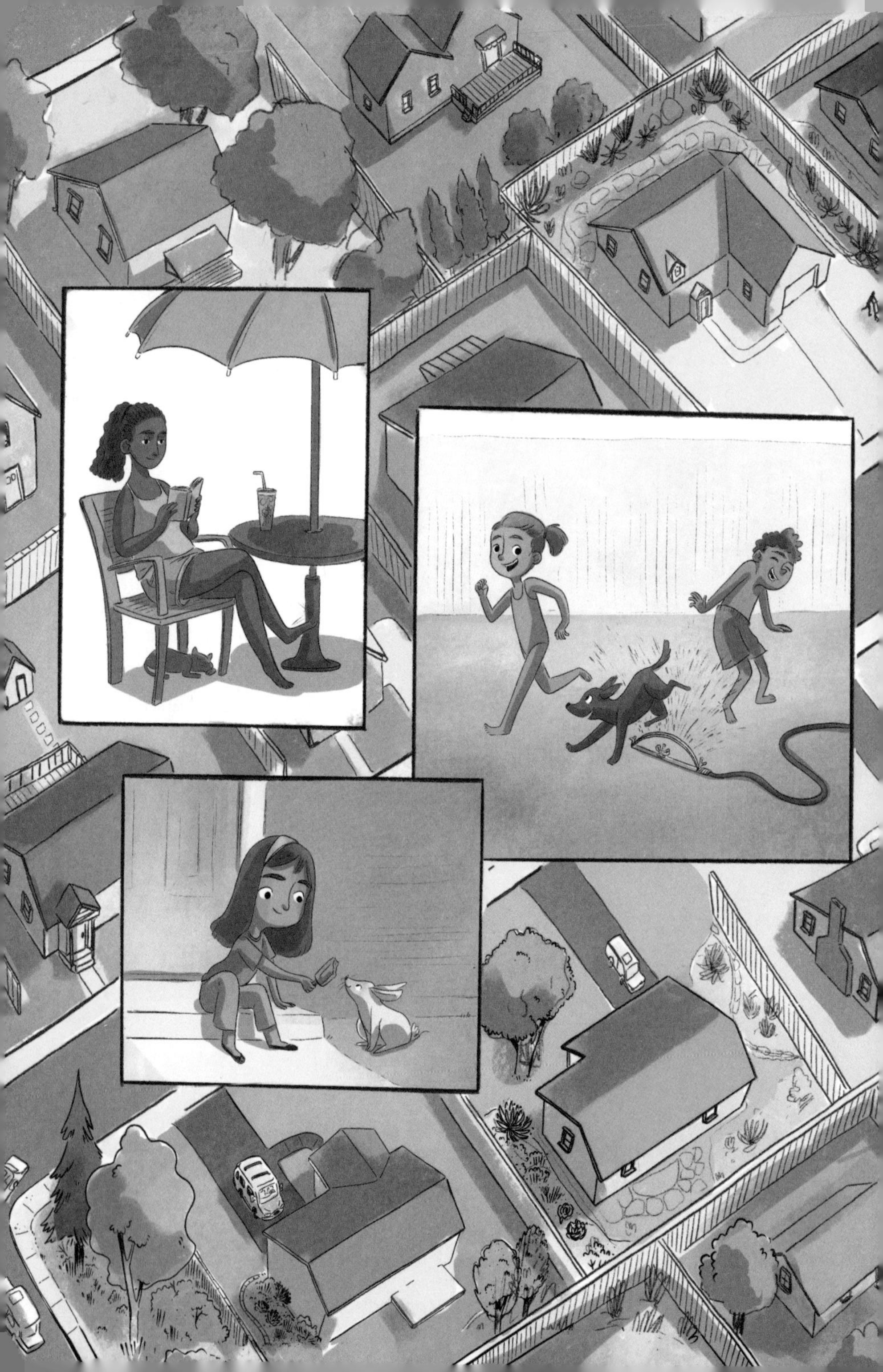

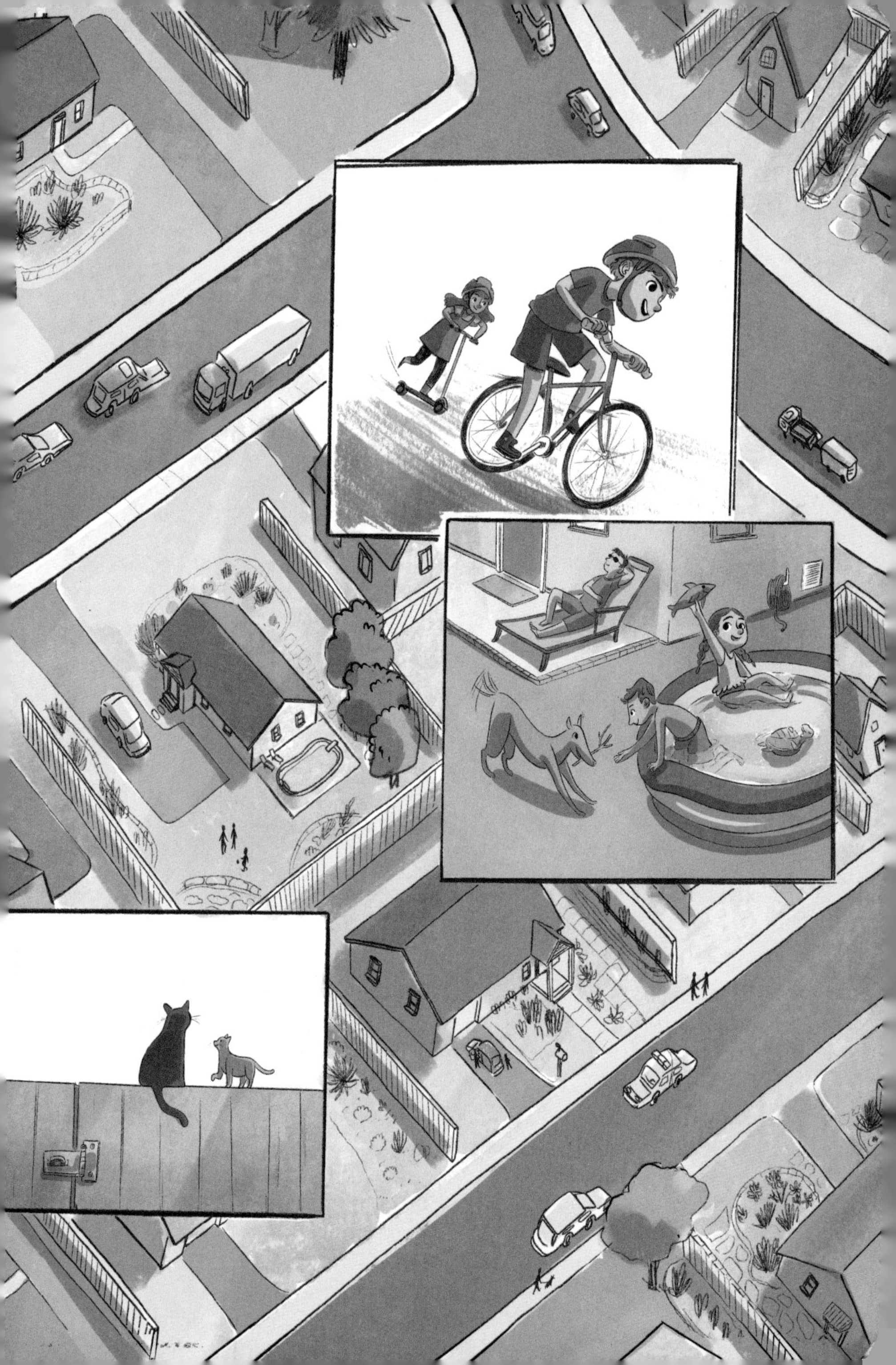

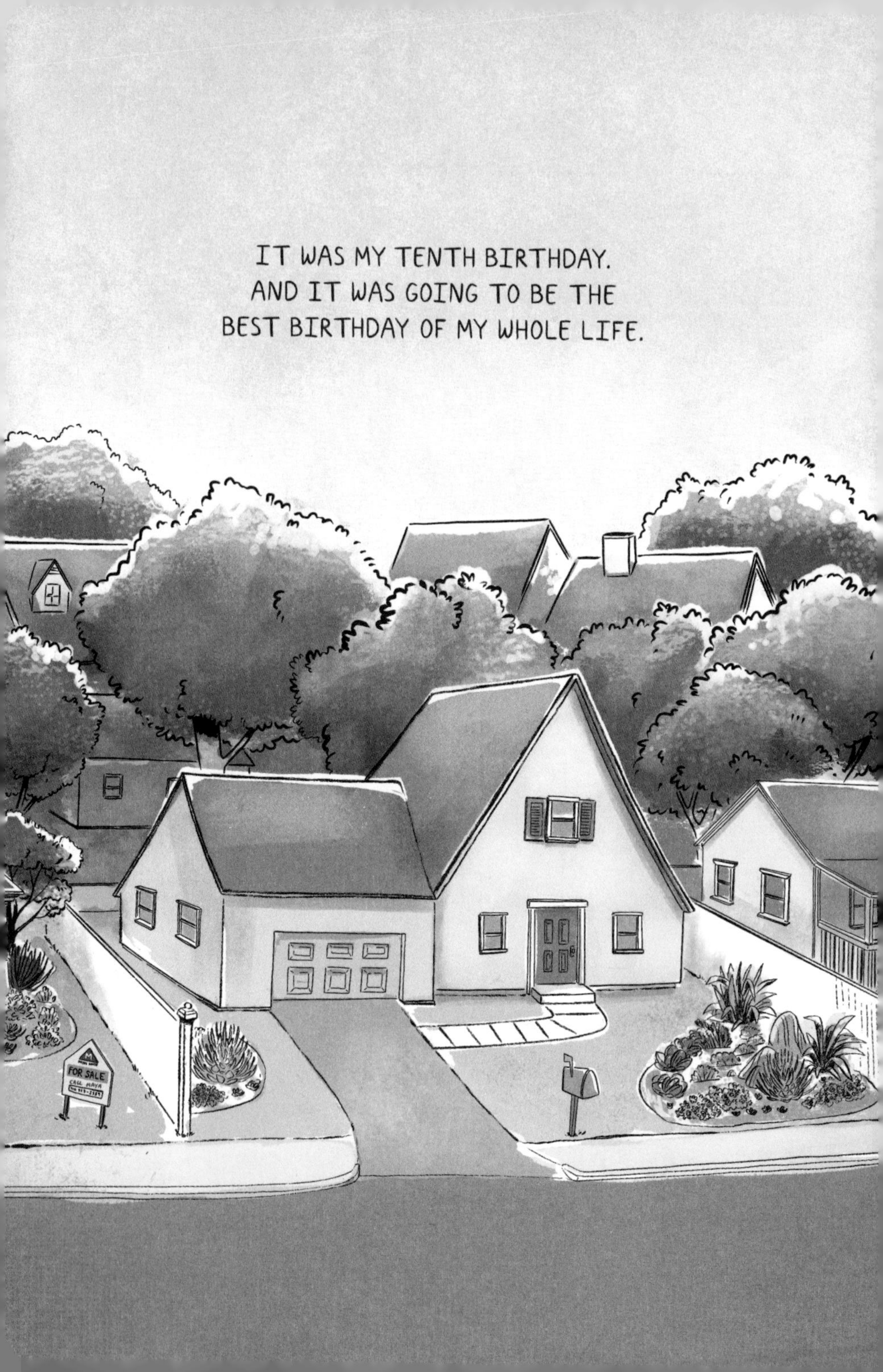
IT WAS MY TENTH BIRTHDAY. AND IT WAS GOING TO BE THE BEST BIRTHDAY OF MY WHOLE LIFE.
FOR SALE

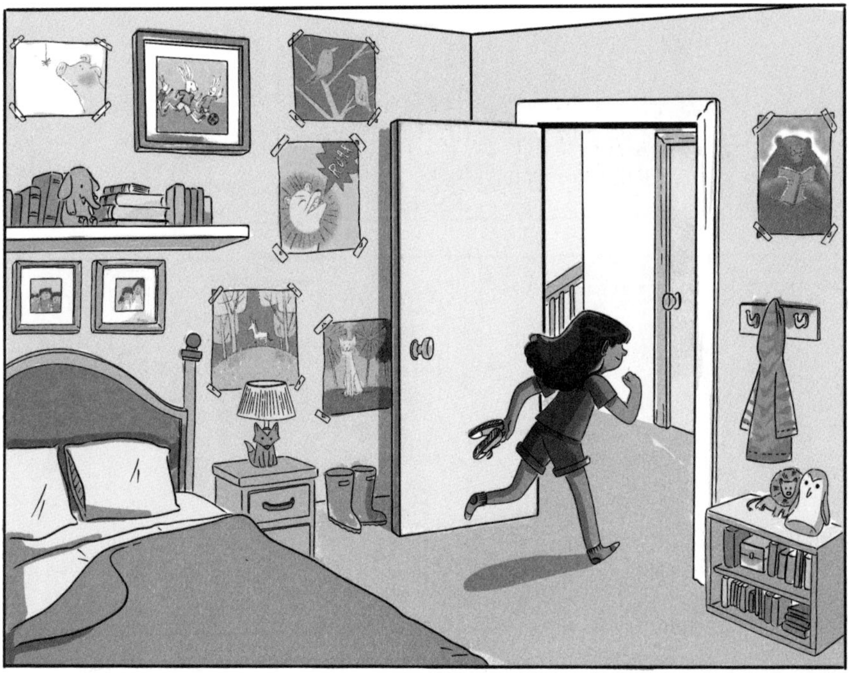

THE BEST **DAY** OF MY ENTIRE LIFE, PERIOD.

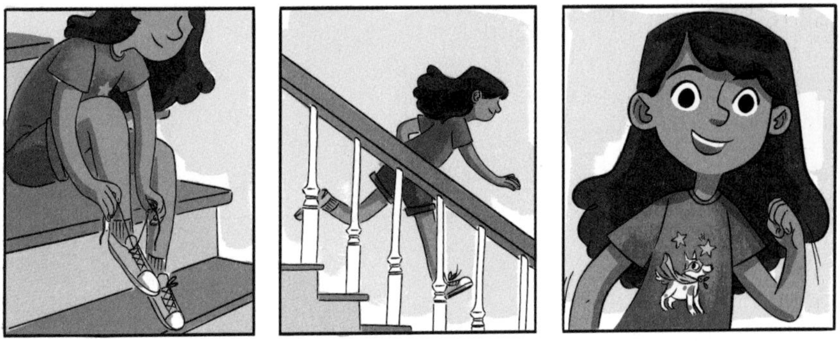

I WAS SURE OF IT.

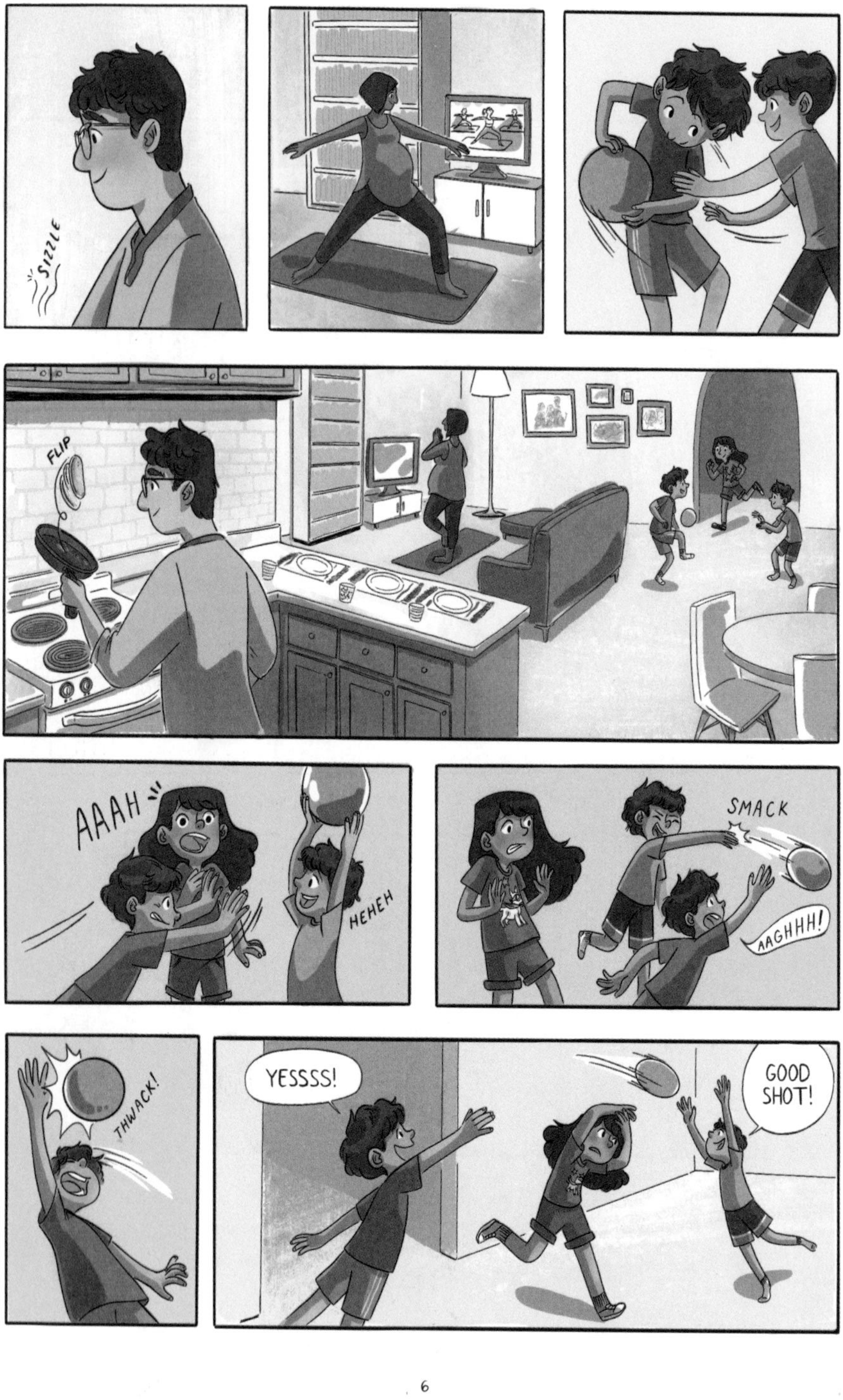
SIZZLE
FLIP
AAAH
HEHEH
SMACK
AAGHHH!
THWACK!
YESSSS!
GOOD SHOT!

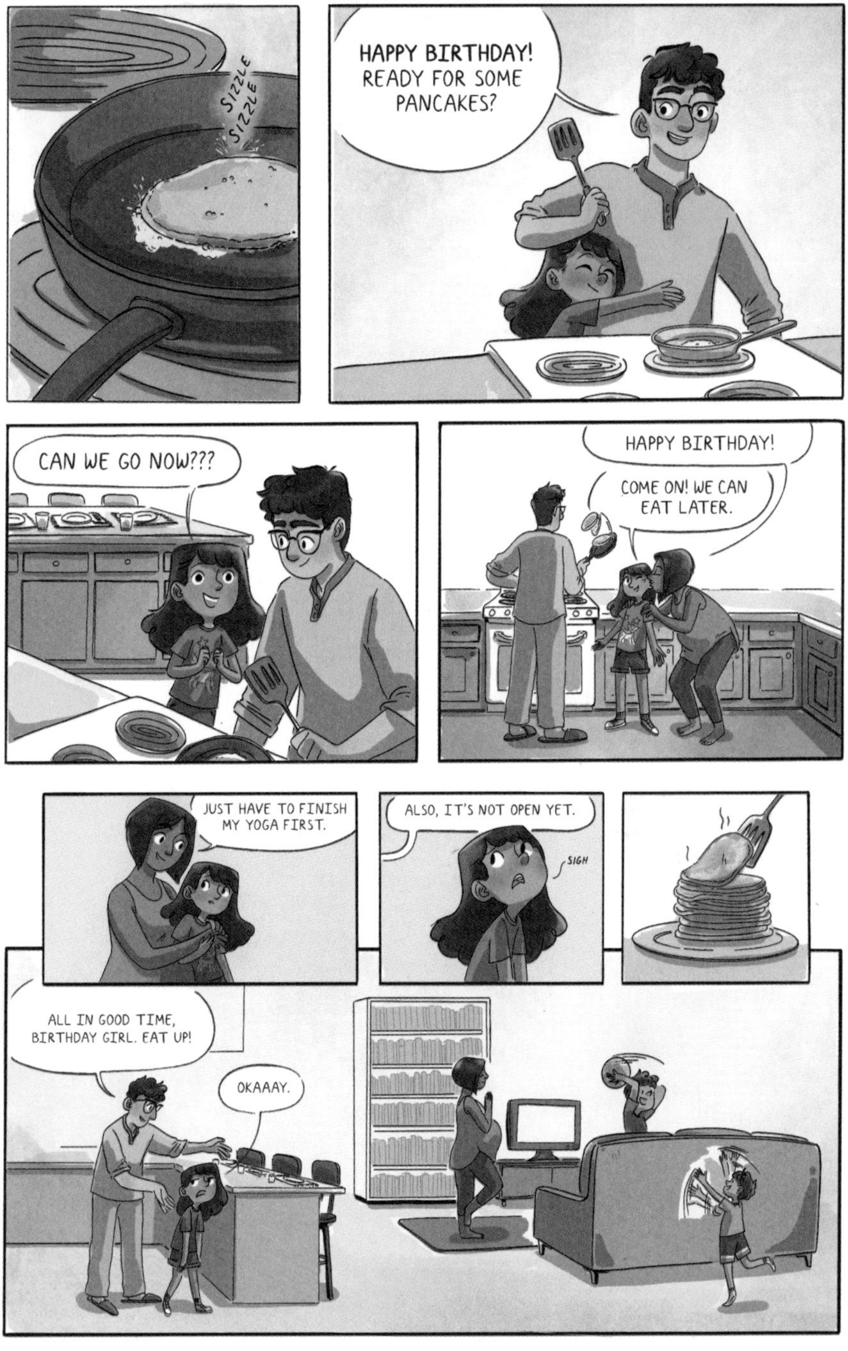
SIZZLE
SIZZLE
HAPPY BIRTHDAY! READY FOR SOME PANCAKES?
CAN WE GO NOW???
HAPPY BIRTHDAY!
COME ON! WE CAN EAT LATER.
JUST HAVE TO FINISH MY YOGA FIRST.
ALSO, IT'S NOT OPEN YET.
SIGH
ALL IN GOOD TIME, BIRTHDAY GIRL. EAT UP!
OKAAAY.

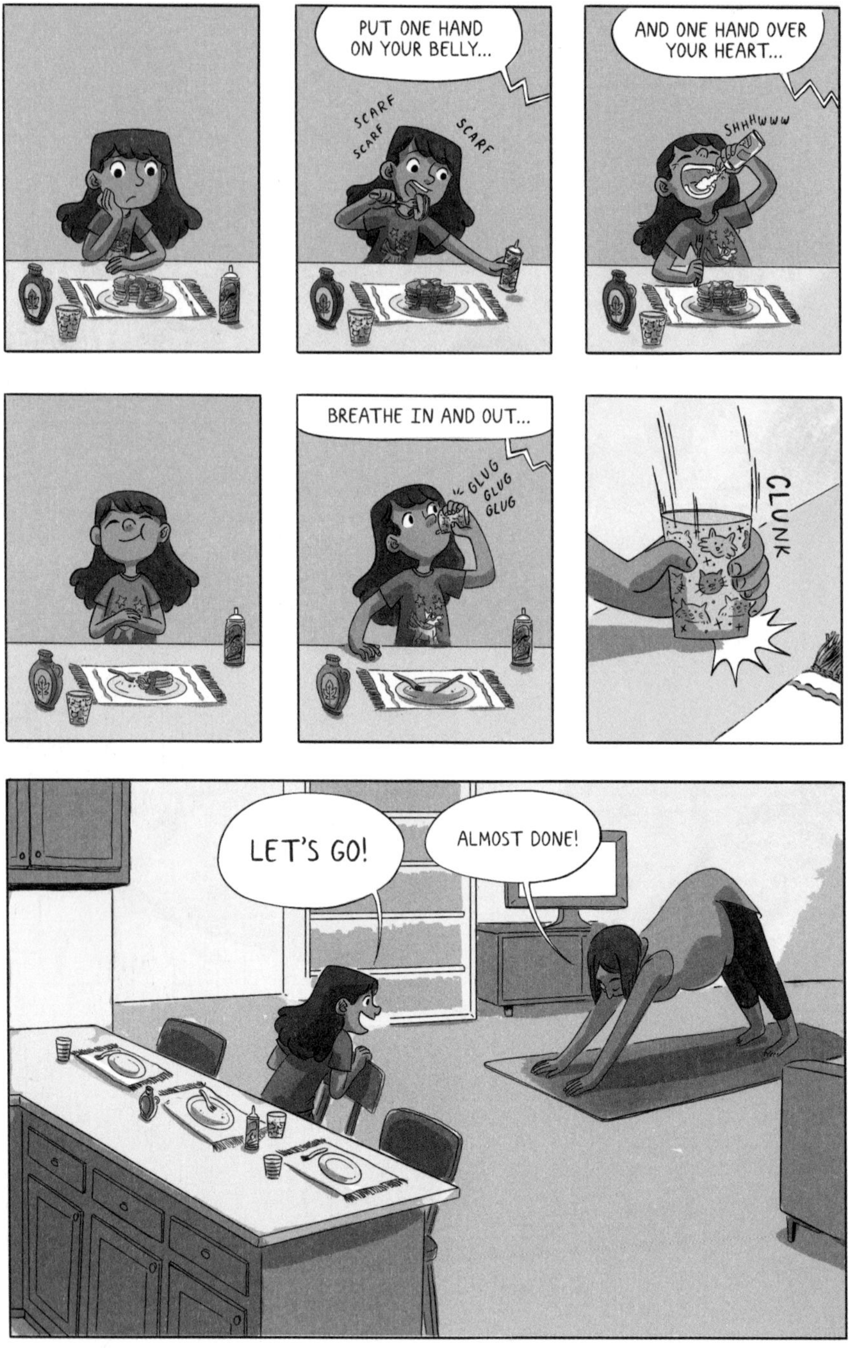
PUT ONE HAND ON YOUR BELLY...
SCARF SCARF
SCARF
AND ONE HAND OVER YOUR HEART...
SHHHWWW
BREATHE IN AND OUT...
GLUG GLUG GLUG
CLUNK
LET'S GO!
ALMOST DONE!

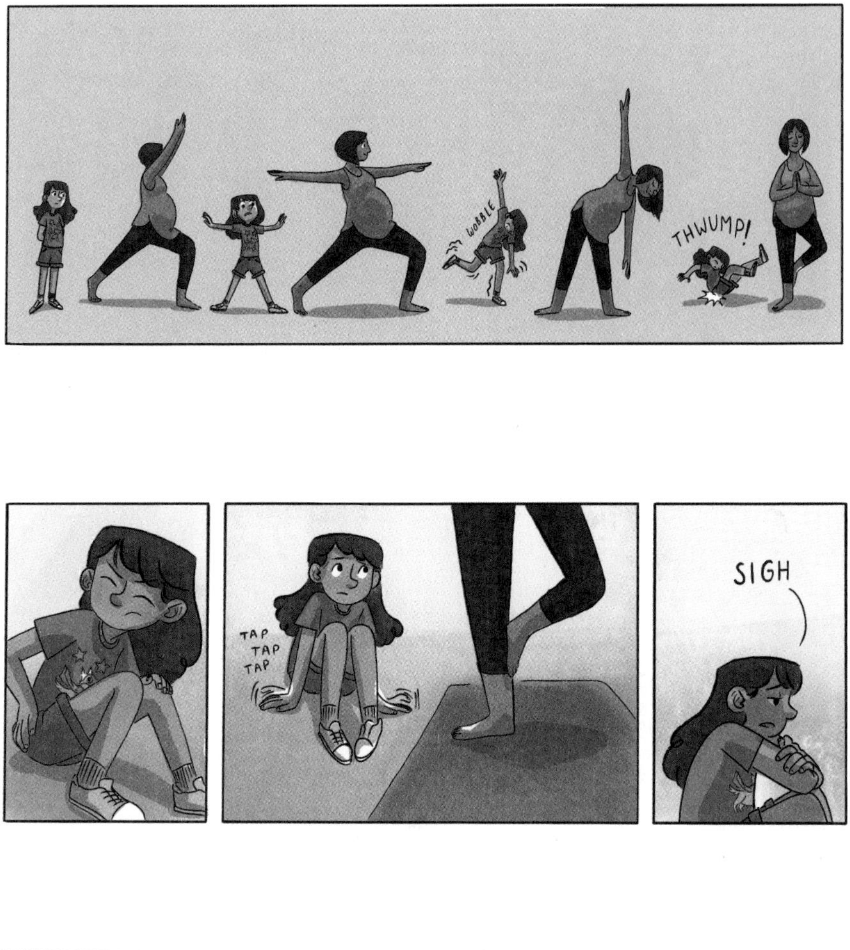
WOBBLE
THWUMP!
TAP
TAP
TAP
SIGH
NOM
NOM
NOM
NOM
SSSHHK
TRY TO APPRECIATE THIS MOMENT. FEEL YOUR HEART EXPAND.

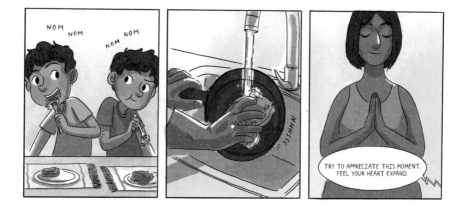

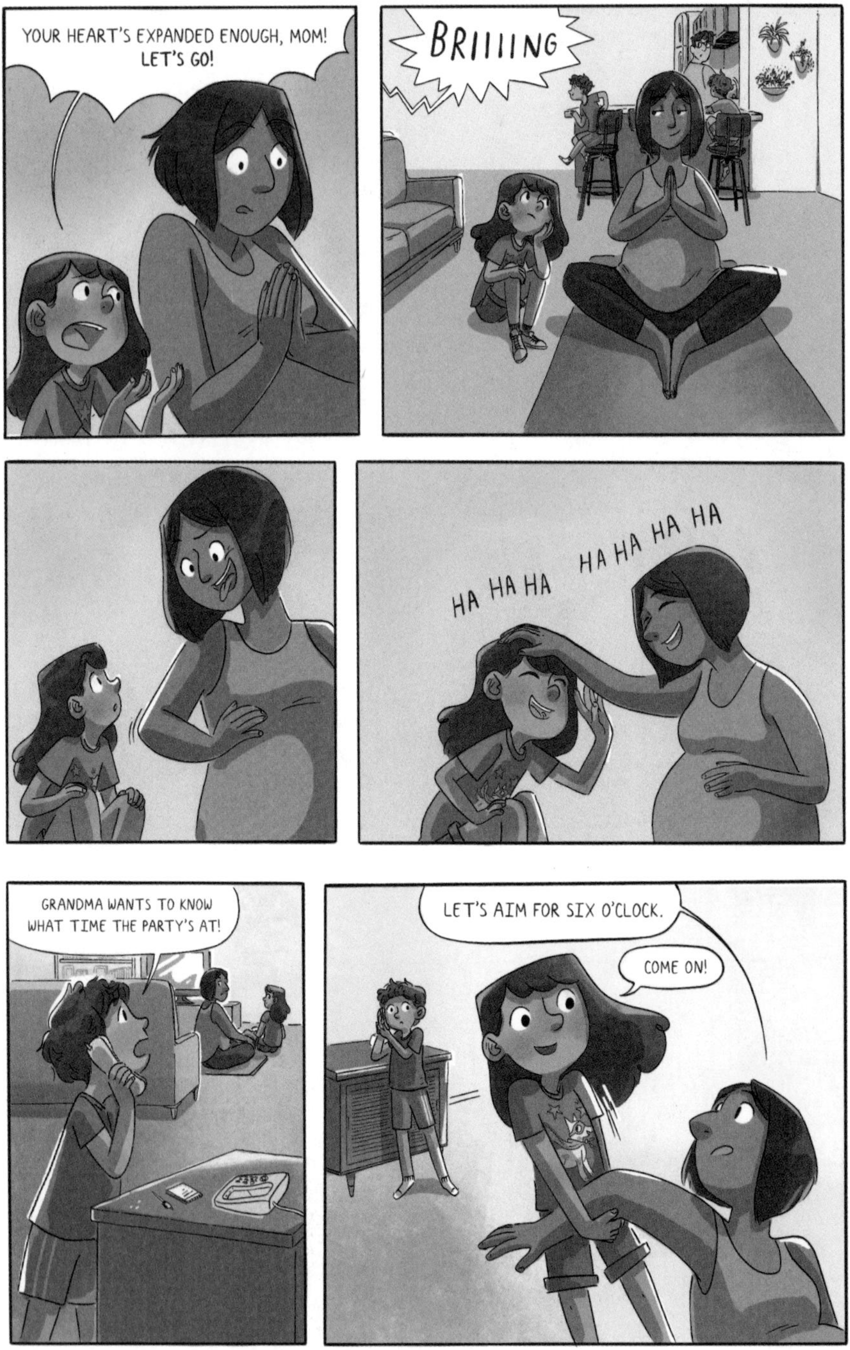
YOUR HEART'S EXPANDED ENOUGH, MOM! LET'S GO!
BRIIIING
HA HA HA
HA HA HA HA
GRANDMA WANTS TO KNOW WHAT TIME THE PARTY'S AT!
LET'S AIM FOR SIX O'CLOCK.
COME ON!

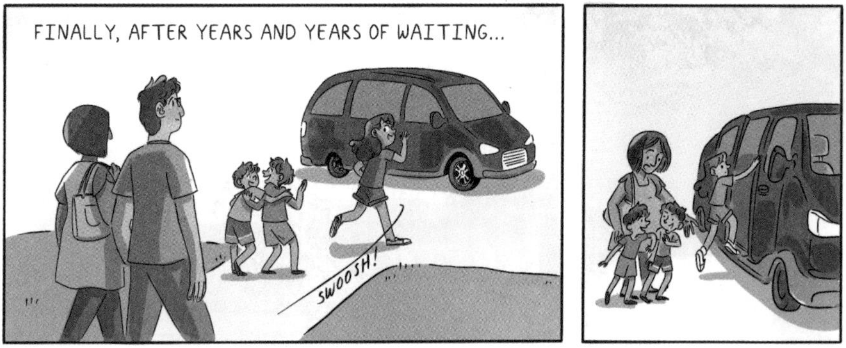
FINALLY, AFTER YEARS AND YEARS OF WAITING...
SWOOSH!

OF WISHING AND HOPING AND BEGGING...

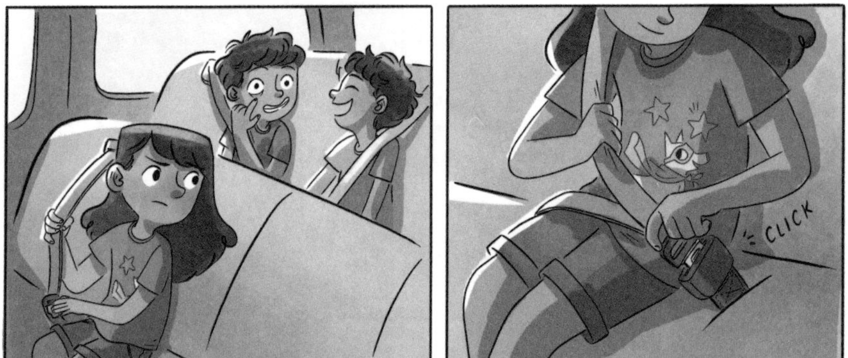
CLICK

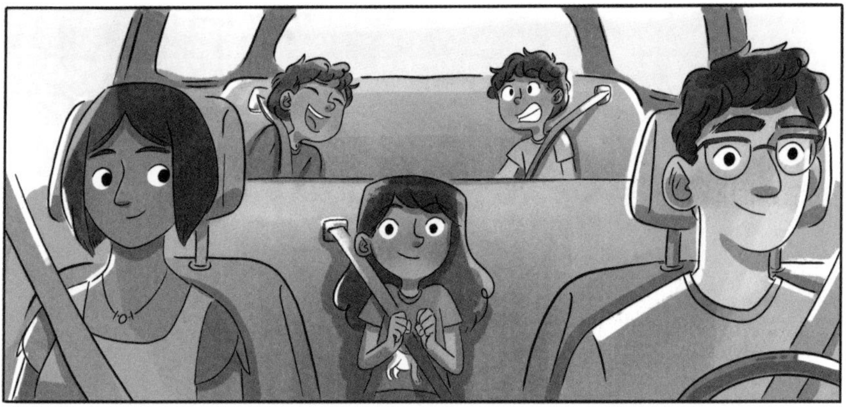

AT LAST, I WAS GETTING MY VERY OWN DOG.

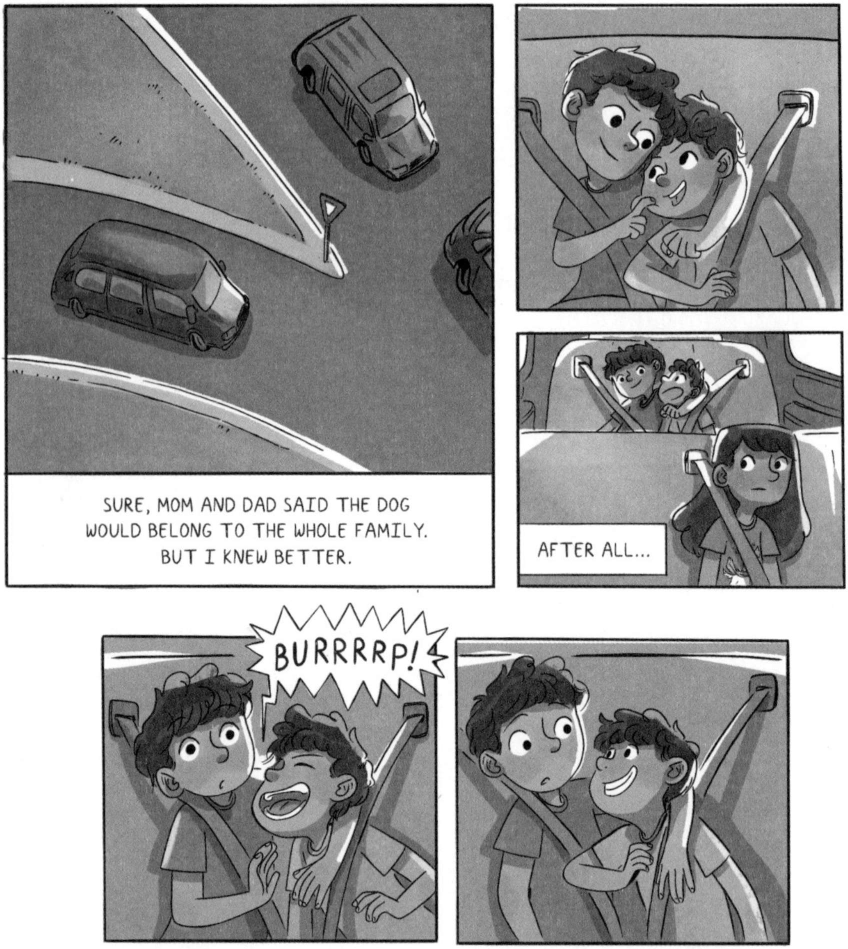
SURE, MOM AND DAD SAID THE DOG WOULD BELONG TO THE WHOLE FAMILY. BUT I KNEW BETTER.
AFTER ALL...
BURRRRP!

LIAM AND NOAH DIDN'T REALLY PAY ATTENTION TO ANYONE...

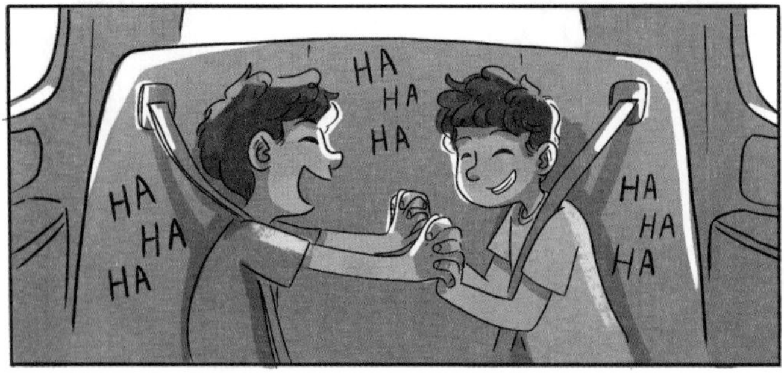
HA HA HA
HA HA HA
HA HA HA

BUT EACH OTHER.

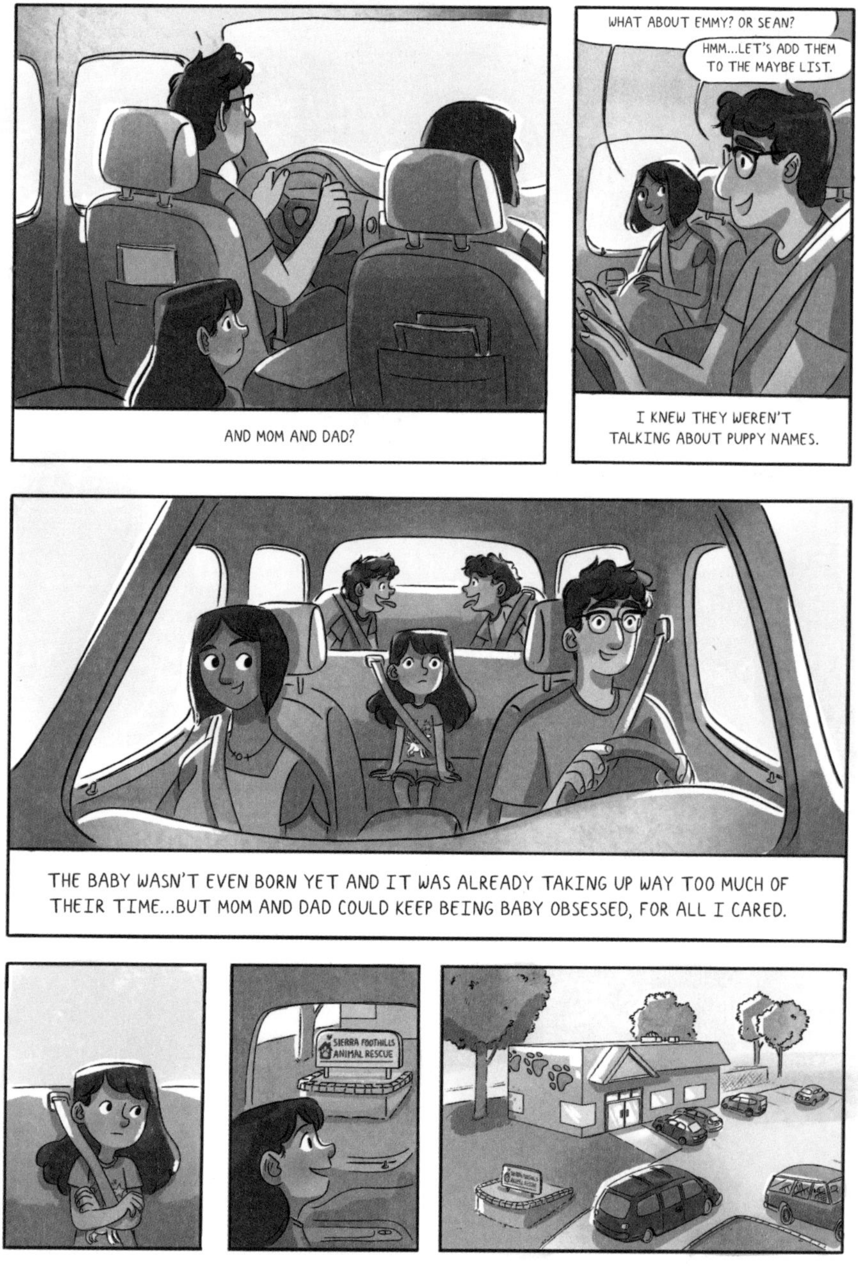
AND MOM AND DAD?
WHAT ABOUT EMMY? OR SEAN?
HMM...LET'S ADD THEM TO THE MAYBE LIST.
I KNEW THEY WEREN'T TALKING ABOUT PUPPY NAMES.
THE BABY WASN'T EVEN BORN YET AND IT WAS ALREADY TAKING UP WAY TOO MUCH OF THEIR TIME...BUT MOM AND DAD COULD KEEP BEING BABY OBSESSED, FOR ALL I CARED.
SIERRA FOOTHILLS ANIMAL RESCUE

THAT JUST MEANT THE DOG WOULD BE MINE.

ALL MINE.

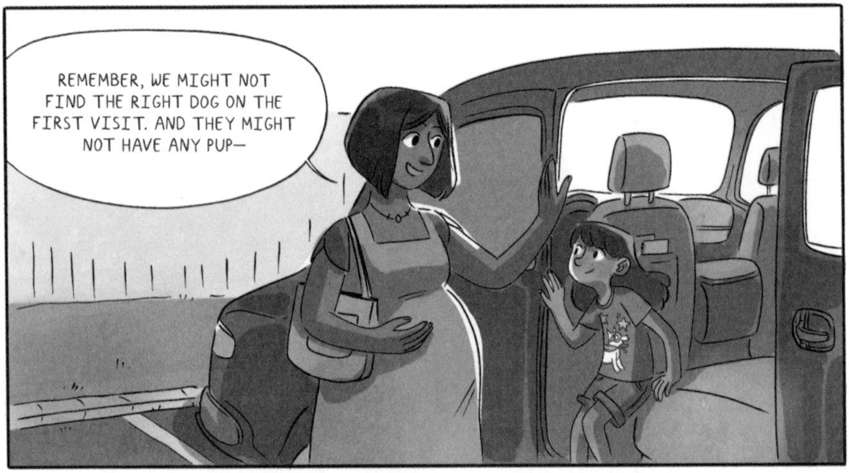
REMEMBER, WE MIGHT NOT FIND THE RIGHT DOG ON THE FIRST VISIT. AND THEY MIGHT NOT HAVE ANY PUP—

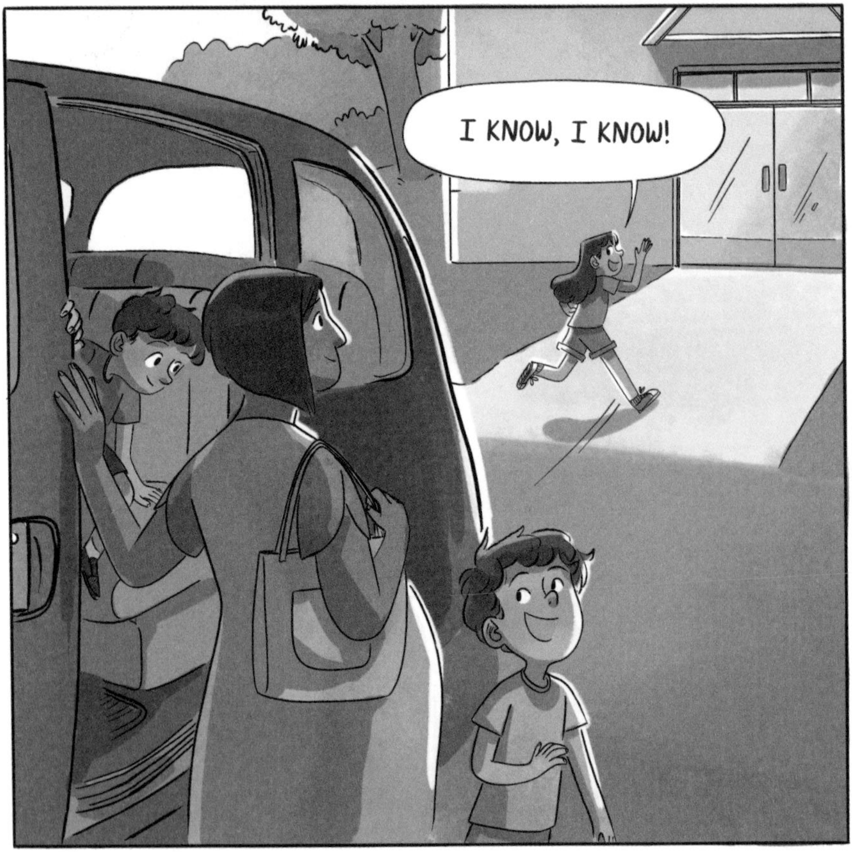
I KNOW, I KNOW!

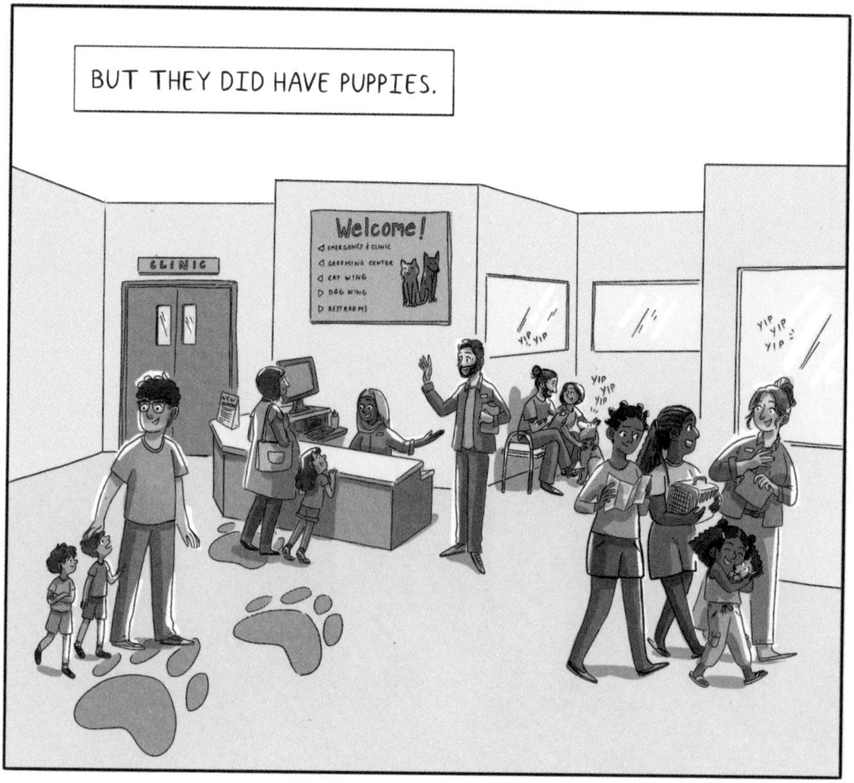
BUT THEY DID HAVE PUPPIES.
CLINIC
Welcome!
EMERGENCY & CLINIC
GROOMING CENTER
CAT WING
DOG WING
RESTROOMS
YIP YIP
YIP YIP YIP
YIP YIP YIP

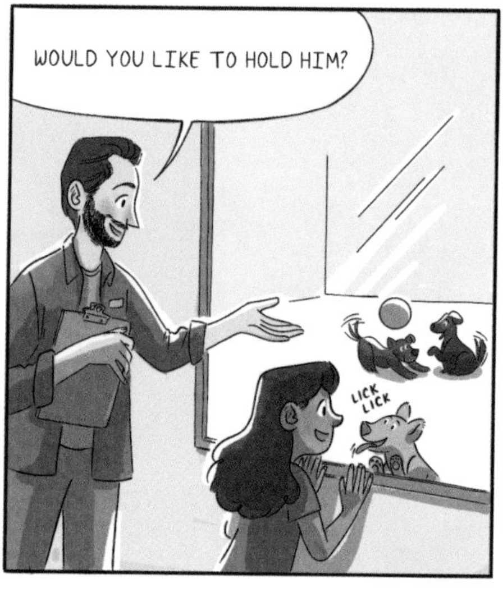
WOULD YOU LIKE TO HOLD HIM?
LICK LICK

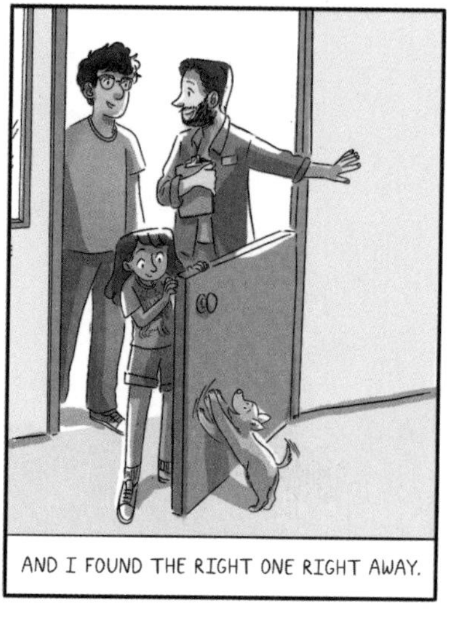
AND I FOUND THE RIGHT ONE RIGHT AWAY.

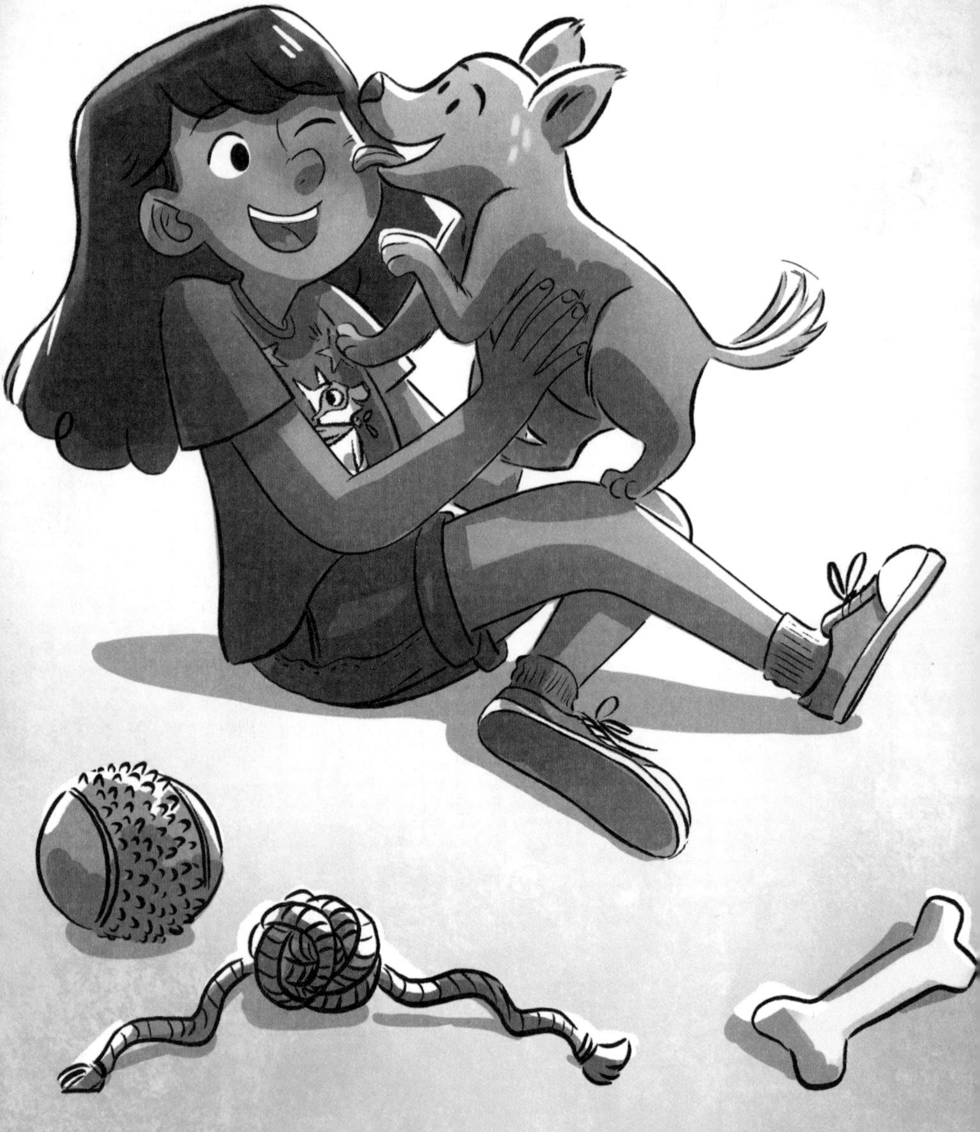

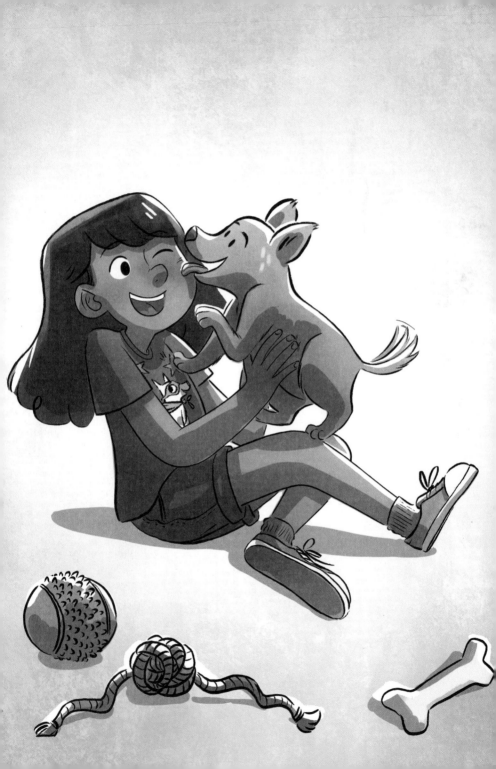

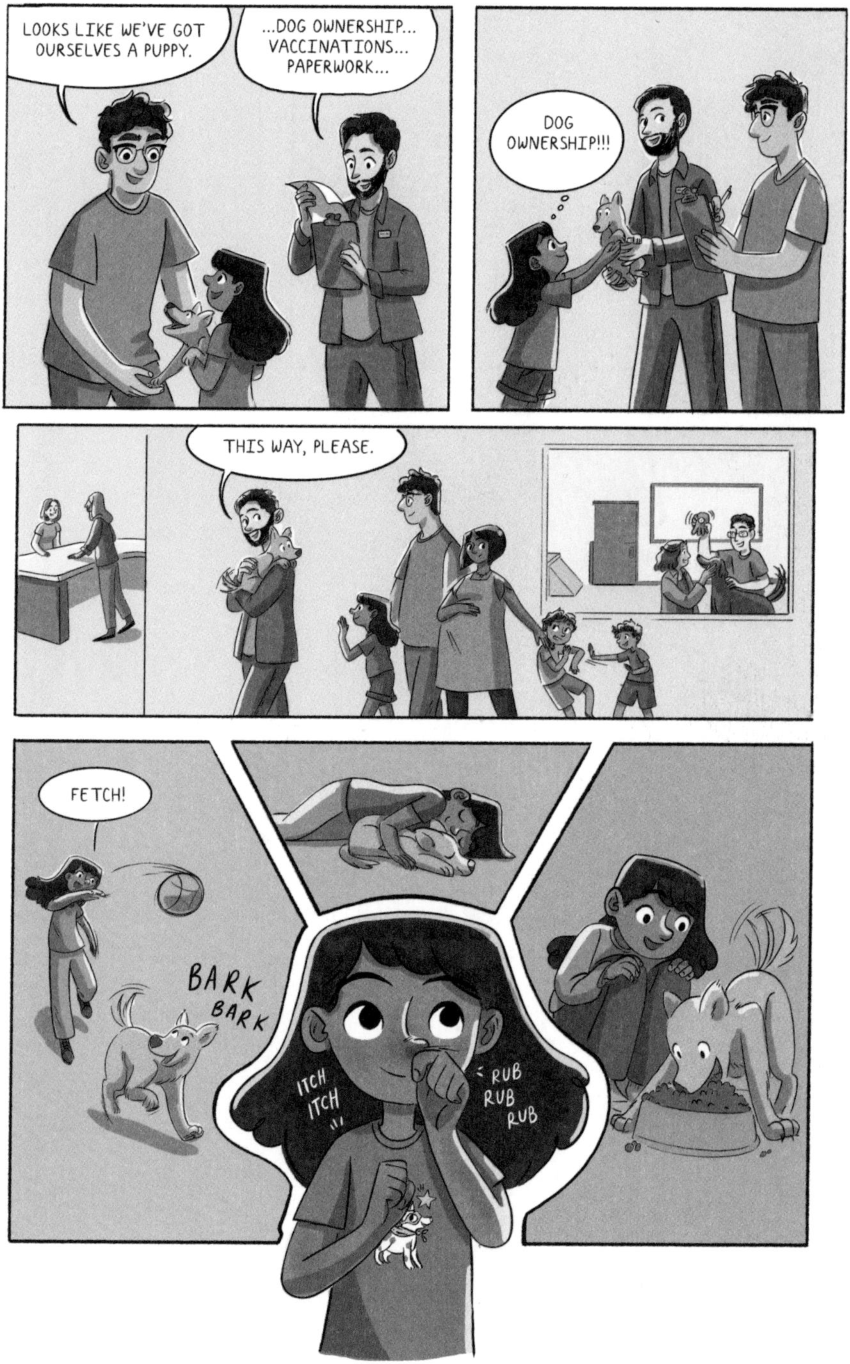
LOOKS LIKE WE'VE GOT OURSELVES A PUPPY.
...DOG OWNERSHIP... VACCINATIONS... PAPERWORK...
DOG OWNERSHIP!!!
THIS WAY, PLEASE.
FETCH!
BARK BARK
ITCH ITCH
RUB RUB RUB

ALL I WANTED TO THINK ABOUT WAS MY PUPPY.

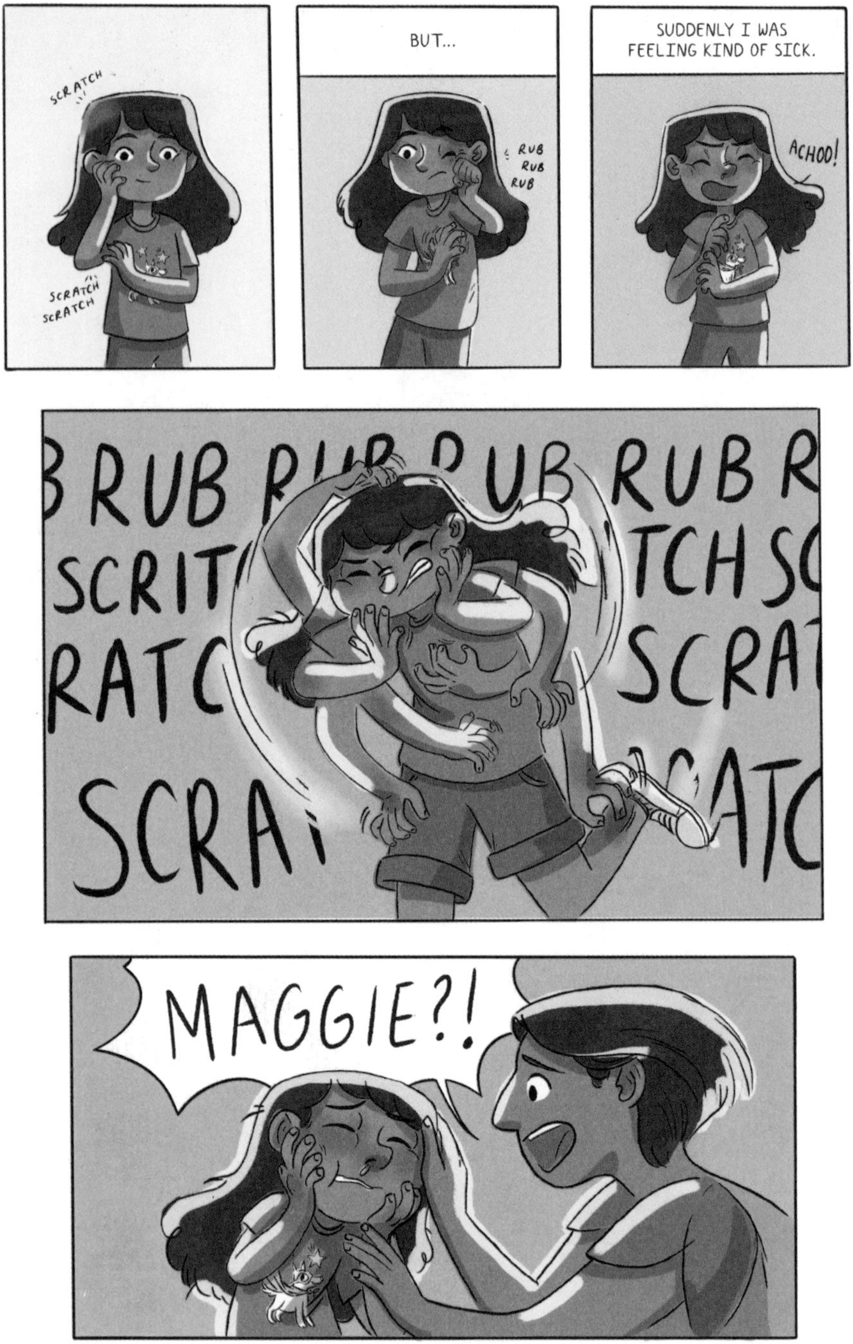
SCRATCH
SCRATCH SCRATCH
BUT...
RUB RUB RUB
SUDDENLY I WAS FEELING KIND OF SICK.
ACHOO!
RUB RUB RUB
SCRATCH
MAGGIE?!

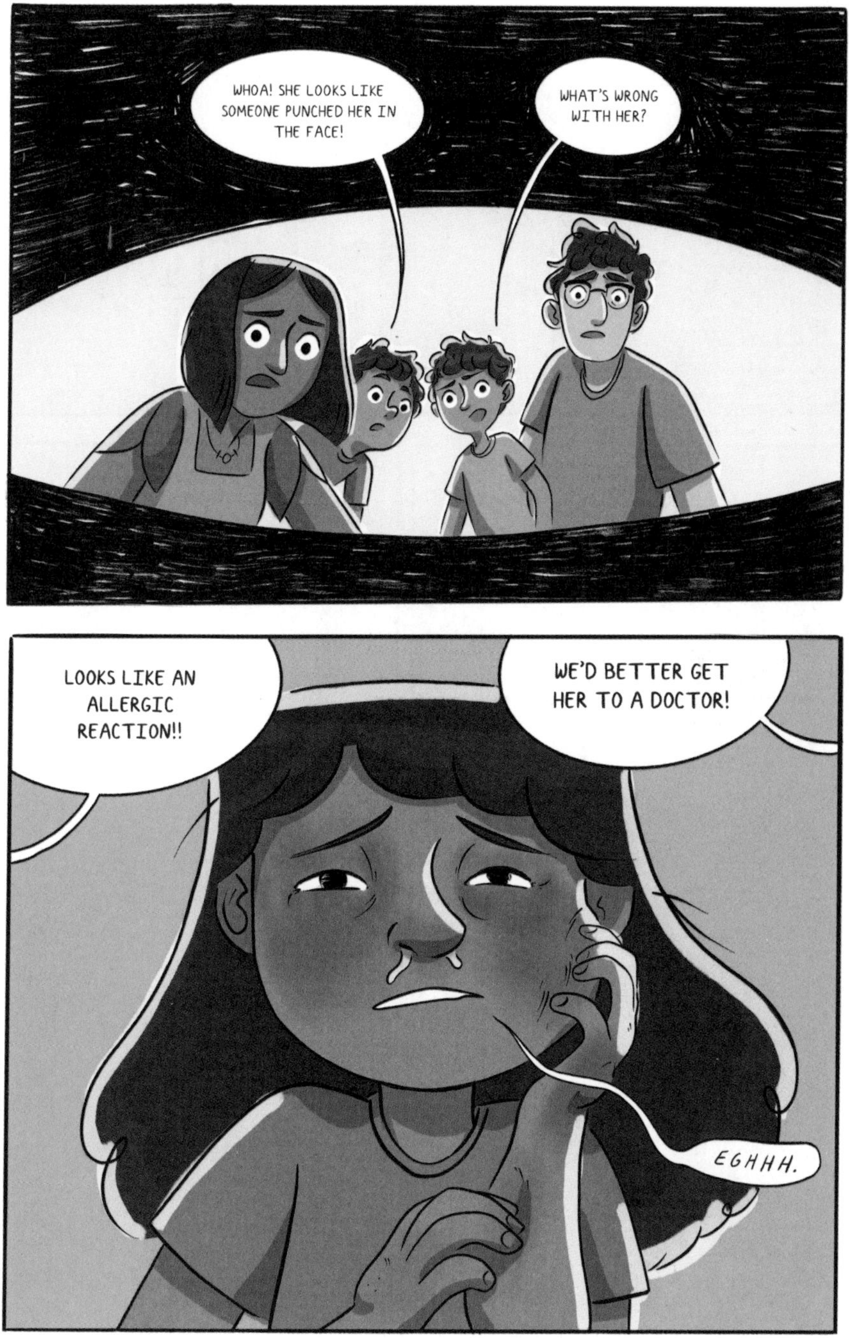
WHOA! SHE LOOKS LIKE SOMEONE PUNCHED HER IN THE FACE!
WHAT'S WRONG WITH HER?
LOOKS LIKE AN ALLERGIC REACTION!!
WE'D BETTER GET HER TO A DOCTOR!
EGHHH.

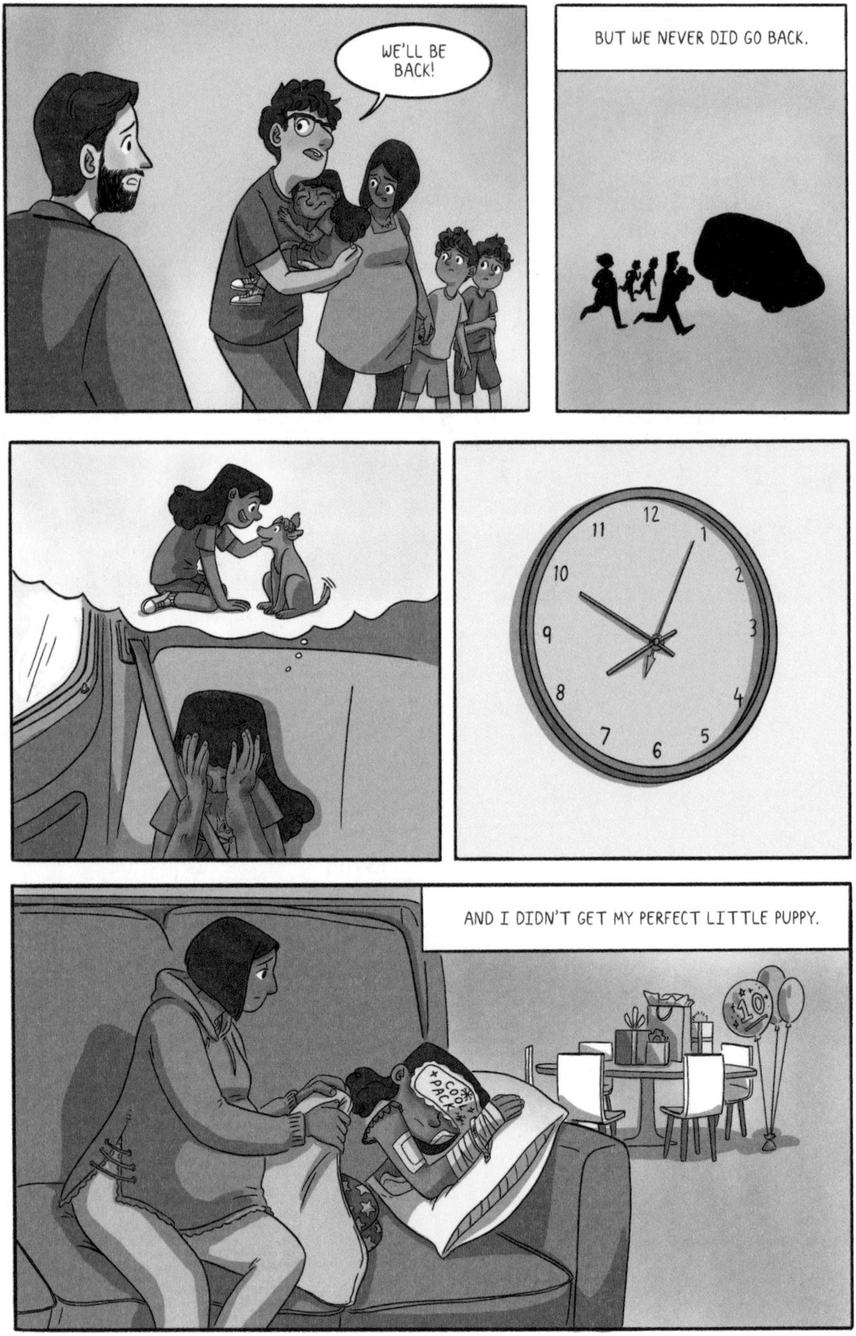
WE'LL BE BACK!
BUT WE NEVER DID GO BACK.
AND I DIDN'T GET MY PERFECT LITTLE PUPPY.
COOL PACK

Chapter Two

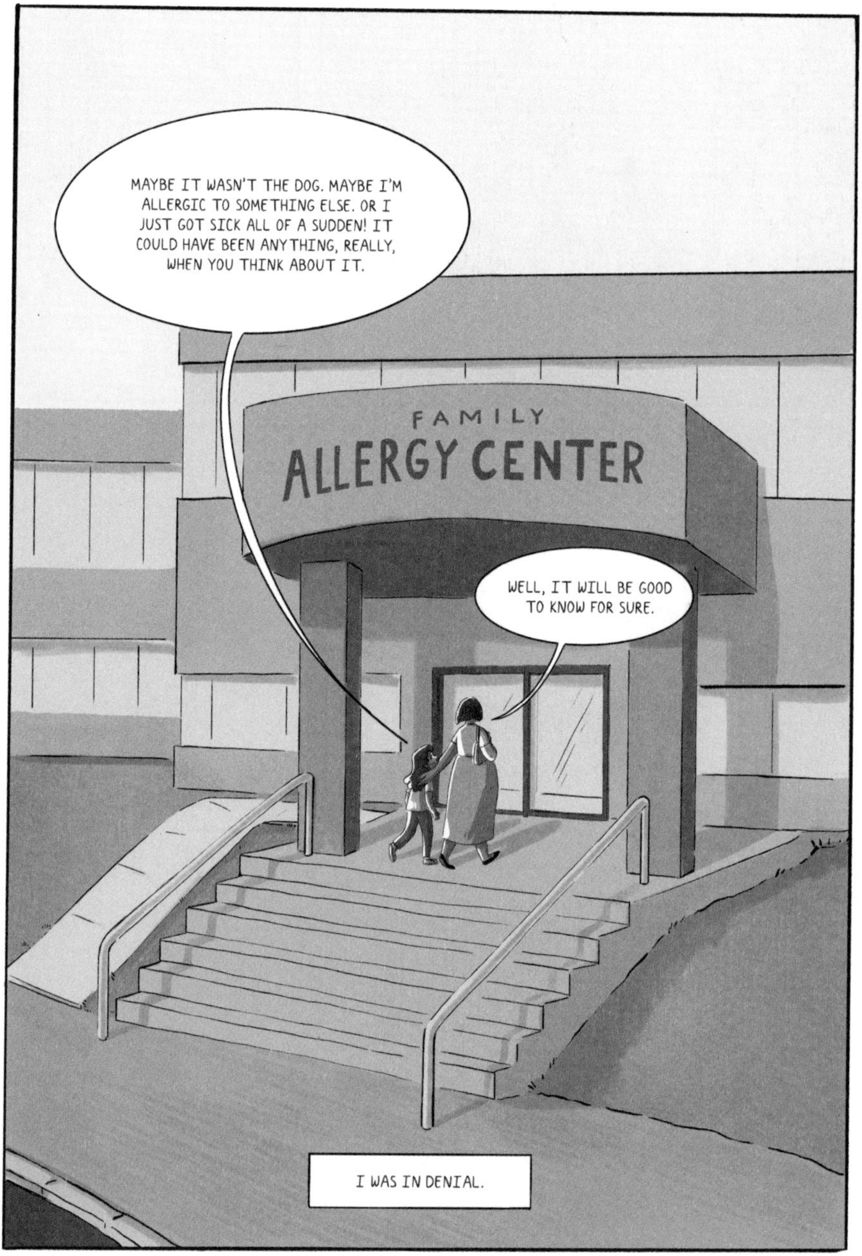

FAMILY ALLERGY CENTER
MAYBE IT WASN'T THE DOG. MAYBE I'M ALLERGIC TO SOMETHING ELSE. OR I JUST GOT SICK ALL OF A SUDDEN! IT COULD HAVE BEEN ANYTHING, REALLY, WHEN YOU THINK ABOUT IT.
WELL, IT WILL BE GOOD TO KNOW FOR SURE.
I WAS IN DENIAL.

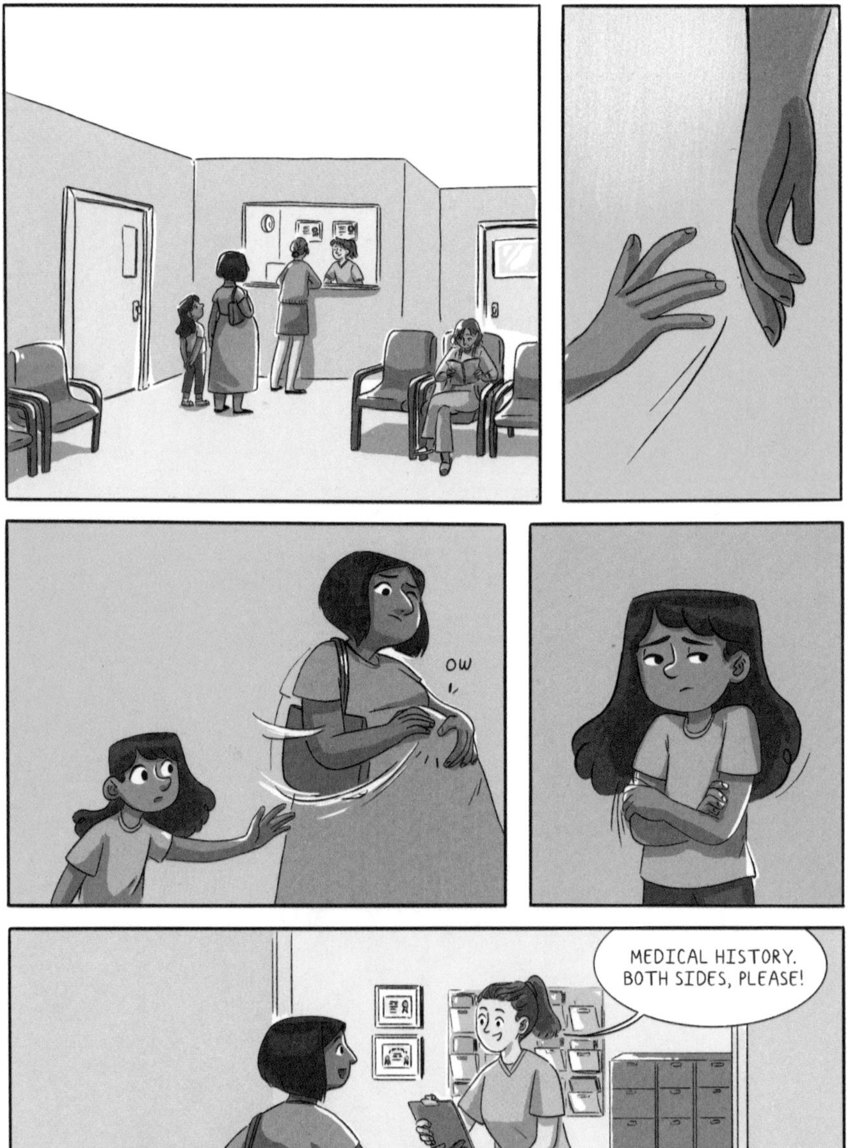
OW
MEDICAL HISTORY. BOTH SIDES, PLEASE!

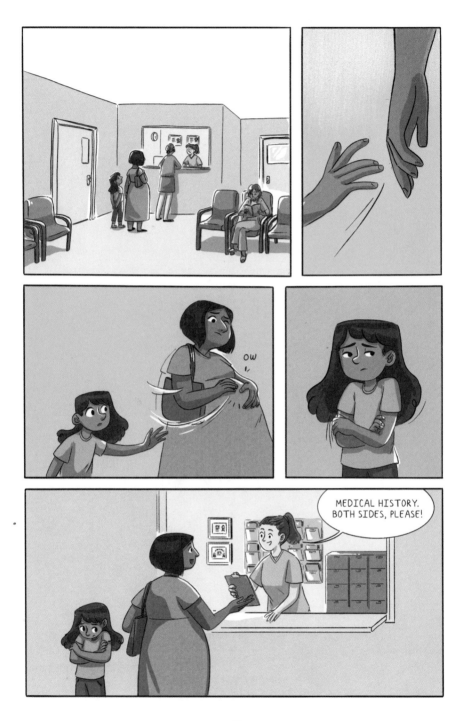

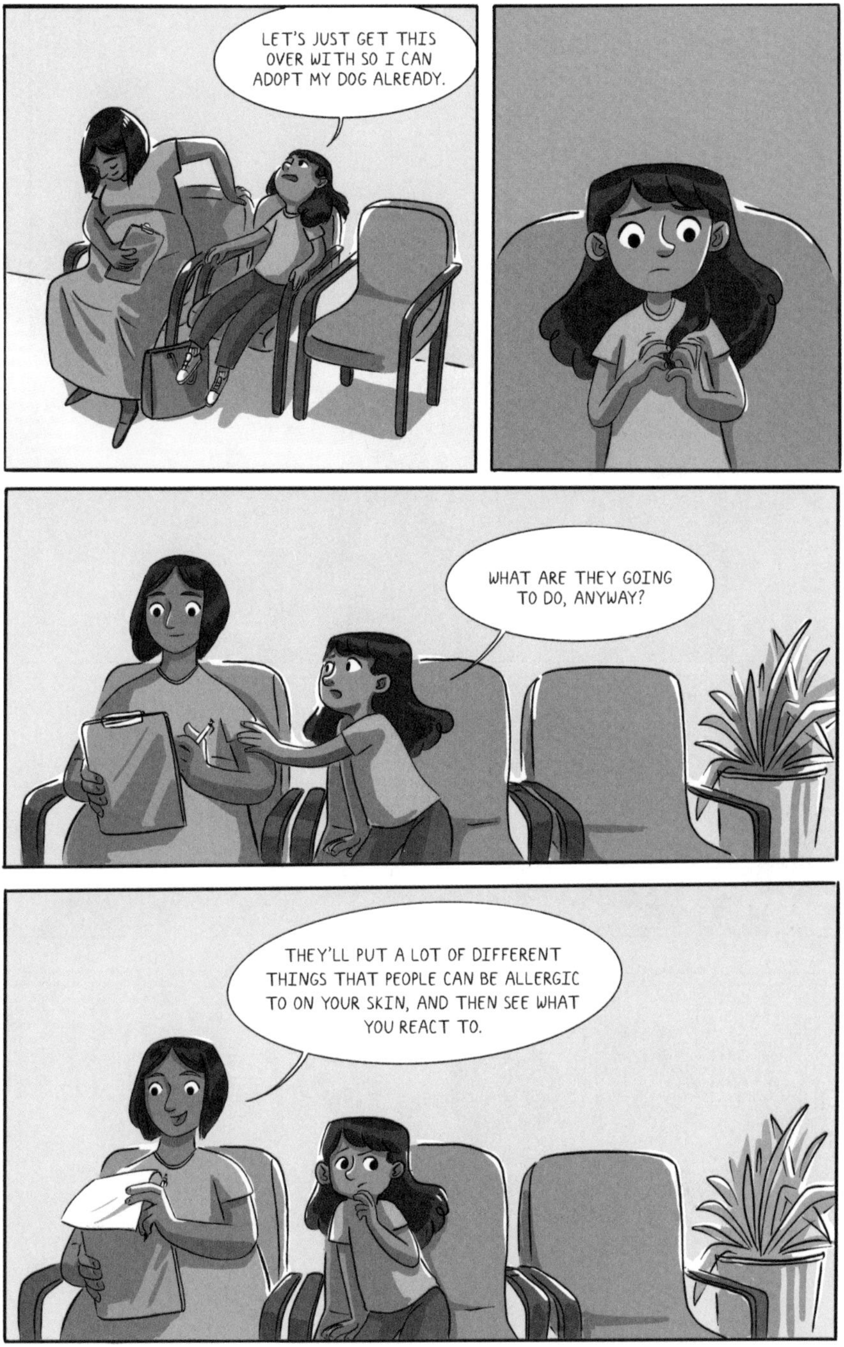
LET'S JUST GET THIS OVER WITH SO I CAN ADOPT MY DOG ALREADY.
WHAT ARE THEY GOING TO DO, ANYWAY?
THEY'LL PUT A LOT OF DIFFERENT THINGS THAT PEOPLE CAN BE ALLERGIC TO ON YOUR SKIN, AND THEN SEE WHAT YOU REACT TO.

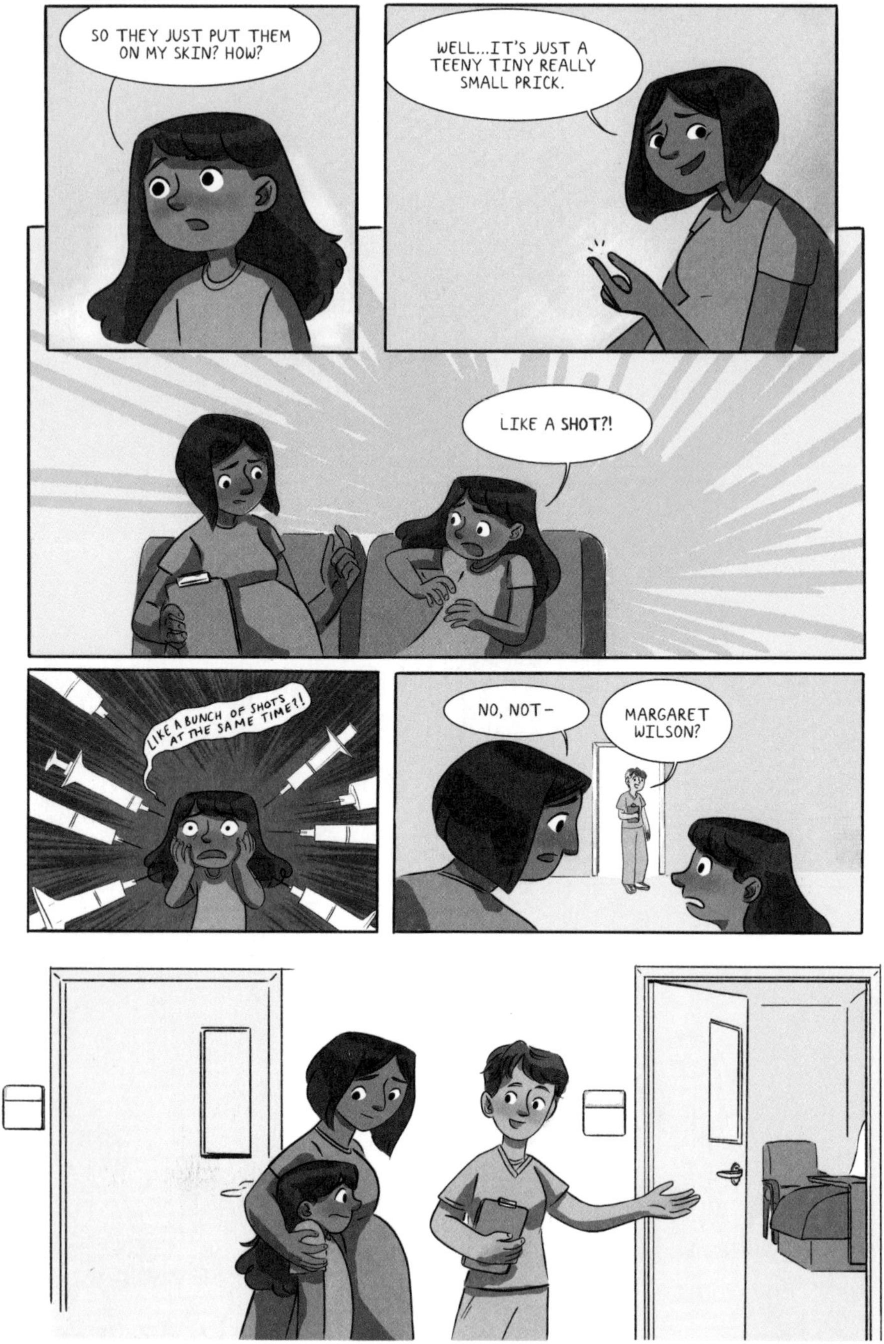
SO THEY JUST PUT THEM ON MY SKIN? HOW?
WELL...IT'S JUST A TEENY TINY REALLY SMALL PRICK.
LIKE A SHOT?!
LIKE A BUNCH OF SHOTS AT THE SAME TIME?!
NO, NOT–
MARGARET WILSON?

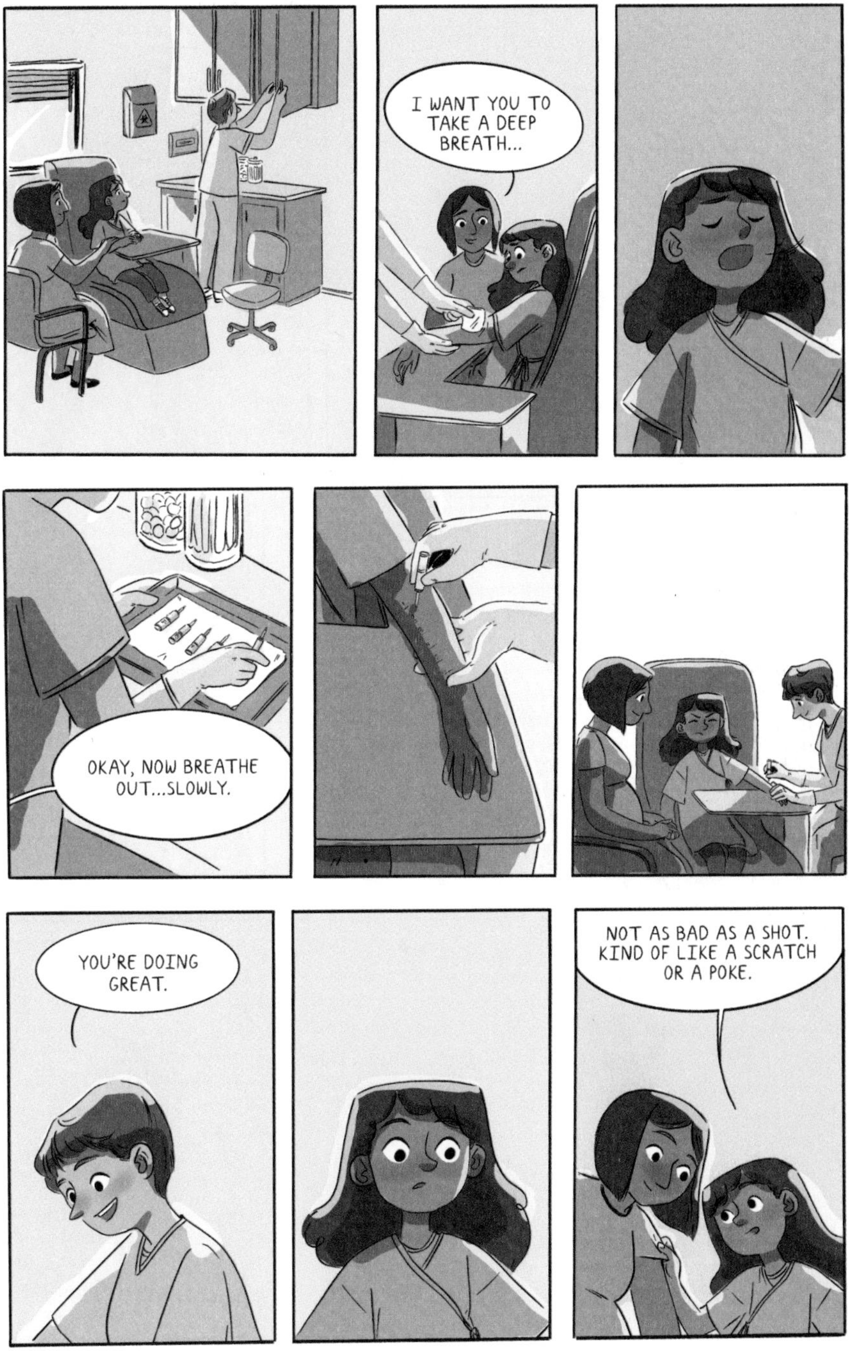
I WANT YOU TO TAKE A DEEP BREATH...
OKAY, NOW BREATHE OUT...SLOWLY.
YOU'RE DOING GREAT.
NOT AS BAD AS A SHOT. KIND OF LIKE A SCRATCH OR A POKE.

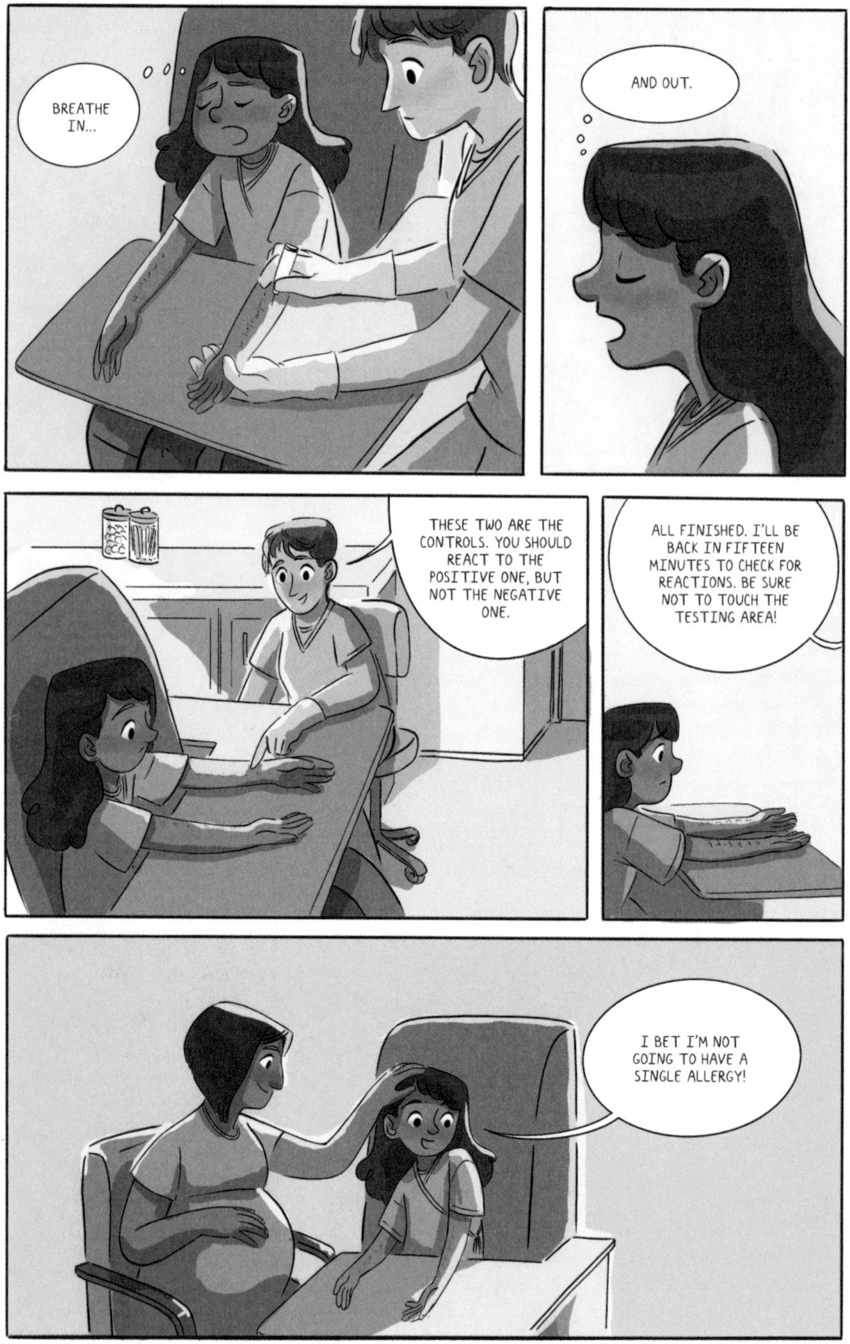
BREATHE IN...
AND OUT.
THESE TWO ARE THE CONTROLS. YOU SHOULD REACT TO THE POSITIVE ONE, BUT NOT THE NEGATIVE ONE.
ALL FINISHED. I'LL BE BACK IN FIFTEEN MINUTES TO CHECK FOR REACTIONS. BE SURE NOT TO TOUCH THE TESTING AREA!
I BET I'M NOT GOING TO HAVE A SINGLE ALLERGY!

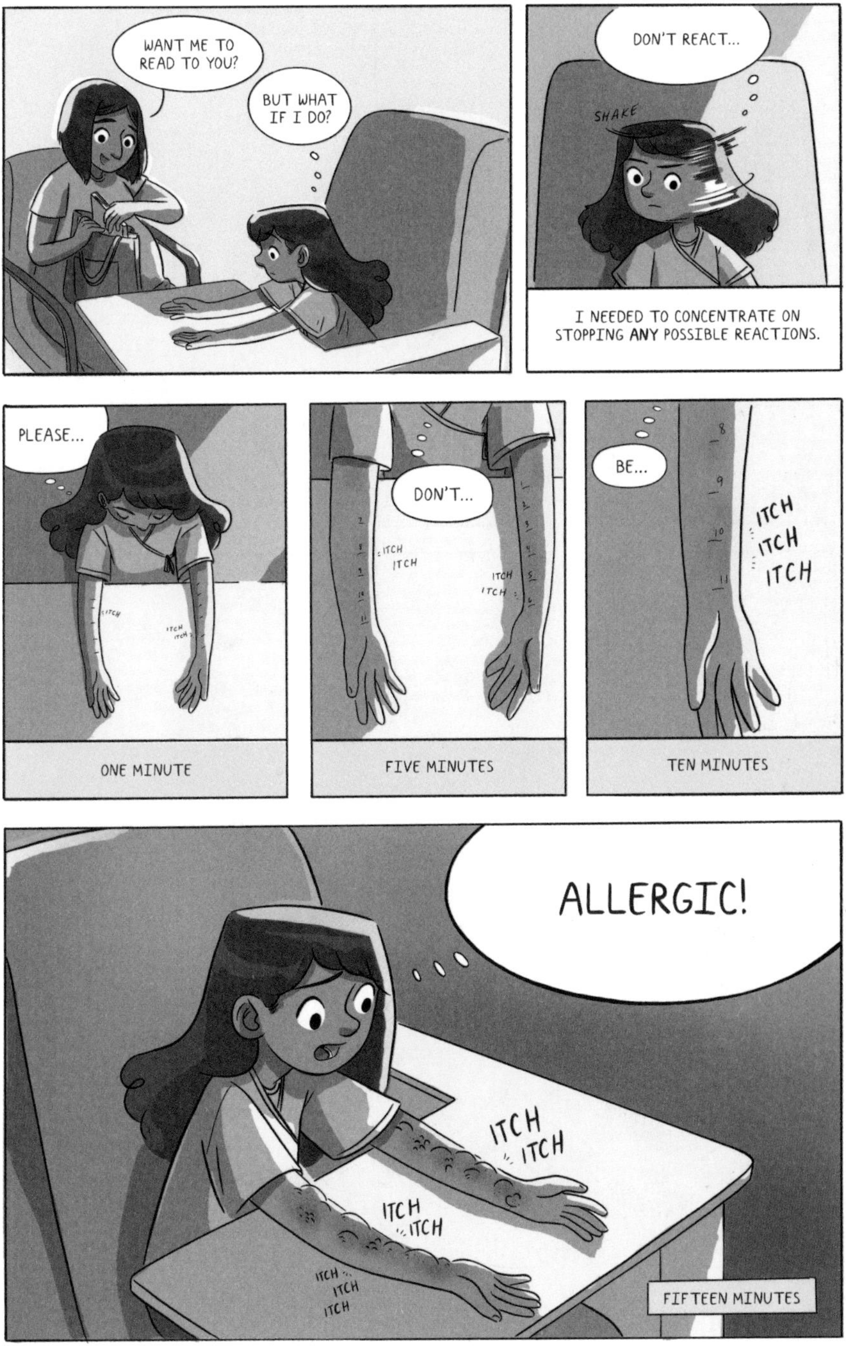
WANT ME TO READ TO YOU?
BUT WHAT IF I DO?
DON'T REACT...
SHAKE
I NEEDED TO CONCENTRATE ON STOPPING **ANY** POSSIBLE REACTIONS.
PLEASE...
ONE MINUTE
DON'T...
ITCH
ITCH
ITCH
ITCH
FIVE MINUTES
BE...
ITCH
ITCH
ITCH
TEN MINUTES
ALLERGIC!
ITCH
ITCH
ITCH
ITCH
ITCH
ITCH
ITCH
FIFTEEN MINUTES

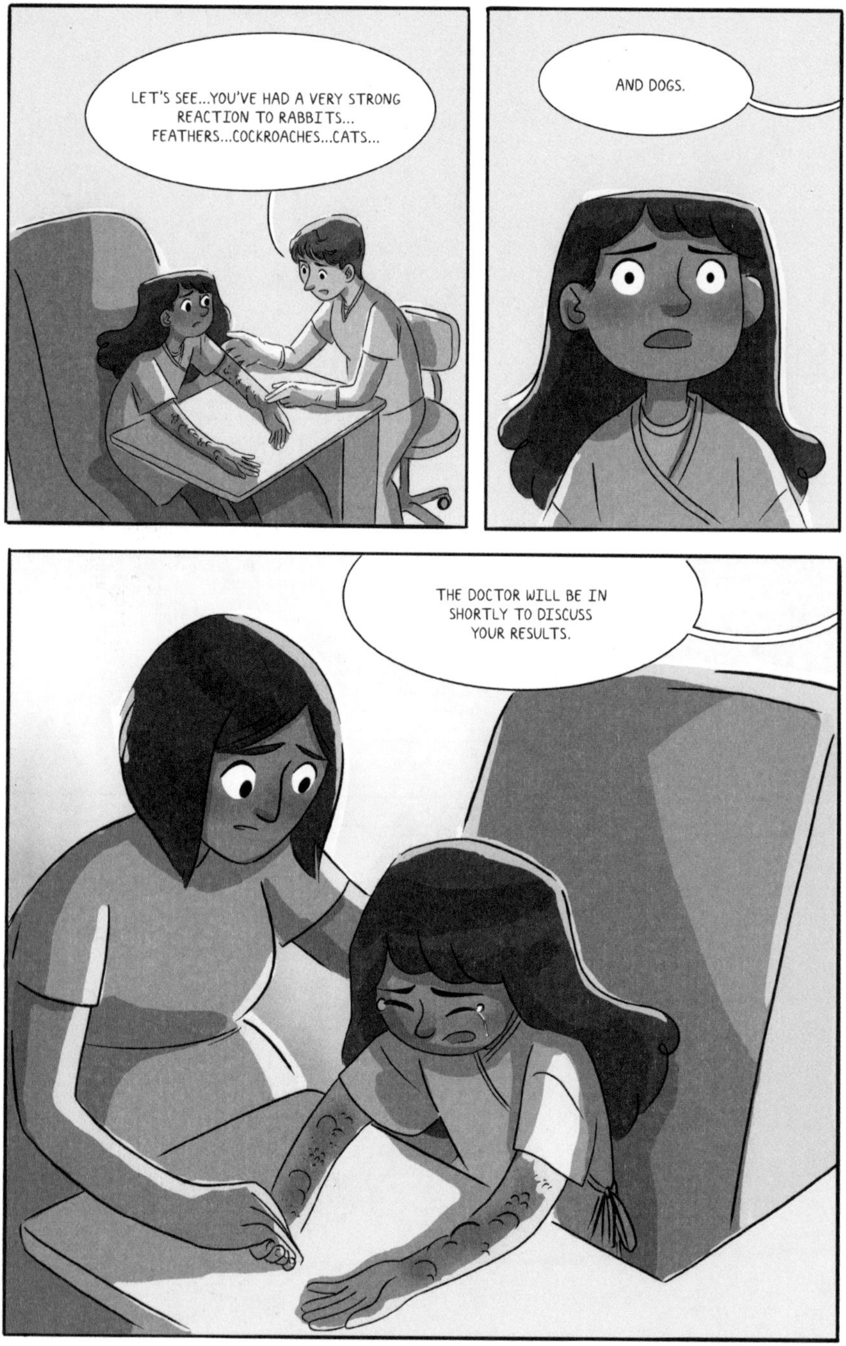
LET'S SEE...YOU'VE HAD A VERY STRONG REACTION TO RABBITS... FEATHERS...COCKROACHES...CATS...
AND DOGS.
THE DOCTOR WILL BE IN SHORTLY TO DISCUSS YOUR RESULTS.

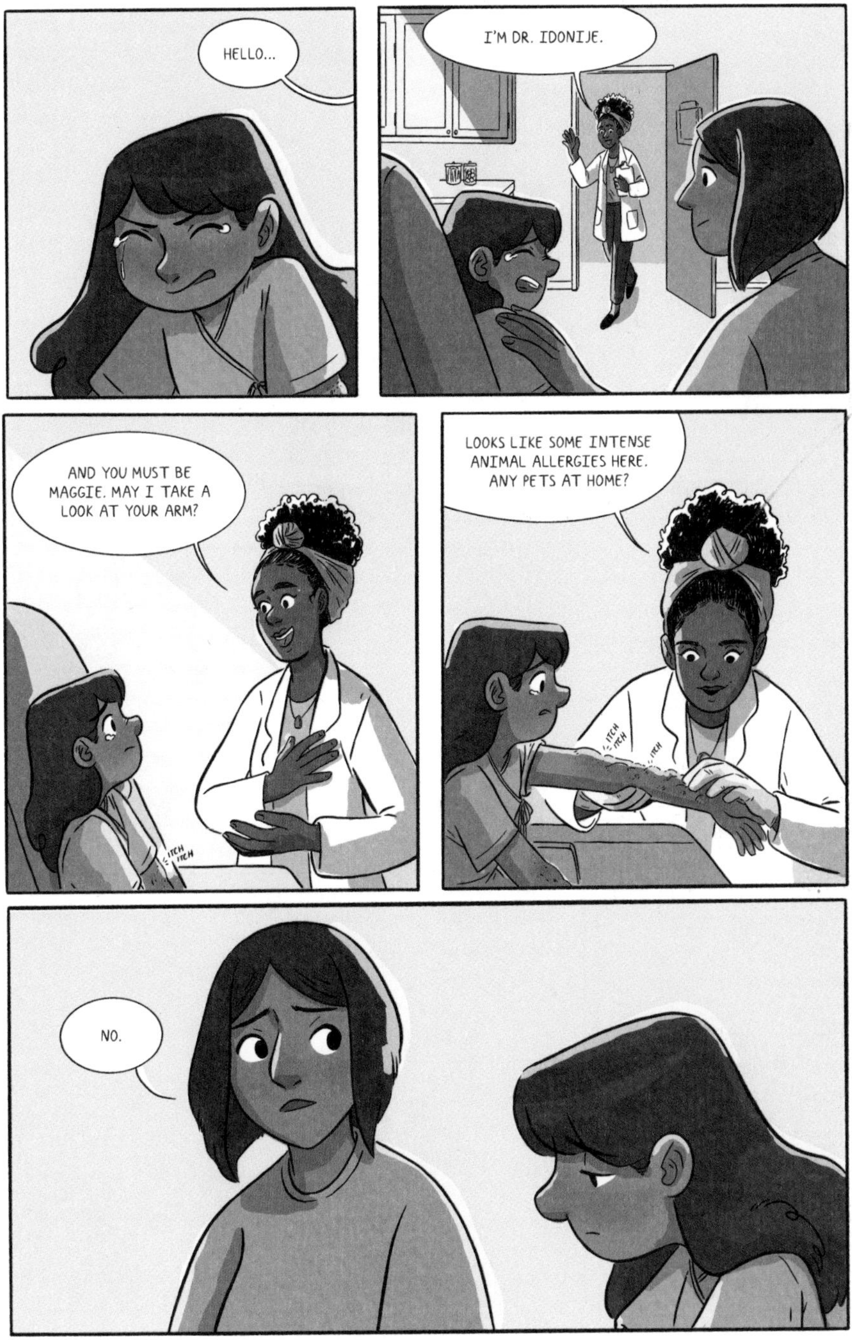
HELLO...
I'M DR. IDONIJE.
AND YOU MUST BE MAGGIE. MAY I TAKE A LOOK AT YOUR ARM?
ITCH ITCH
LOOKS LIKE SOME INTENSE ANIMAL ALLERGIES HERE. ANY PETS AT HOME?
ITCH ITCH
ITCH
NO.

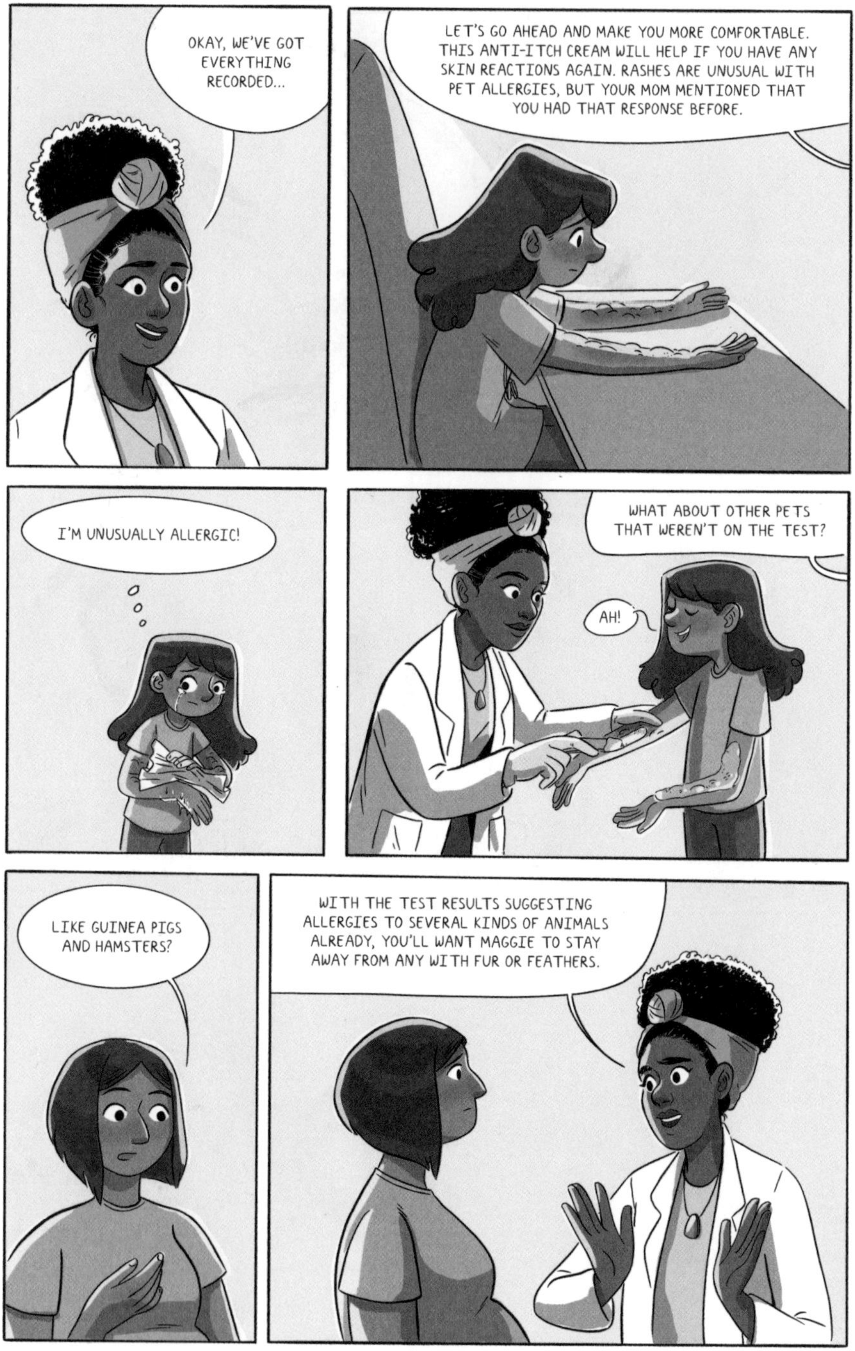
OKAY, WE'VE GOT EVERYTHING RECORDED...
LET'S GO AHEAD AND MAKE YOU MORE COMFORTABLE. THIS ANTI-ITCH CREAM WILL HELP IF YOU HAVE ANY SKIN REACTIONS AGAIN. RASHES ARE UNUSUAL WITH PET ALLERGIES, BUT YOUR MOM MENTIONED THAT YOU HAD THAT RESPONSE BEFORE.
I'M UNUSUALLY ALLERGIC!
WHAT ABOUT OTHER PETS THAT WEREN'T ON THE TEST?
AH!
LIKE GUINEA PIGS AND HAMSTERS?
WITH THE TEST RESULTS SUGGESTING ALLERGIES TO SEVERAL KINDS OF ANIMALS ALREADY, YOU'LL WANT MAGGIE TO STAY AWAY FROM ANY WITH FUR OR FEATHERS.

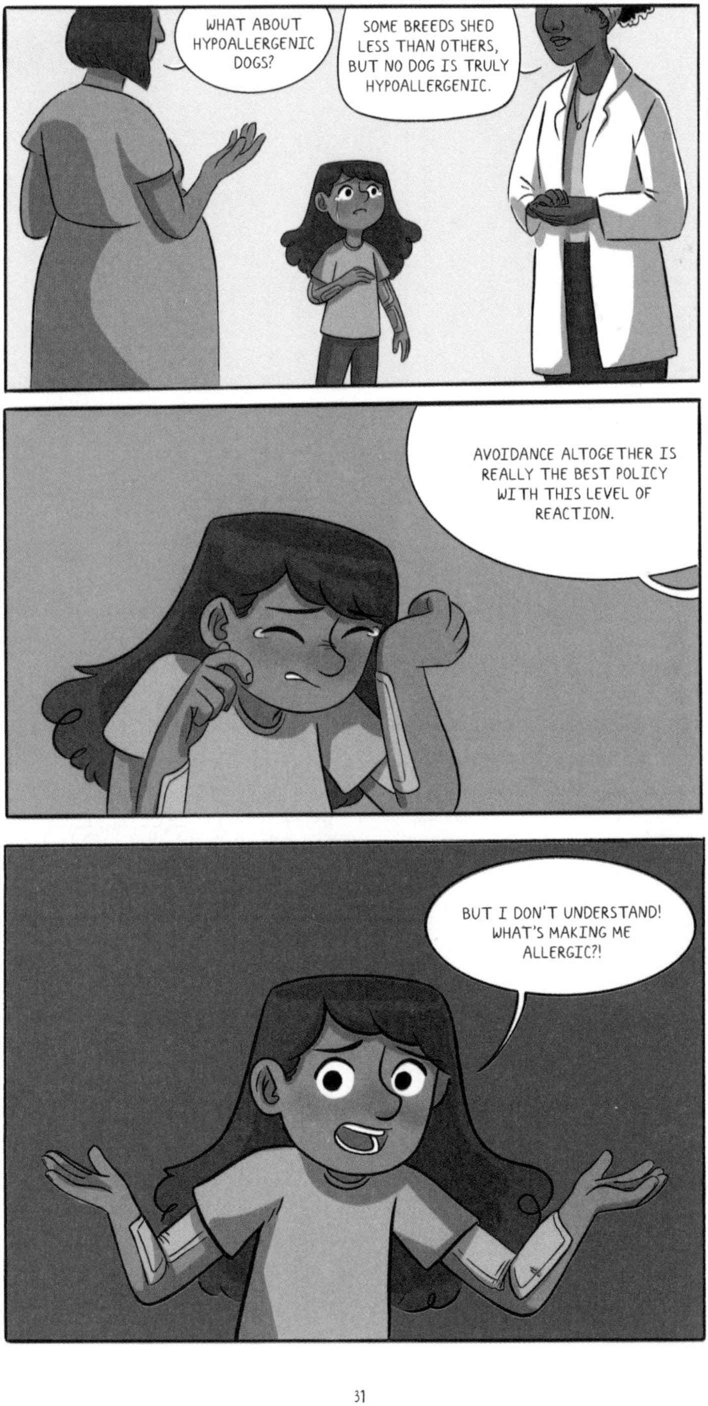
WHAT ABOUT HYPOALLERGENIC DOGS?
SOME BREEDS SHED LESS THAN OTHERS, BUT NO DOG IS TRULY HYPOALLERGENIC.
AVOIDANCE ALTOGETHER IS REALLY THE BEST POLICY WITH THIS LEVEL OF REACTION.
BUT I DON'T UNDERSTAND! WHAT'S MAKING ME ALLERGIC?!

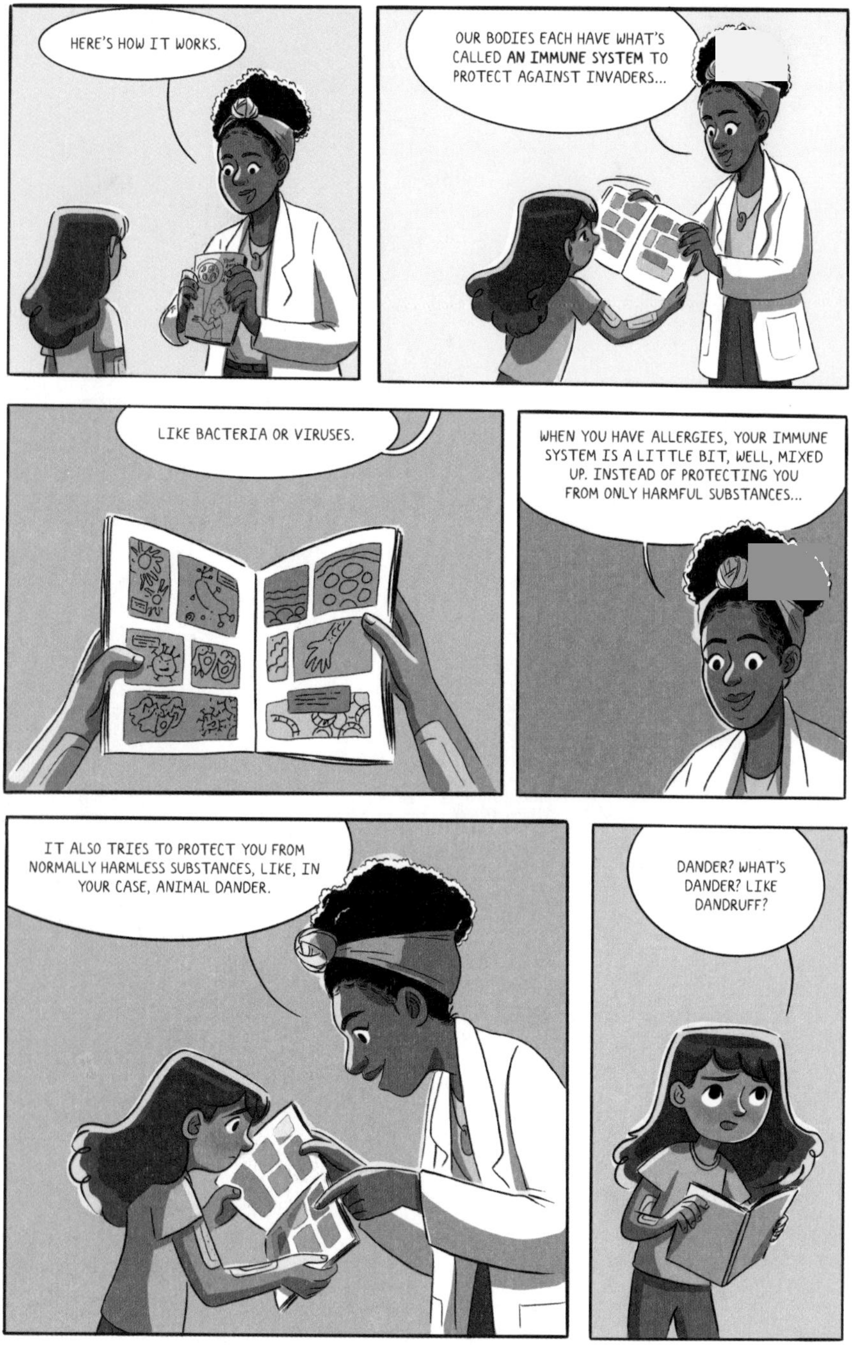
HERE'S HOW IT WORKS.
OUR BODIES EACH HAVE WHAT'S CALLED **AN IMMUNE SYSTEM** TO PROTECT AGAINST INVADERS...
LIKE BACTERIA OR VIRUSES.
WHEN YOU HAVE ALLERGIES, YOUR IMMUNE SYSTEM IS A LITTLE BIT, WELL, MIXED UP. INSTEAD OF PROTECTING YOU FROM ONLY HARMFUL SUBSTANCES...
IT ALSO TRIES TO PROTECT YOU FROM NORMALLY HARMLESS SUBSTANCES, LIKE, IN YOUR CASE, ANIMAL DANDER.
DANDER? WHAT'S DANDER? LIKE DANDRUFF?

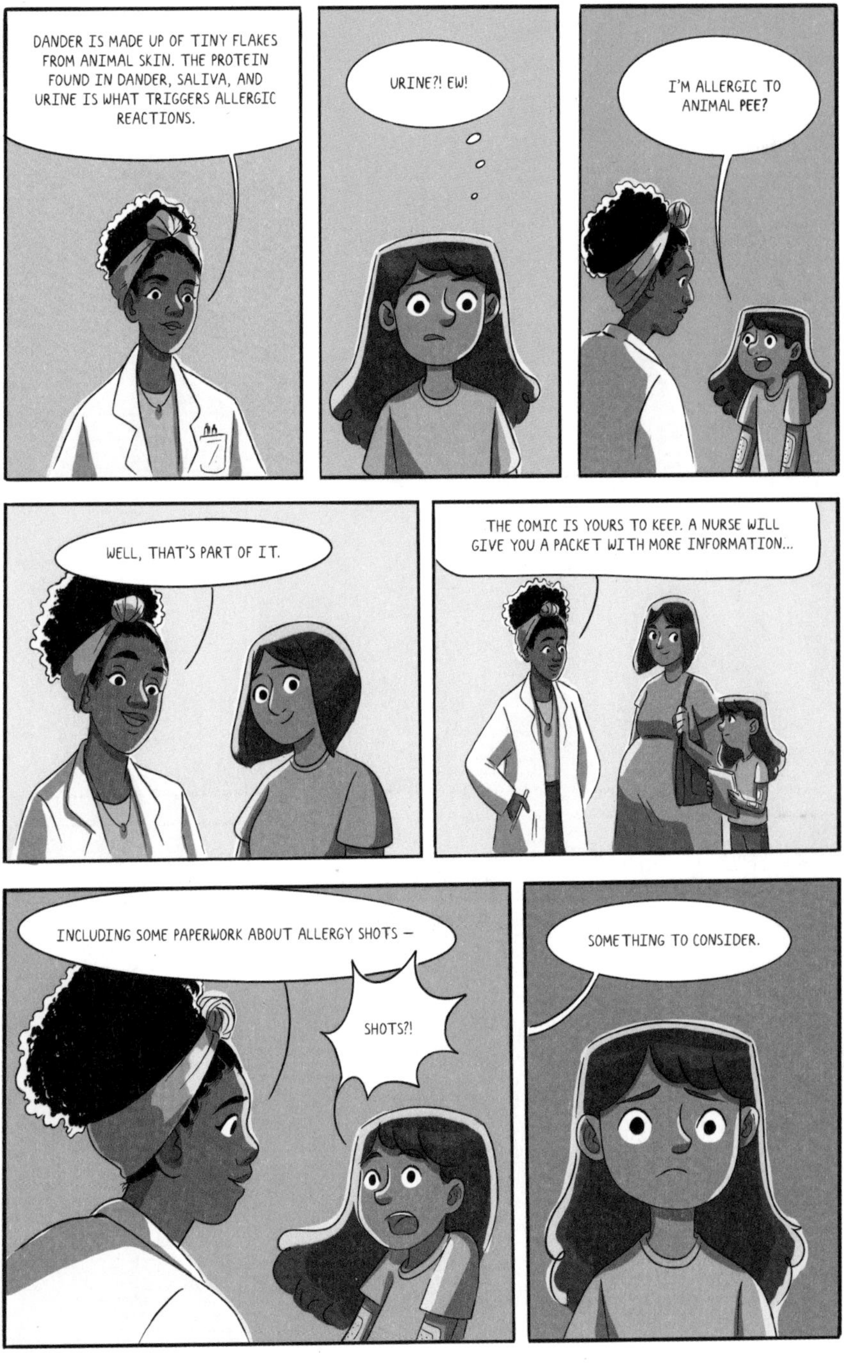
DANDER IS MADE UP OF TINY FLAKES FROM ANIMAL SKIN. THE PROTEIN FOUND IN DANDER, SALIVA, AND URINE IS WHAT TRIGGERS ALLERGIC REACTIONS.
URINE?! EW!
I'M ALLERGIC TO ANIMAL PEE?
WELL, THAT'S PART OF IT.
THE COMIC IS YOURS TO KEEP. A NURSE WILL GIVE YOU A PACKET WITH MORE INFORMATION...
INCLUDING SOME PAPERWORK ABOUT ALLERGY SHOTS —
SHOTS?!
SOMETHING TO CONSIDER.

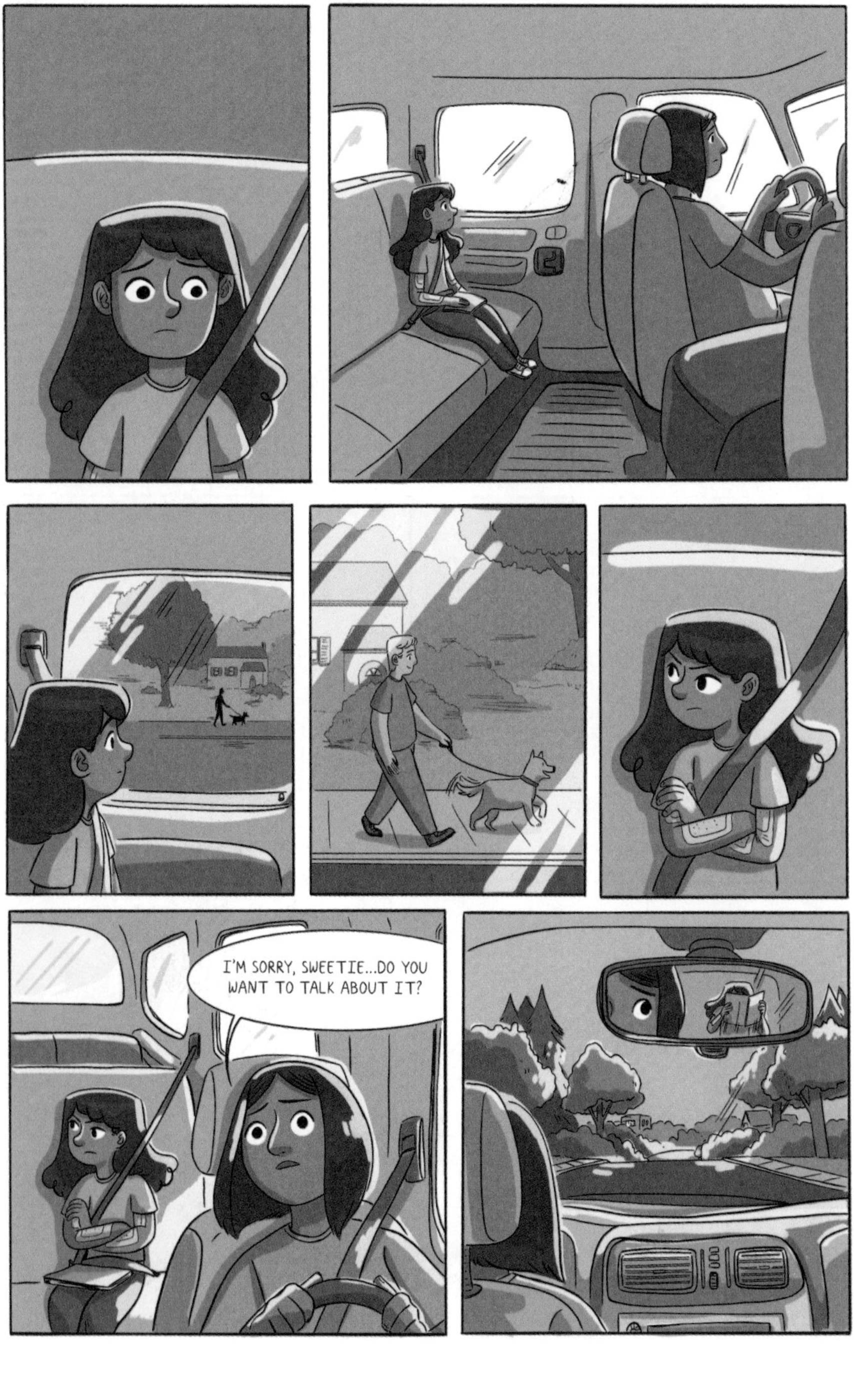
I'M SORRY, SWEETIE...DO YOU WANT TO TALK ABOUT IT?

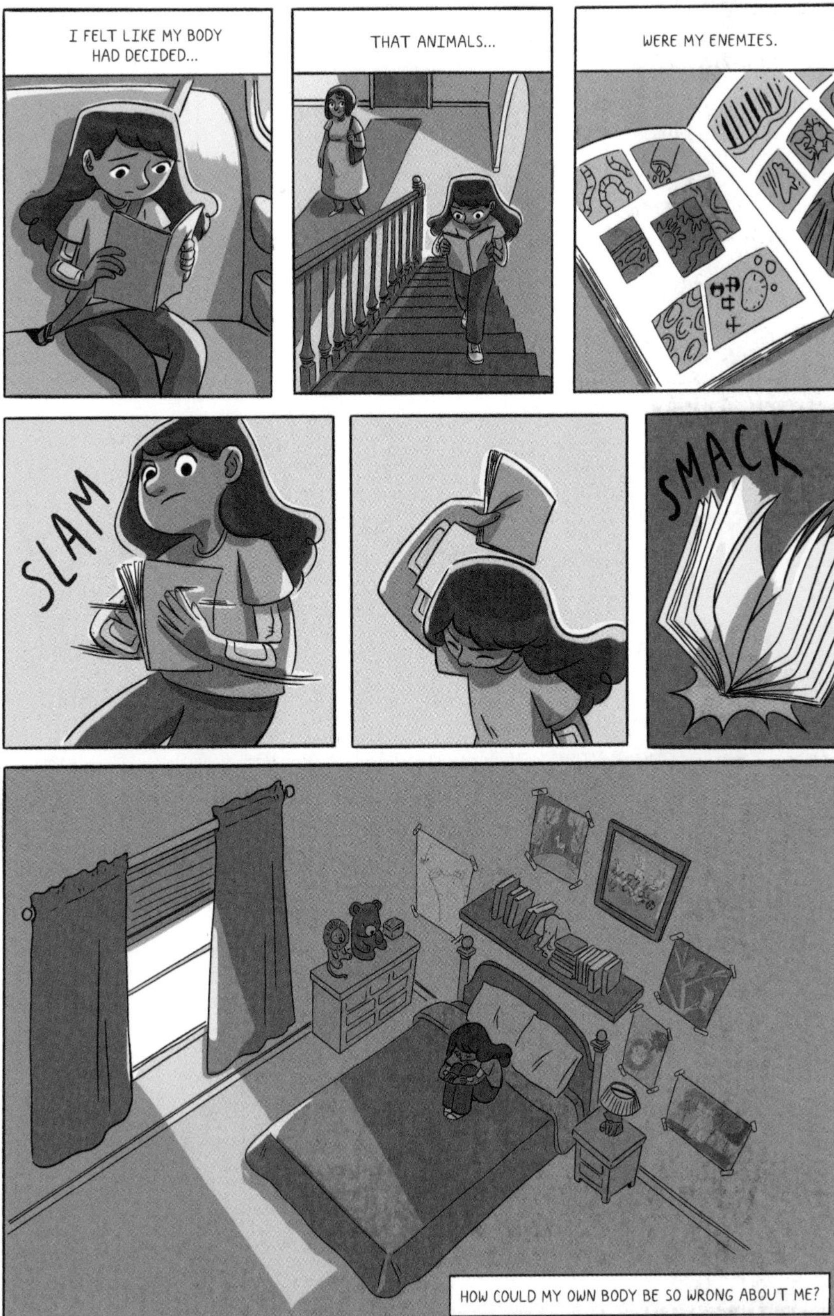
I FELT LIKE MY BODY HAD DECIDED...
THAT ANIMALS...
WERE MY ENEMIES.
SLAM
SMACK
HOW COULD MY OWN BODY BE SO WRONG ABOUT ME?

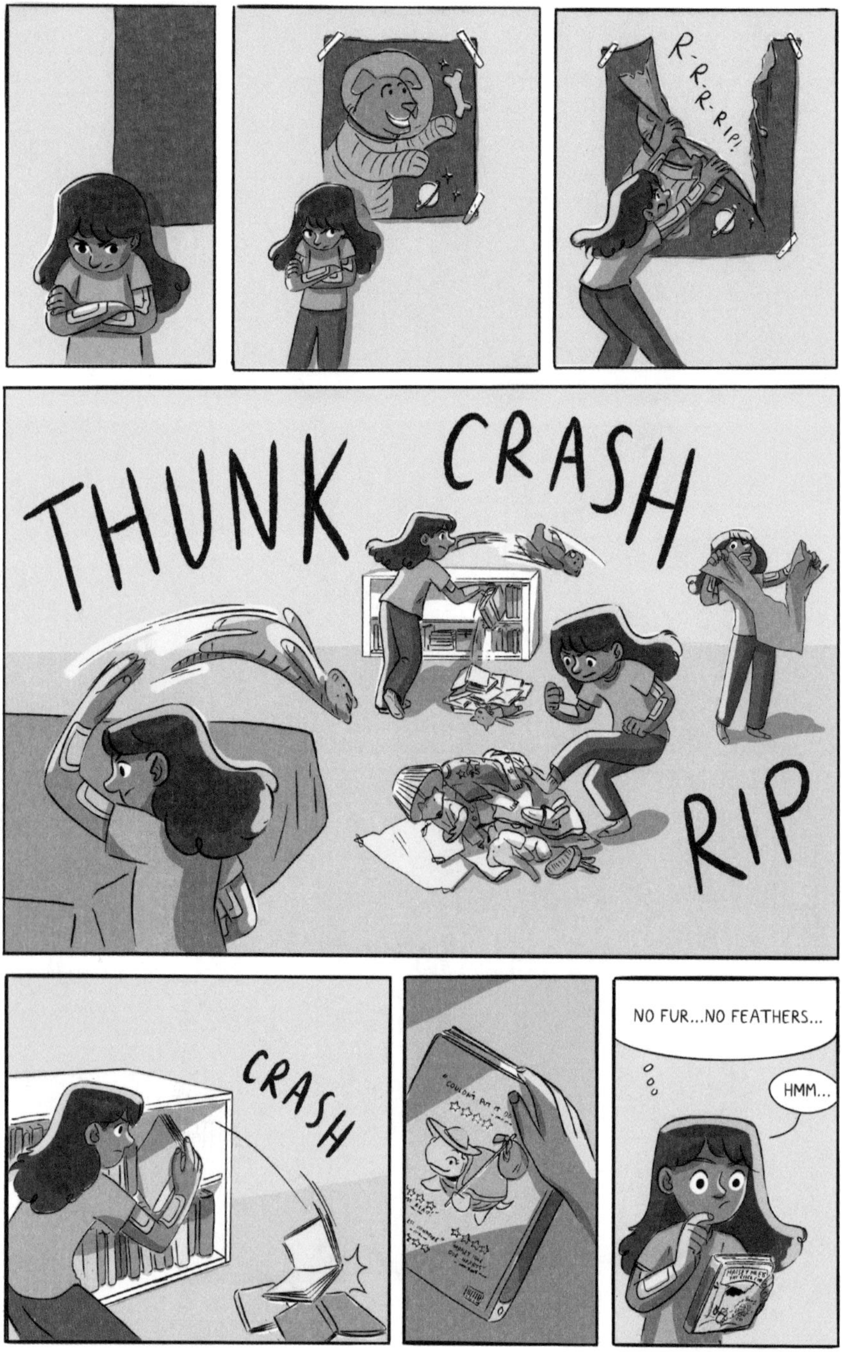
R-R-R-RIP!
THUNK
CRASH
RIP
CRASH
NO FUR...NO FEATHERS...
HMM...

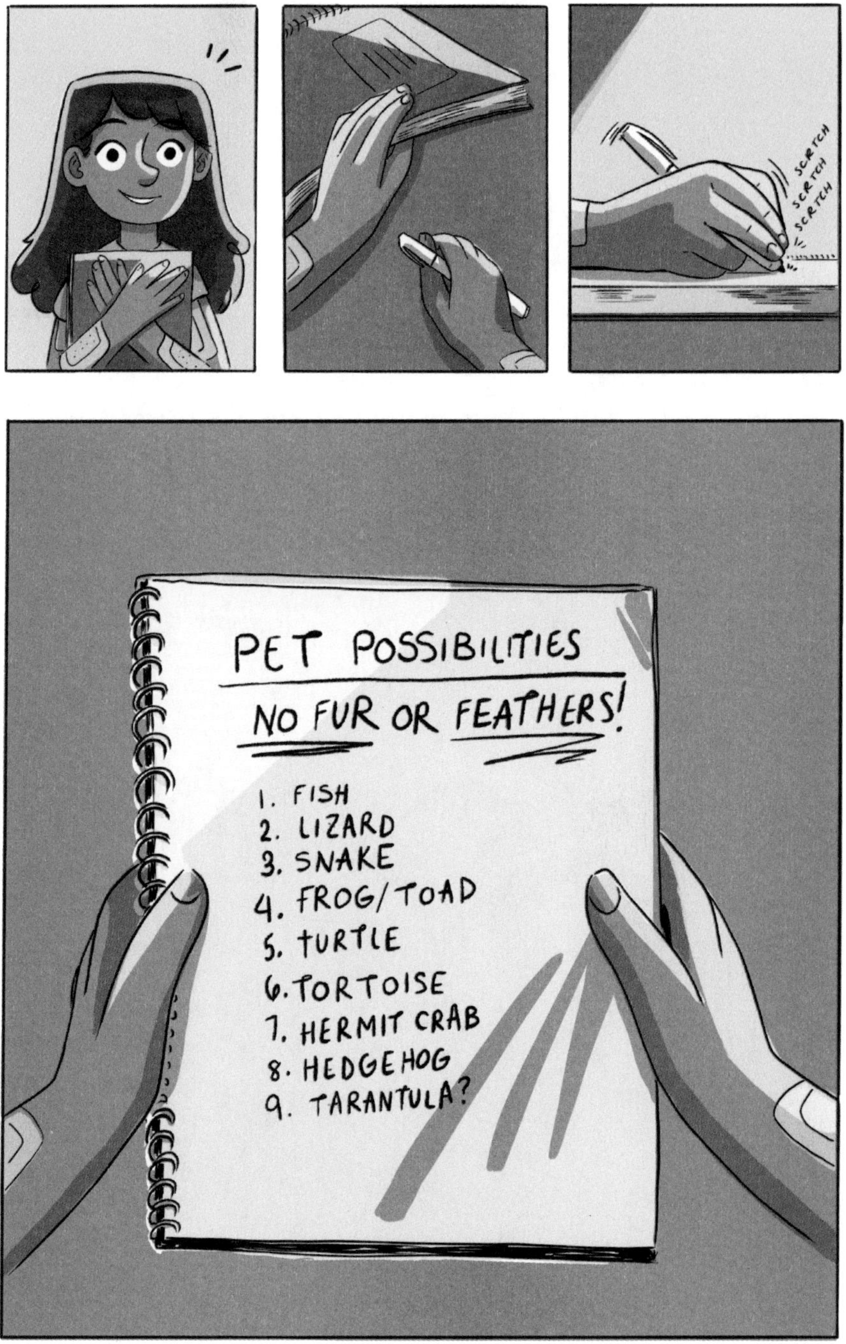
SCRTCH
SCRTCH
SCRTCH
PET POSSIBILITIES
NO FUR OR FEATHERS!
1. FISH
2. LIZARD
3. SNAKE
4. FROG/TOAD
5. TURTLE
6. TORTOISE
7. HERMIT CRAB
8. HEDGEHOG
9. TARANTULA?

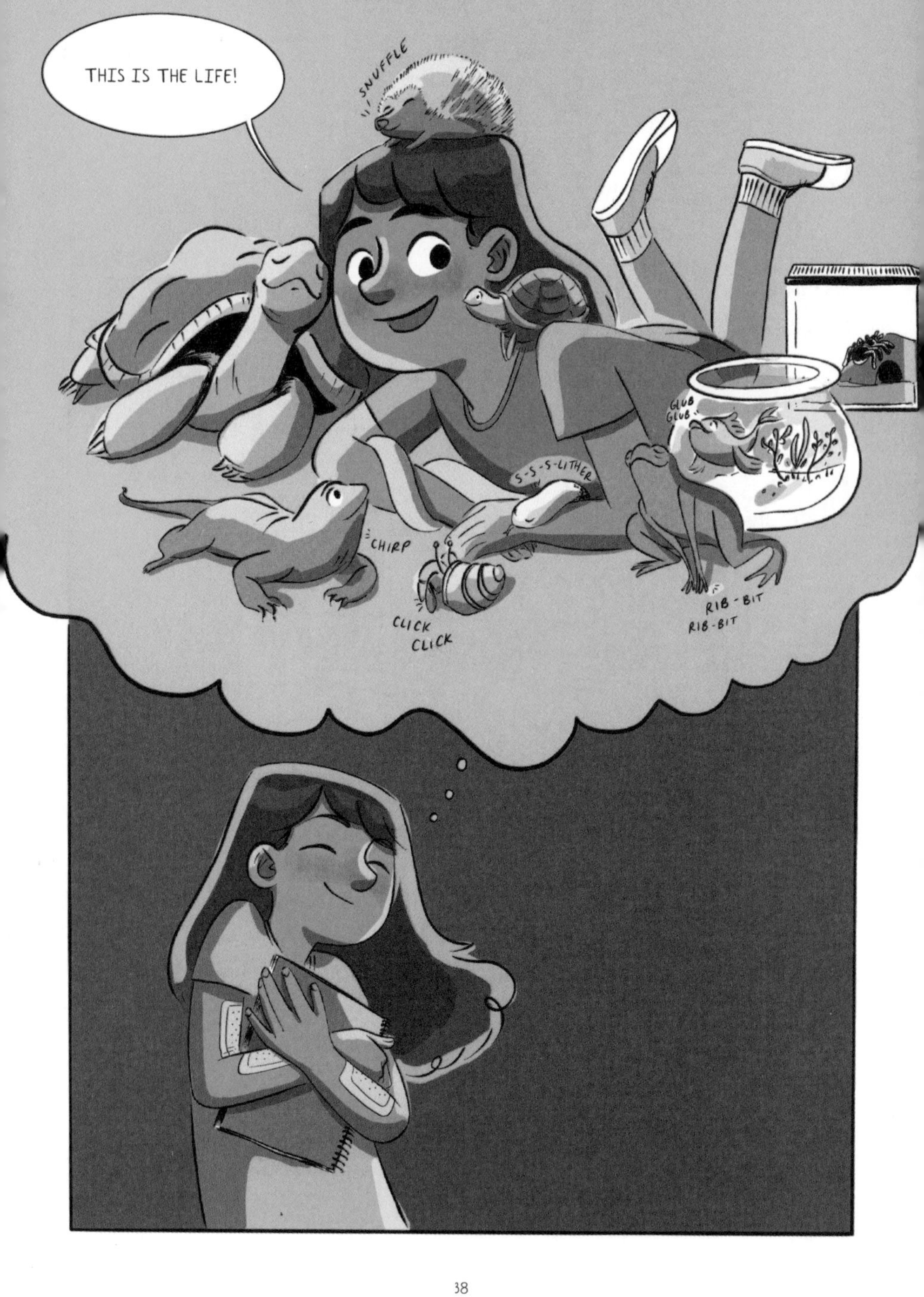
THIS IS THE LIFE!
SNUFFLE
GLUB GLUB
S-S-S-LITHER
CHIRP
CLICK CLICK
RIB-BIT RIB-BIT

Chapter Three

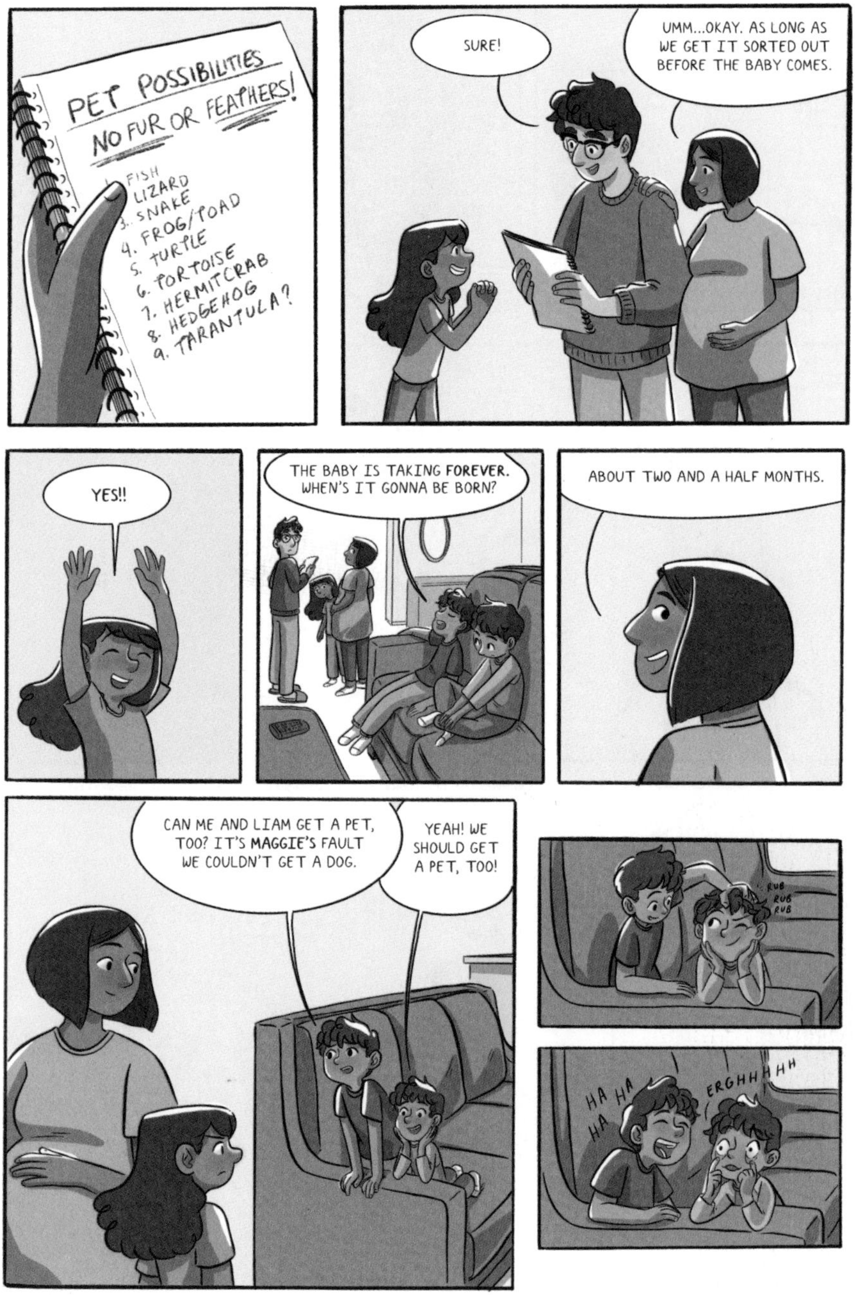
PET POSSIBILITIES
NO FUR OR FEATHERS!
FISH
LIZARD
3. SNAKE
4. FROG/TOAD
5. TURTLE
6. TORTOISE
7. HERMITCRAB
8. HEDGEHOG
9. TARANTULA?
SURE!
UMM...OKAY. AS LONG AS WE GET IT SORTED OUT BEFORE THE BABY COMES.
YES!!
THE BABY IS TAKING **FOREVER.** WHEN'S IT GONNA BE BORN?
ABOUT TWO AND A HALF MONTHS.
CAN ME AND LIAM GET A PET, TOO? IT'S **MAGGIE'S** FAULT WE COULDN'T GET A DOG.
YEAH! WE SHOULD GET A PET, TOO!
RUB RUB RUB
HA HA HA HA
ERGHHHHHH

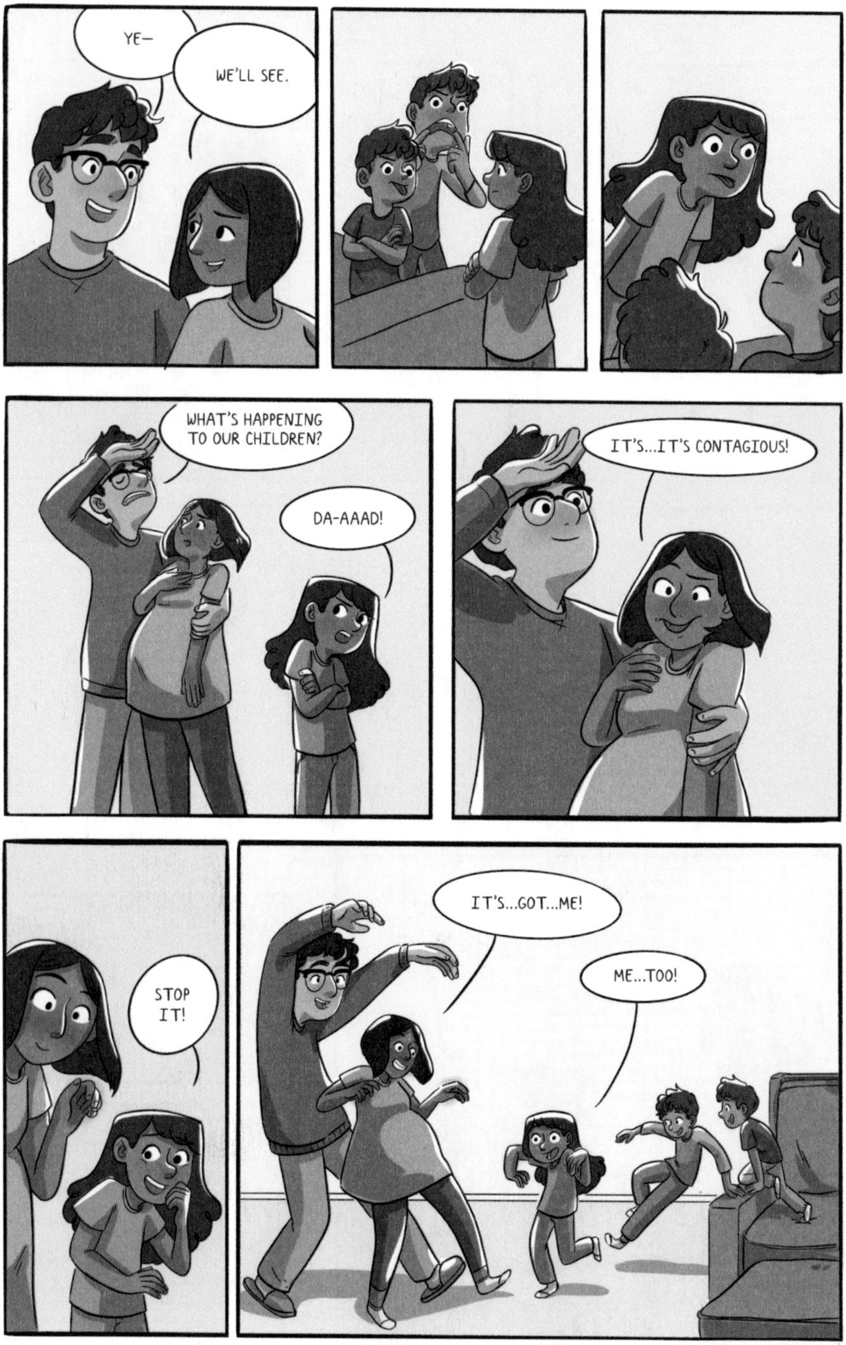
YE—
WE'LL SEE.
WHAT'S HAPPENING TO OUR CHILDREN?
DA-AAAD!
IT'S...IT'S CONTAGIOUS!
STOP IT!
IT'S...GOT...ME!
ME...TOO!

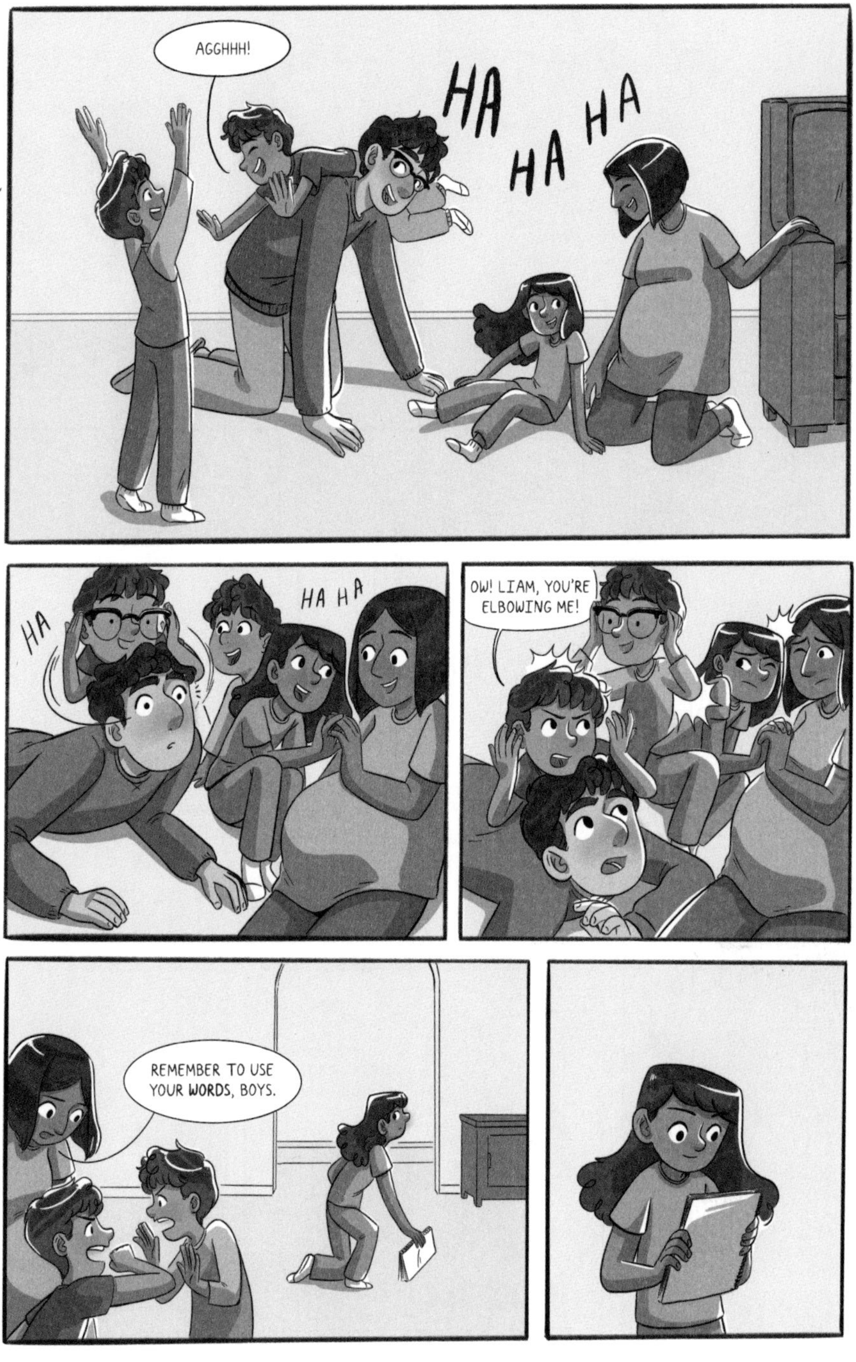
AGGHHH!
HA HA HA
HA
HA HA
OW! LIAM, YOU'RE ELBOWING ME!
REMEMBER TO USE YOUR WORDS, BOYS.

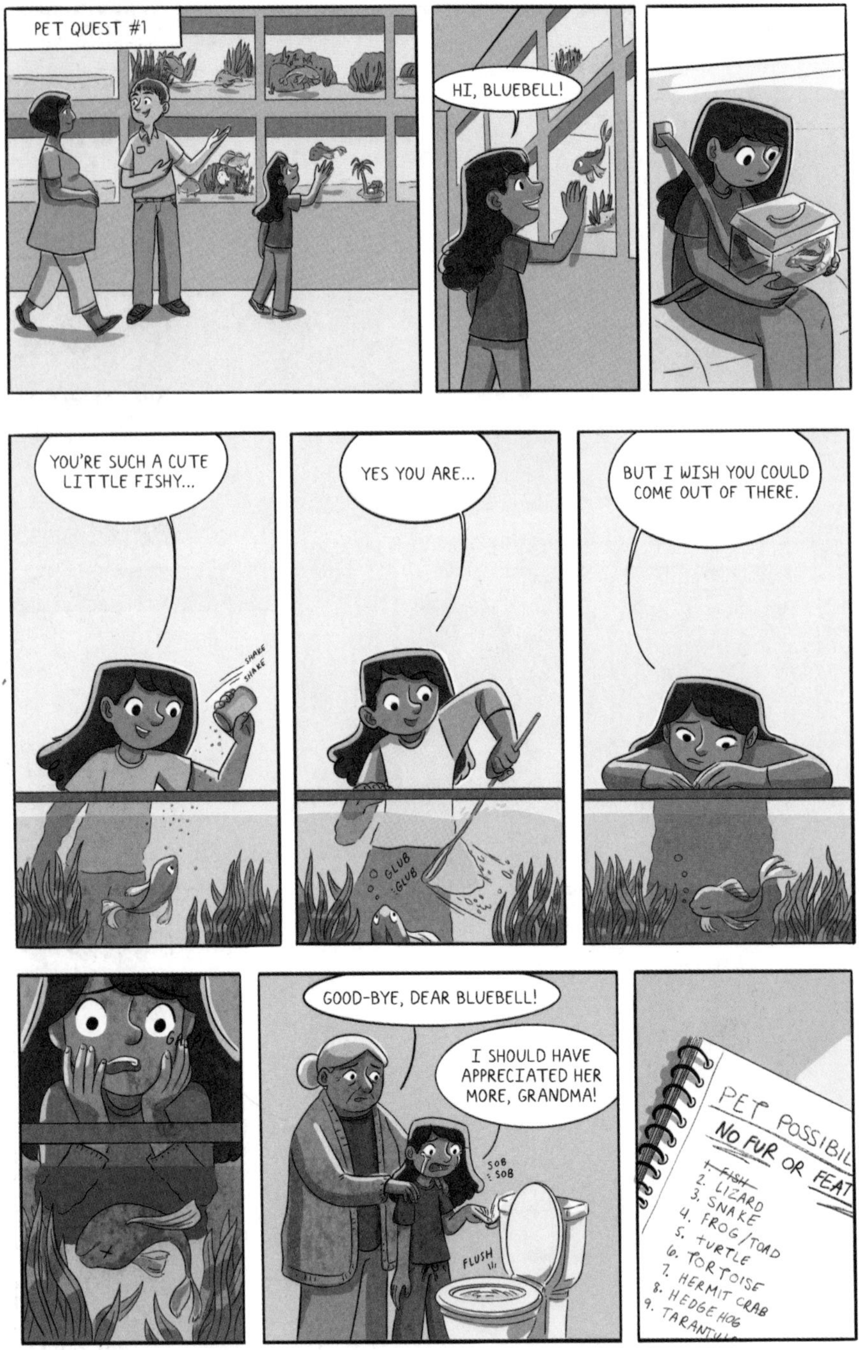
PET QUEST #1
HI, BLUEBELL!
YOU'RE SUCH A CUTE LITTLE FISHY...
SHAKE
SHAKE
YES YOU ARE...
GLUB
GLUB
BUT I WISH YOU COULD COME OUT OF THERE.
GOOD-BYE, DEAR BLUEBELL!
I SHOULD HAVE APPRECIATED HER MORE, GRANDMA!
SOB
SOB
FLUSH
PET POSSIBIL
NO FUR OR FEAT
1. FISH
2. LIZARD
3. SNAKE
4. FROG/TOAD
5. TURTLE
6. TORTOISE
7. HERMIT CRAB
8. HEDGEHOG

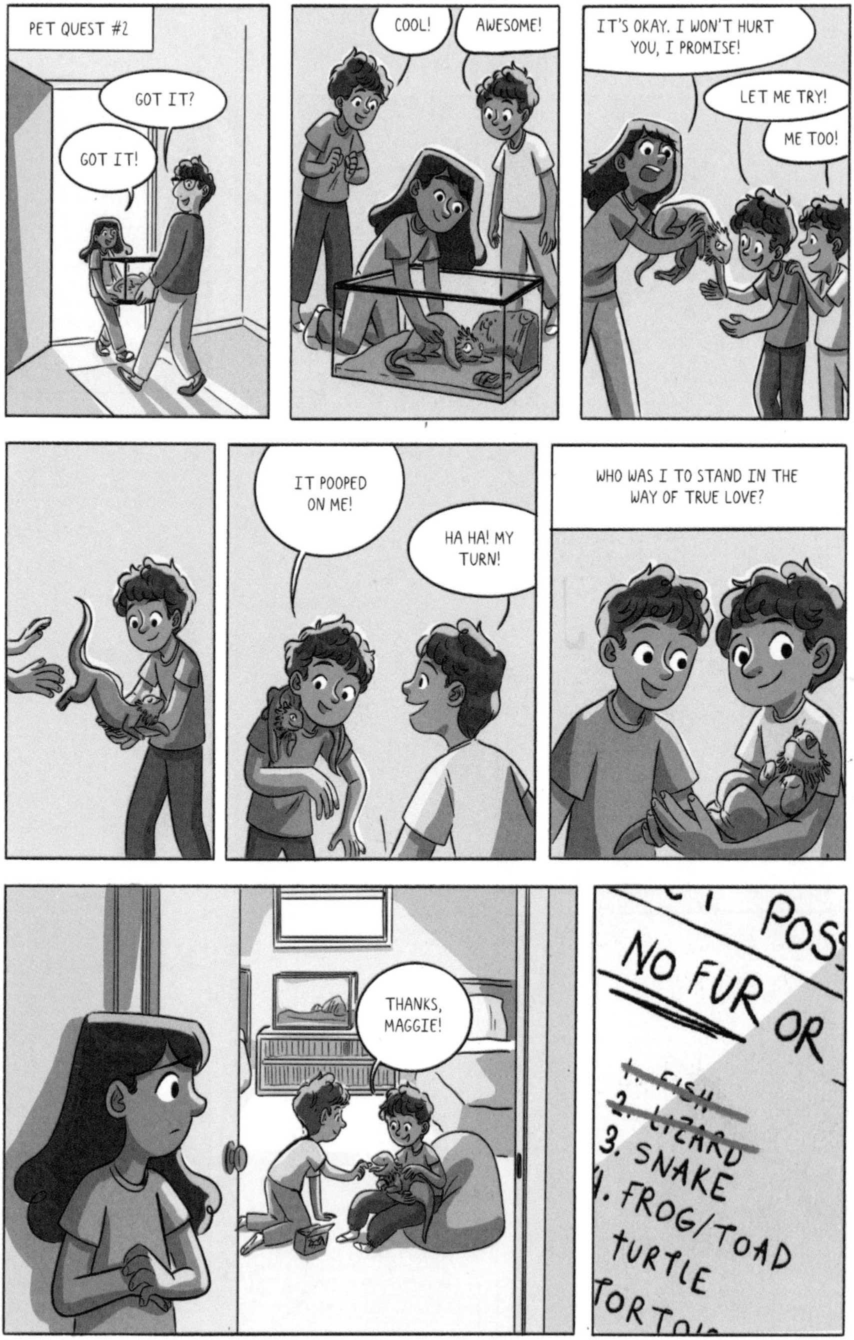
PET QUEST #2
GOT IT?
GOT IT!
COOL!
AWESOME!
IT'S OKAY. I WON'T HURT YOU, I PROMISE!
LET ME TRY!
ME TOO!
IT POOPED ON ME!
HA HA! MY TURN!
WHO WAS I TO STAND IN THE WAY OF TRUE LOVE?
THANKS, MAGGIE!
POSS
NO FUR OR
1. FISH
2. LIZARD
3. SNAKE
4. FROG/TOAD
TURTLE
TORTOI

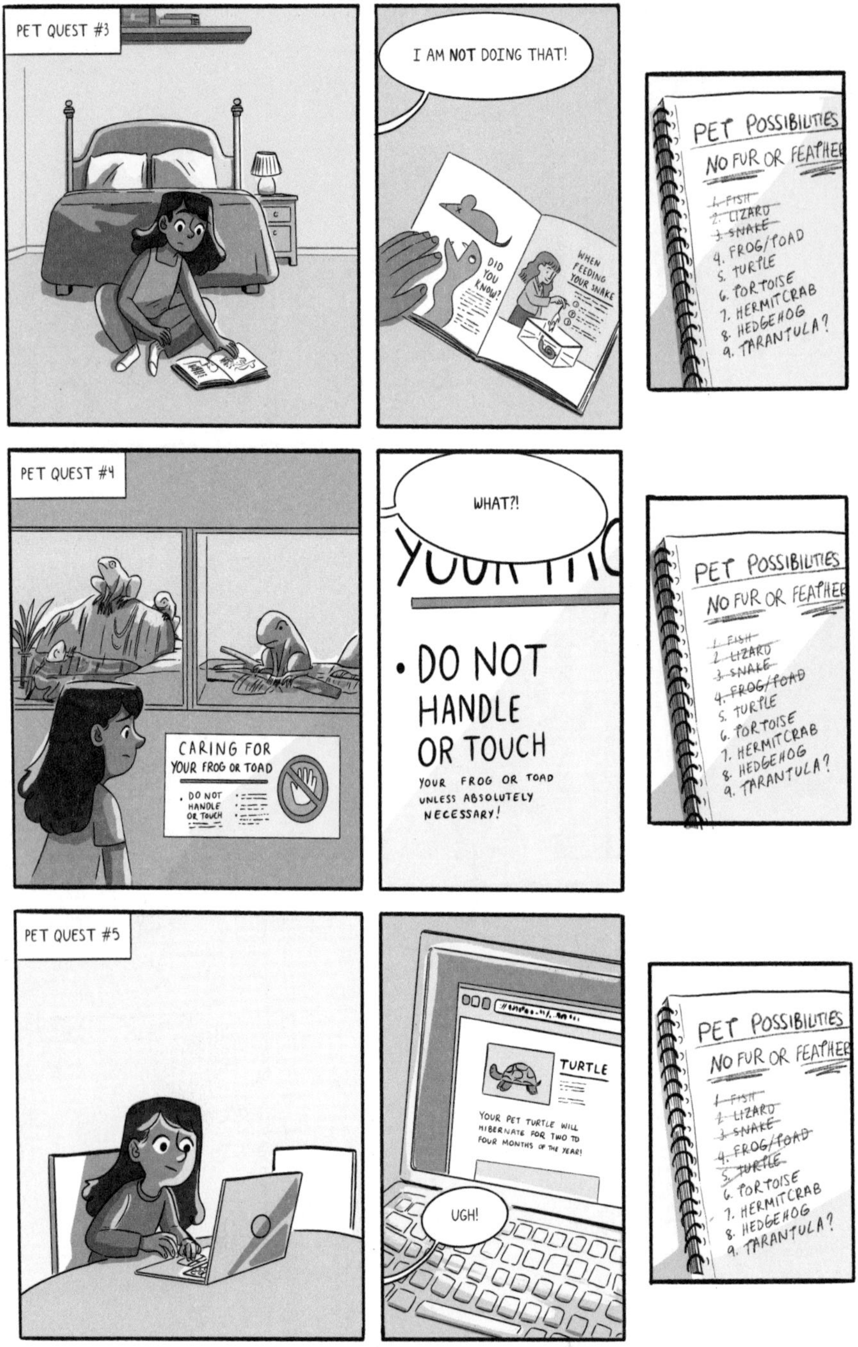
PET QUEST #3
I AM NOT DOING THAT!
DID YOU KNOW?
WHEN FEEDING YOUR SNAKE
PET POSSIBILITIES
NO FUR OR FEATHER
1. FISH
2. LIZARD
3. SNAKE
4. FROG/TOAD
5. TURTLE
6. TORTOISE
7. HERMITCRAB
8. HEDGEHOG
9. TARANTULA?
PET QUEST #4
CARING FOR YOUR FROG OR TOAD
• DO NOT HANDLE OR TOUCH
WHAT?!
• DO NOT HANDLE OR TOUCH
YOUR FROG OR TOAD UNLESS ABSOLUTELY NECESSARY!
PET POSSIBILITIES
NO FUR OR FEATHER
1. FISH
2. LIZARD
3. SNAKE
4. FROG/TOAD
5. TURTLE
6. TORTOISE
7. HERMITCRAB
8. HEDGEHOG
9. TARANTULA?
PET QUEST #5
TURTLE
YOUR PET TURTLE WILL HIBERNATE FOR TWO TO FOUR MONTHS OF THE YEAR!
UGH!
PET POSSIBILITIES
NO FUR OR FEATHER
1. FISH
2. LIZARD
3. SNAKE
4. FROG/TOAD
5. TURTLE
6. TORTOISE
7. HERMITCRAB
8. HEDGEHOG
9. TARANTULA?

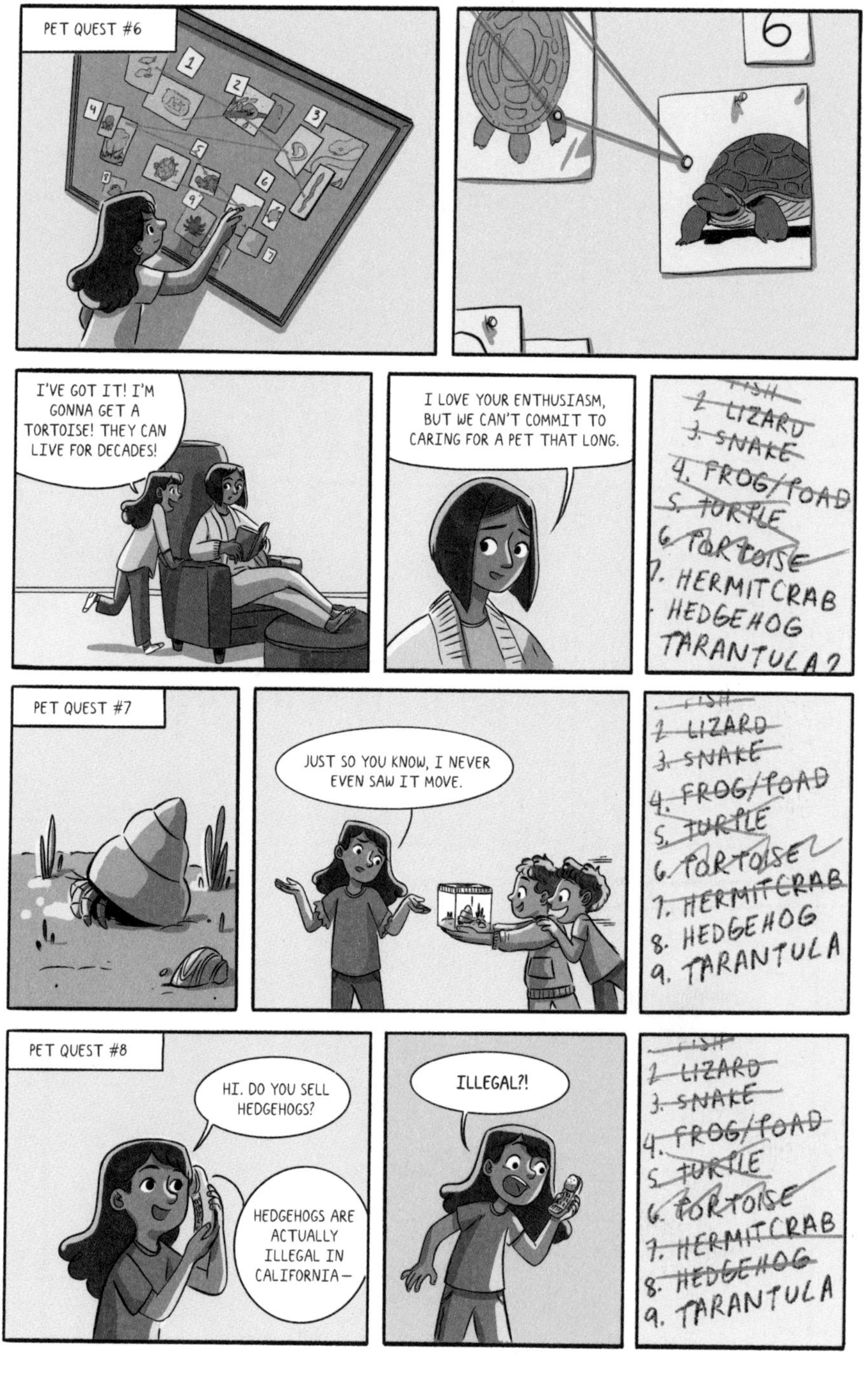
PET QUEST #6
1
2
3
4
5
6
7
8
9
6
I'VE GOT IT! I'M GONNA GET A TORTOISE! THEY CAN LIVE FOR DECADES!
I LOVE YOUR ENTHUSIASM, BUT WE CAN'T COMMIT TO CARING FOR A PET THAT LONG.
2. LIZARD
3. SNAKE
4. FROG/TOAD
5. TURTLE
6. TORTOISE
7. HERMITCRAB
HEDGEHOG
TARANTULA?
PET QUEST #7
JUST SO YOU KNOW, I NEVER EVEN SAW IT MOVE.
2. LIZARD
3. SNAKE
4. FROG/TOAD
5. TURTLE
6. TORTOISE
7. HERMITCRAB
8. HEDGEHOG
9. TARANTULA
PET QUEST #8
HI. DO YOU SELL HEDGEHOGS?
HEDGEHOGS ARE ACTUALLY ILLEGAL IN CALIFORNIA—
ILLEGAL?!
2. LIZARD
3. SNAKE
4. FROG/TOAD
5. TURTLE
6. TORTOISE
7. HERMITCRAB
8. HEDGEHOG
9. TARANTULA

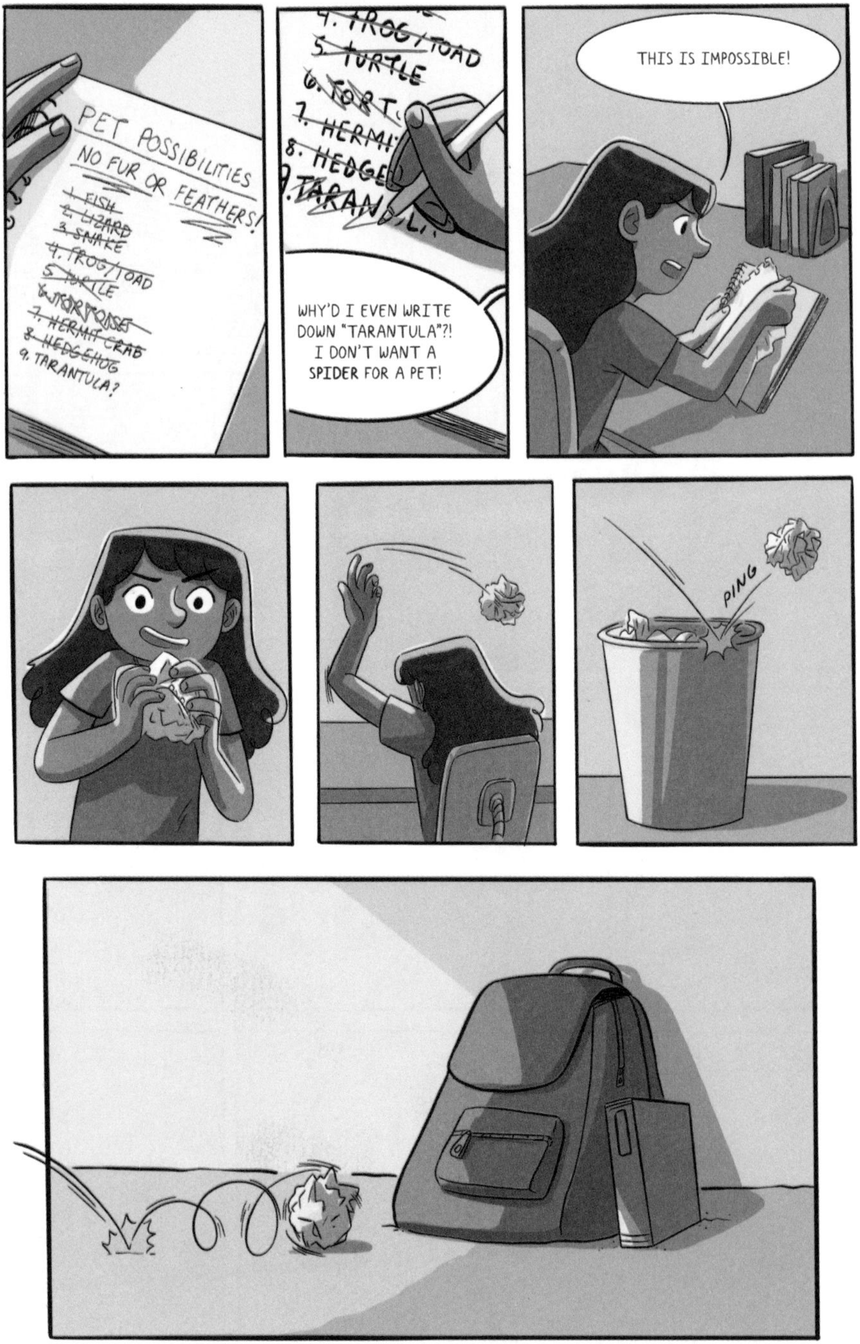
PET POSSIBILITIES
NO FUR OR FEATHERS!
1. FISH
2. LIZARD
3. SNAKE
4. FROG/TOAD
5. TURTLE
7. HERMIT CRAB
8. HEDGEHOG
9. TARANTULA?
WHY'D I EVEN WRITE DOWN "TARANTULA"?! I DON'T WANT A SPIDER FOR A PET!
THIS IS IMPOSSIBLE!
PING

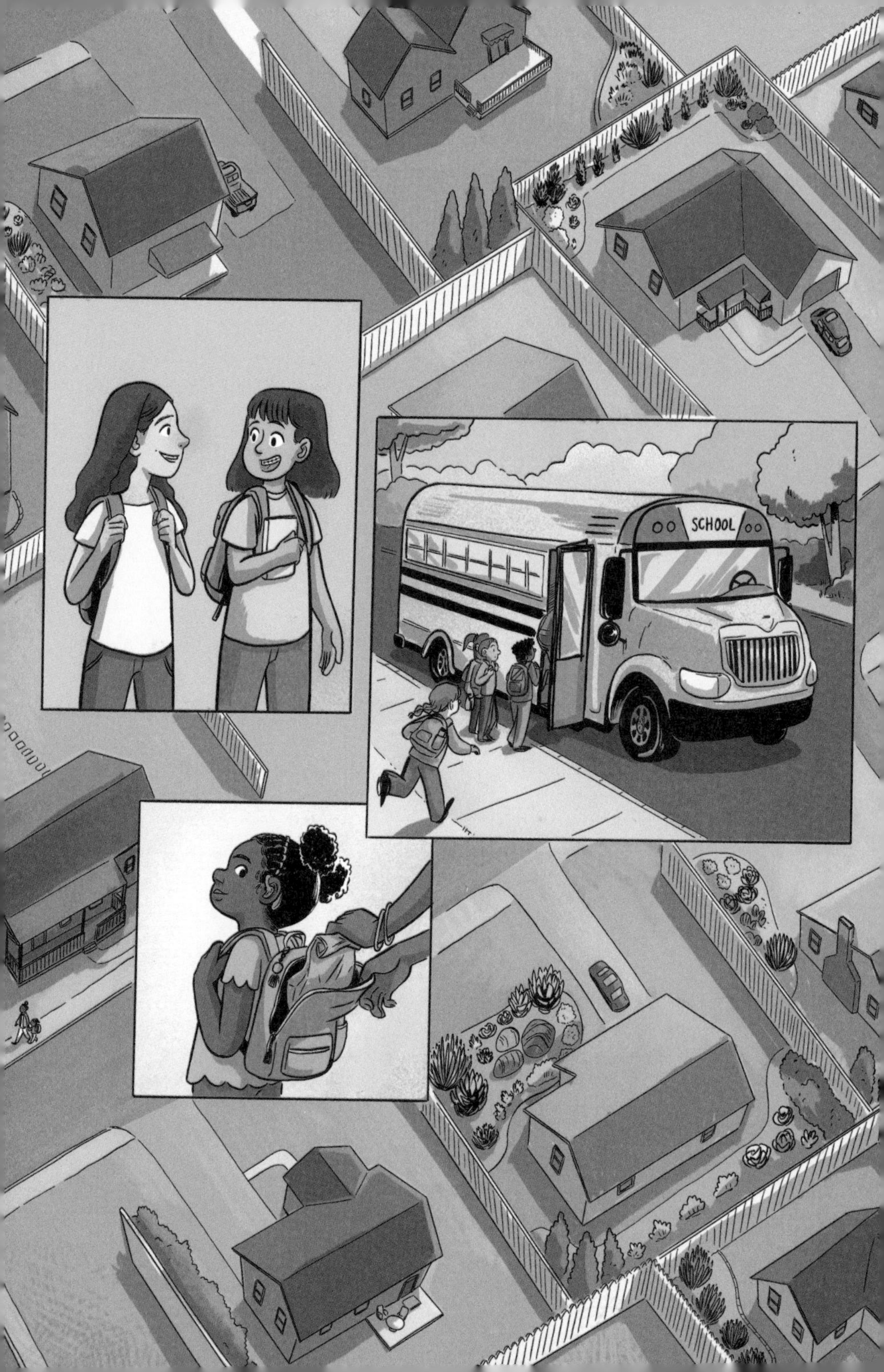
SCHOOL

Chapter Four

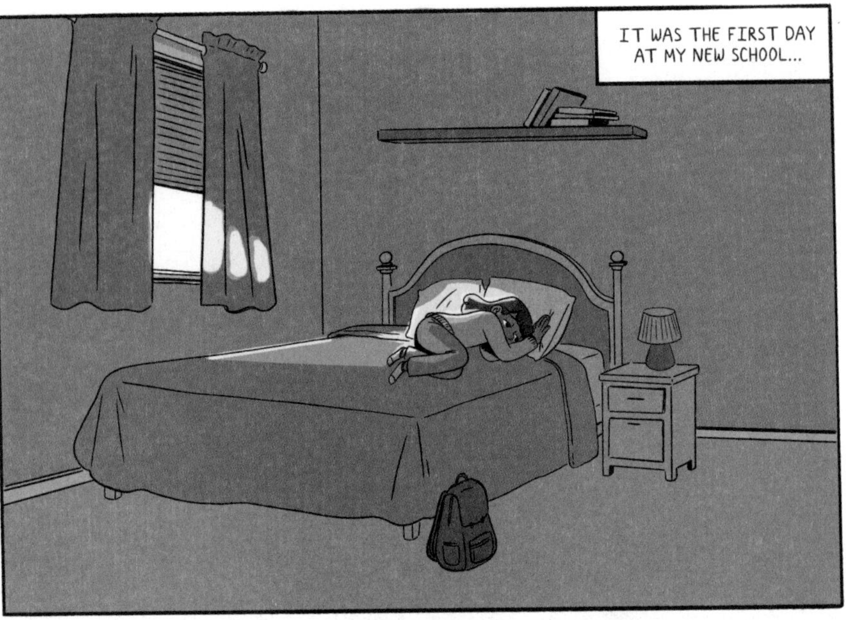
IT WAS THE FIRST DAY AT MY NEW SCHOOL...

AND IT WAS GOING TO BE THE **WORST** DAY EVER.

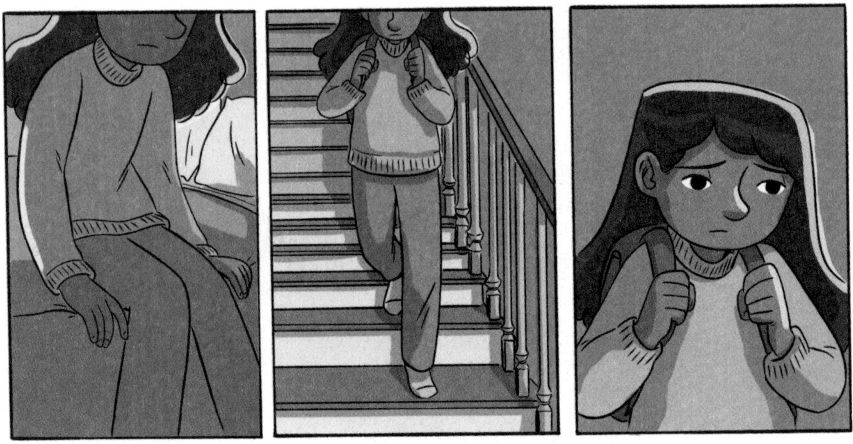

I WAS SURE OF IT.

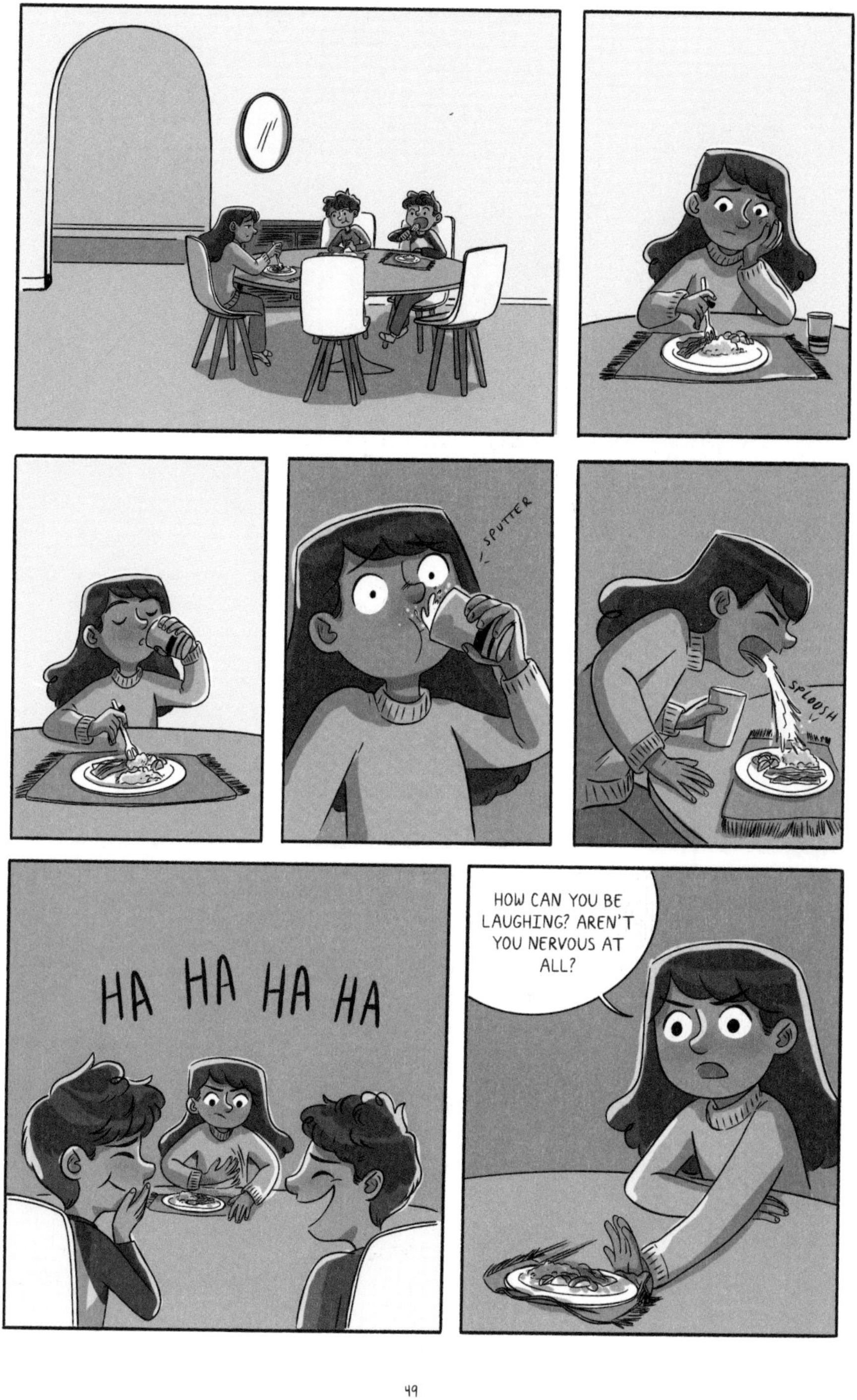
SPUTTER
SPLOOSH
HA HA HA HA
HOW CAN YOU BE LAUGHING? AREN'T YOU NERVOUS AT ALL?

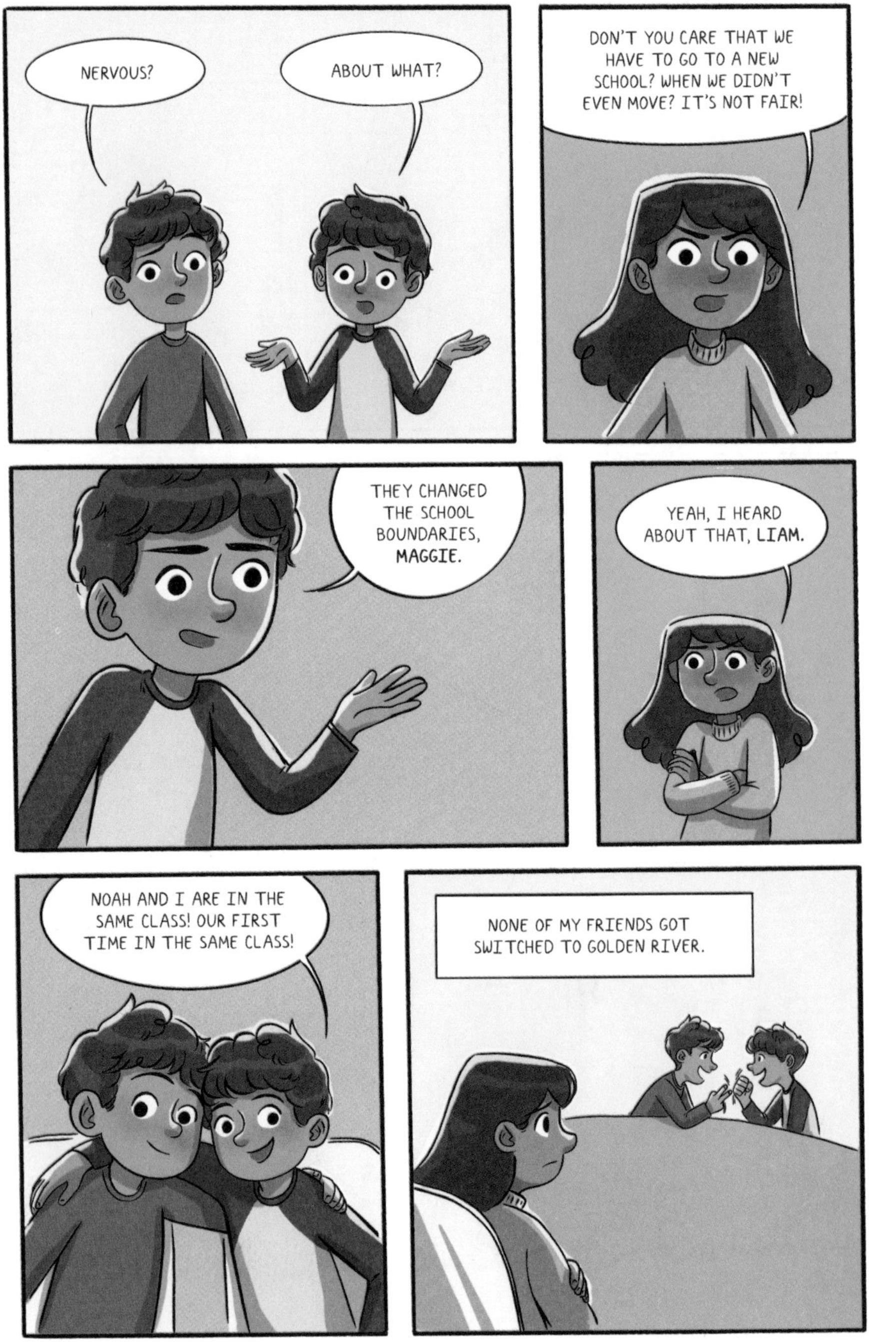
NERVOUS?
ABOUT WHAT?
DON'T YOU CARE THAT WE HAVE TO GO TO A NEW SCHOOL? WHEN WE DIDN'T EVEN MOVE? IT'S NOT FAIR!
THEY CHANGED THE SCHOOL BOUNDARIES, MAGGIE.
YEAH, I HEARD ABOUT THAT, LIAM.
NOAH AND I ARE IN THE SAME CLASS! OUR FIRST TIME IN THE SAME CLASS!
NONE OF MY FRIENDS GOT SWITCHED TO GOLDEN RIVER.

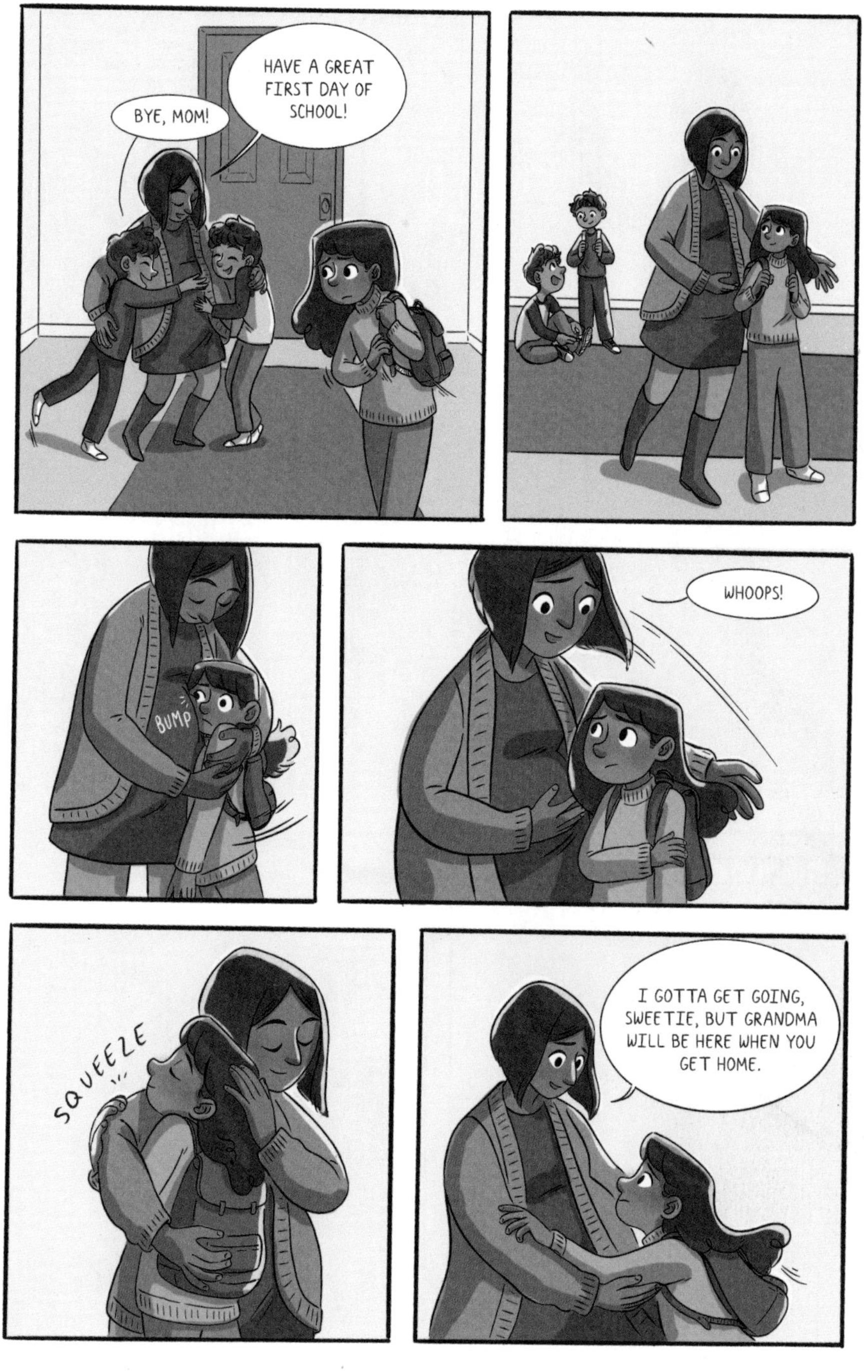
BYE, MOM!
HAVE A GREAT FIRST DAY OF SCHOOL!
BUMP
WHOOPS!
SQUEEZE
I GOTTA GET GOING, SWEETIE, BUT GRANDMA WILL BE HERE WHEN YOU GET HOME.

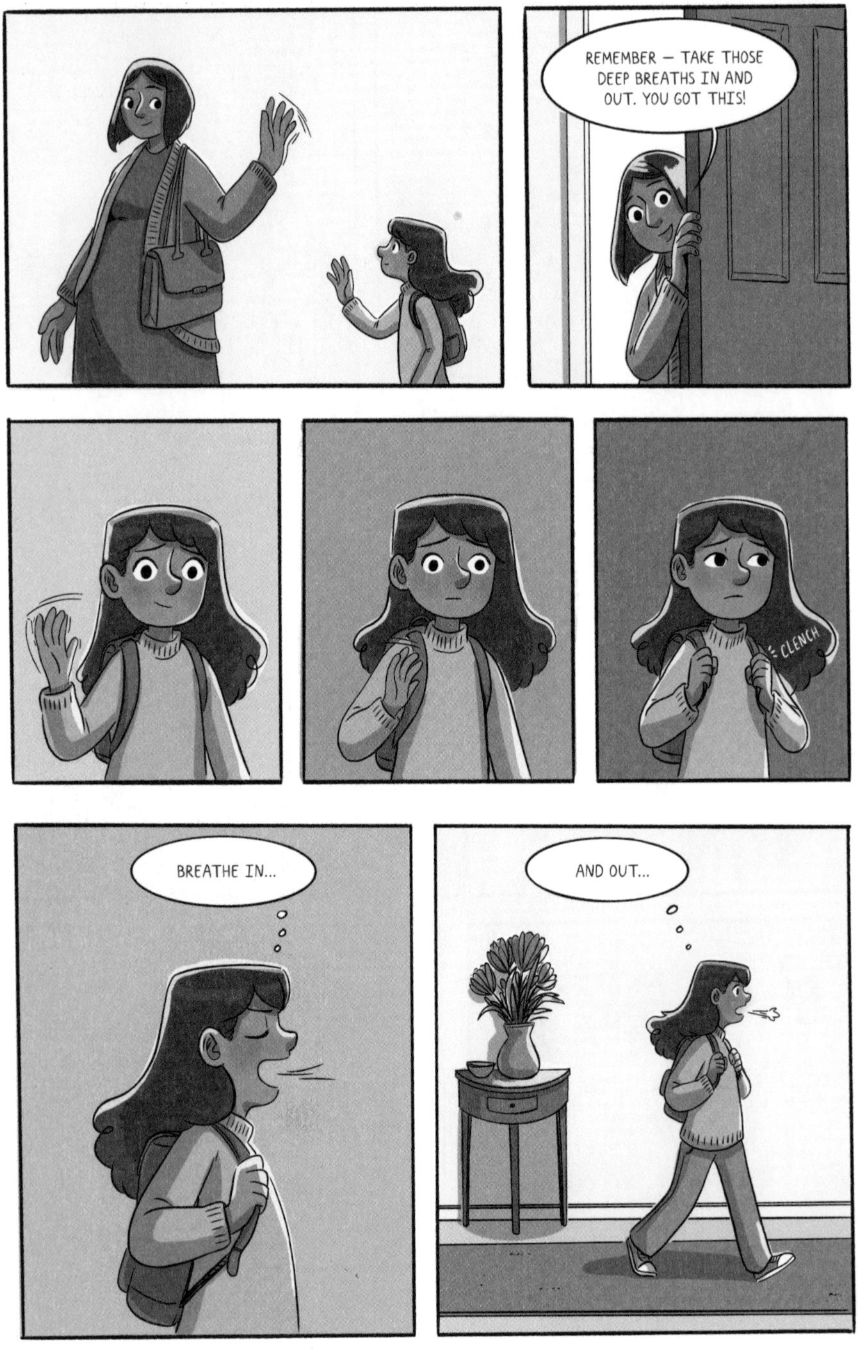
REMEMBER — TAKE THOSE DEEP BREATHS IN AND OUT. YOU GOT THIS!
CLENCH
BREATHE IN...
AND OUT...

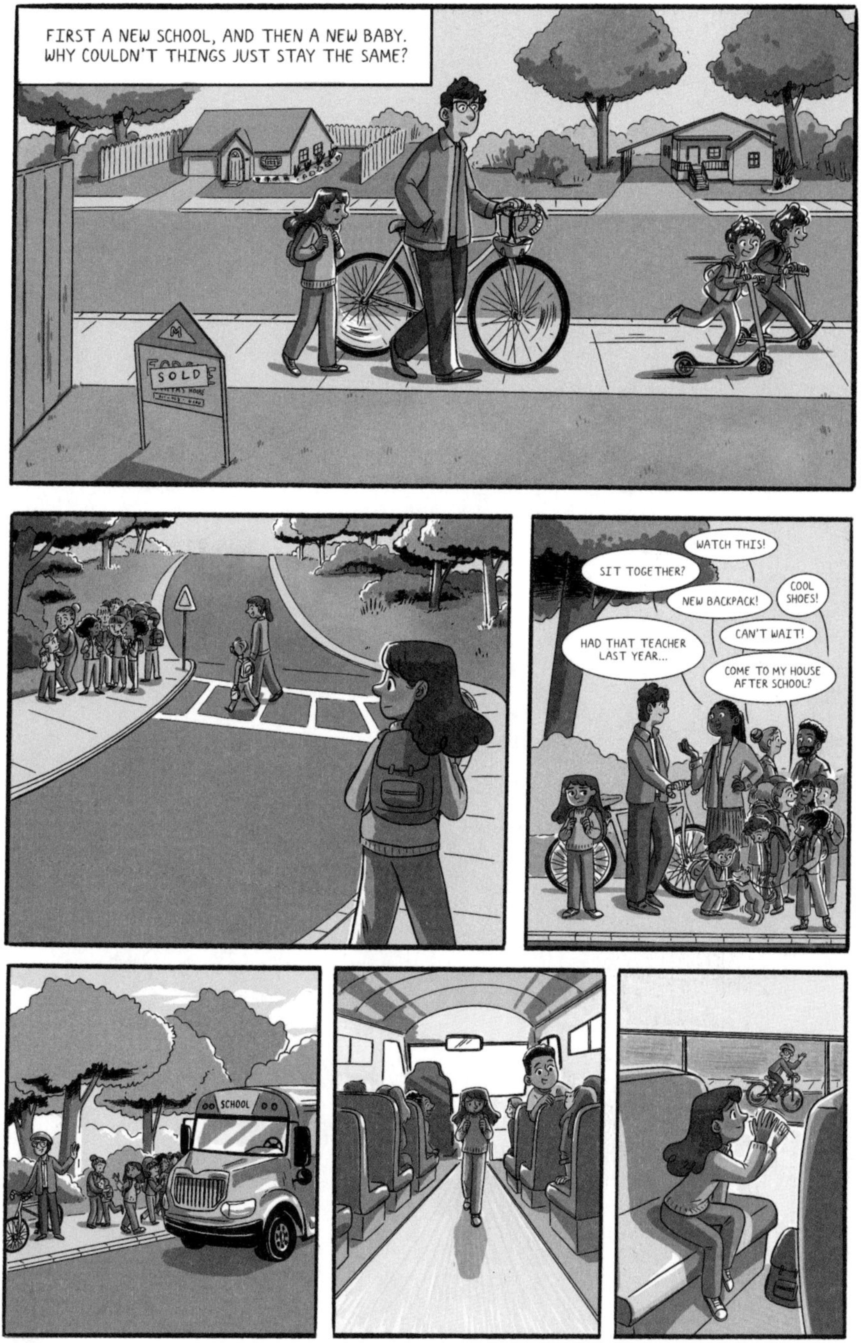
FIRST A NEW SCHOOL, AND THEN A NEW BABY. WHY COULDN'T THINGS JUST STAY THE SAME?
SOLD
SIT TOGETHER?
WATCH THIS!
NEW BACKPACK!
COOL SHOES!
HAD THAT TEACHER LAST YEAR...
CAN'T WAIT!
COME TO MY HOUSE AFTER SCHOOL?
SCHOOL

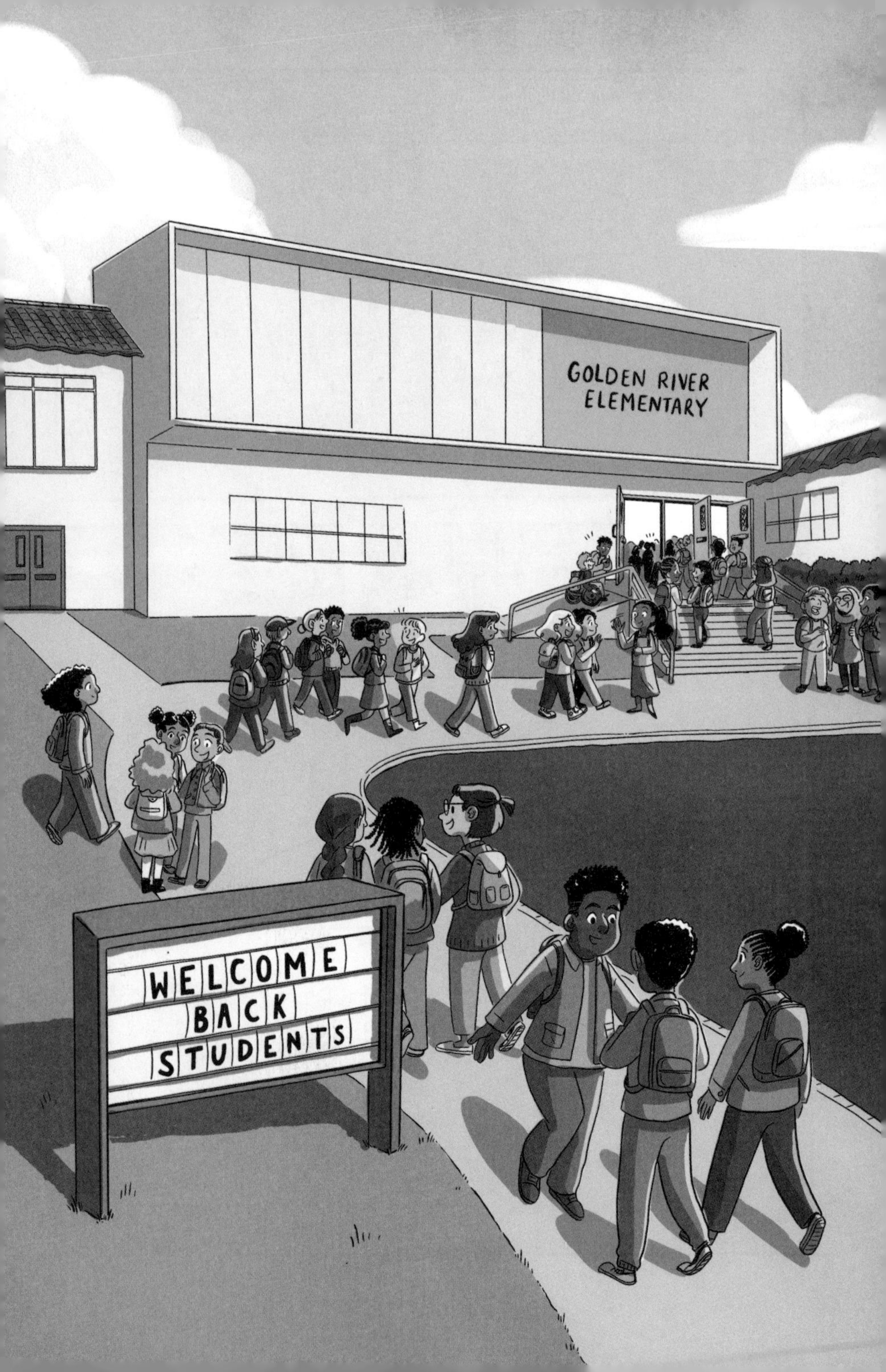
GOLDEN RIVER ELEMENTARY
WELCOME BACK STUDENTS

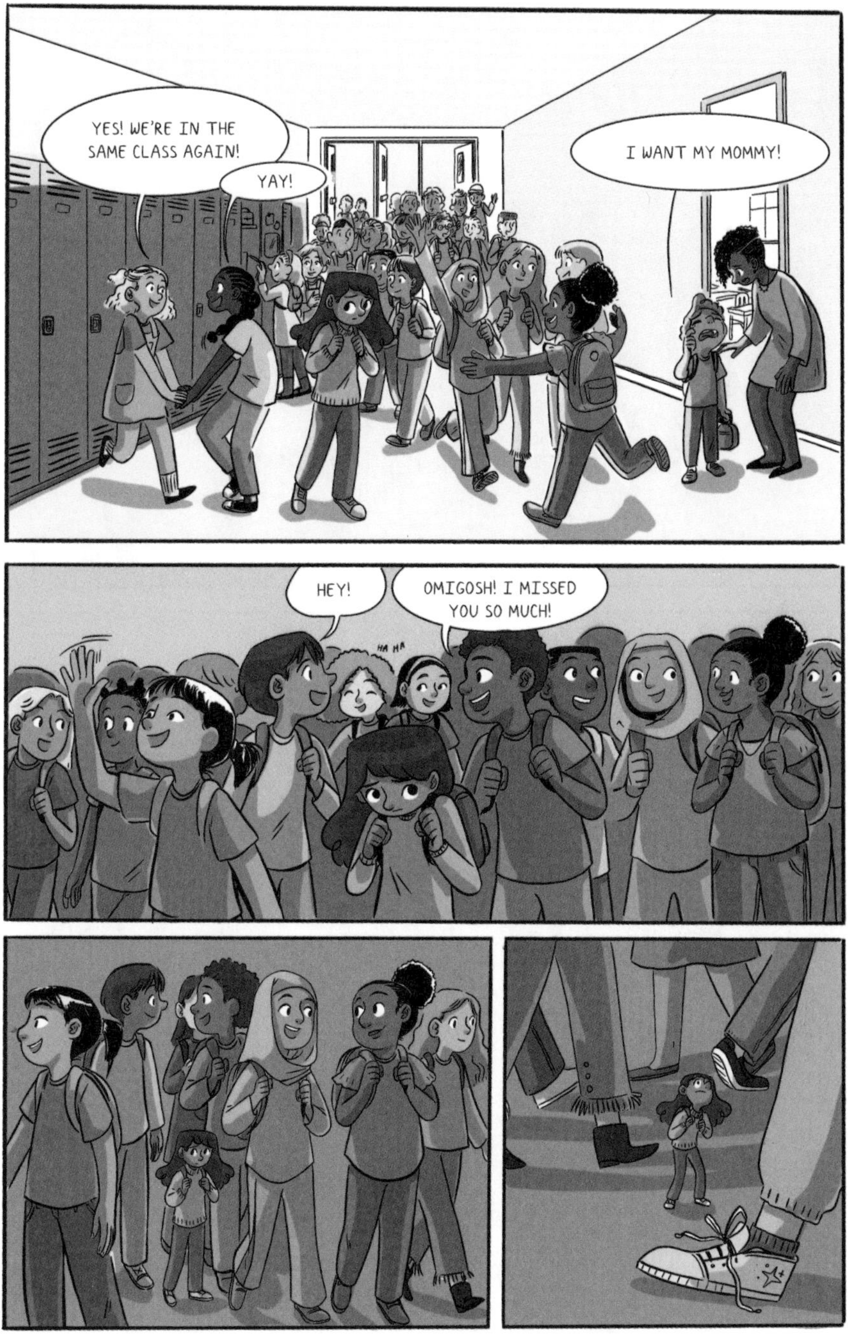
YES! WE'RE IN THE SAME CLASS AGAIN!
YAY!
I WANT MY MOMMY!
HEY!
HA HA
OMIGOSH! I MISSED YOU SO MUCH!

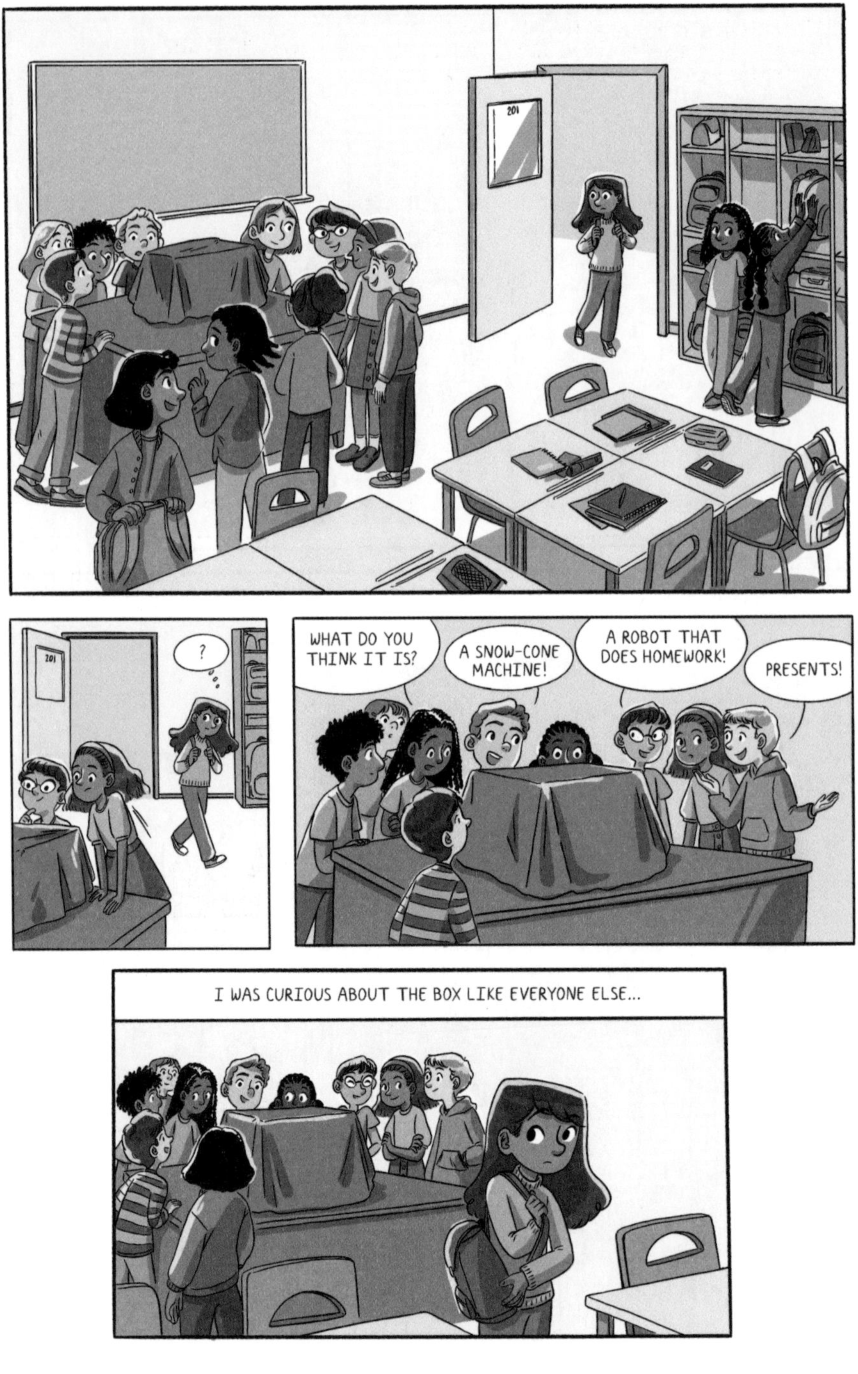
?
WHAT DO YOU THINK IT IS?
A SNOW-CONE MACHINE!
A ROBOT THAT DOES HOMEWORK!
PRESENTS!
I WAS CURIOUS ABOUT THE BOX LIKE EVERYONE ELSE...

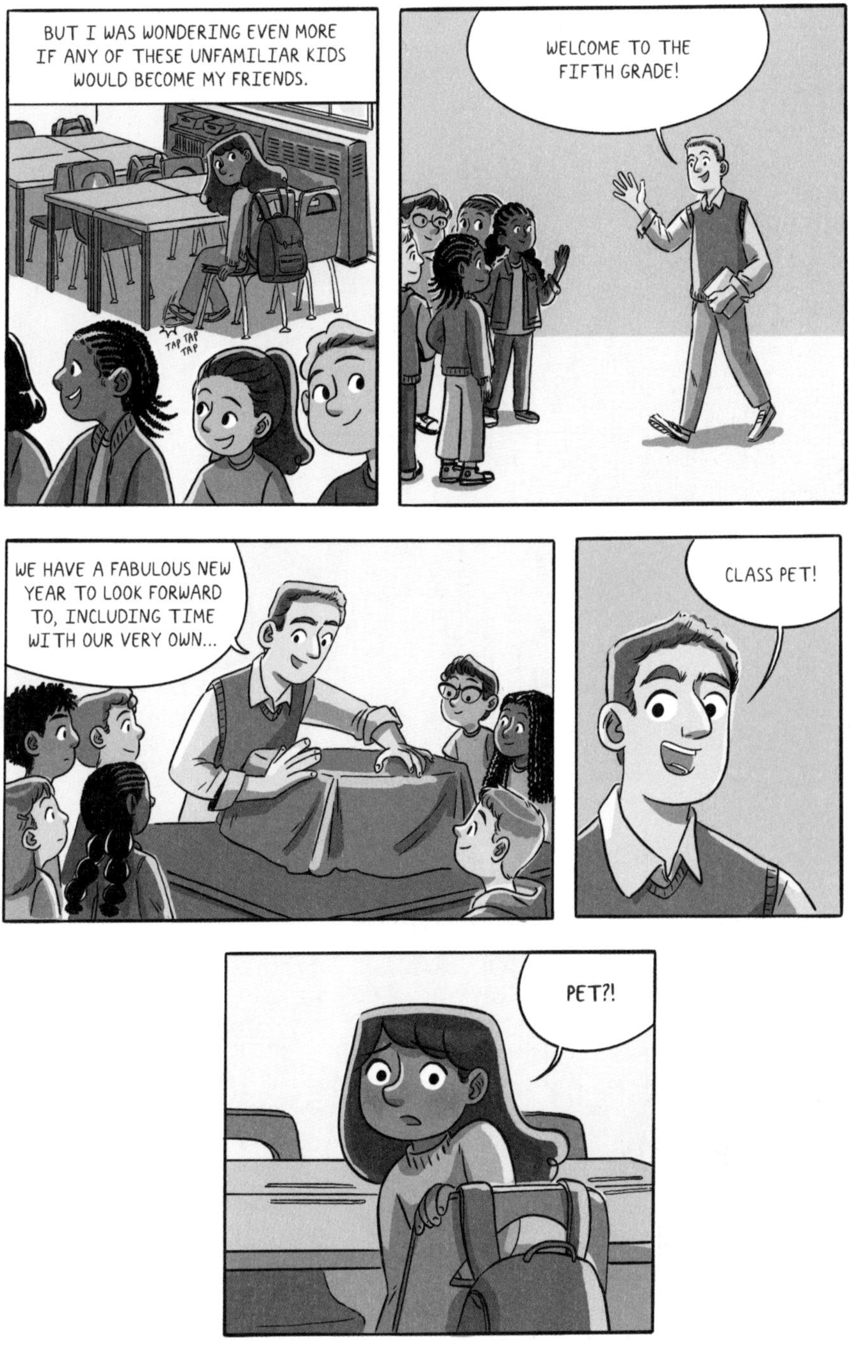
BUT I WAS WONDERING EVEN MORE IF ANY OF THESE UNFAMILIAR KIDS WOULD BECOME MY FRIENDS.
TAP TAP TAP
WELCOME TO THE FIFTH GRADE!
WE HAVE A FABULOUS NEW YEAR TO LOOK FORWARD TO, INCLUDING TIME WITH OUR VERY OWN...
CLASS PET!
PET?!

SWISH

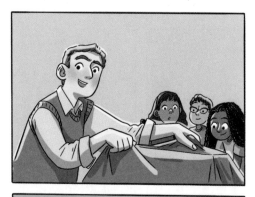

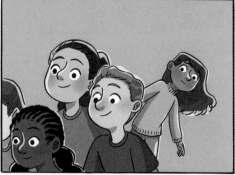

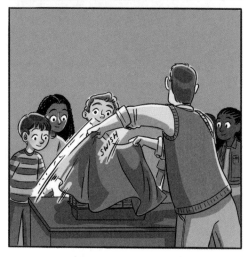

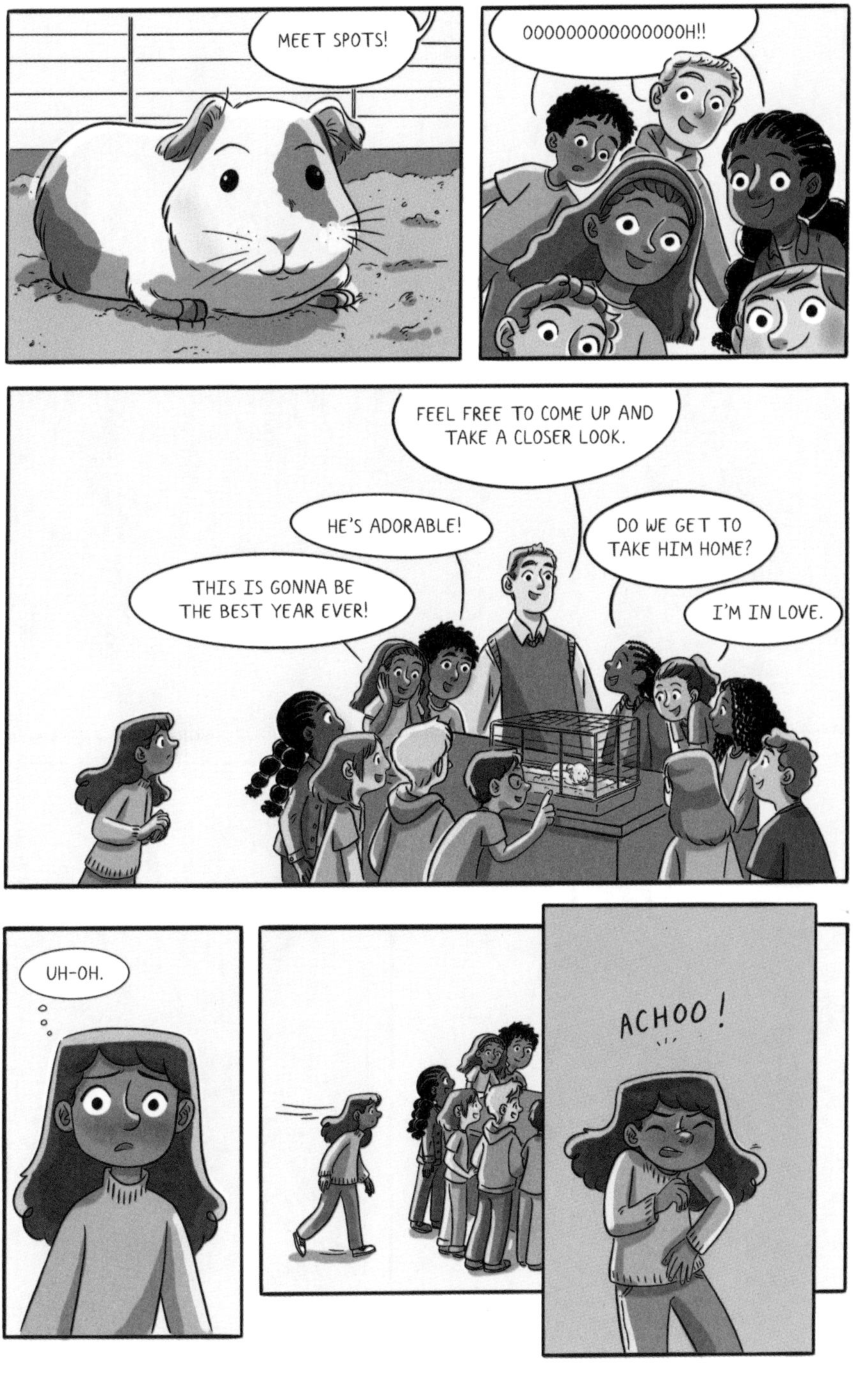
MEET SPOTS!
OOOOOOOOOOOOOOOH!!
FEEL FREE TO COME UP AND TAKE A CLOSER LOOK.
HE'S ADORABLE!
DO WE GET TO TAKE HIM HOME?
THIS IS GONNA BE THE BEST YEAR EVER!
I'M IN LOVE.
UH-OH.
ACHOO!

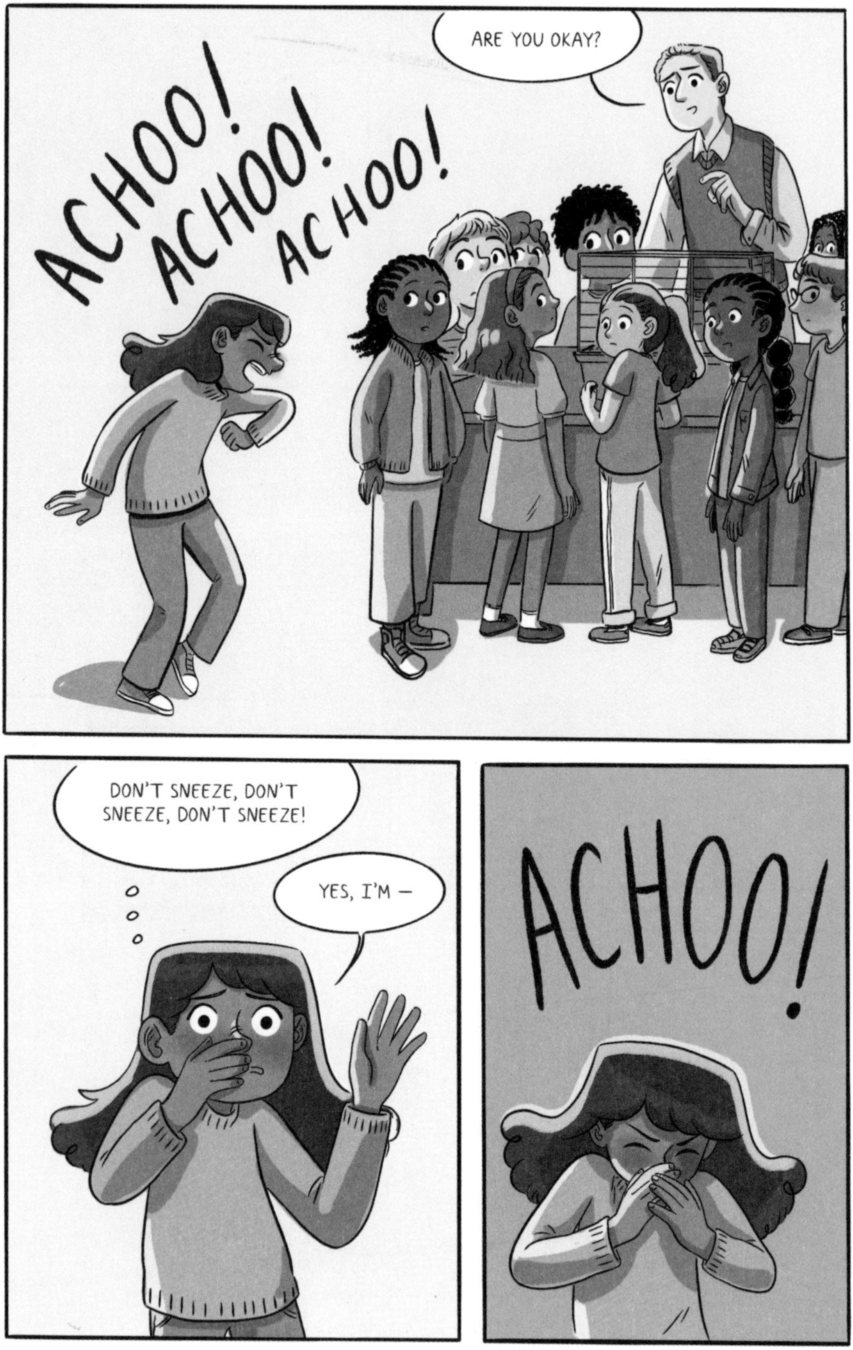
ACHOO! ACHOO! ACHOO!
ARE YOU OKAY?
DON'T SNEEZE, DON'T SNEEZE, DON'T SNEEZE!
YES, I'M —
ACHOO!

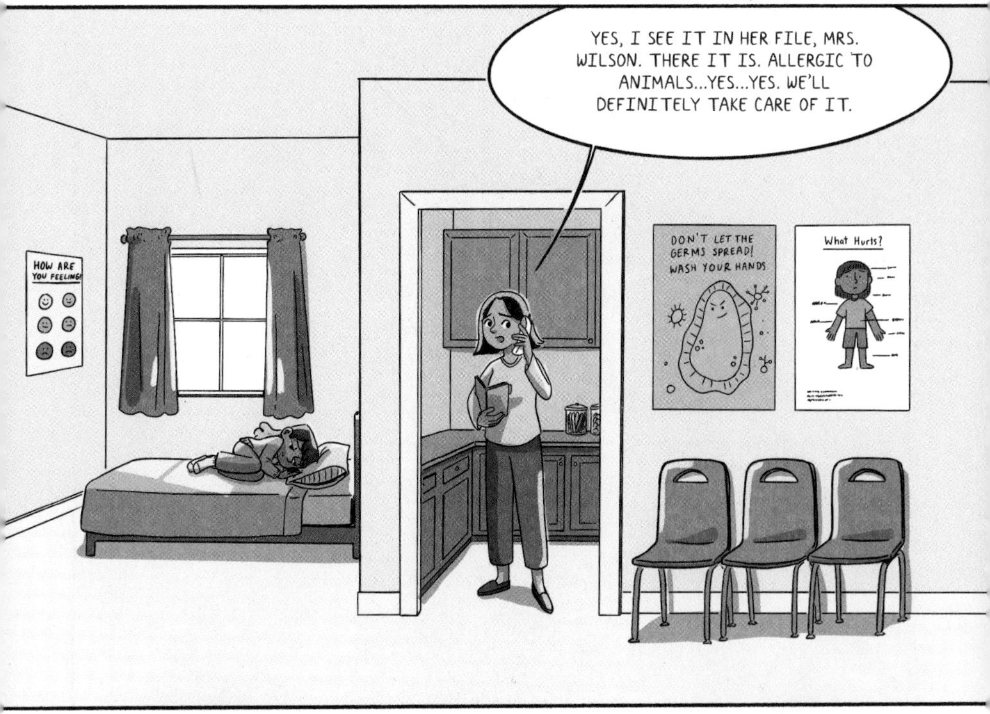
YES, I SEE IT IN HER FILE, MRS. WILSON. THERE IT IS. ALLERGIC TO ANIMALS...YES...YES. WE'LL DEFINITELY TAKE CARE OF IT.
HOW ARE YOU FEELING?
DON'T LET THE GERMS SPREAD! WASH YOUR HANDS.
What Hurts?

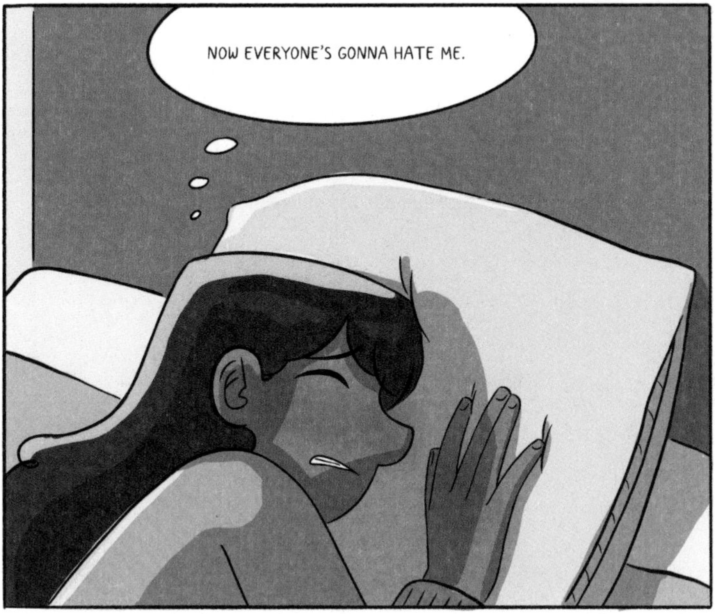
NOW EVERYONE'S GONNA HATE ME.

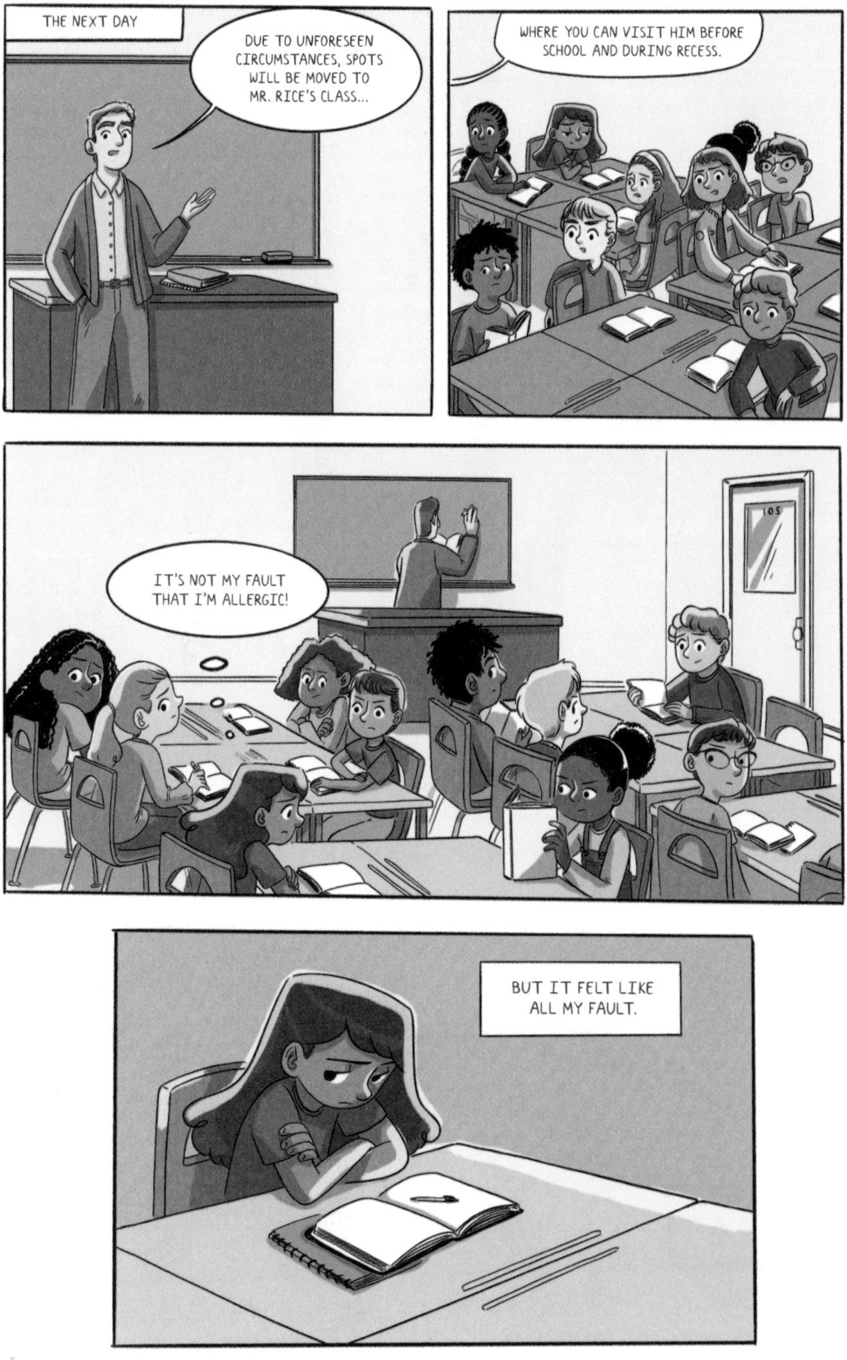
THE NEXT DAY
DUE TO UNFORESEEN CIRCUMSTANCES, SPOTS WILL BE MOVED TO MR. RICE'S CLASS...
WHERE YOU CAN VISIT HIM BEFORE SCHOOL AND DURING RECESS.
105
IT'S NOT MY FAULT THAT I'M ALLERGIC!
BUT IT FELT LIKE ALL MY FAULT.

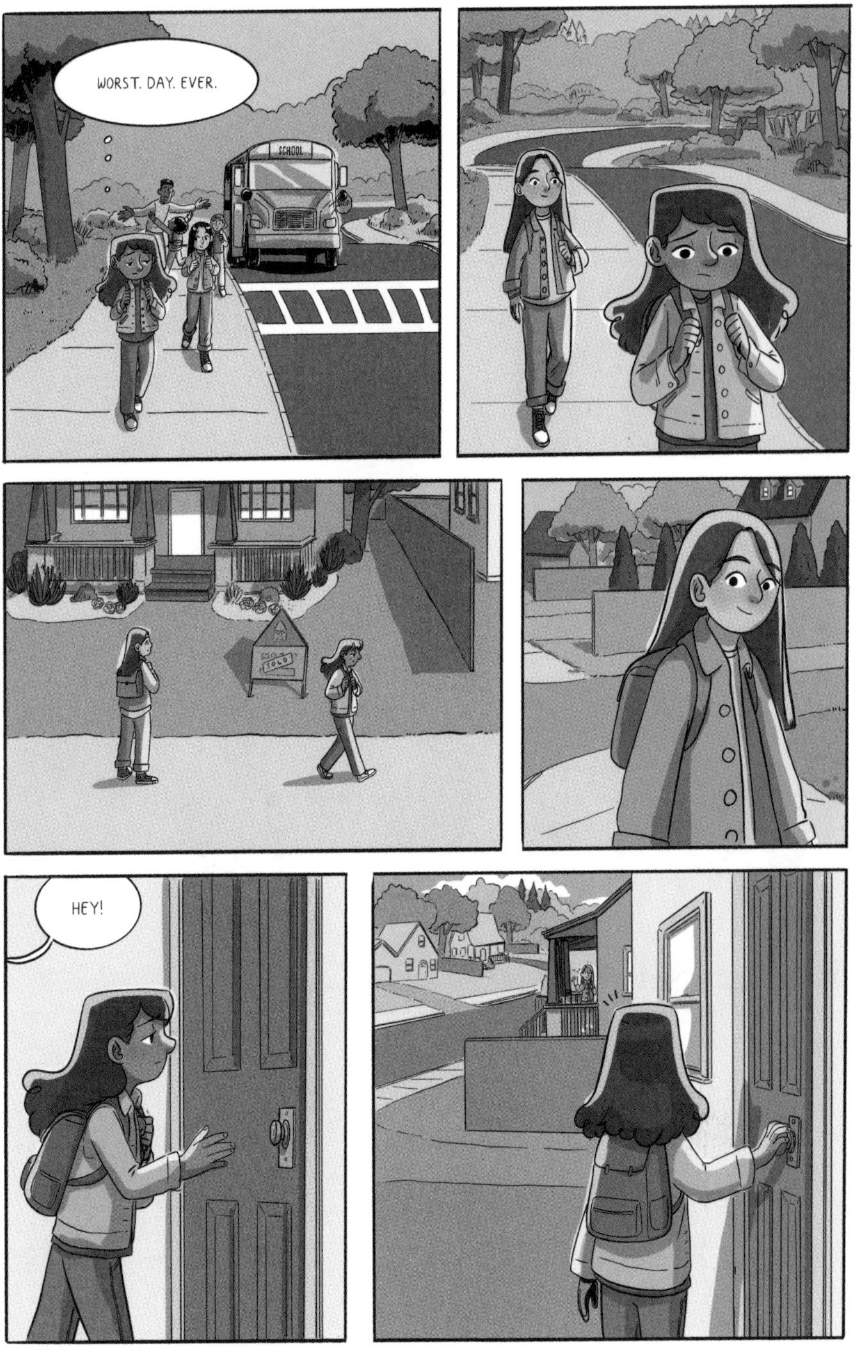
WORST. DAY. EVER.
SCHOOL
SOLD
HEY!

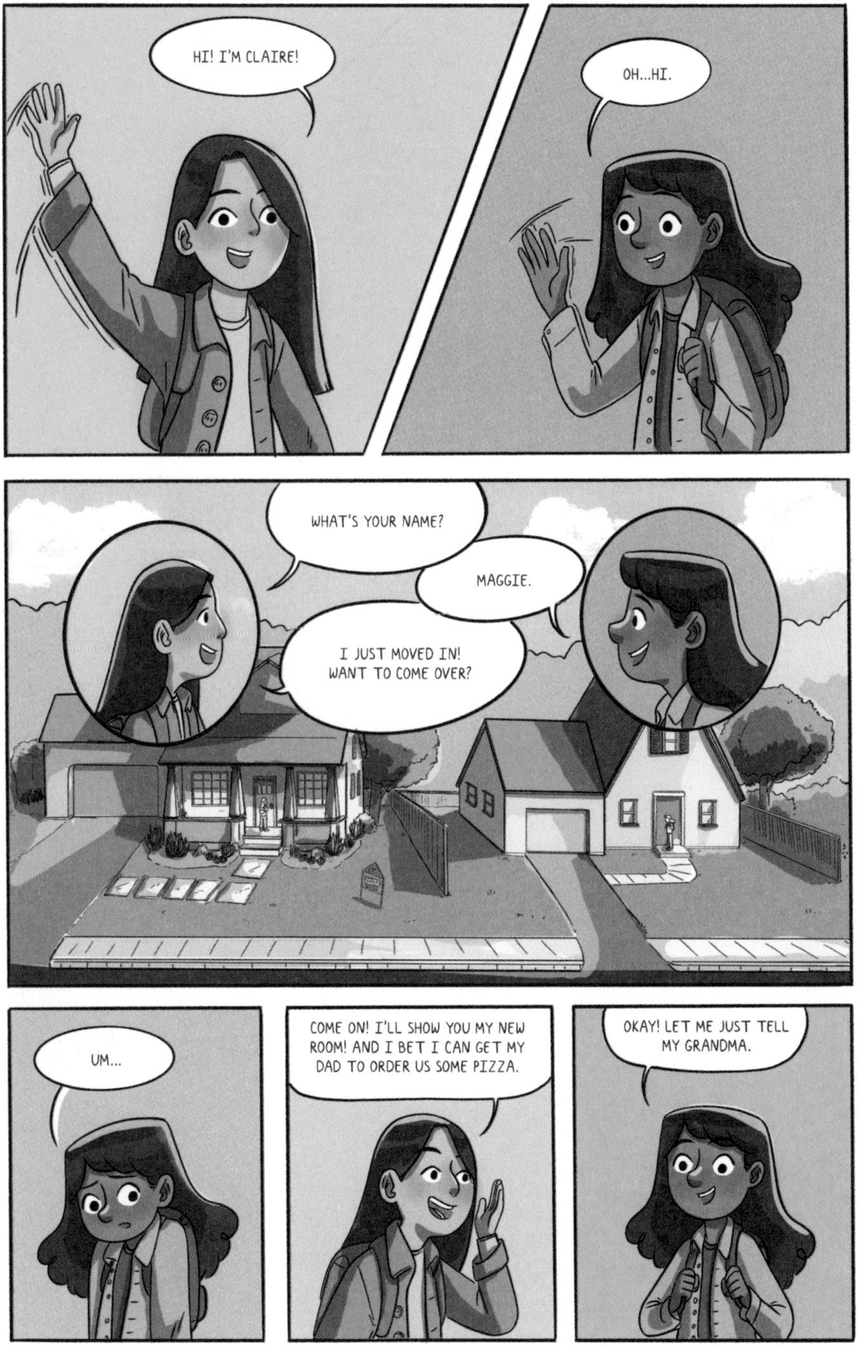
HI! I'M CLAIRE!
OH...HI.
WHAT'S YOUR NAME?
MAGGIE.
I JUST MOVED IN! WANT TO COME OVER?
UM...
COME ON! I'LL SHOW YOU MY NEW ROOM! AND I BET I CAN GET MY DAD TO ORDER US SOME PIZZA.
OKAY! LET ME JUST TELL MY GRANDMA.

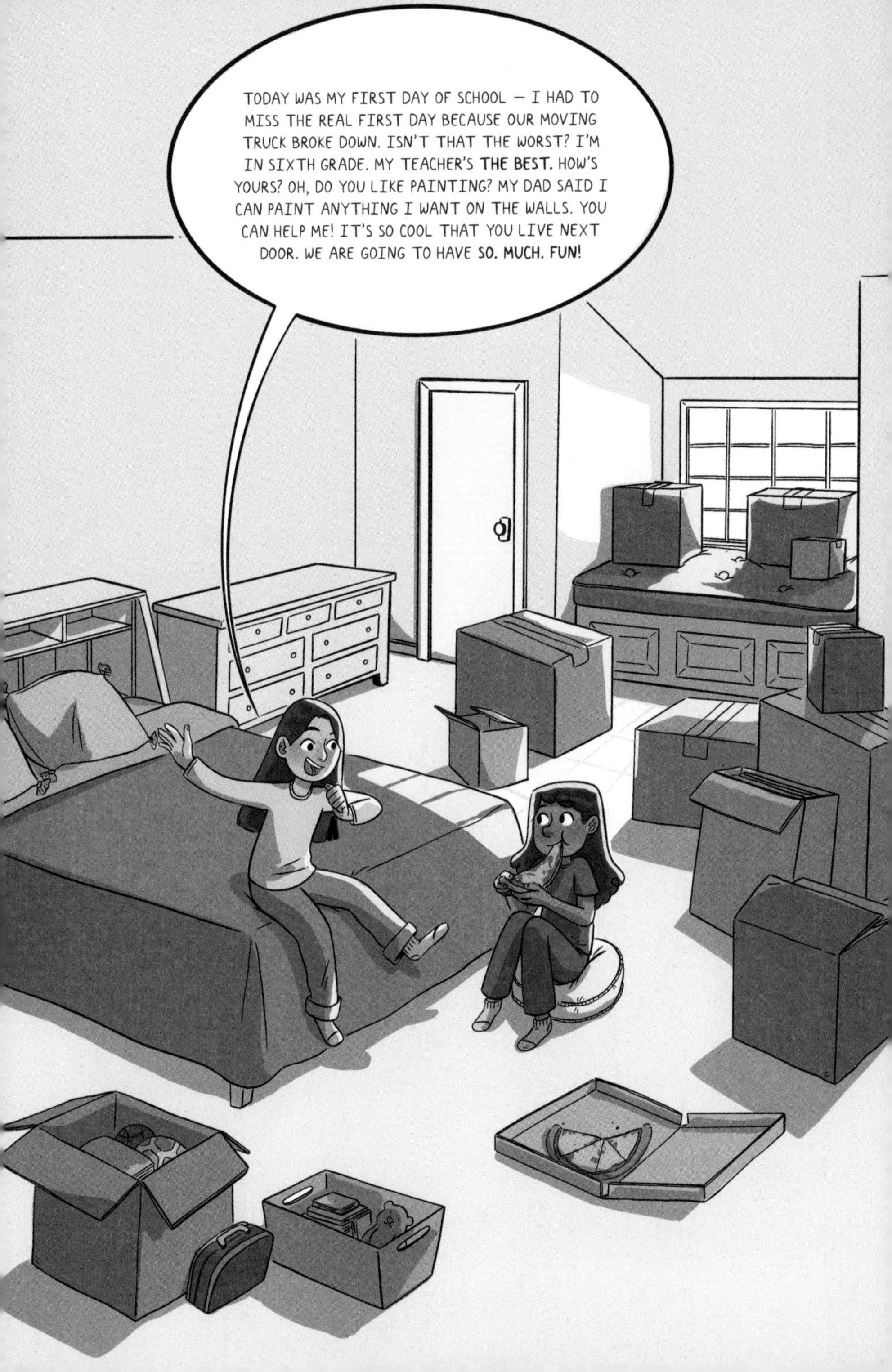
TODAY WAS MY FIRST DAY OF SCHOOL — I HAD TO MISS THE REAL FIRST DAY BECAUSE OUR MOVING TRUCK BROKE DOWN. ISN'T THAT THE WORST? I'M IN SIXTH GRADE. MY TEACHER'S **THE BEST.** HOW'S YOURS? OH, DO YOU LIKE PAINTING? MY DAD SAID I CAN PAINT ANYTHING I WANT ON THE WALLS. YOU CAN HELP ME! IT'S SO COOL THAT YOU LIVE NEXT DOOR. WE ARE GOING TO HAVE **SO. MUCH. FUN!**

Chapter Five

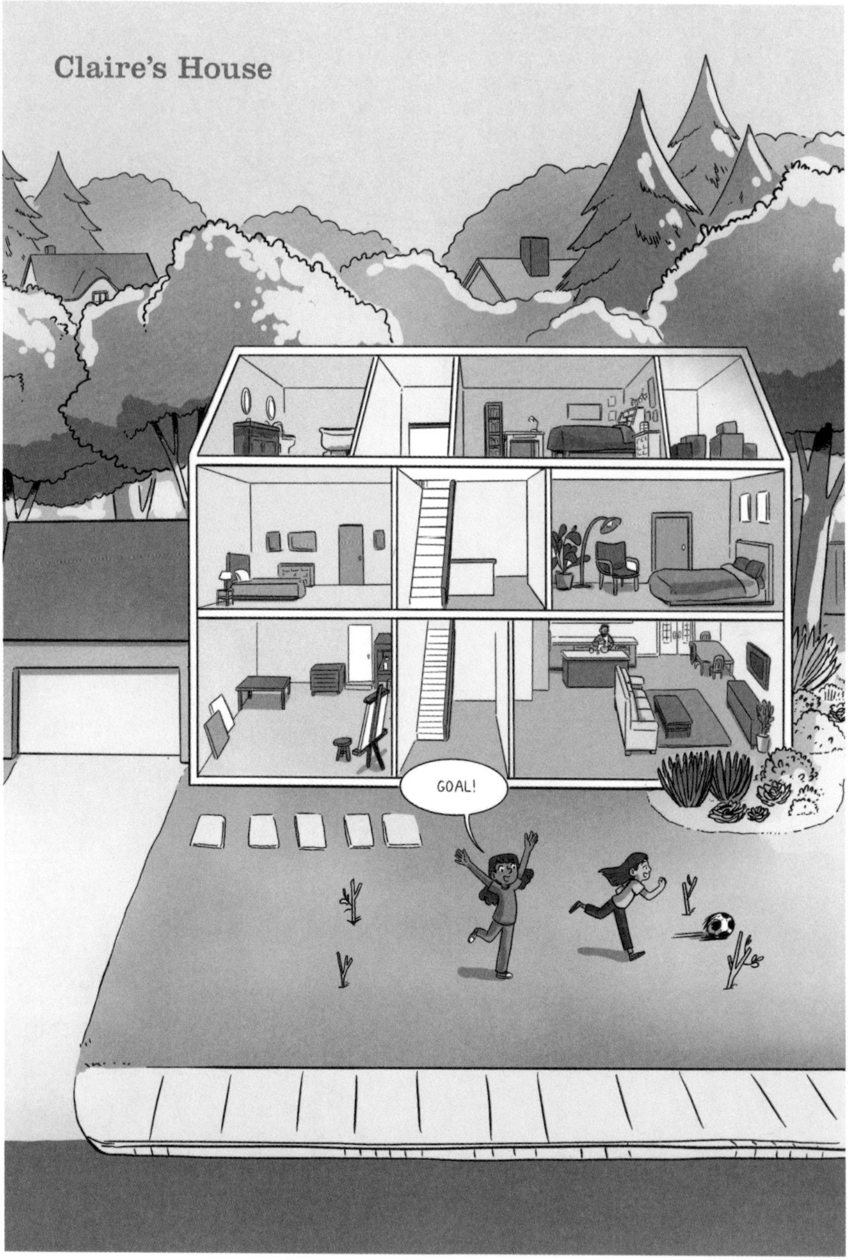
Claire's House
GOAL!

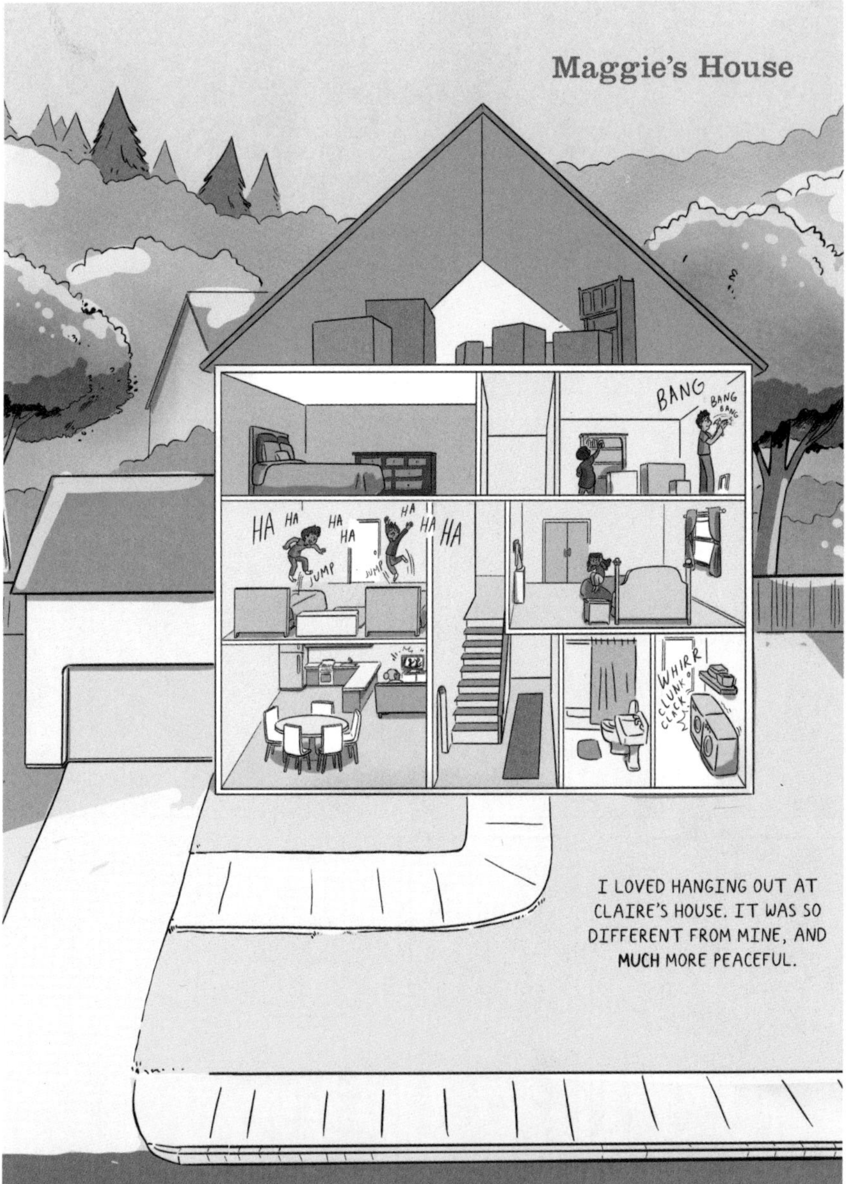
Maggie's House
BANG
BANG BANG
HA HA HA HA HA HA HA HA
JUMP
JUMP
WHIRR CLUNK CLACK
I LOVED HANGING OUT AT CLAIRE'S HOUSE. IT WAS SO DIFFERENT FROM MINE, AND **MUCH** MORE PEACEFUL.

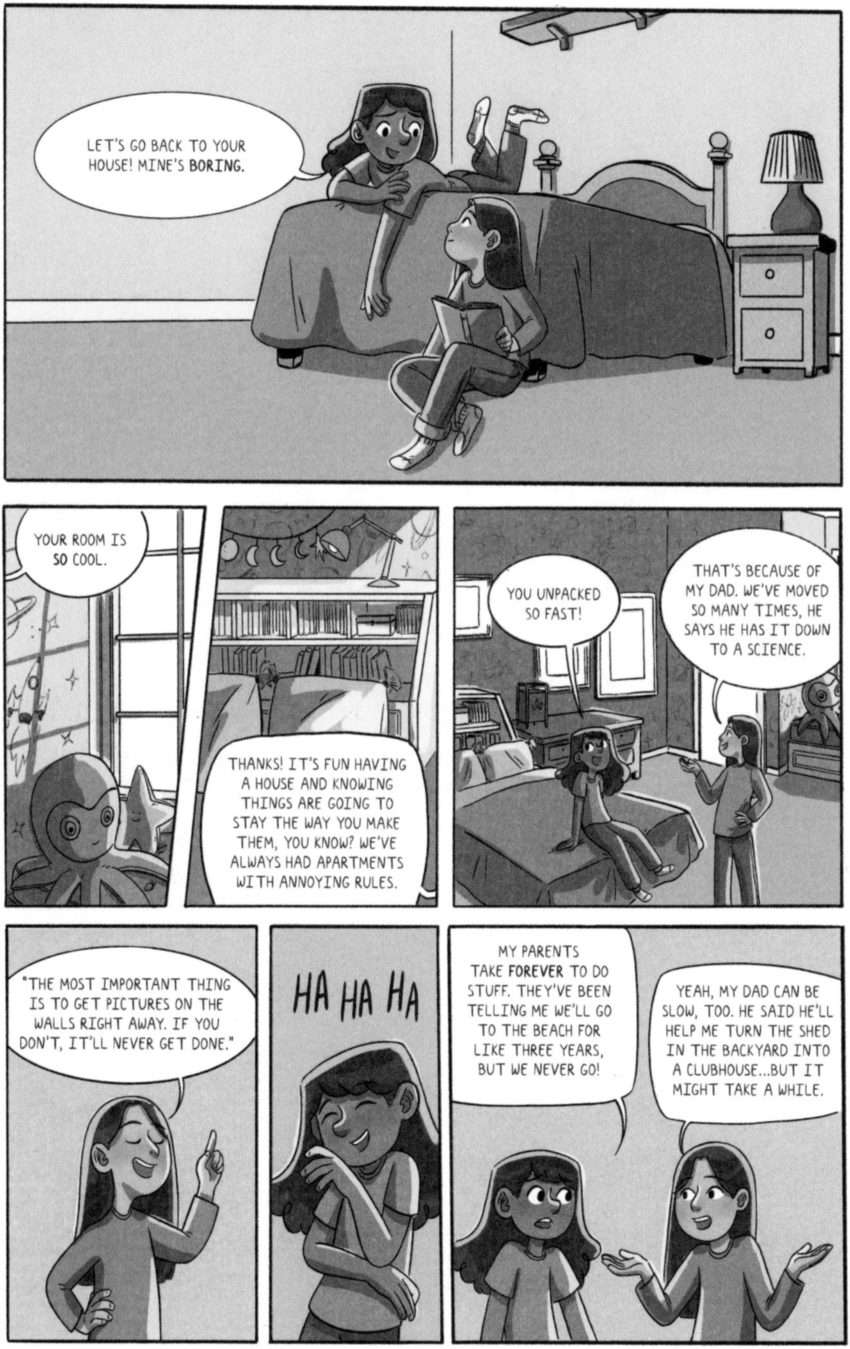
LET'S GO BACK TO YOUR HOUSE! MINE'S **BORING.**
YOUR ROOM IS **SO** COOL.
THANKS! IT'S FUN HAVING A HOUSE AND KNOWING THINGS ARE GOING TO STAY THE WAY YOU MAKE THEM, YOU KNOW? WE'VE ALWAYS HAD APARTMENTS WITH ANNOYING RULES.
YOU UNPACKED SO FAST!
THAT'S BECAUSE OF MY DAD. WE'VE MOVED SO MANY TIMES, HE SAYS HE HAS IT DOWN TO A SCIENCE.
"THE MOST IMPORTANT THING IS TO GET PICTURES ON THE WALLS RIGHT AWAY. IF YOU DON'T, IT'LL NEVER GET DONE."
HA HA HA
MY PARENTS TAKE **FOREVER** TO DO STUFF. THEY'VE BEEN TELLING ME WE'LL GO TO THE BEACH FOR LIKE THREE YEARS, BUT WE NEVER GO!
YEAH, MY DAD CAN BE SLOW, TOO. HE SAID HE'LL HELP ME TURN THE SHED IN THE BACKYARD INTO A CLUBHOUSE...BUT IT MIGHT TAKE A WHILE.

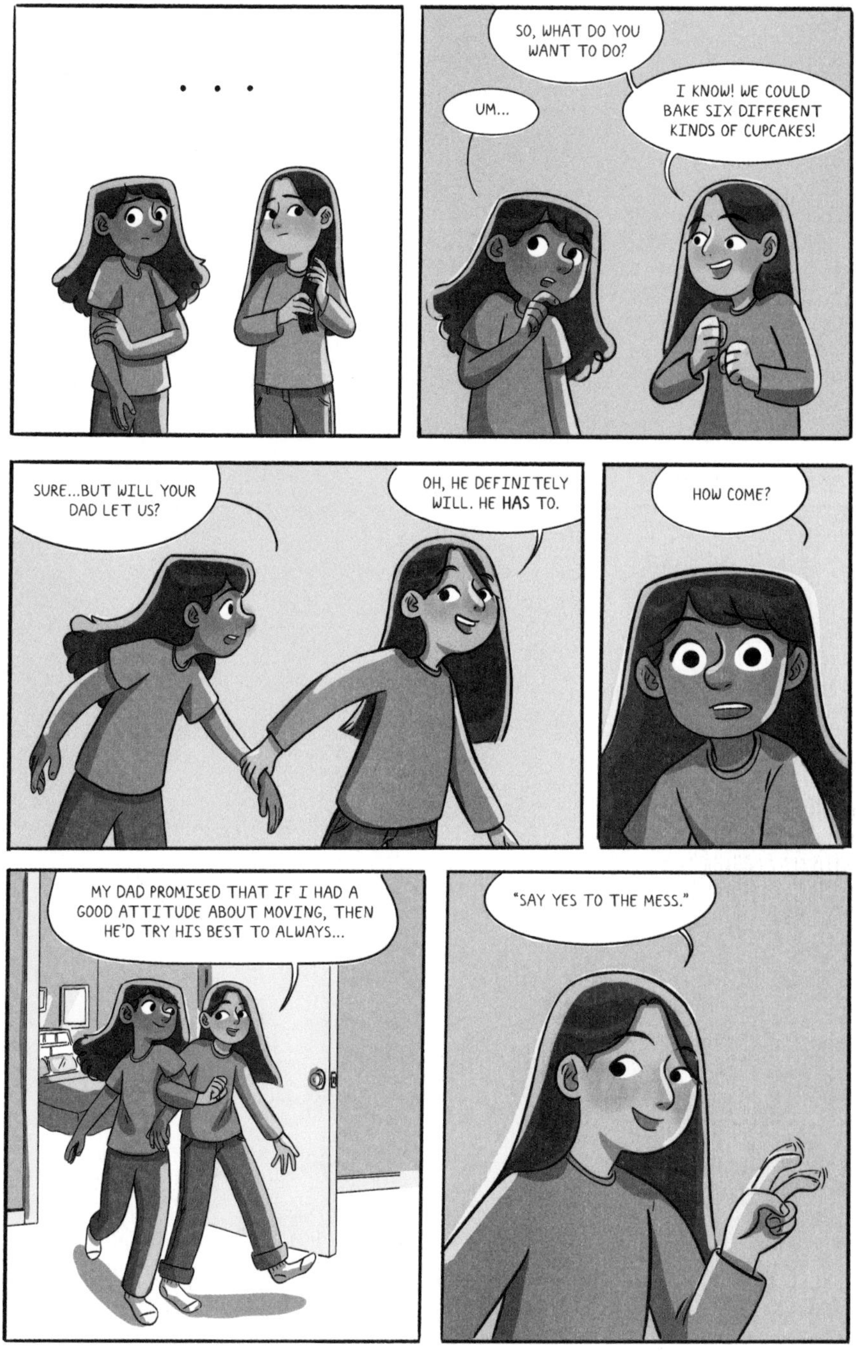
. . .
SO, WHAT DO YOU WANT TO DO?
UM...
I KNOW! WE COULD BAKE SIX DIFFERENT KINDS OF CUPCAKES!
SURE...BUT WILL YOUR DAD LET US?
OH, HE DEFINITELY WILL. HE HAS TO.
HOW COME?
MY DAD PROMISED THAT IF I HAD A GOOD ATTITUDE ABOUT MOVING, THEN HE'D TRY HIS BEST TO ALWAYS...
"SAY YES TO THE MESS."

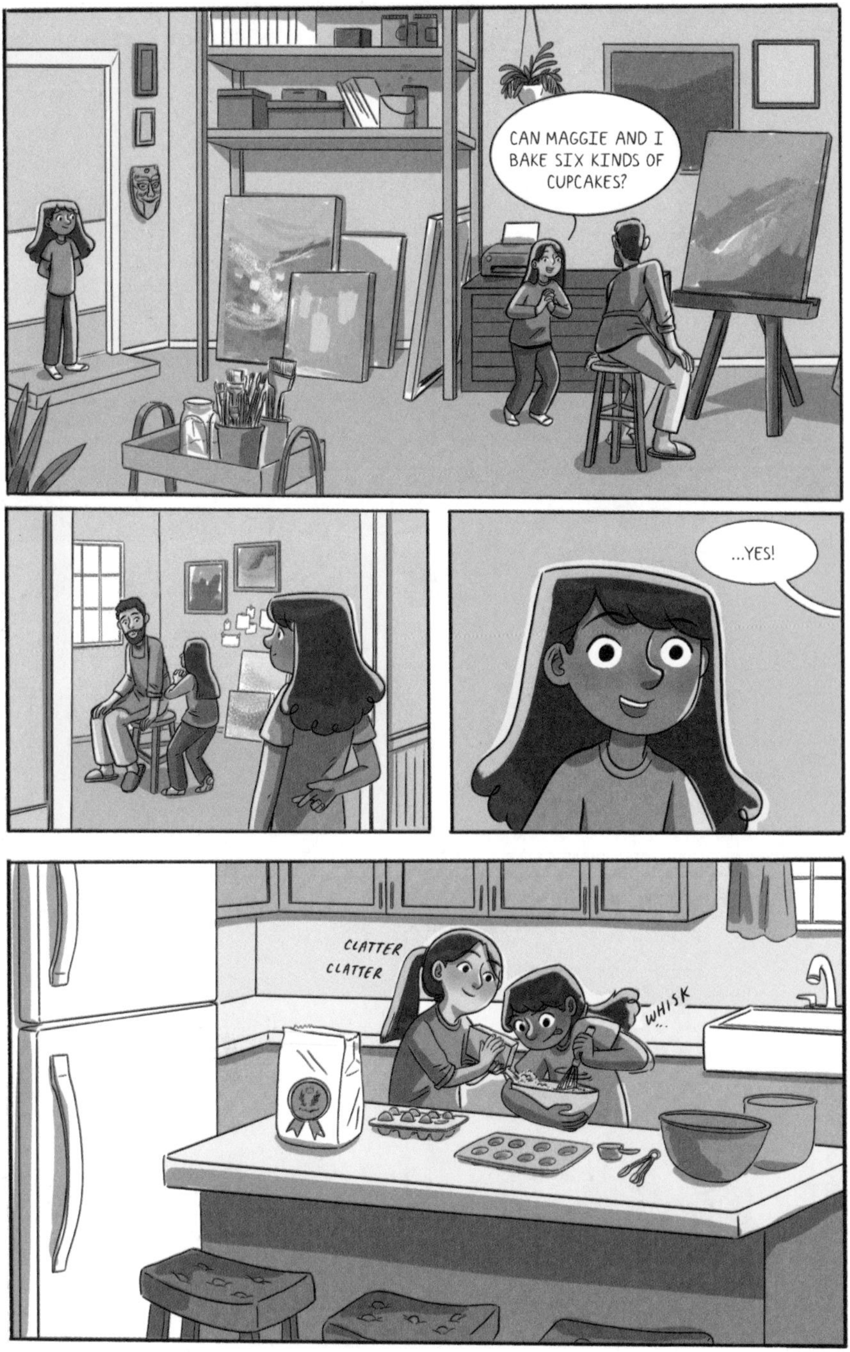
CAN MAGGIE AND I BAKE SIX KINDS OF CUPCAKES?
...YES!
CLATTER
CLATTER
WHISK
...

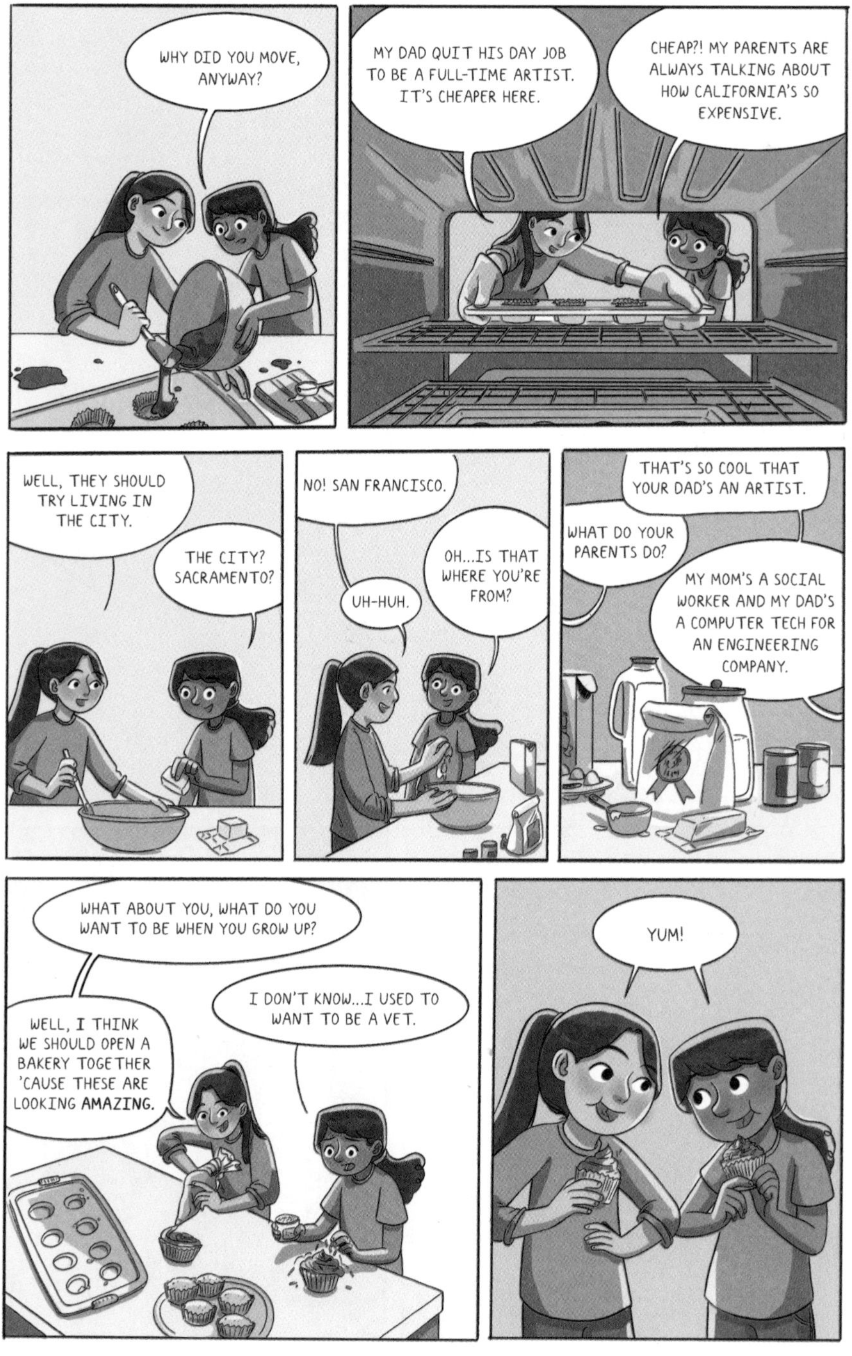
WHY DID YOU MOVE, ANYWAY?
MY DAD QUIT HIS DAY JOB TO BE A FULL-TIME ARTIST. IT'S CHEAPER HERE.
CHEAP?! MY PARENTS ARE ALWAYS TALKING ABOUT HOW CALIFORNIA'S SO EXPENSIVE.
WELL, THEY SHOULD TRY LIVING IN THE CITY.
THE CITY? SACRAMENTO?
NO! SAN FRANCISCO.
OH...IS THAT WHERE YOU'RE FROM?
UH-HUH.
THAT'S SO COOL THAT YOUR DAD'S AN ARTIST.
WHAT DO YOUR PARENTS DO?
MY MOM'S A SOCIAL WORKER AND MY DAD'S A COMPUTER TECH FOR AN ENGINEERING COMPANY.
WHAT ABOUT YOU, WHAT DO YOU WANT TO BE WHEN YOU GROW UP?
I DON'T KNOW...I USED TO WANT TO BE A VET.
WELL, I THINK WE SHOULD OPEN A BAKERY TOGETHER 'CAUSE THESE ARE LOOKING **AMAZING.**
YUM!

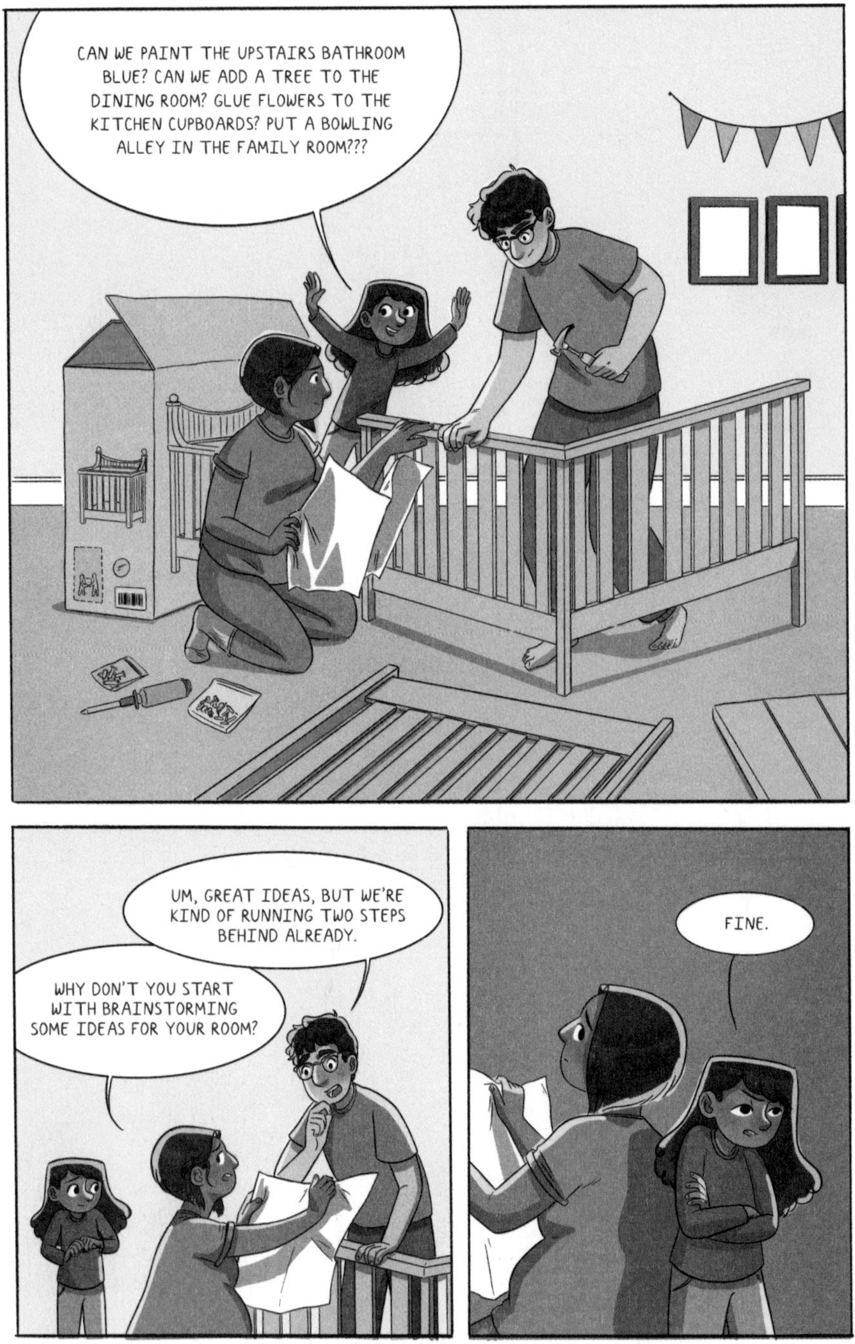

CAN WE PAINT THE UPSTAIRS BATHROOM BLUE? CAN WE ADD A TREE TO THE DINING ROOM? GLUE FLOWERS TO THE KITCHEN CUPBOARDS? PUT A BOWLING ALLEY IN THE FAMILY ROOM???
UM, GREAT IDEAS, BUT WE'RE KIND OF RUNNING TWO STEPS BEHIND ALREADY.
WHY DON'T YOU START WITH BRAINSTORMING SOME IDEAS FOR YOUR ROOM?
FINE.

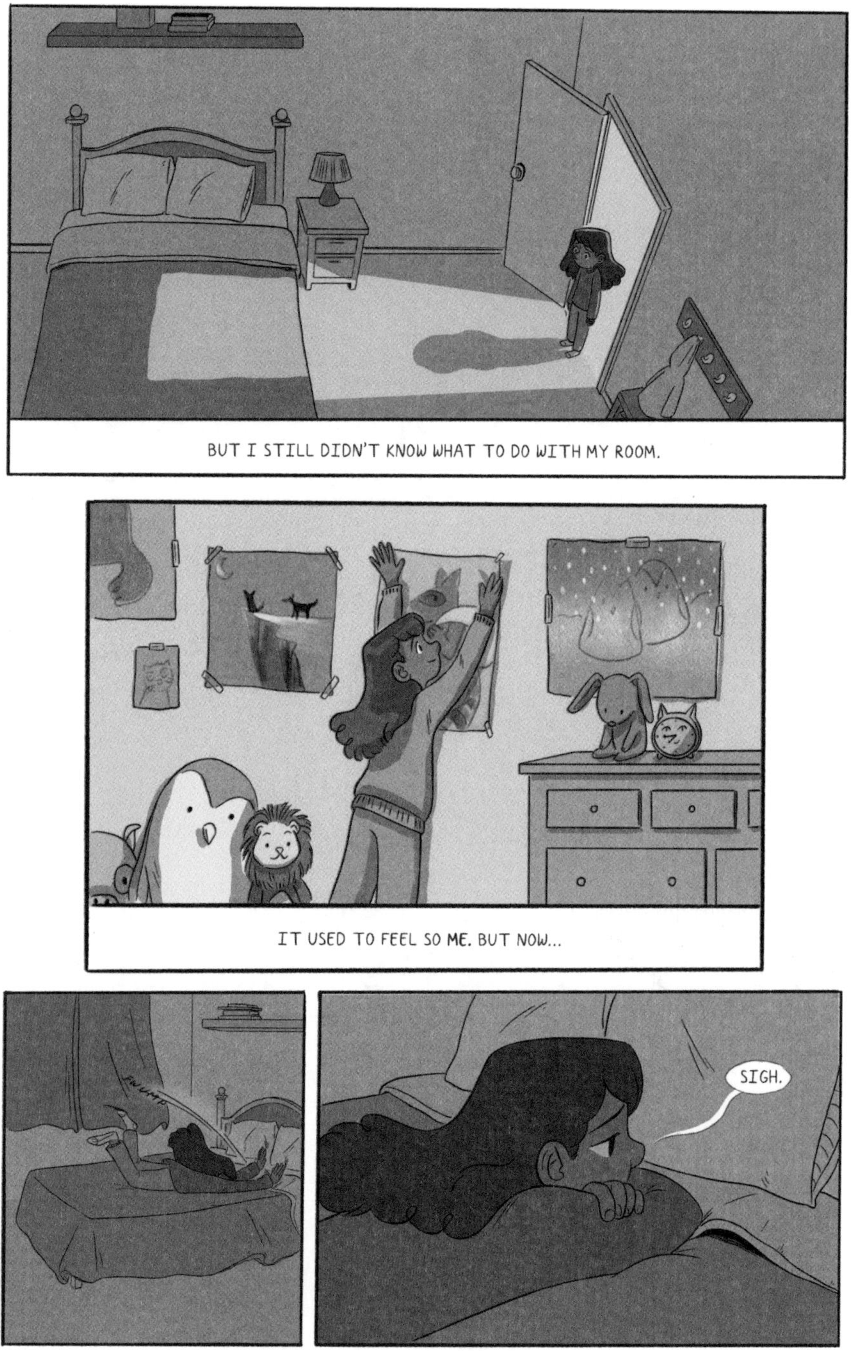
BUT I STILL DIDN'T KNOW WHAT TO DO WITH MY ROOM.
IT USED TO FEEL SO **ME**. BUT NOW...
FWUMP
SIGH.

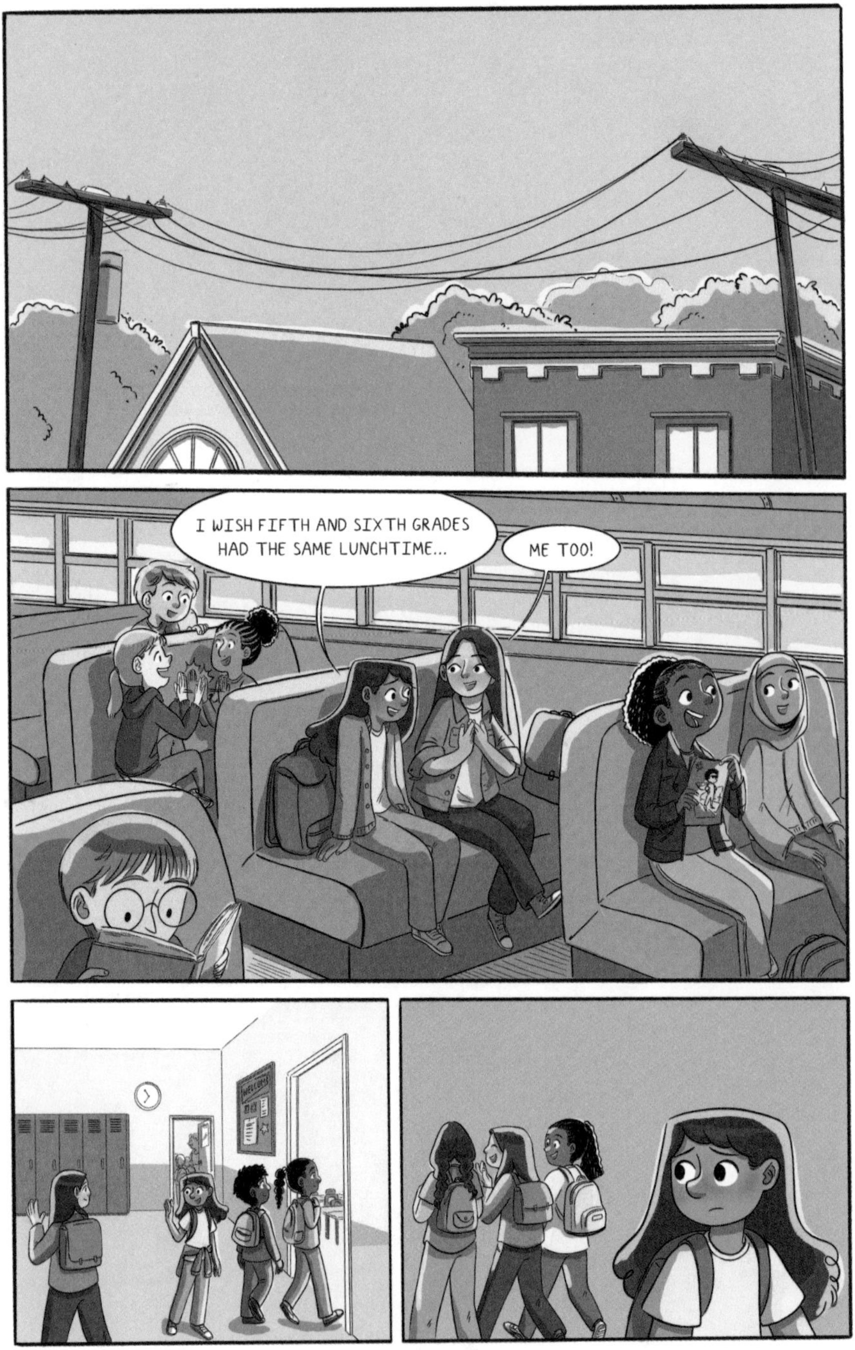
I WISH FIFTH AND SIXTH GRADES HAD THE SAME LUNCHTIME...
ME TOO!

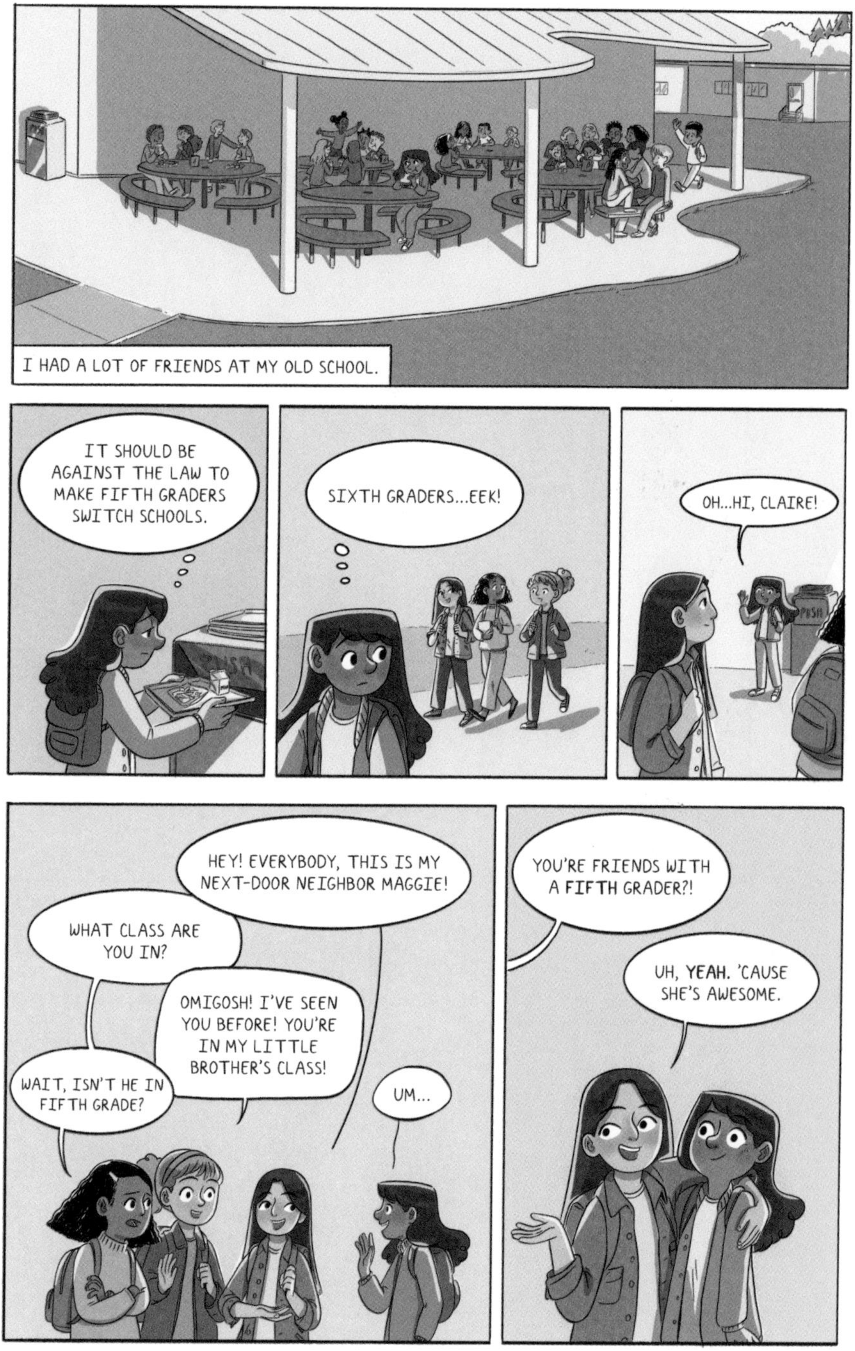

I HAD A LOT OF FRIENDS AT MY OLD SCHOOL.
IT SHOULD BE AGAINST THE LAW TO MAKE FIFTH GRADERS SWITCH SCHOOLS.
SIXTH GRADERS...EEK!
OH...HI, CLAIRE!
HEY! EVERYBODY, THIS IS MY NEXT-DOOR NEIGHBOR MAGGIE!
WHAT CLASS ARE YOU IN?
OMIGOSH! I'VE SEEN YOU BEFORE! YOU'RE IN MY LITTLE BROTHER'S CLASS!
WAIT, ISN'T HE IN FIFTH GRADE?
UM...
YOU'RE FRIENDS WITH A **FIFTH** GRADER?!
UH, **YEAH.** 'CAUSE SHE'S AWESOME.

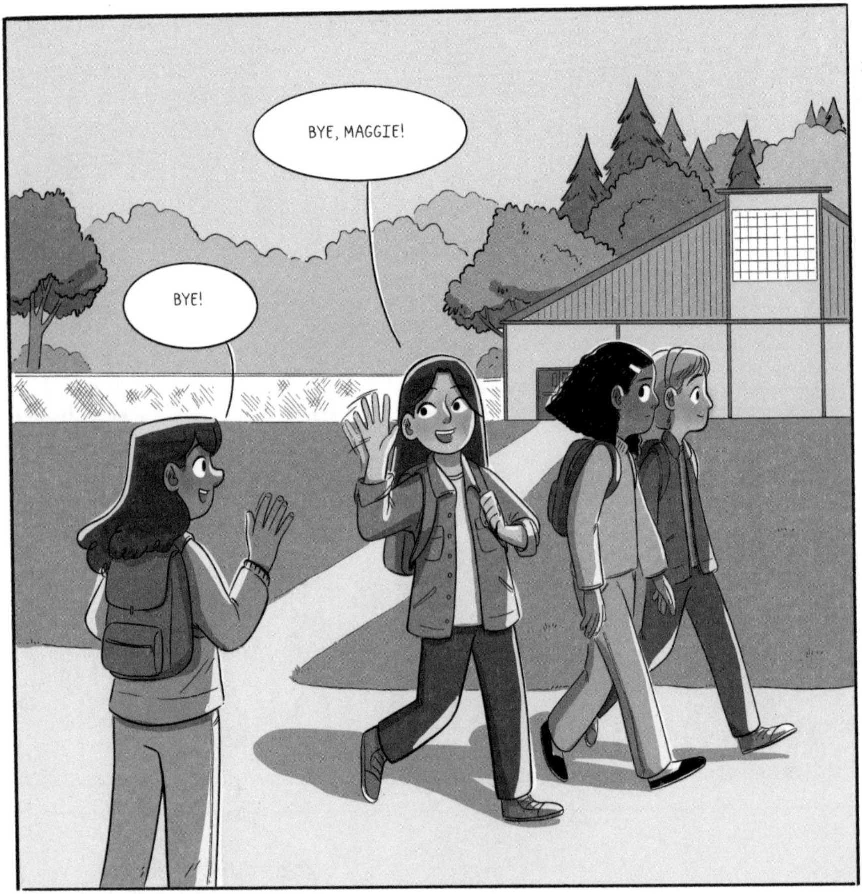
BYE, MAGGIE!
BYE!

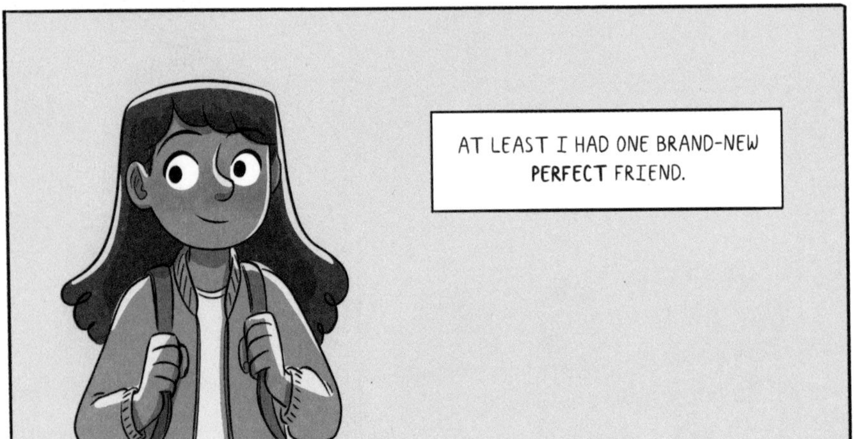
AT LEAST I HAD ONE BRAND-NEW **PERFECT** FRIEND.

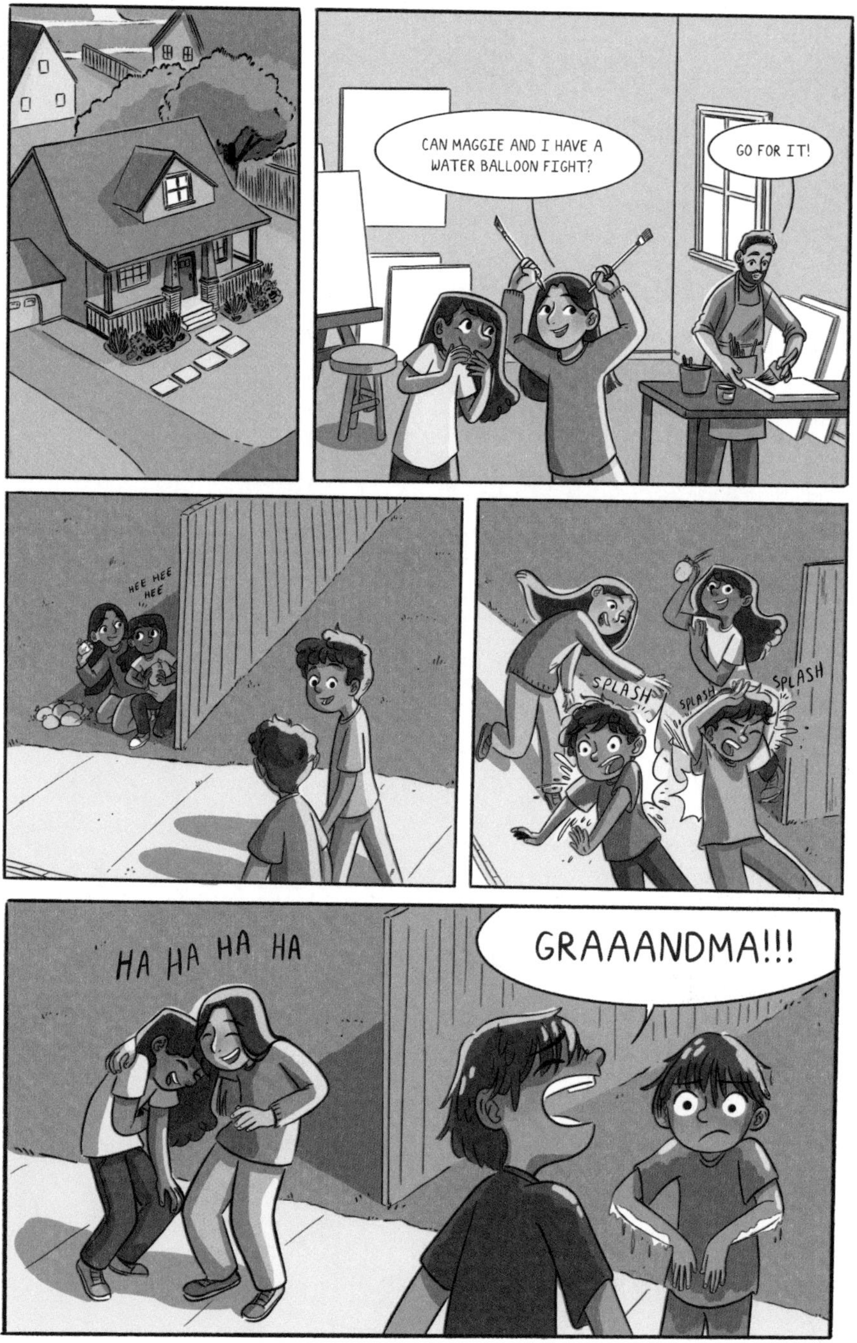
CAN MAGGIE AND I HAVE A WATER BALLOON FIGHT?
GO FOR IT!
HEE HEE HEE
SPLASH
SPLASH
SPLASH
HA HA HA HA
GRAAANDMA!!!

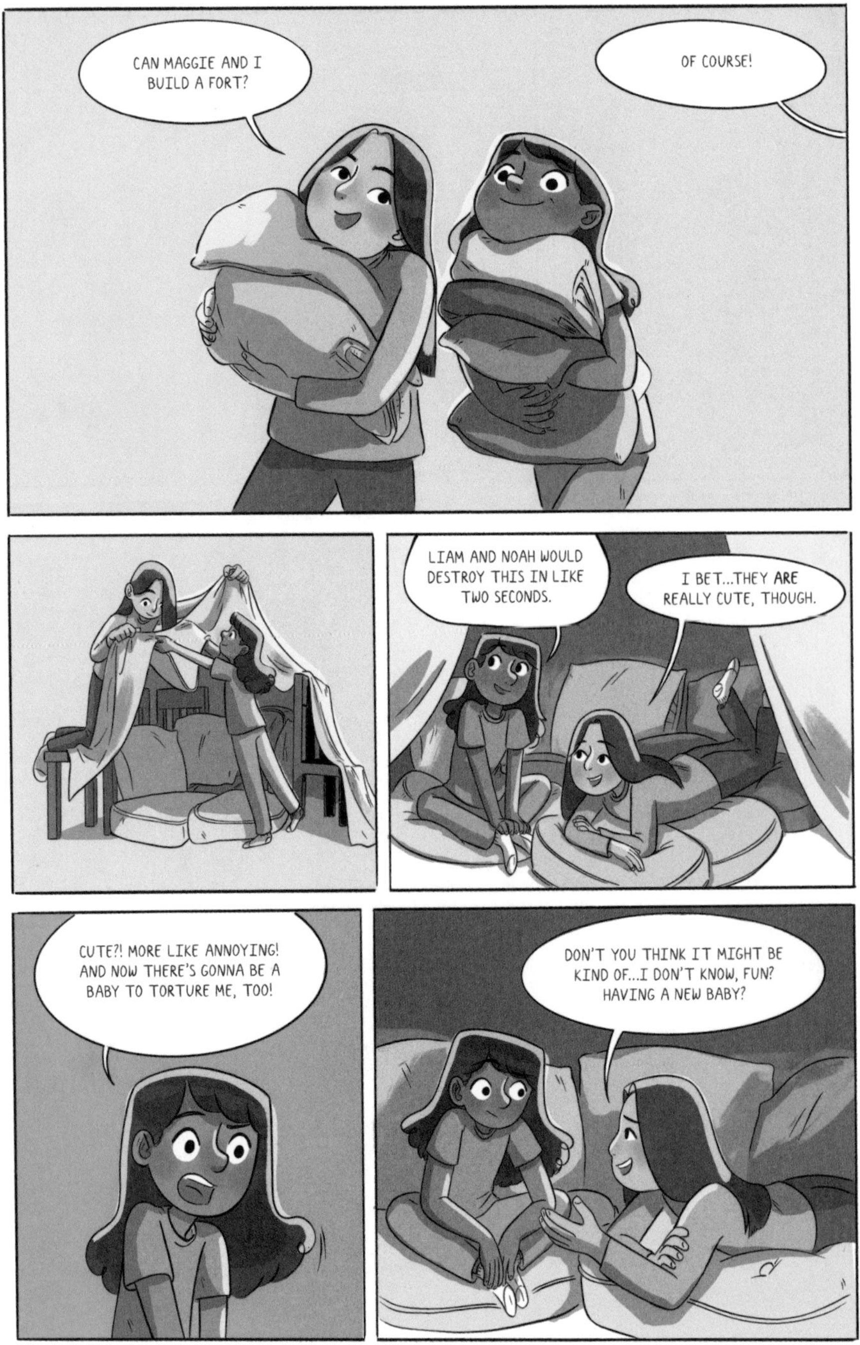
CAN MAGGIE AND I BUILD A FORT?
OF COURSE!
LIAM AND NOAH WOULD DESTROY THIS IN LIKE TWO SECONDS.
I BET...THEY **ARE** REALLY CUTE, THOUGH.
CUTE?! MORE LIKE ANNOYING! AND NOW THERE'S GONNA BE A BABY TO TORTURE ME, TOO!
DON'T YOU THINK IT MIGHT BE KIND OF...I DON'T KNOW, FUN? HAVING A NEW BABY?

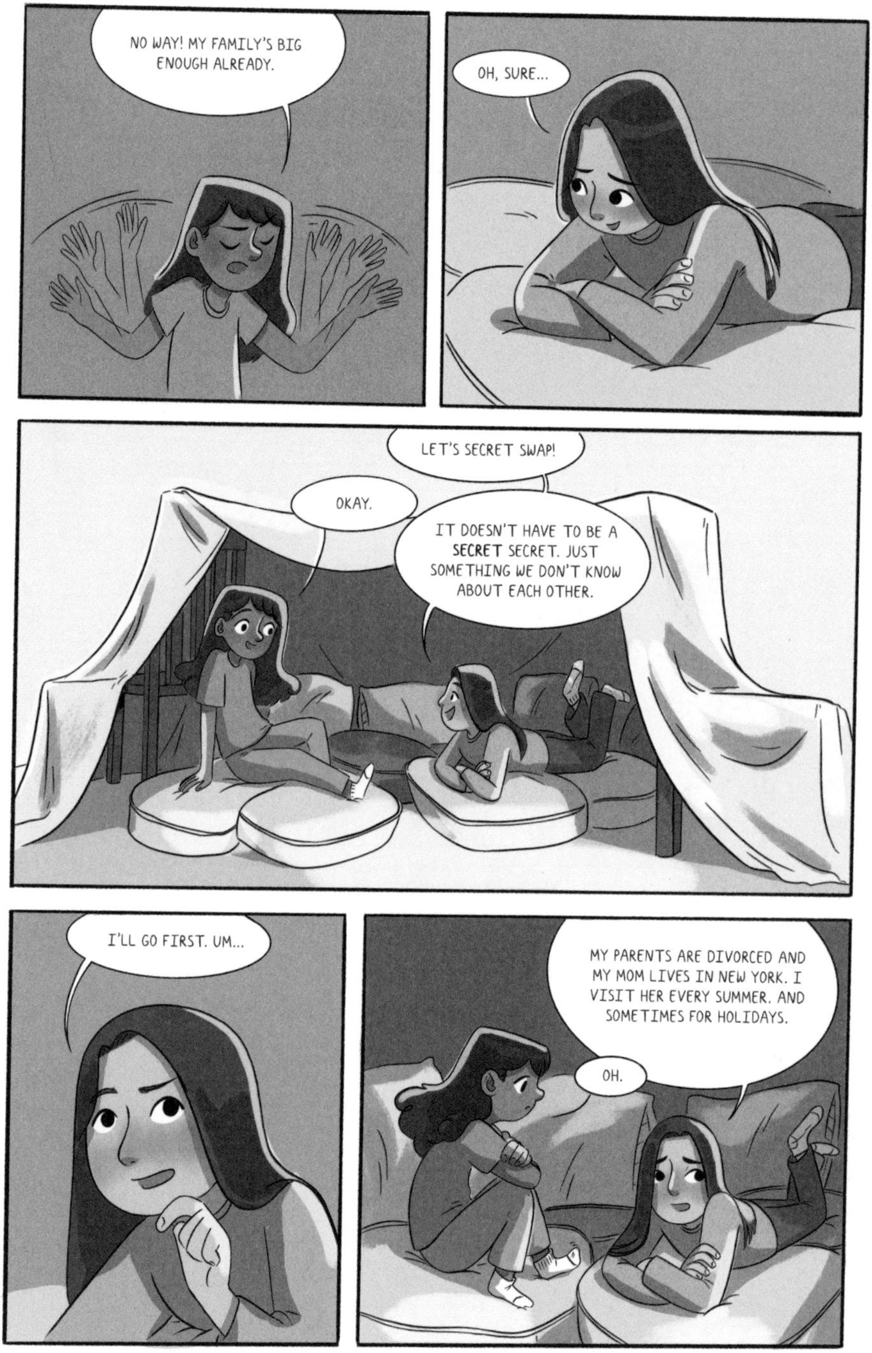
NO WAY! MY FAMILY'S BIG ENOUGH ALREADY.
OH, SURE...
LET'S SECRET SWAP!
OKAY.
IT DOESN'T HAVE TO BE A **SECRET** SECRET. JUST SOMETHING WE DON'T KNOW ABOUT EACH OTHER.
I'LL GO FIRST. UM...
MY PARENTS ARE DIVORCED AND MY MOM LIVES IN NEW YORK. I VISIT HER EVERY SUMMER. AND SOMETIMES FOR HOLIDAYS.
OH.

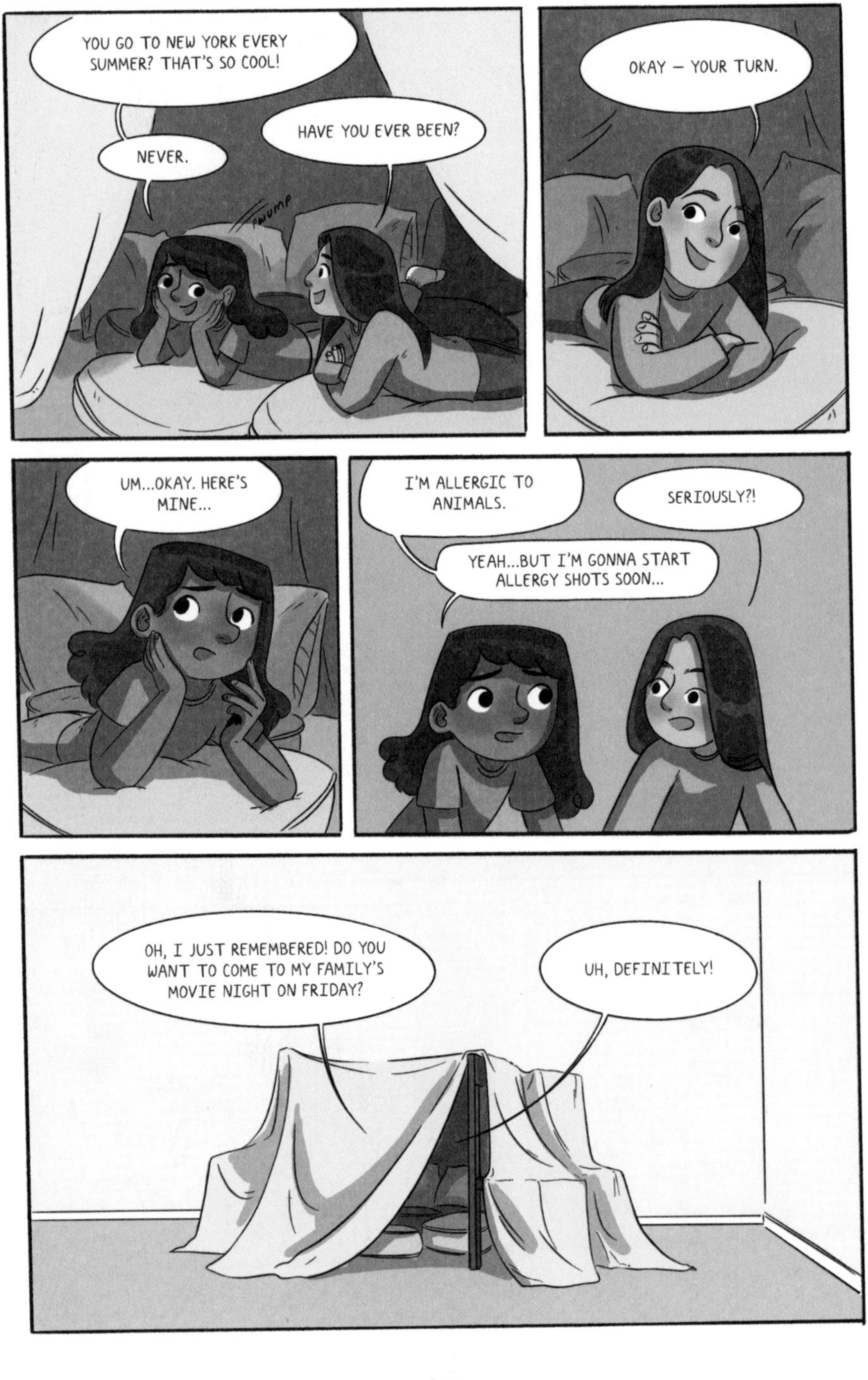
YOU GO TO NEW YORK EVERY SUMMER? THAT'S SO COOL!
NEVER.
HAVE YOU EVER BEEN?
FWUMP
OKAY — YOUR TURN.
UM...OKAY. HERE'S MINE...
I'M ALLERGIC TO ANIMALS.
SERIOUSLY?!
YEAH...BUT I'M GONNA START ALLERGY SHOTS SOON...
OH, I JUST REMEMBERED! DO YOU WANT TO COME TO MY FAMILY'S MOVIE NIGHT ON FRIDAY?
UH, DEFINITELY!

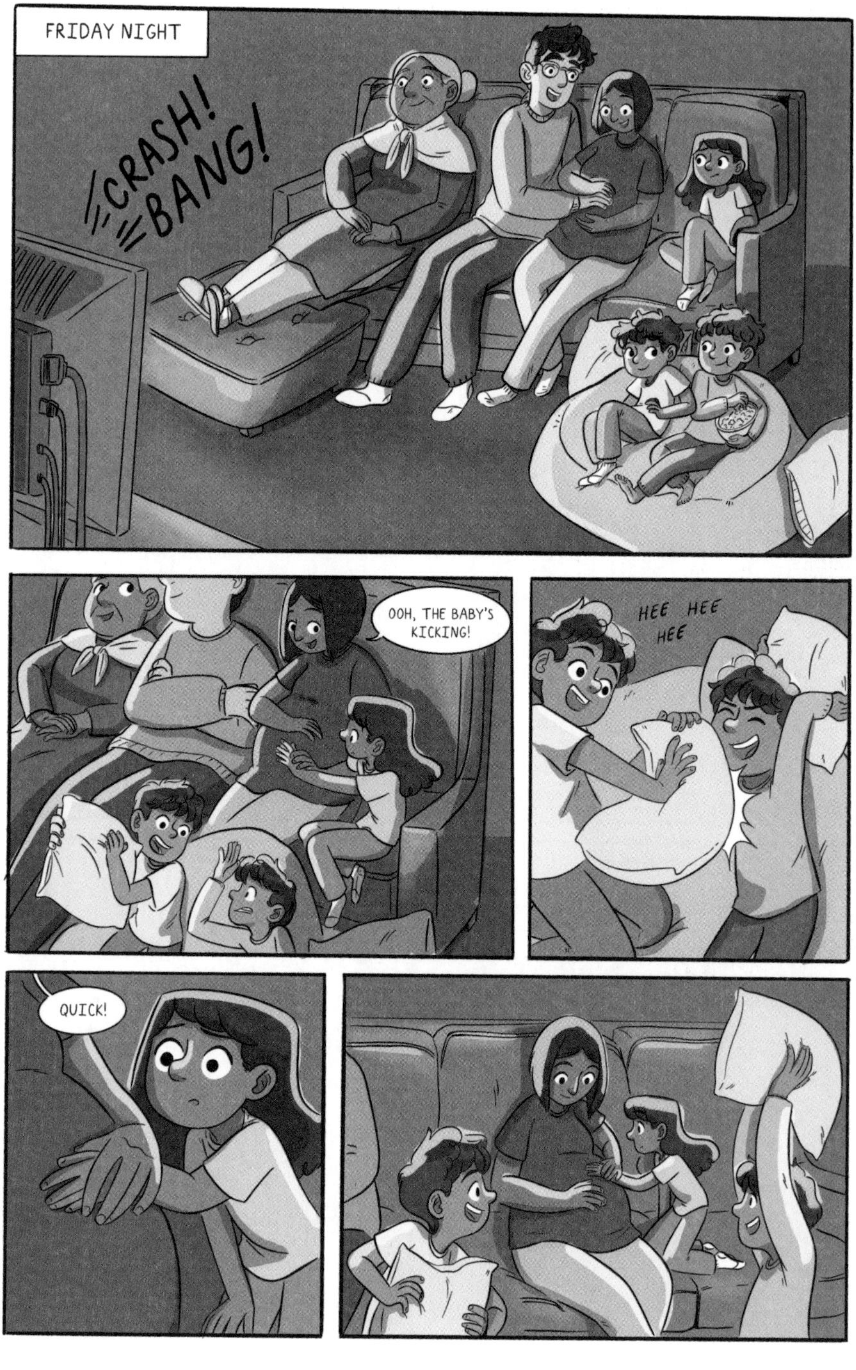
FRIDAY NIGHT
CRASH! BANG!
OOH, THE BABY'S KICKING!
HEE HEE HEE
QUICK!

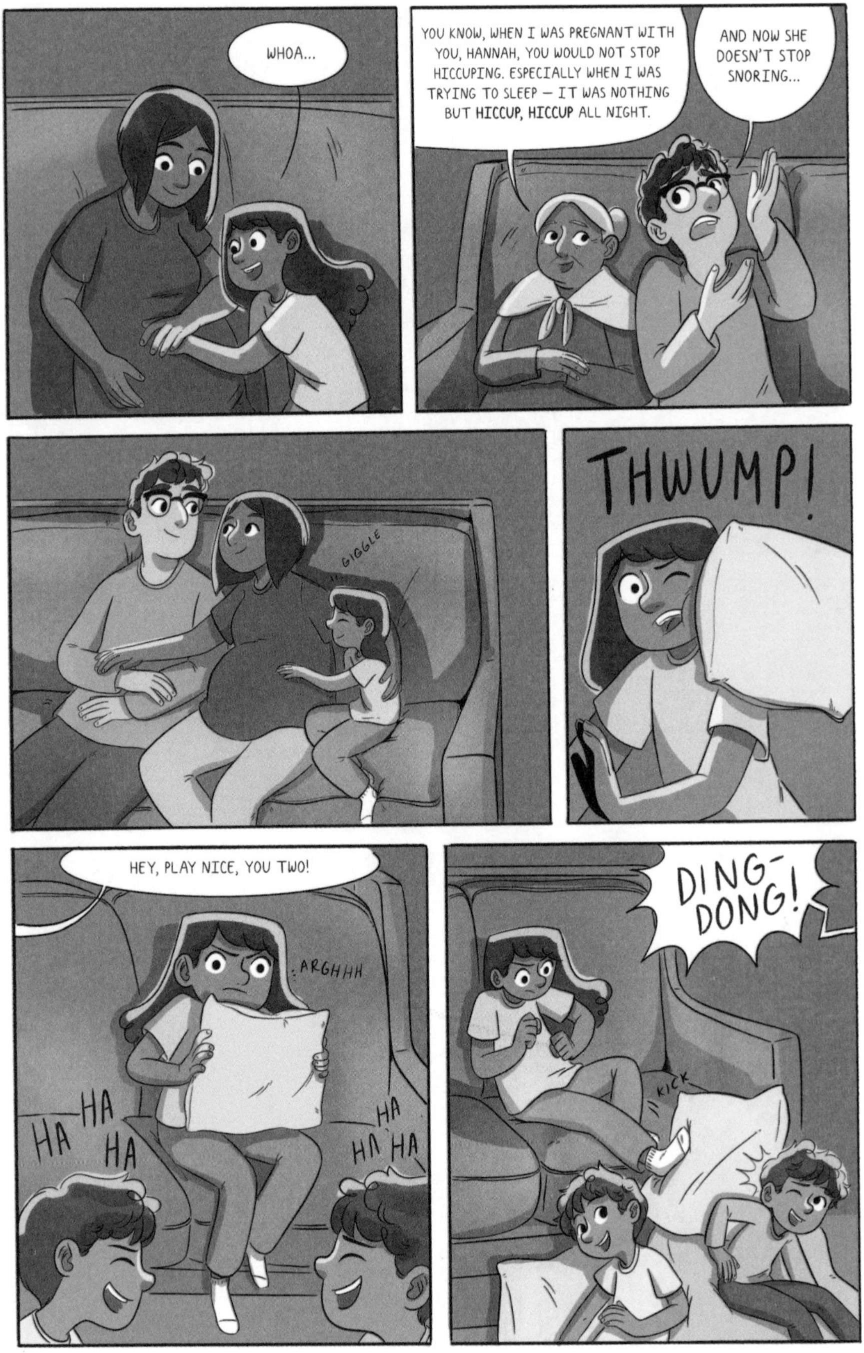
WHOA...
YOU KNOW, WHEN I WAS PREGNANT WITH YOU, HANNAH, YOU WOULD NOT STOP HICCUPING. ESPECIALLY WHEN I WAS TRYING TO SLEEP — IT WAS NOTHING BUT HICCUP, HICCUP ALL NIGHT.
AND NOW SHE DOESN'T STOP SNORING...
GIGGLE
THWUMP!
HEY, PLAY NICE, YOU TWO!
ARGHHH
HA HA HA
HA HA HA
DING-DONG!
KICK

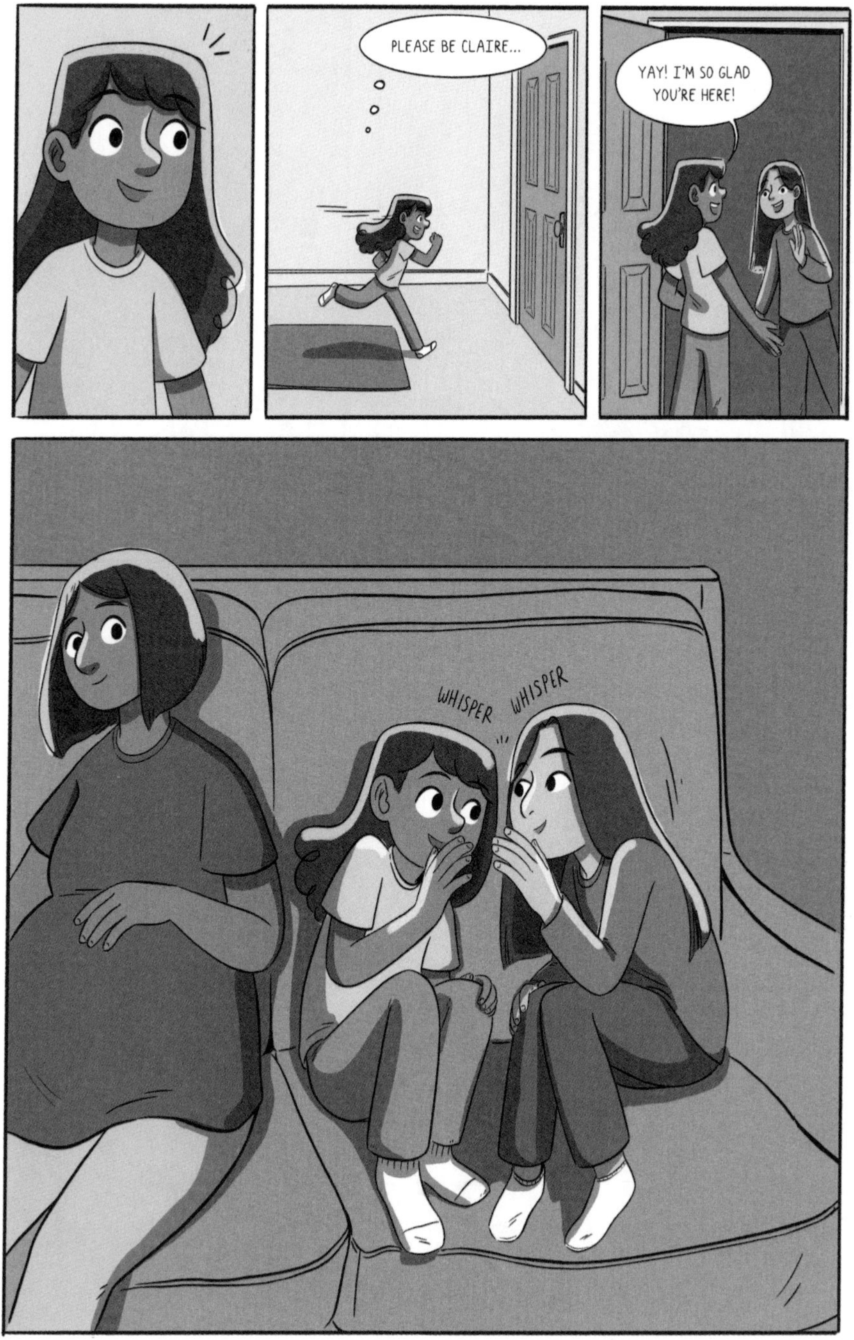
PLEASE BE CLAIRE...
YAY! I'M SO GLAD YOU'RE HERE!
WHISPER WHISPER

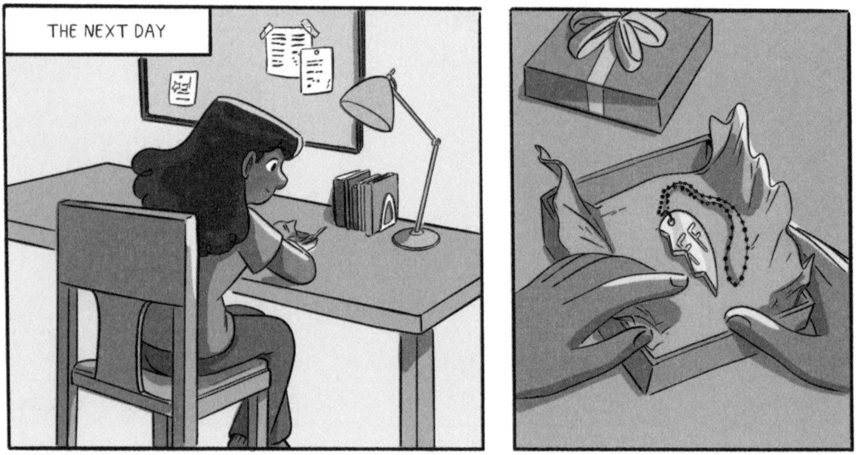
THE NEXT DAY

I'D SAVED UP MY OWN MONEY TO BUY A SURPRISE FOR CLAIRE.

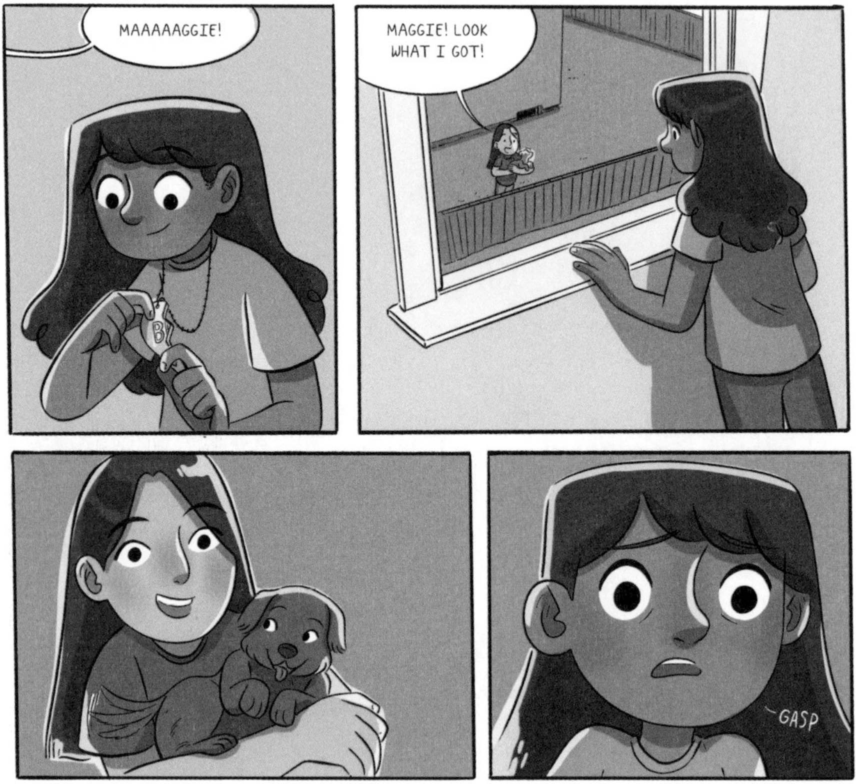
MAAAAAGGIE!
MAGGIE! LOOK WHAT I GOT!
GASP

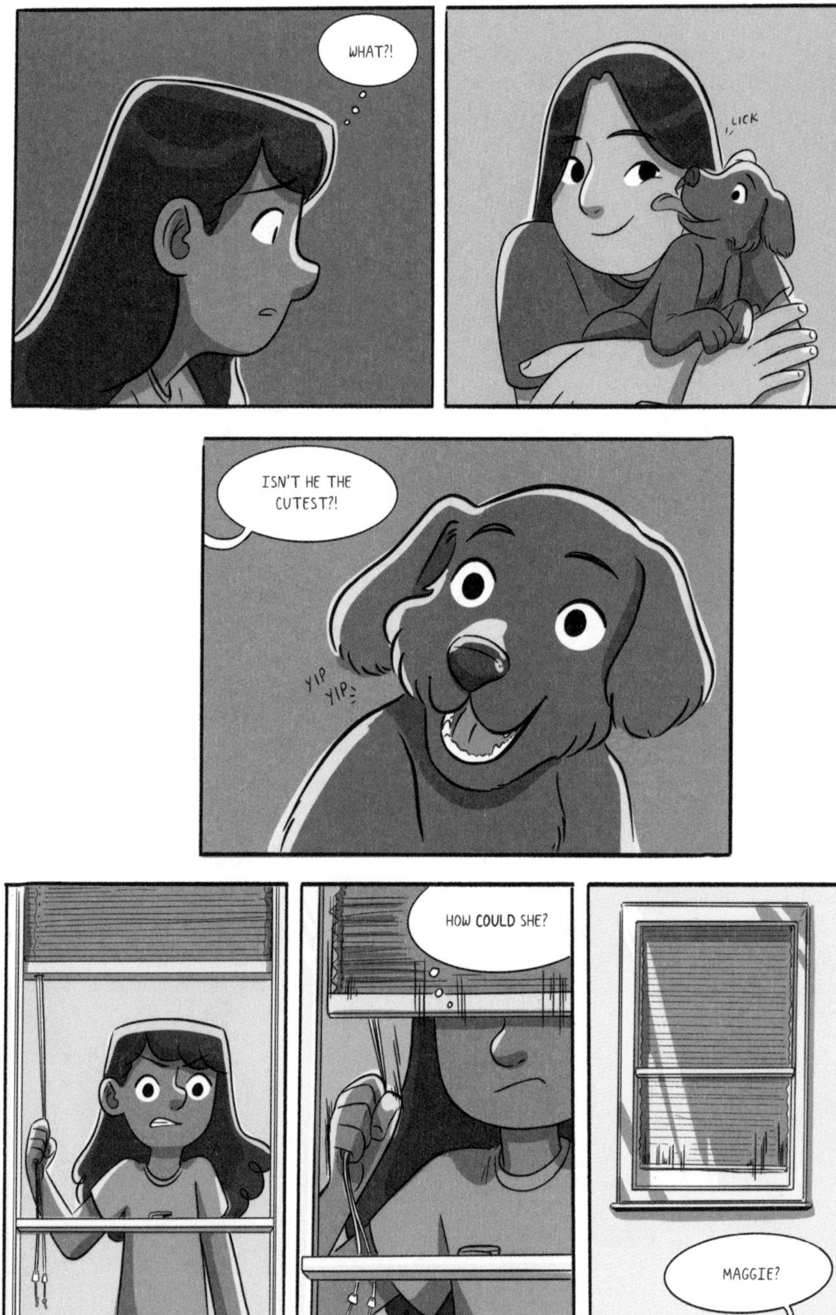
WHAT?!
LICK
ISN'T HE THE CUTEST?!
YIP YIP
HOW COULD SHE?
MAGGIE?

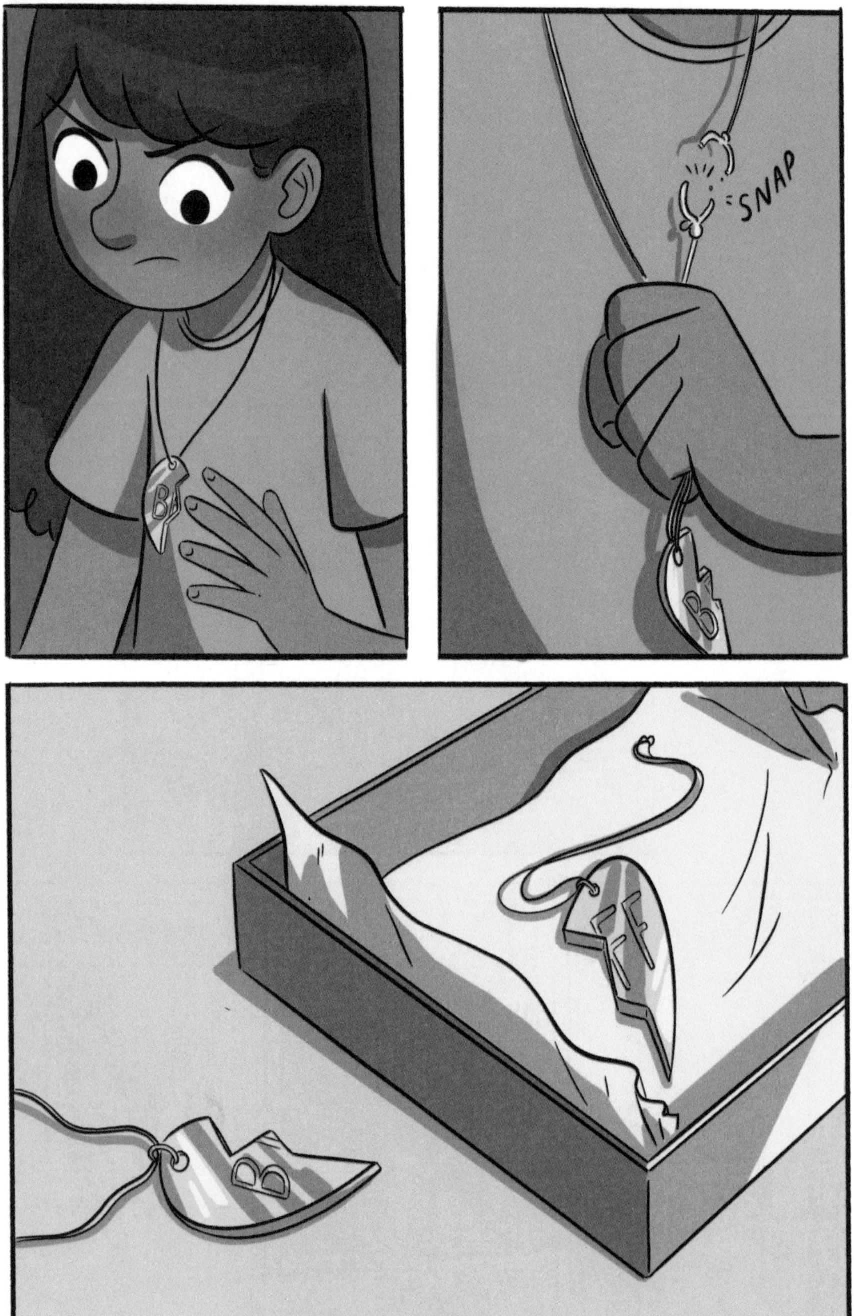
SNAP

Chapter Six

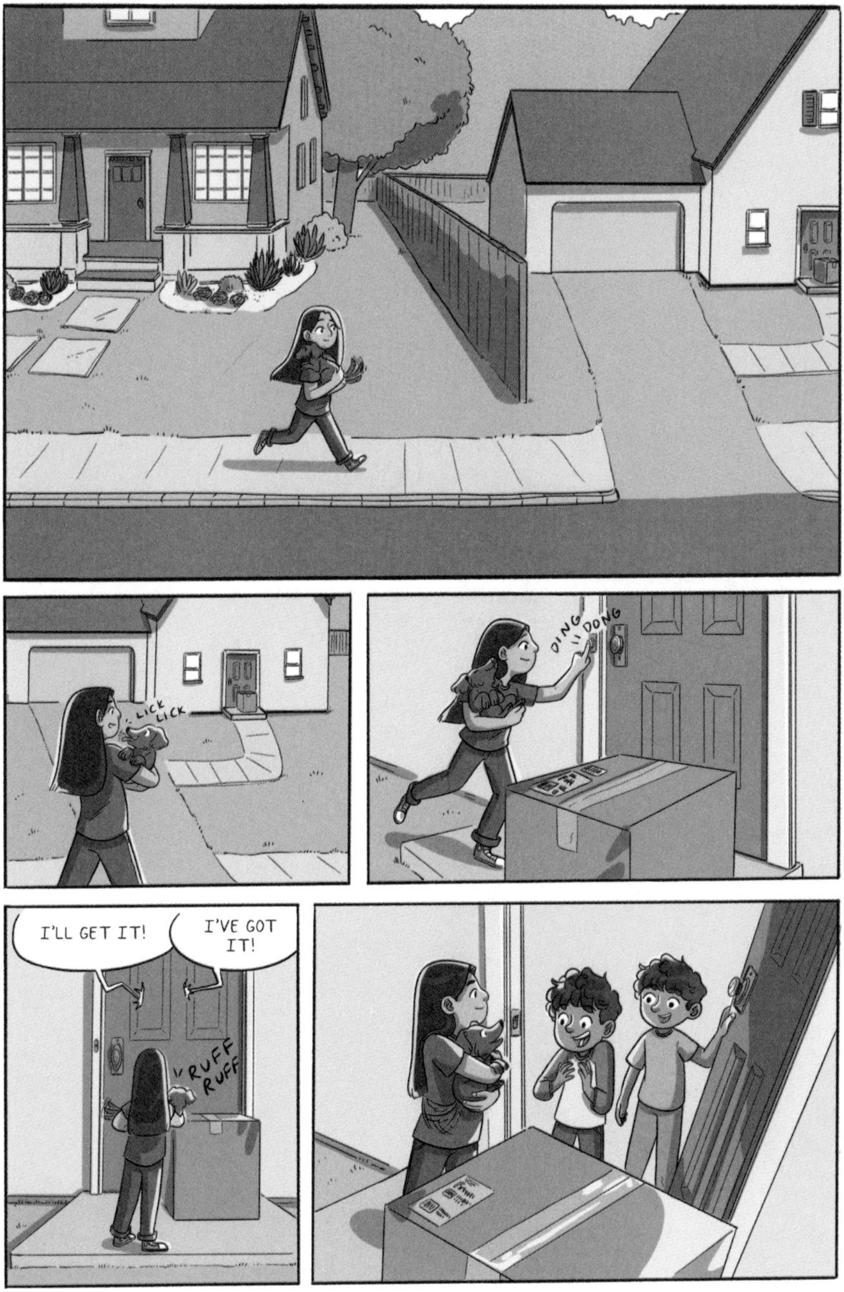
LICK LICK
DING DONG
I'LL GET IT!
I'VE GOT IT!
RUFF RUFF

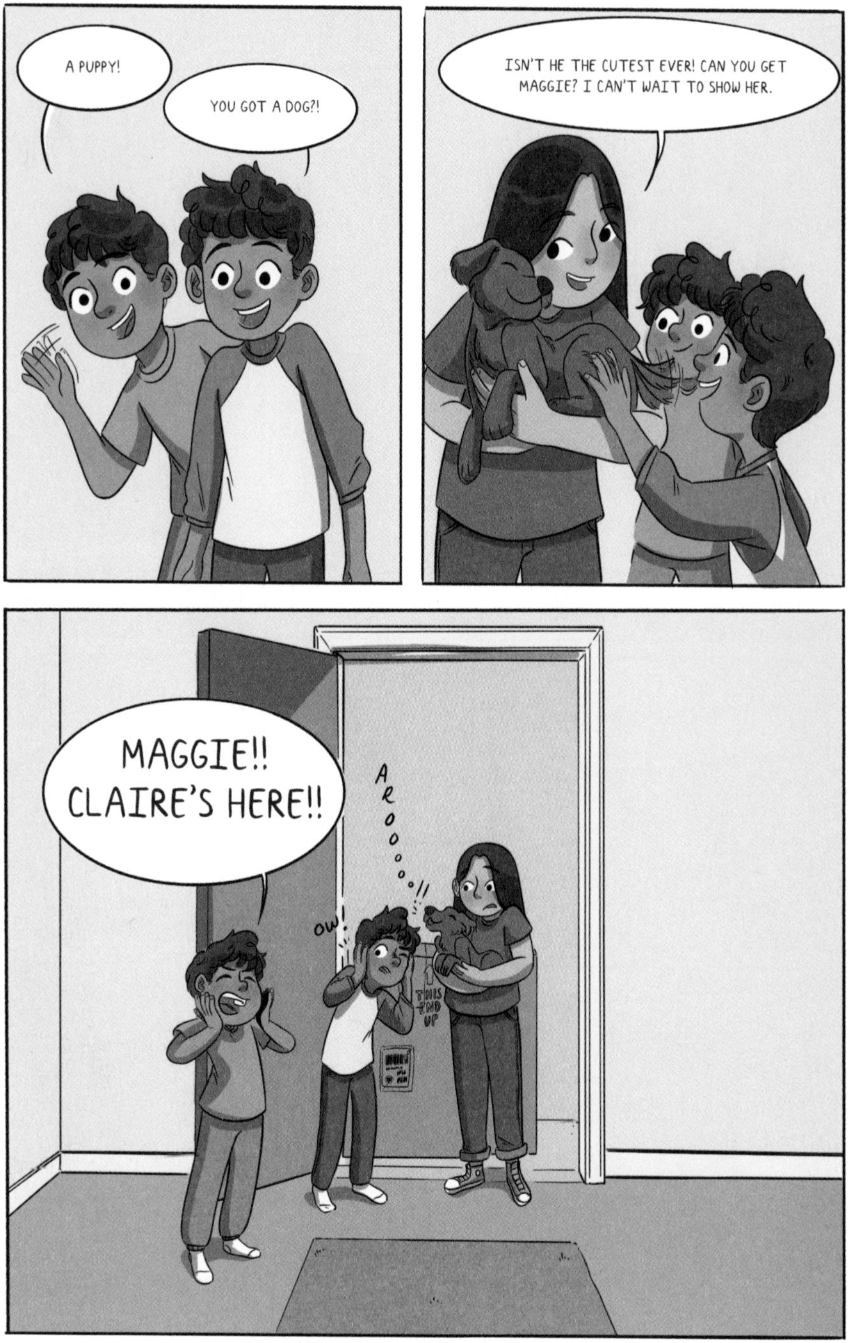
A PUPPY!
YOU GOT A DOG?!
ISN'T HE THE CUTEST EVER! CAN YOU GET MAGGIE? I CAN'T WAIT TO SHOW HER.
MAGGIE!! CLAIRE'S HERE!!
AROOooo!!
OW!
THIS END UP

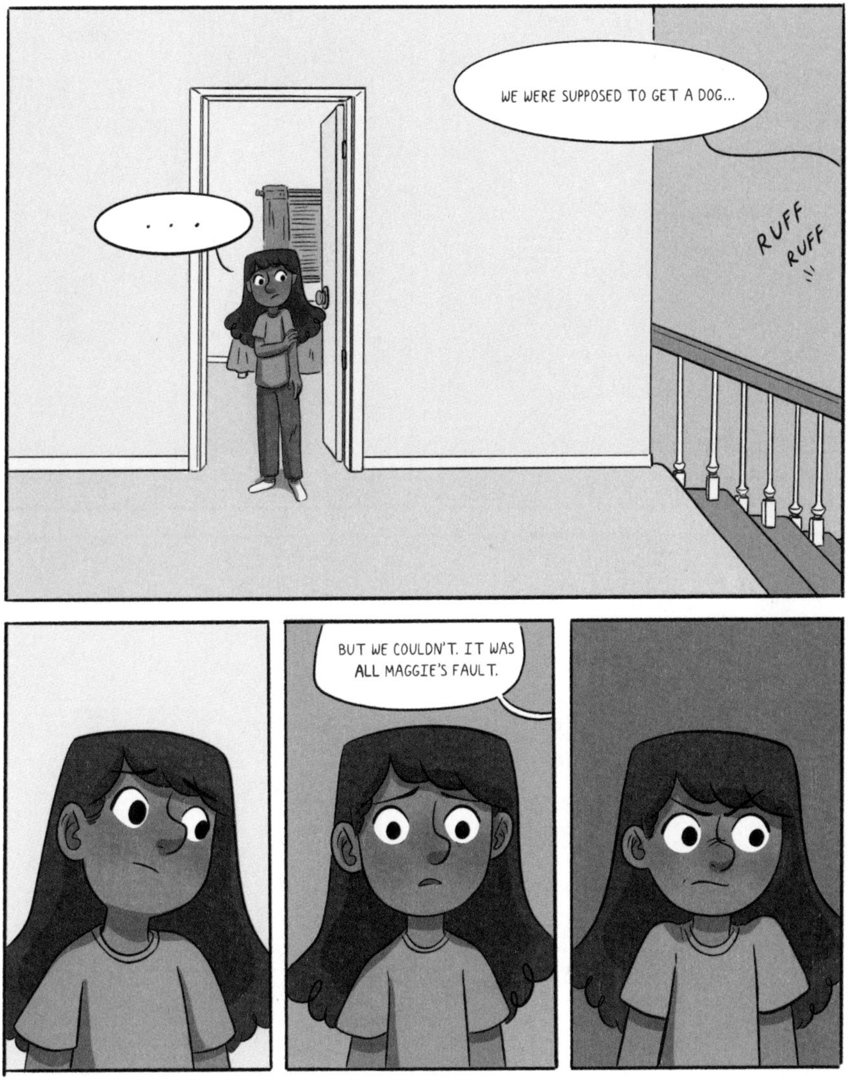
. . .
WE WERE SUPPOSED TO GET A DOG...
RUFF RUFF
BUT WE COULDN'T. IT WAS ALL MAGGIE'S FAULT.

THEY WERE **TRAITORS.** ALL OF THEM.

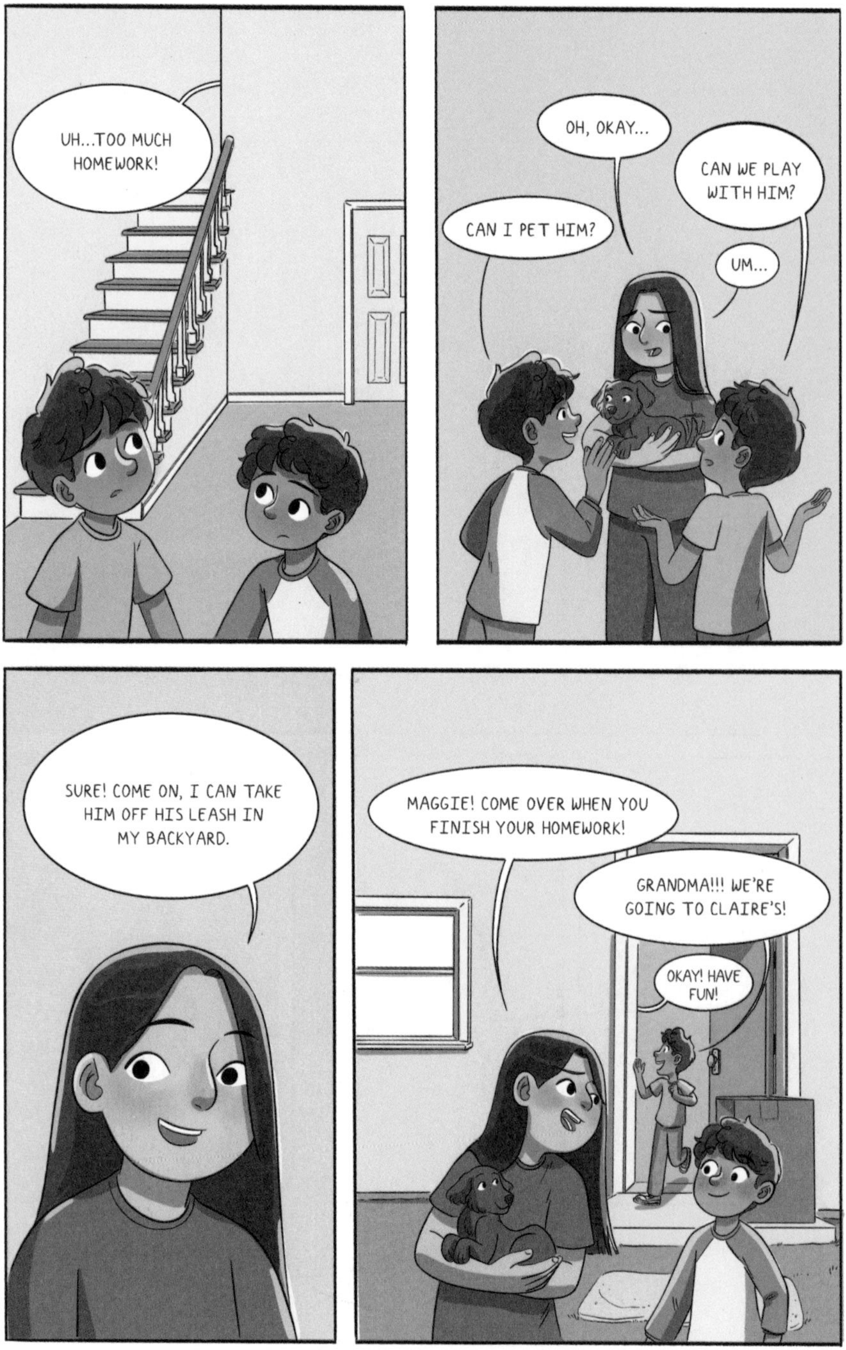
UH...TOO MUCH HOMEWORK!
OH, OKAY...
CAN WE PLAY WITH HIM?
CAN I PET HIM?
UM...
SURE! COME ON, I CAN TAKE HIM OFF HIS LEASH IN MY BACKYARD.
MAGGIE! COME OVER WHEN YOU FINISH YOUR HOMEWORK!
GRANDMA!!! WE'RE GOING TO CLAIRE'S!
OKAY! HAVE FUN!

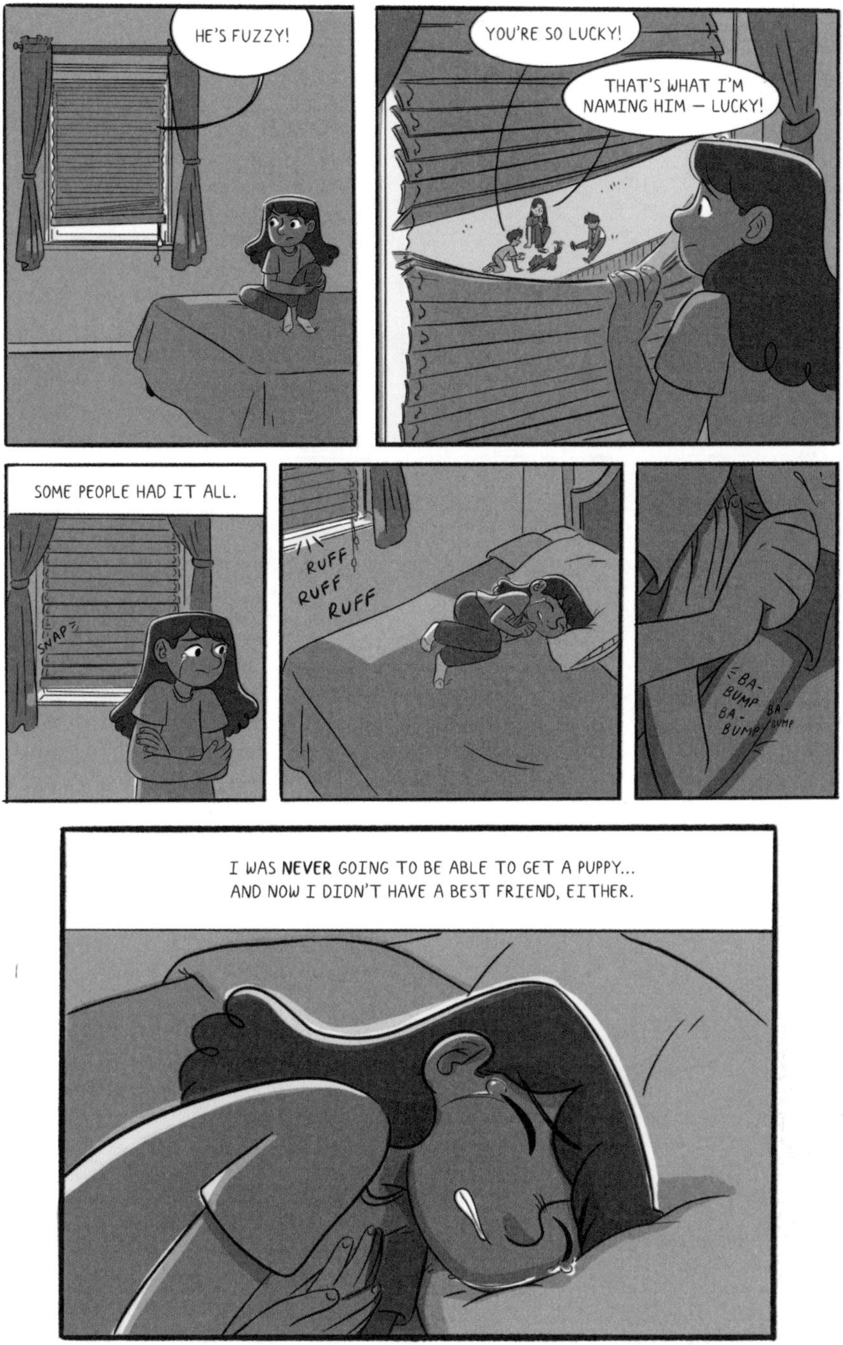
HE'S FUZZY!
YOU'RE SO LUCKY!
THAT'S WHAT I'M NAMING HIM — LUCKY!
SOME PEOPLE HAD IT ALL.
SNAP
RUFF RUFF RUFF
BA-BUMP BA-BUMP BA-BUMP
I WAS **NEVER** GOING TO BE ABLE TO GET A PUPPY...
AND NOW I DIDN'T HAVE A BEST FRIEND, EITHER.

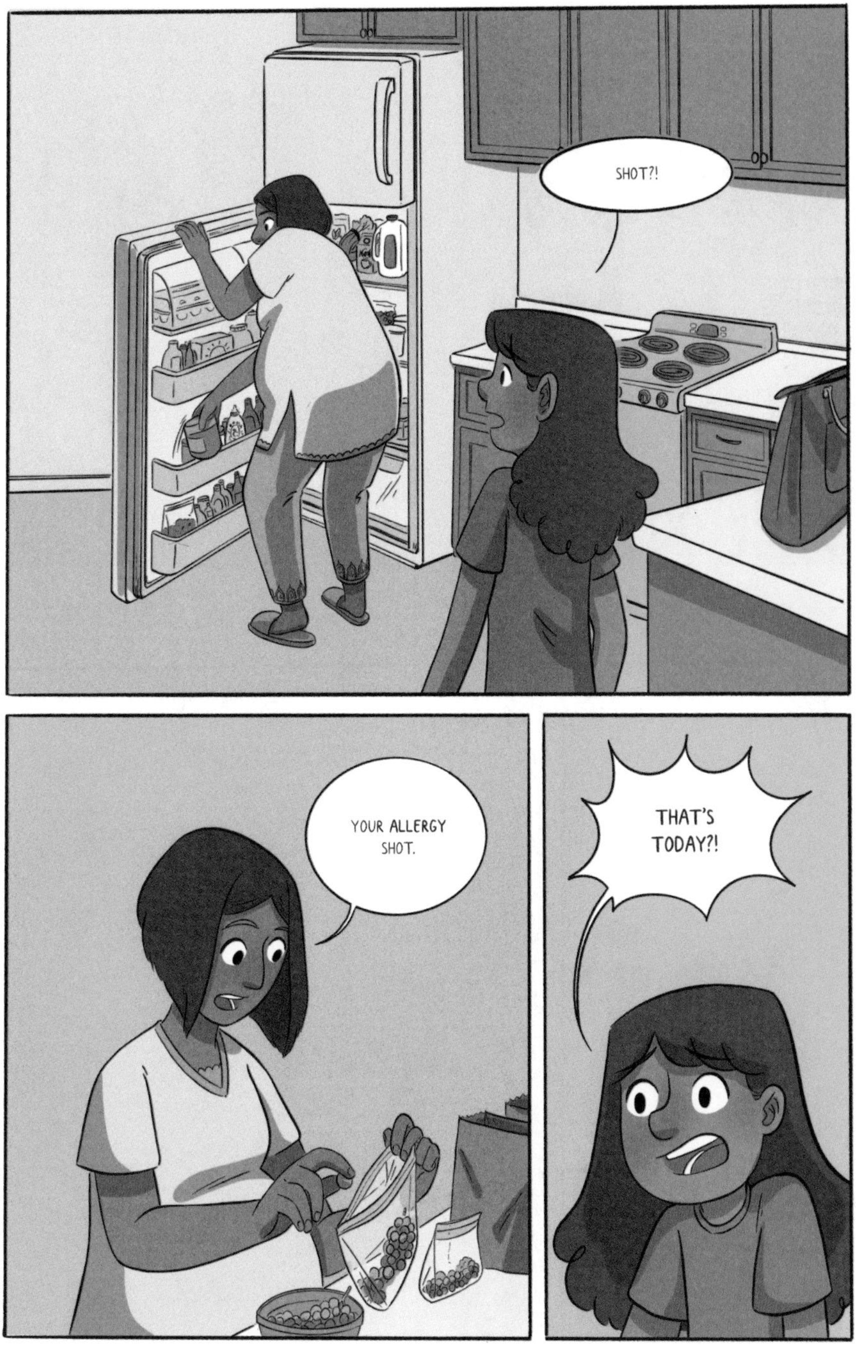
SHOT?!
YOUR ALLERGY SHOT.
THAT'S TODAY?!

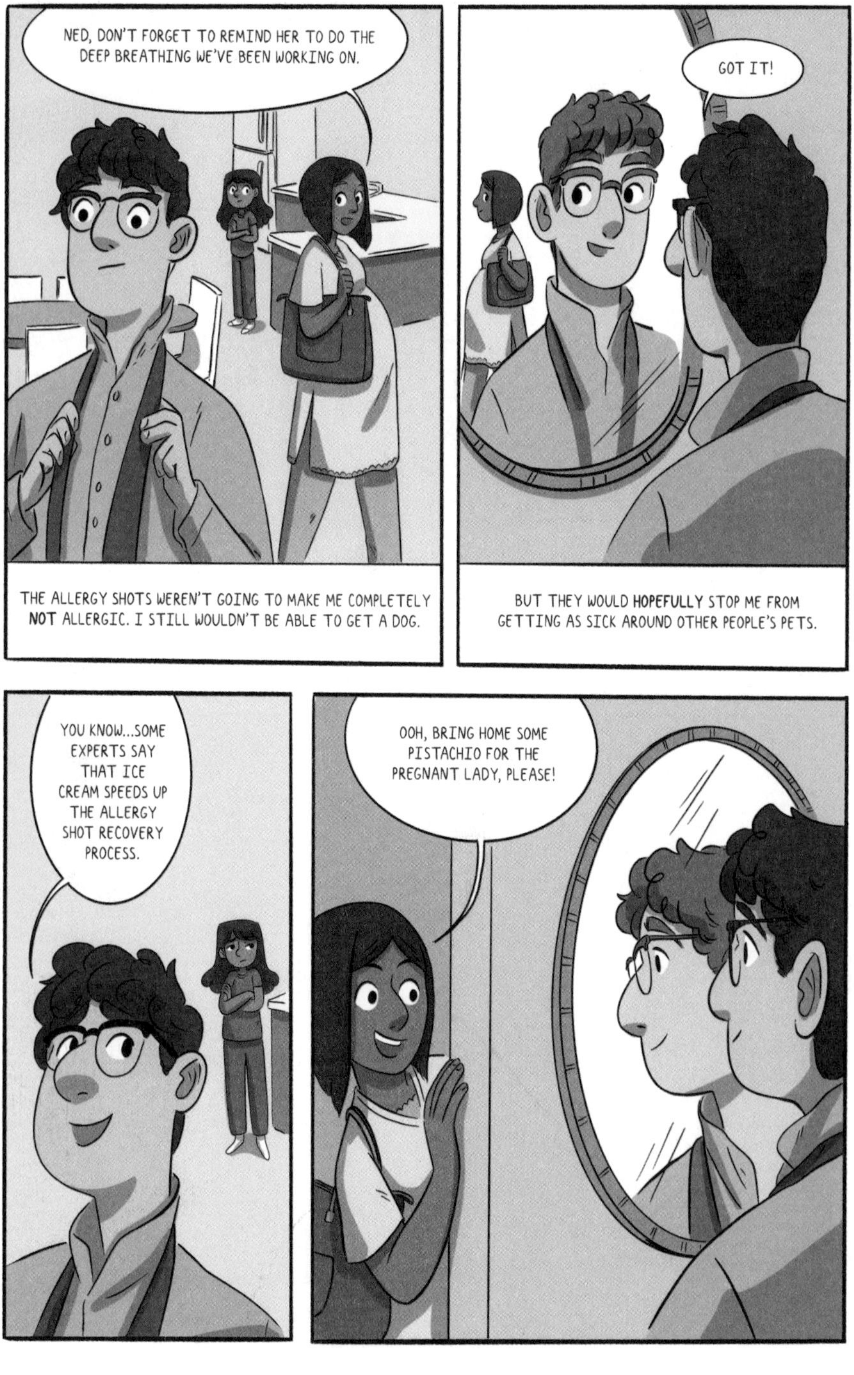
NED, DON'T FORGET TO REMIND HER TO DO THE DEEP BREATHING WE'VE BEEN WORKING ON.
THE ALLERGY SHOTS WEREN'T GOING TO MAKE ME COMPLETELY **NOT** ALLERGIC. I STILL WOULDN'T BE ABLE TO GET A DOG.
GOT IT!
BUT THEY WOULD **HOPEFULLY** STOP ME FROM GETTING AS SICK AROUND OTHER PEOPLE'S PETS.
YOU KNOW...SOME EXPERTS SAY THAT ICE CREAM SPEEDS UP THE ALLERGY SHOT RECOVERY PROCESS.
OOH, BRING HOME SOME PISTACHIO FOR THE PREGNANT LADY, PLEASE!

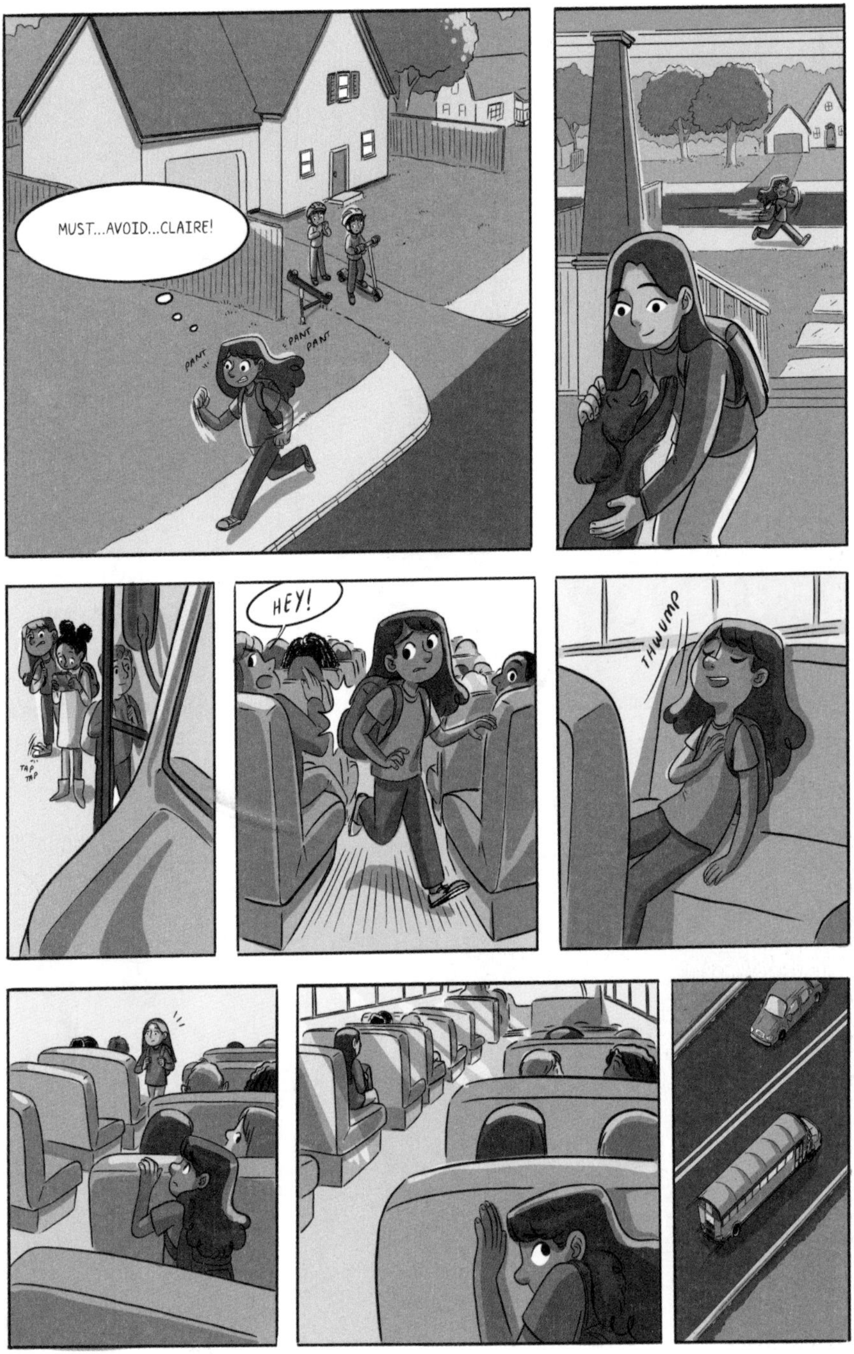
MUST...AVOID...CLAIRE!
PANT
PANT PANT
TAP TAP
HEY!
THWUMP

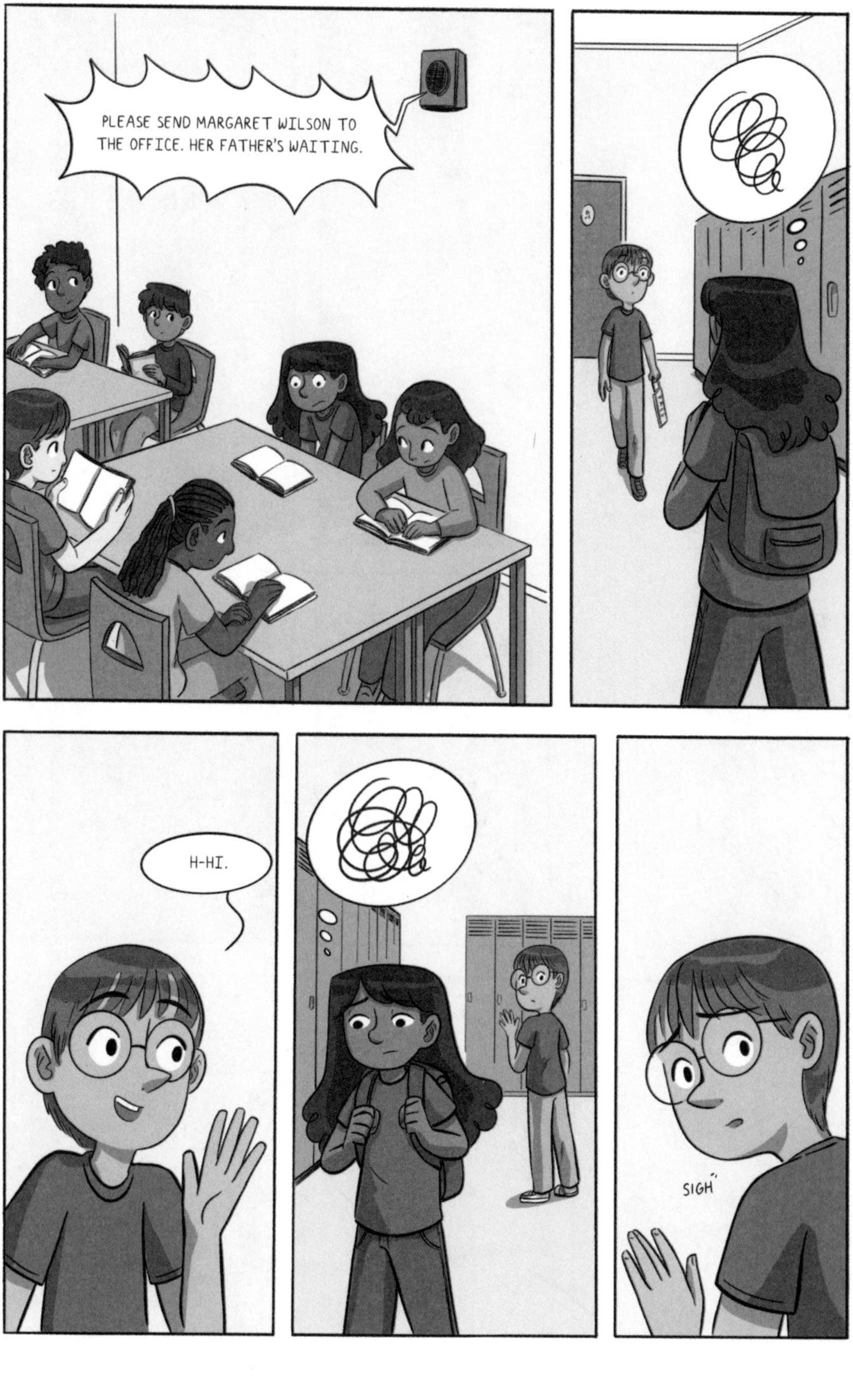
PLEASE SEND MARGARET WILSON TO THE OFFICE. HER FATHER'S WAITING.
H-HI.
SIGH

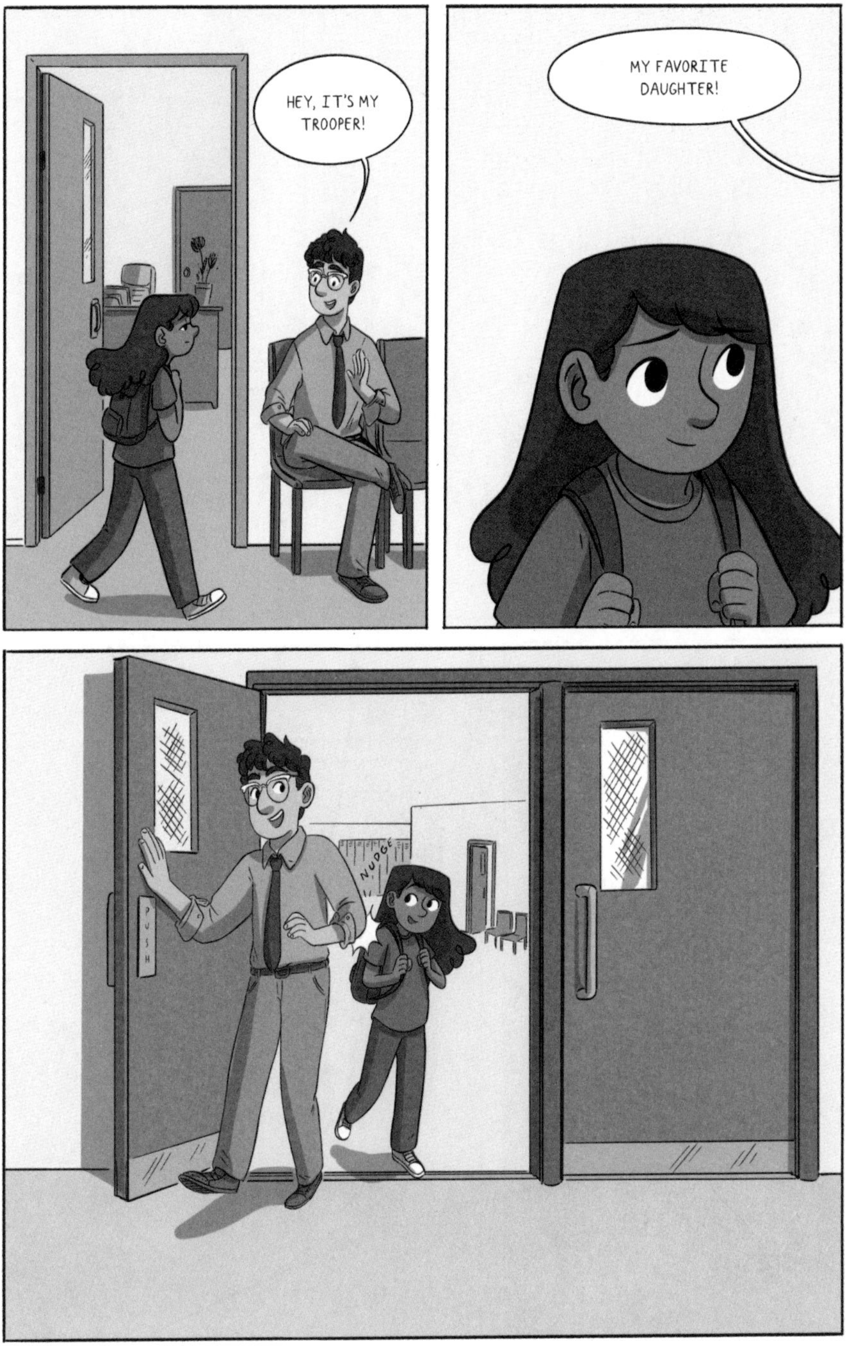
HEY, IT'S MY TROOPER!
MY FAVORITE DAUGHTER!
PUSH
NUDGE

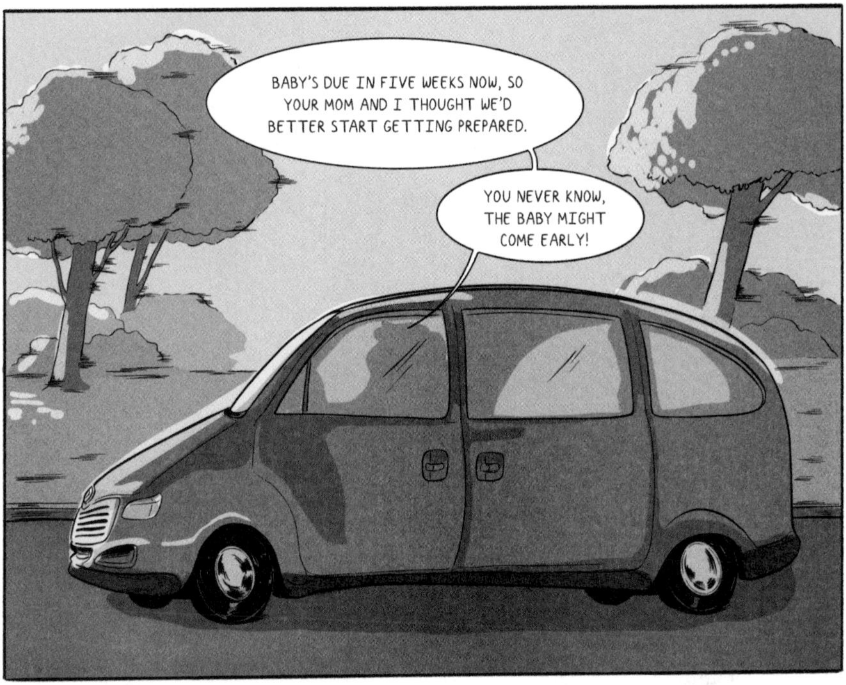
BABY'S DUE IN FIVE WEEKS NOW, SO YOUR MOM AND I THOUGHT WE'D BETTER START GETTING PREPARED.
YOU NEVER KNOW, THE BABY MIGHT COME EARLY!

SOMETHING BAD **WAS** HAPPENING, EVEN IF MOM AND DAD THOUGHT IT WAS GOOD.

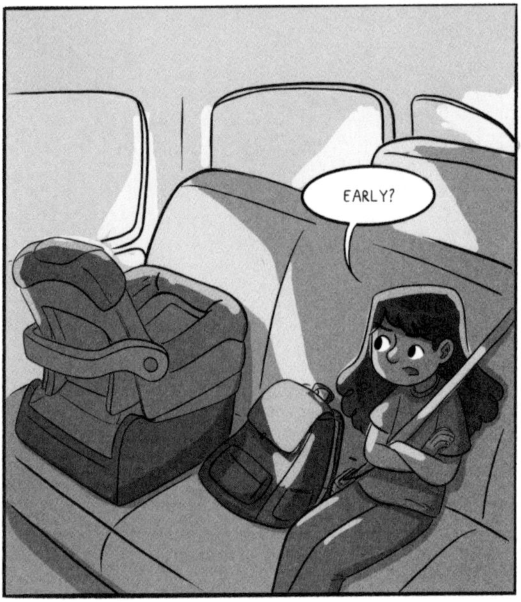
EARLY?

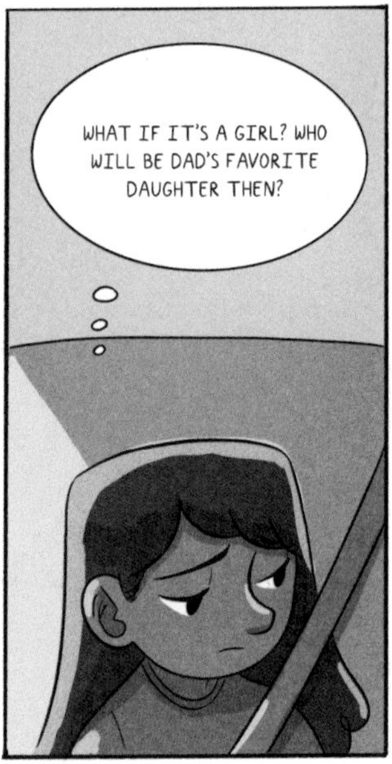
WHAT IF IT'S A GIRL? WHO WILL BE DAD'S FAVORITE DAUGHTER THEN?

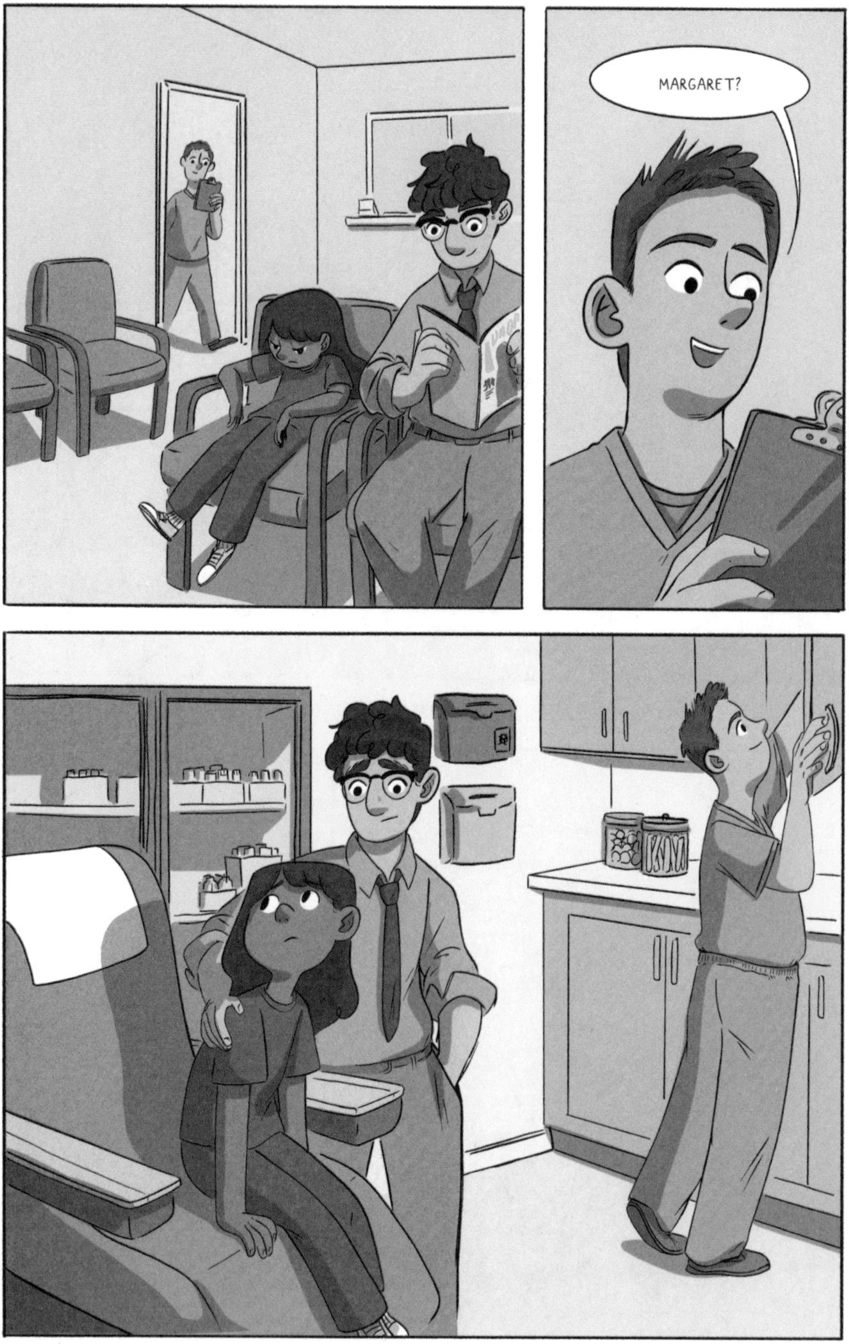
MARGARET?

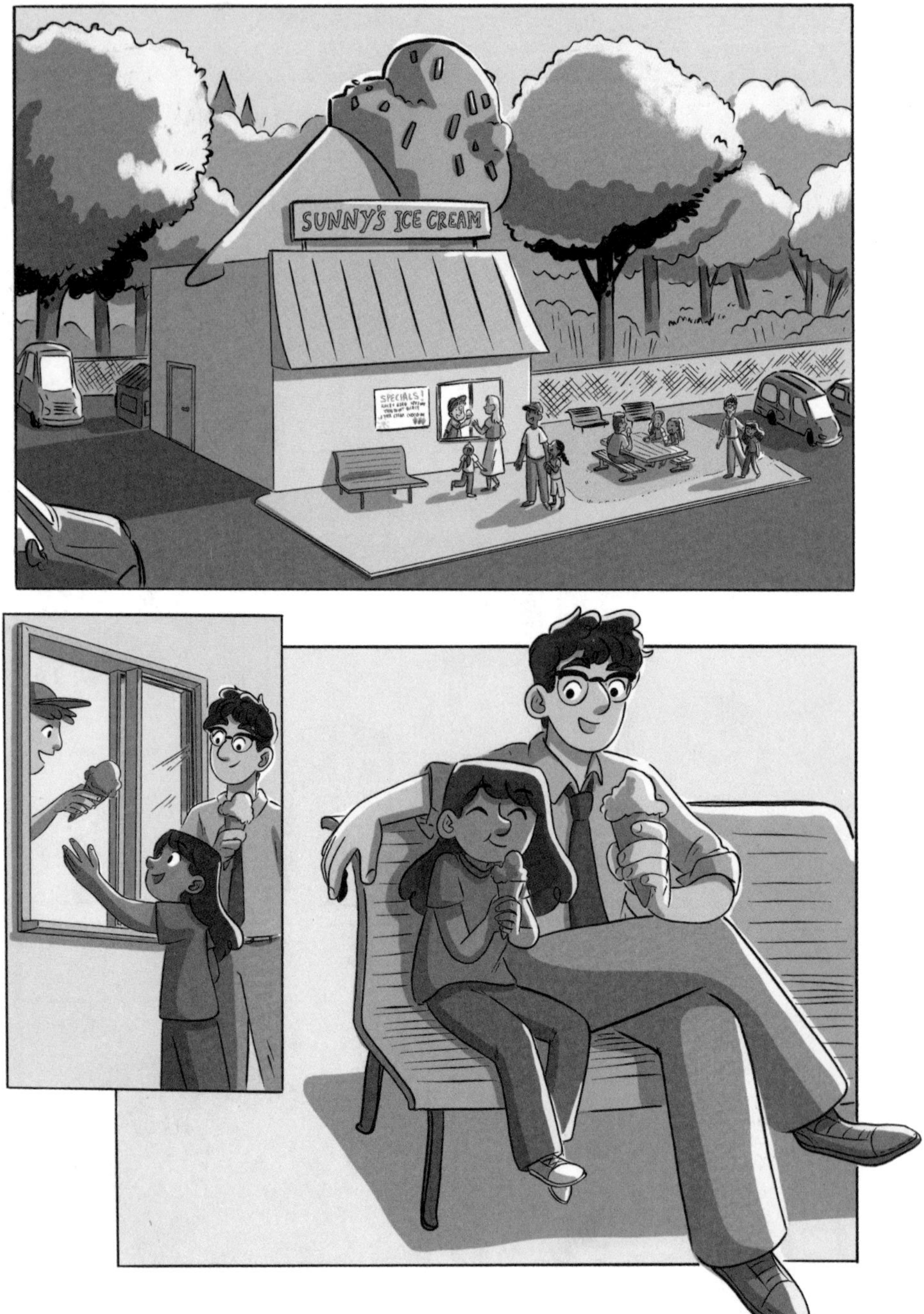
SUNNY'S ICE CREAM
SPECIALS!

Chapter Seven

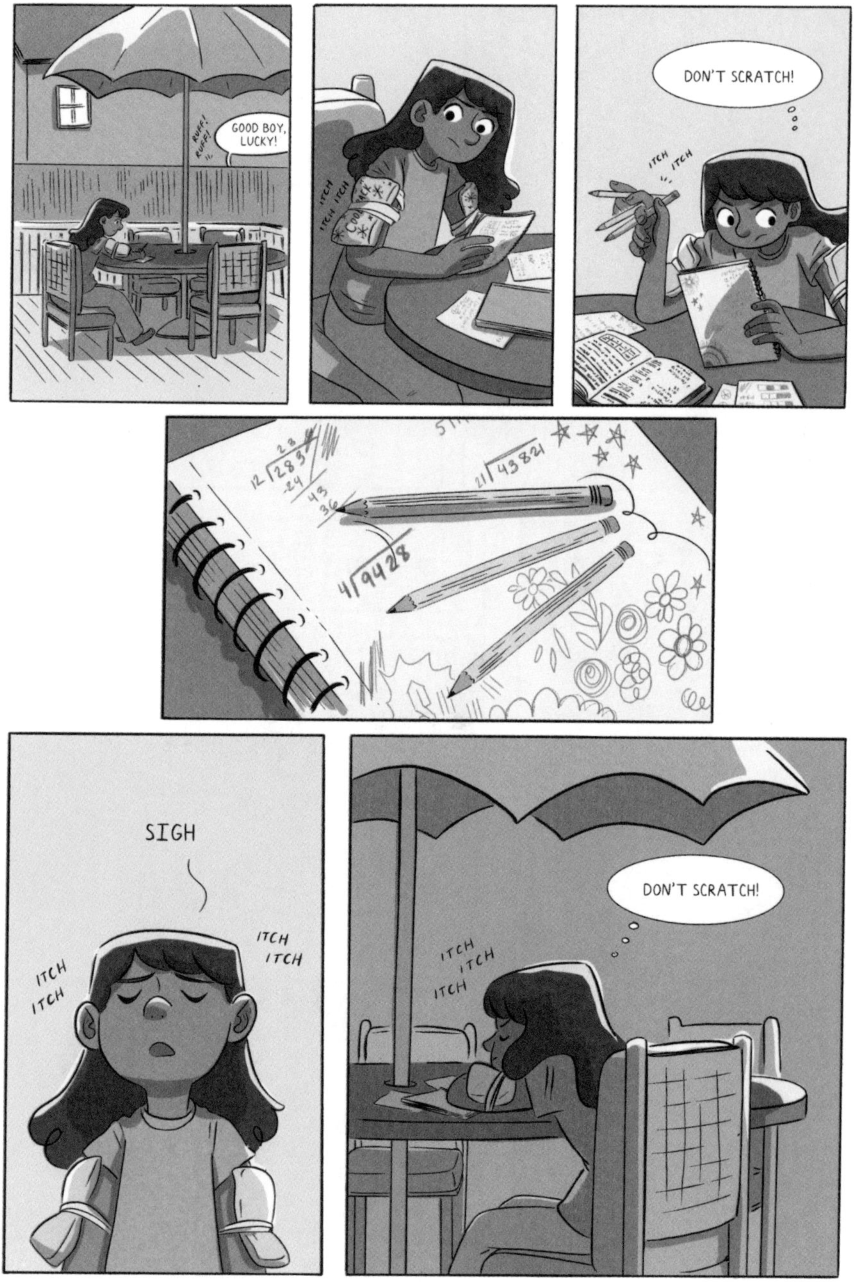
RUFF! RUFF!
GOOD BOY, LUCKY!
ITCH ITCH ITCH
DON'T SCRATCH!
ITCH ITCH
SIGH
ITCH ITCH
ITCH ITCH
DON'T SCRATCH!
ITCH ITCH ITCH

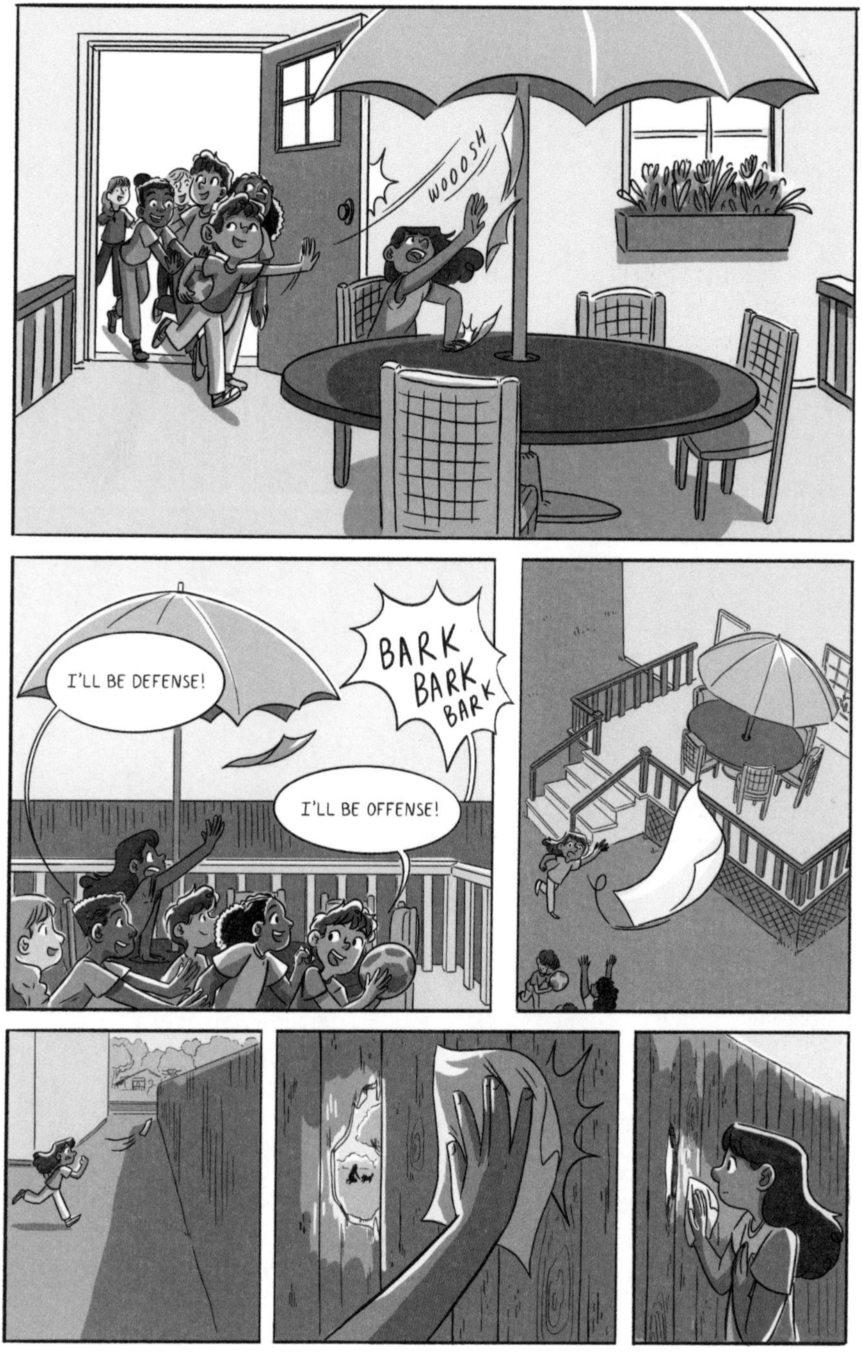
WOOOSH
I'LL BE DEFENSE!
BARK BARK BARK
I'LL BE OFFENSE!

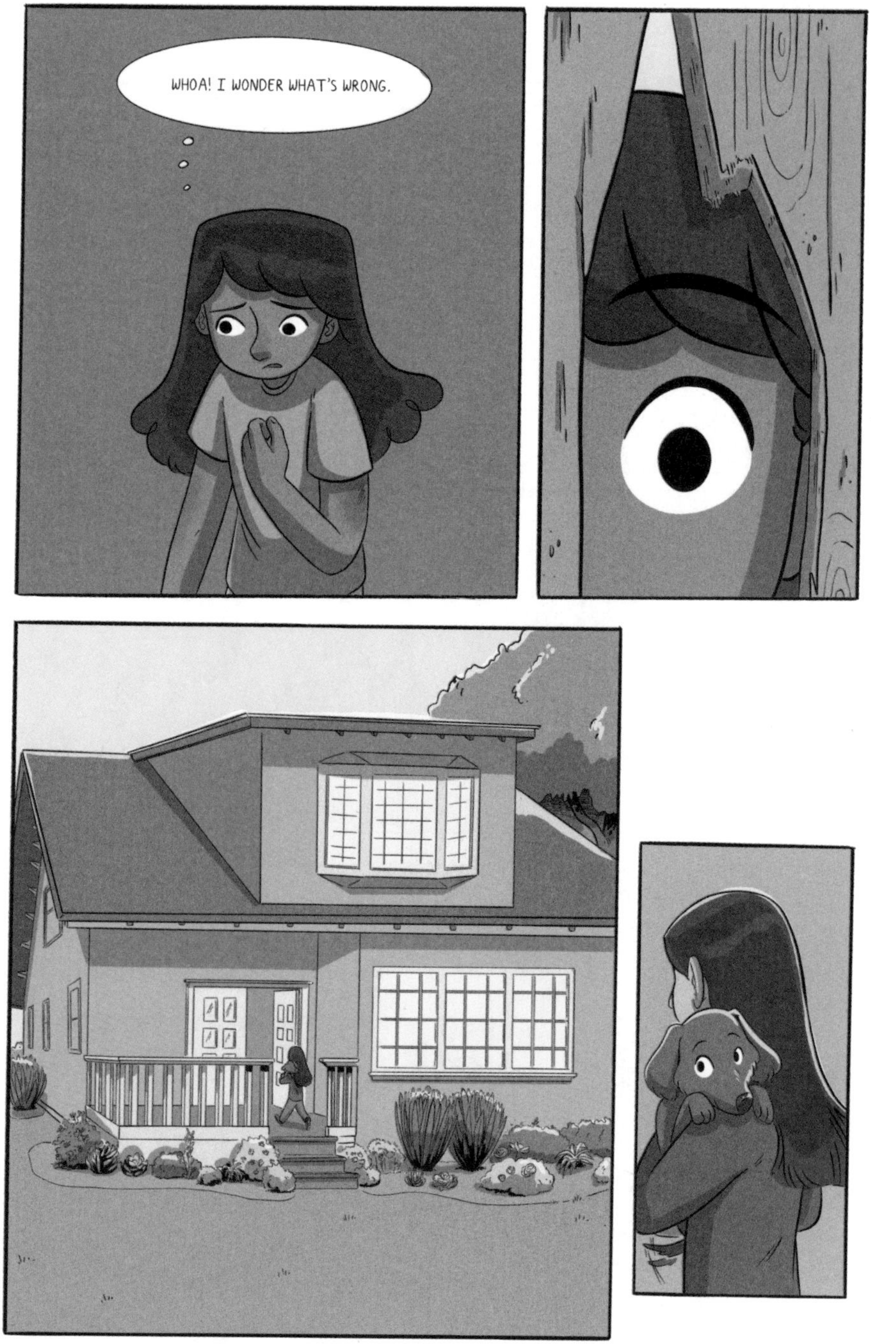
WHOA! I WONDER WHAT'S WRONG.

WAS SHE CRYING BECAUSE OF...ME?

WHACKK

SORRY!

OUCH

IT HADN'T OCCURRED TO ME THAT MAYBE I WASN'T THE ONLY ONE WHO MISSED BEING FRIENDS...

AFTER ALL, NOW THAT CLAIRE HAD LUCKY FOR COMPANY, WHY WOULD SHE NEED ME?

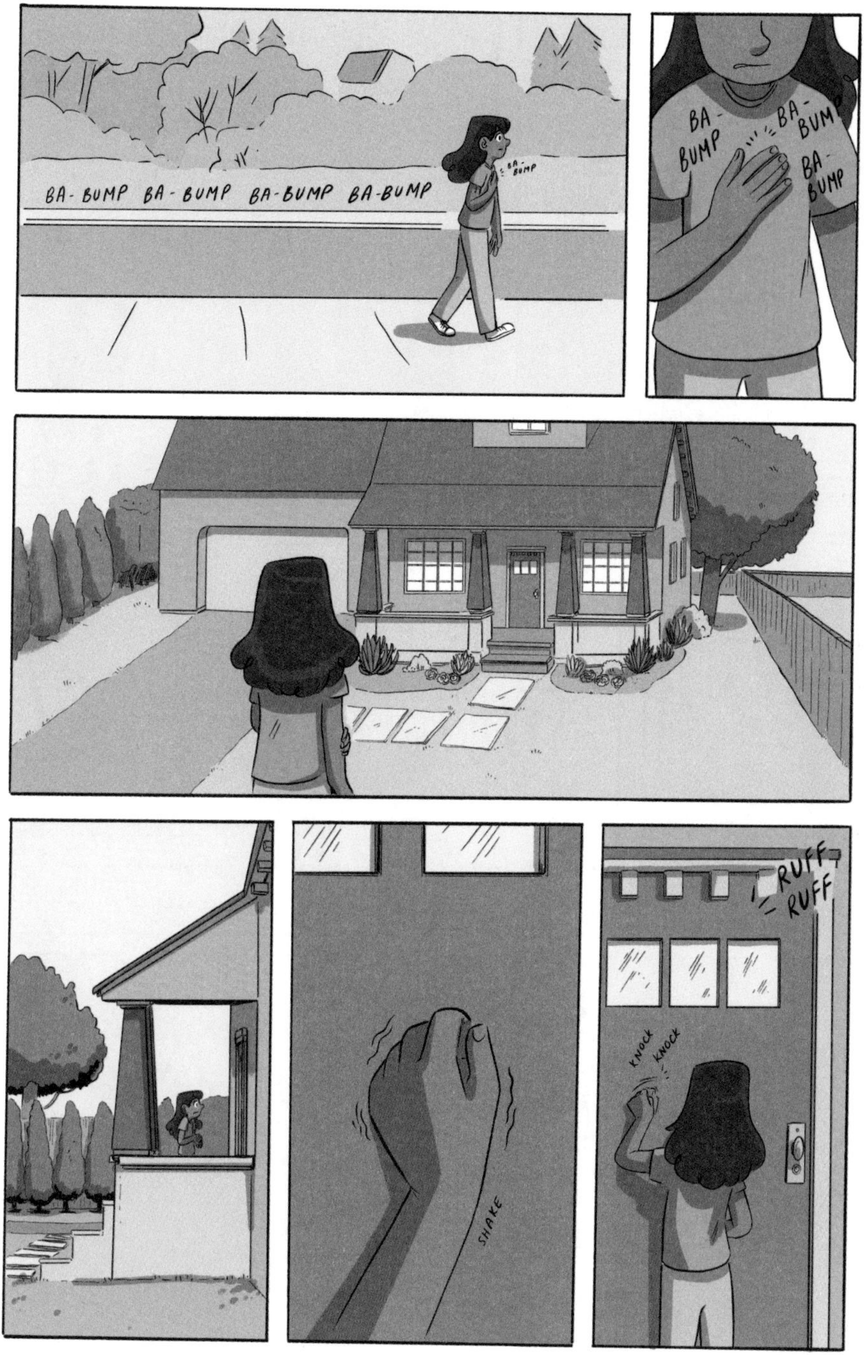
BA-BUMP
BA-BUMP BA-BUMP BA-BUMP BA-BUMP
BA-BUMP
BA-BUMP
BA-BUMP
SHAKE
KNOCK KNOCK
RUFF RUFF

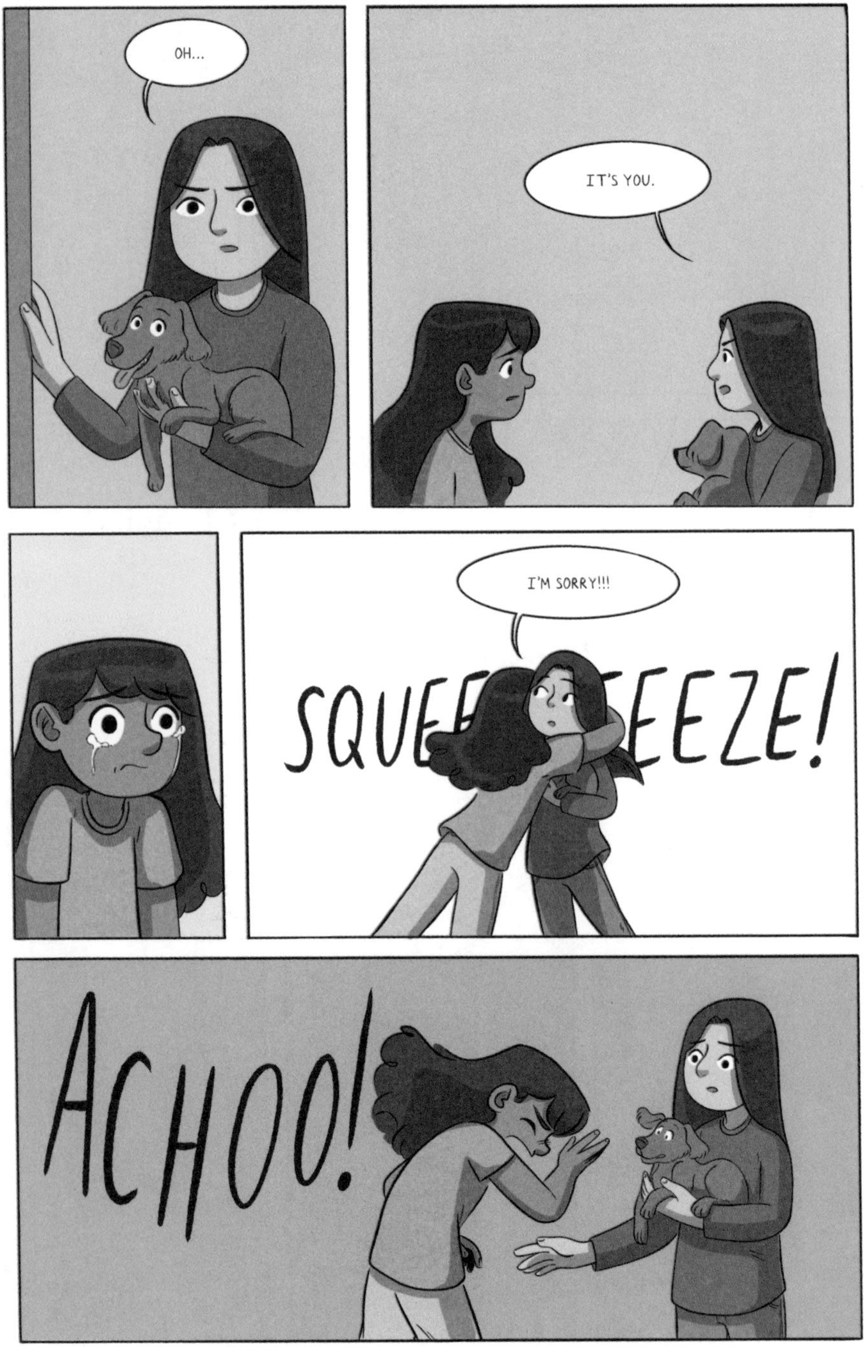
OH...
IT'S YOU.
I'M SORRY!!!
SQUEE
EEZE!
ACHOO!

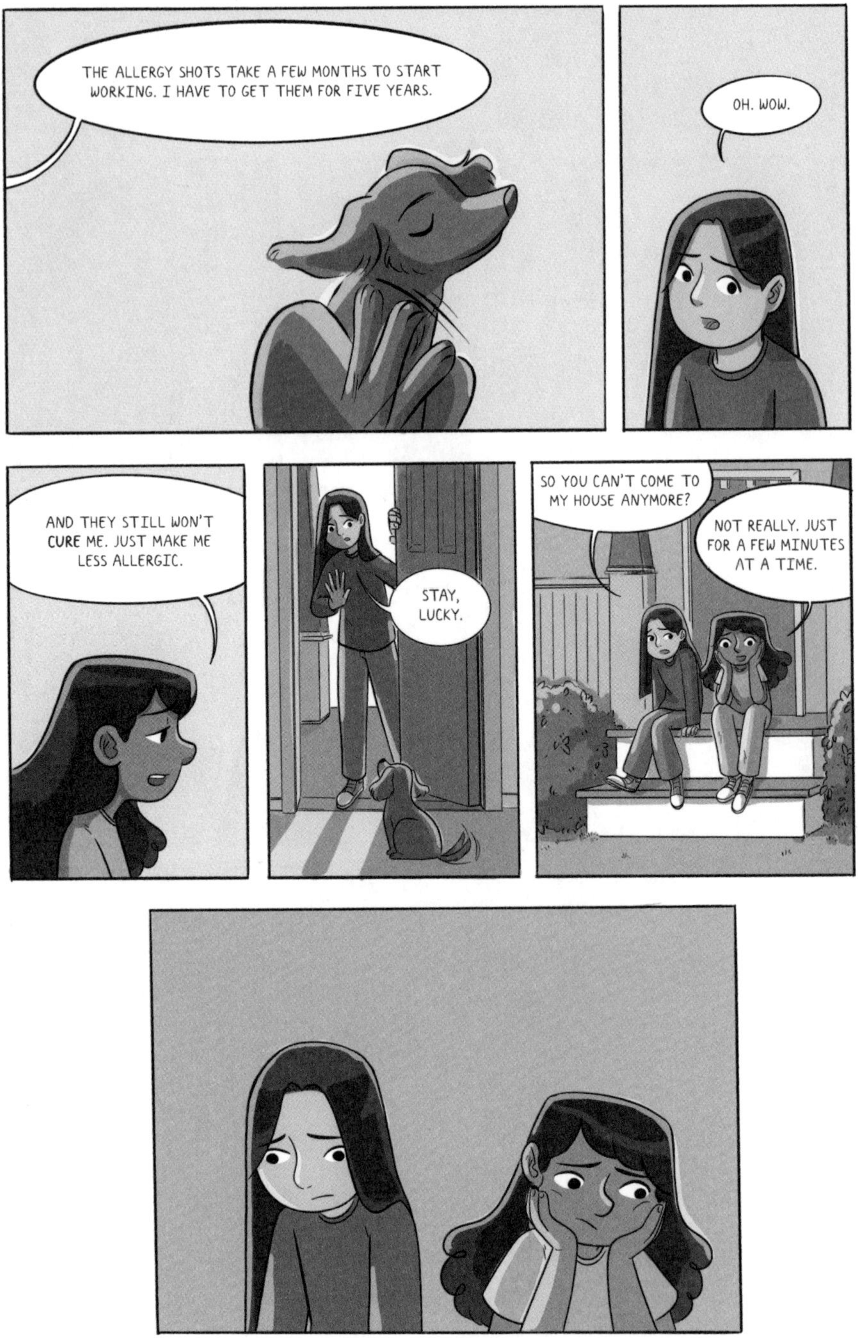
THE ALLERGY SHOTS TAKE A FEW MONTHS TO START WORKING. I HAVE TO GET THEM FOR FIVE YEARS.
OH. WOW.
AND THEY STILL WON'T **CURE** ME. JUST MAKE ME LESS ALLERGIC.
STAY, LUCKY.
SO YOU CAN'T COME TO MY HOUSE ANYMORE?
NOT REALLY. JUST FOR A FEW MINUTES AT A TIME.

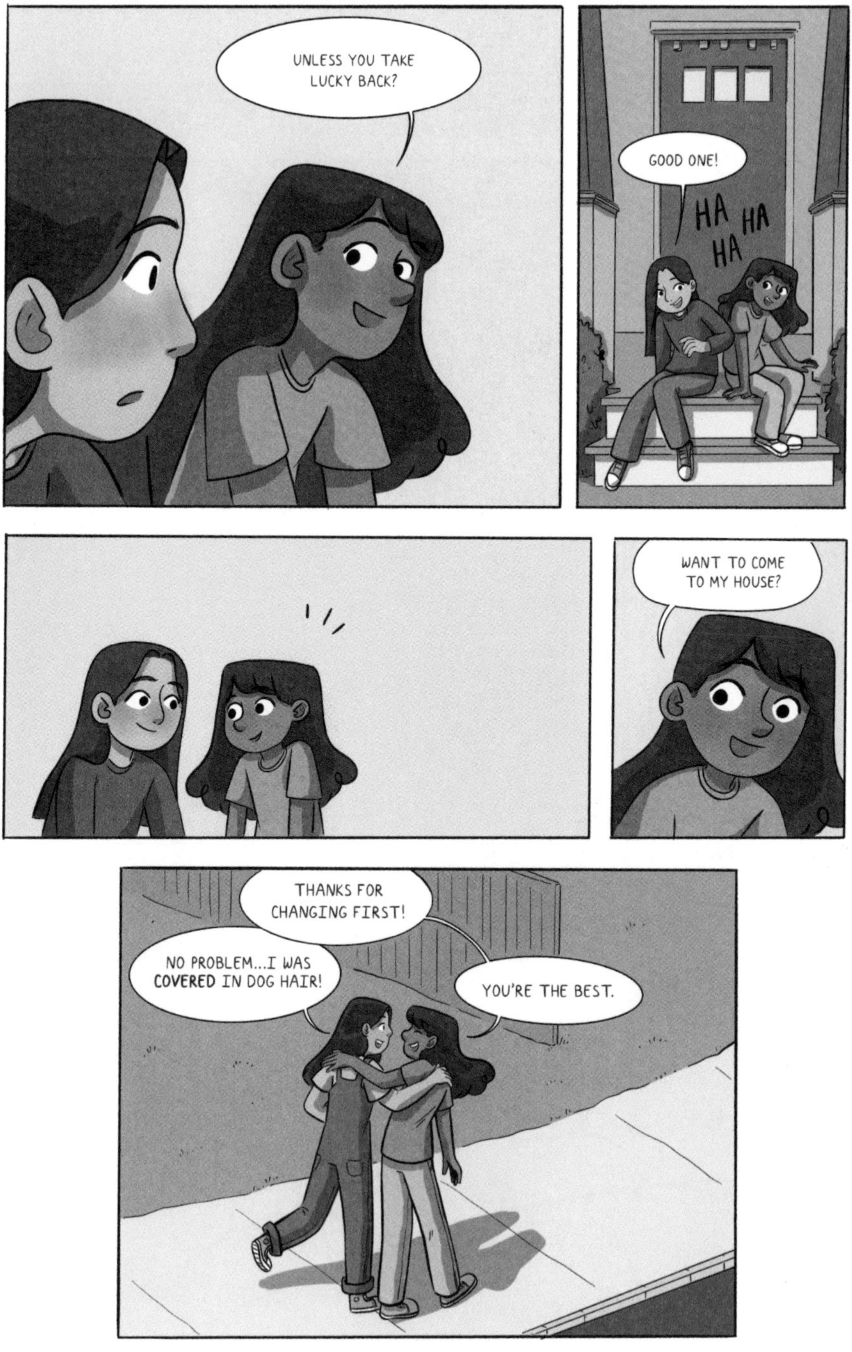
UNLESS YOU TAKE LUCKY BACK?
GOOD ONE!
HA HA HA
WANT TO COME TO MY HOUSE?
THANKS FOR CHANGING FIRST!
NO PROBLEM...I WAS **COVERED** IN DOG HAIR!
YOU'RE THE BEST.

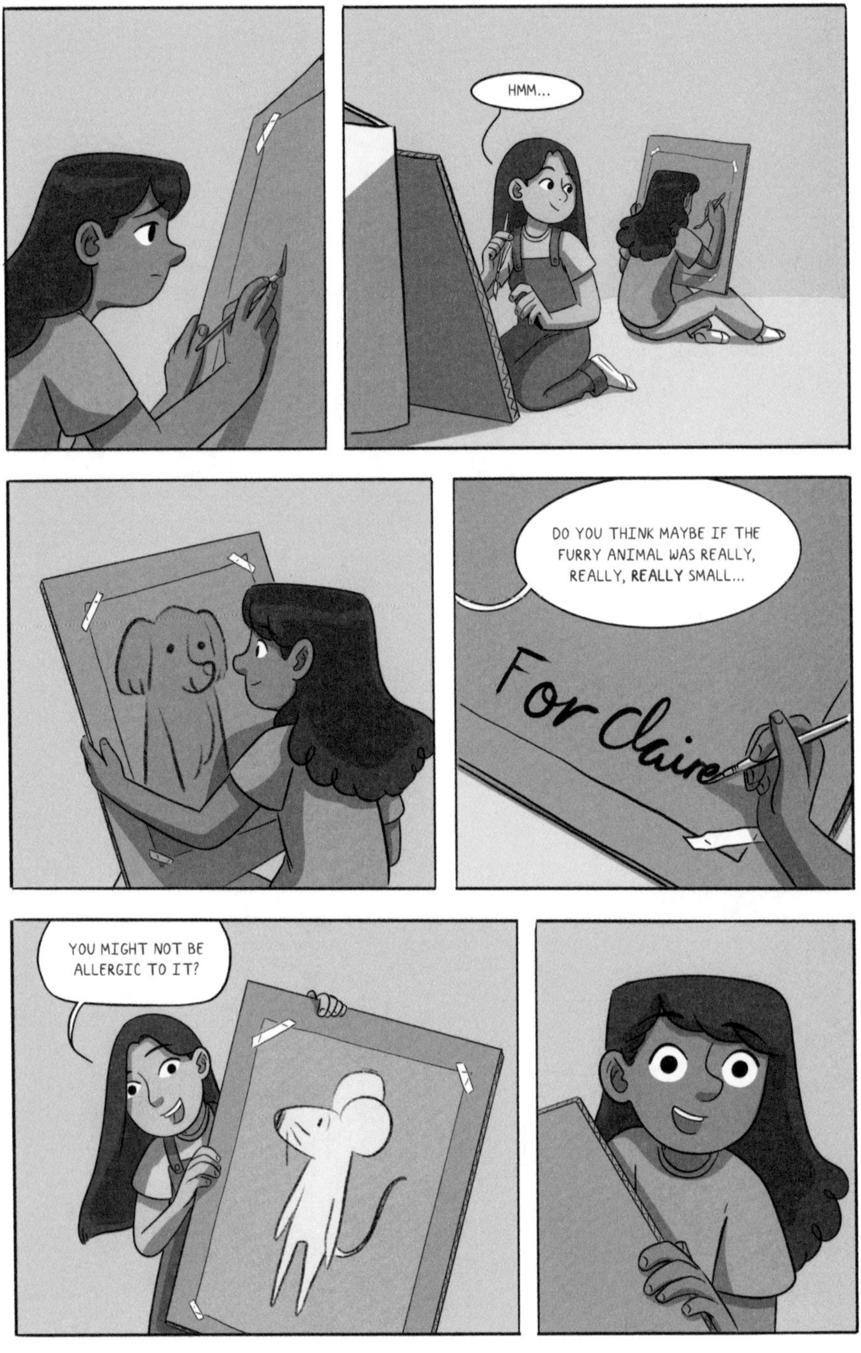
HMM...
DO YOU THINK MAYBE IF THE FURRY ANIMAL WAS REALLY, REALLY, **REALLY** SMALL...
For Claire
YOU MIGHT NOT BE ALLERGIC TO IT?

PET QUEST #9

DO YOU THINK YOU HAVE ENOUGH?

ALMOST.

THERE. THAT SHOULD DO IT.

THANKS!

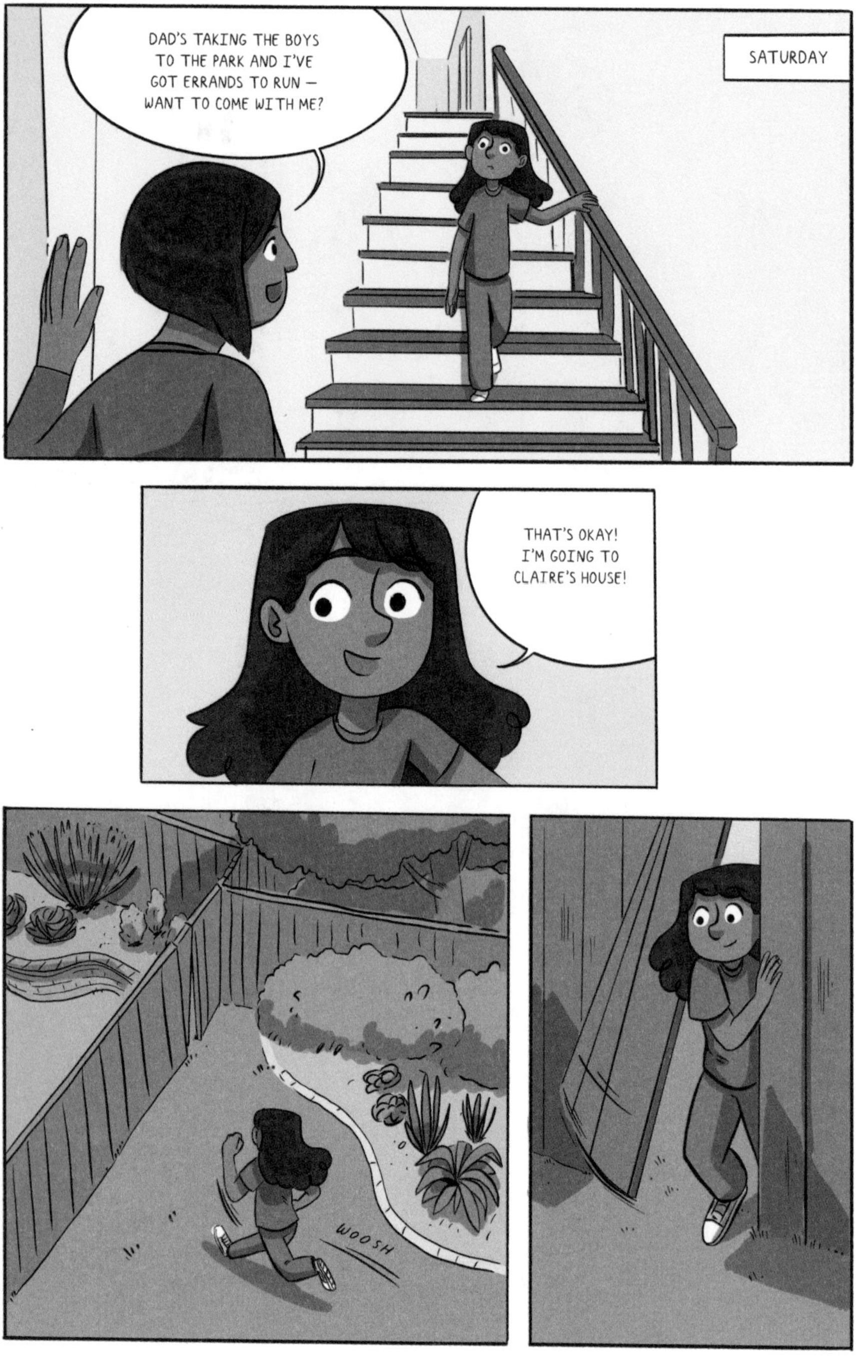
SATURDAY
DAD'S TAKING THE BOYS TO THE PARK AND I'VE GOT ERRANDS TO RUN — WANT TO COME WITH ME?
THAT'S OKAY! I'M GOING TO CLAIRE'S HOUSE!
WOOSH

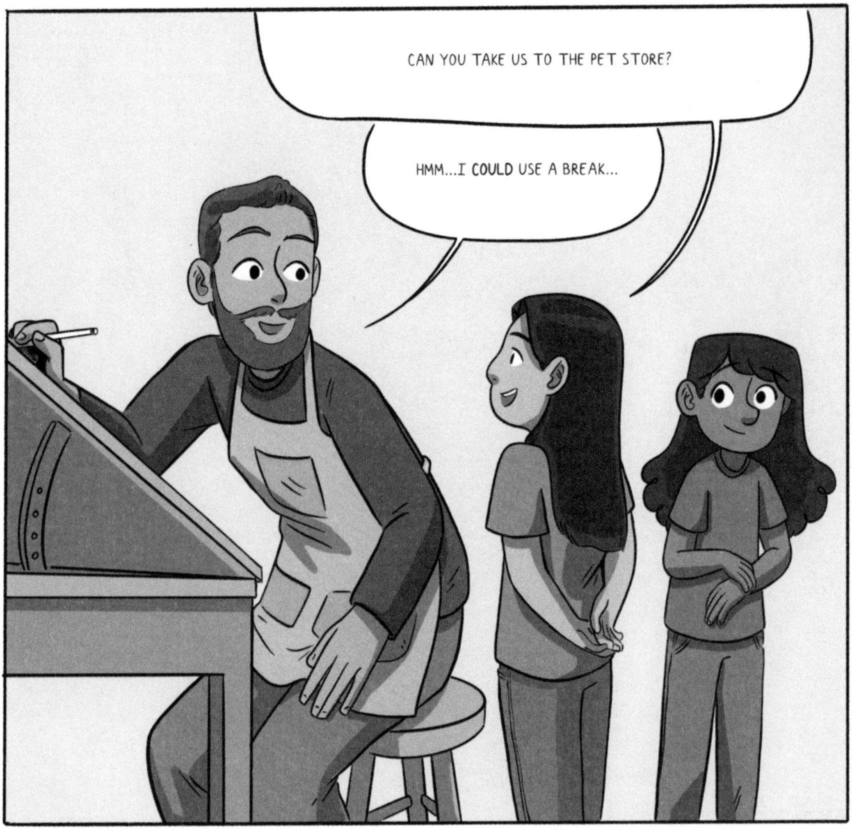
CAN YOU TAKE US TO THE PET STORE?
HMM...I COULD USE A BREAK...

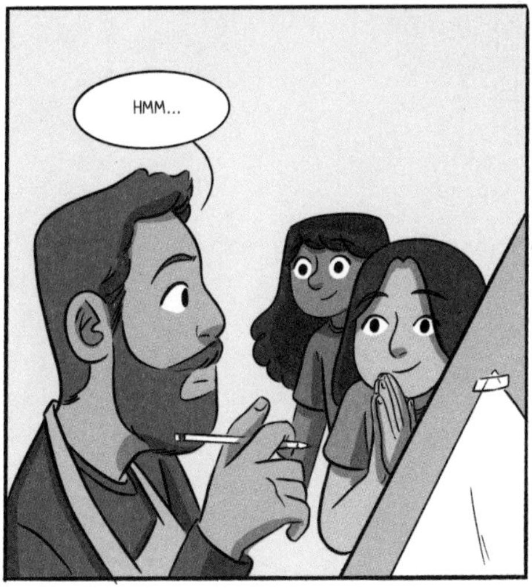
HMM...

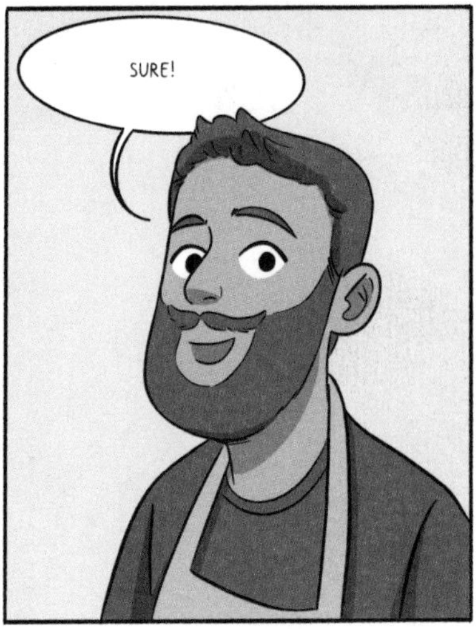
SURE!

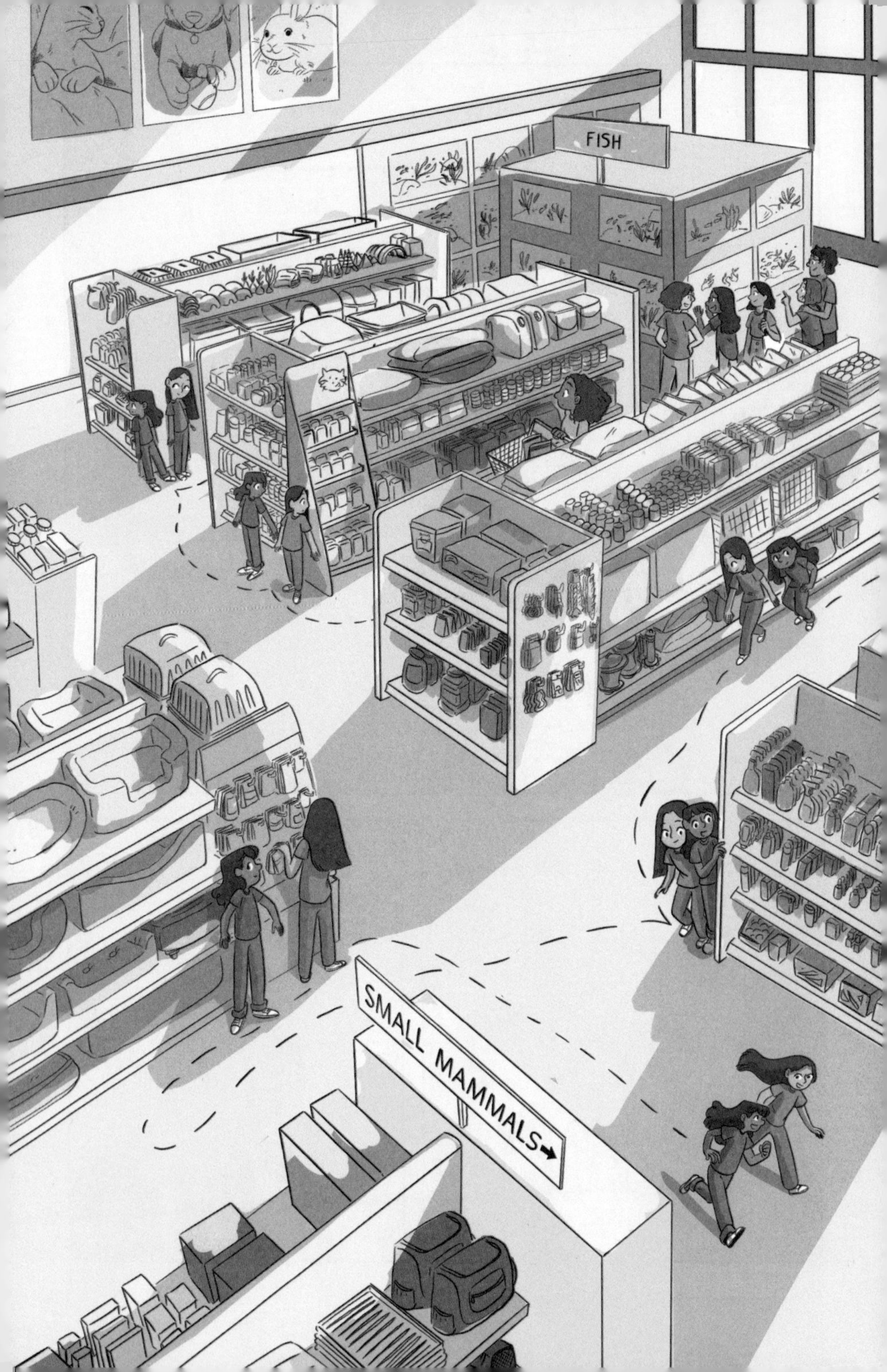
FISH
SMALL MAMMALS→

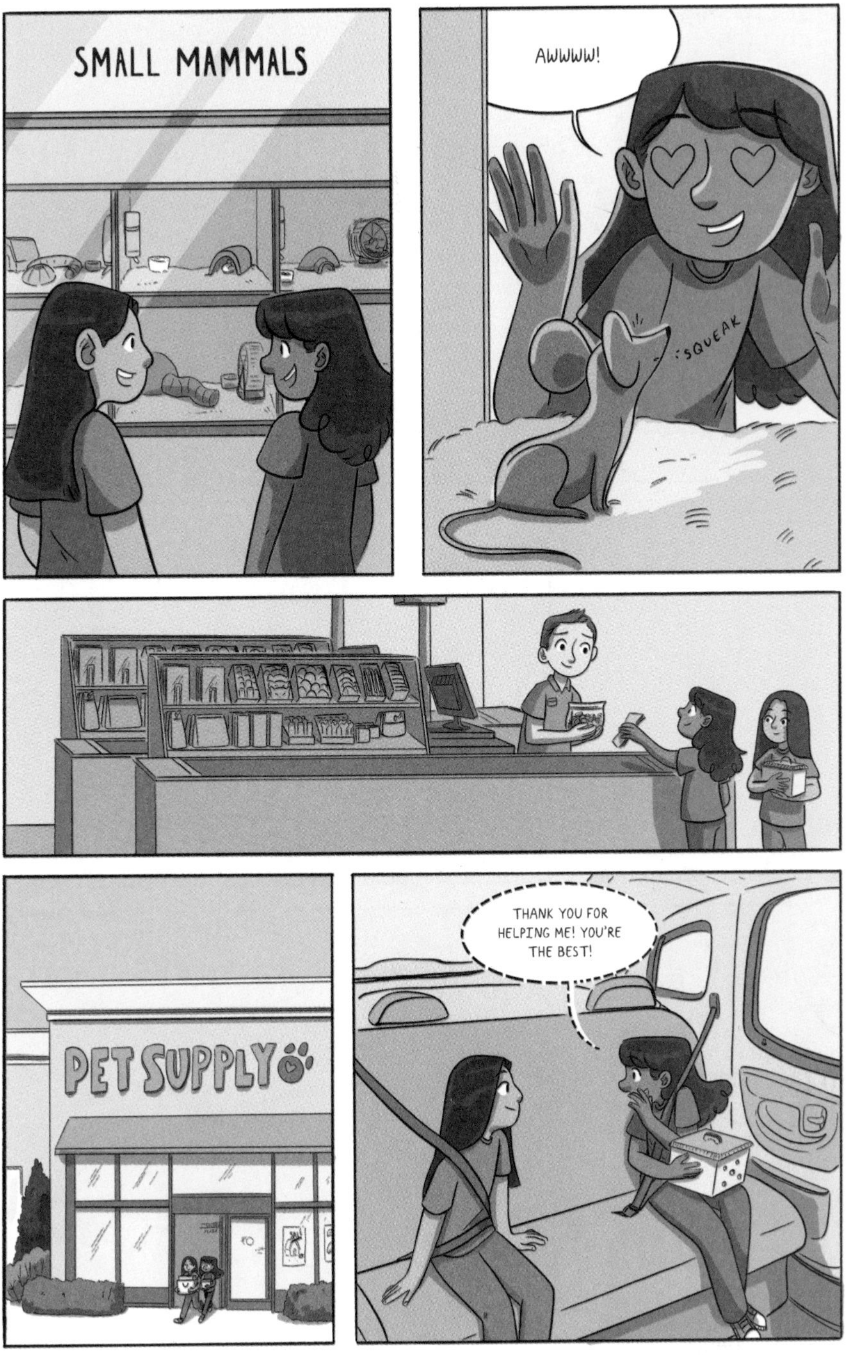
SMALL MAMMALS
AWWWW!
SQUEAK
PET SUPPLY
THANK YOU FOR HELPING ME! YOU'RE THE BEST!

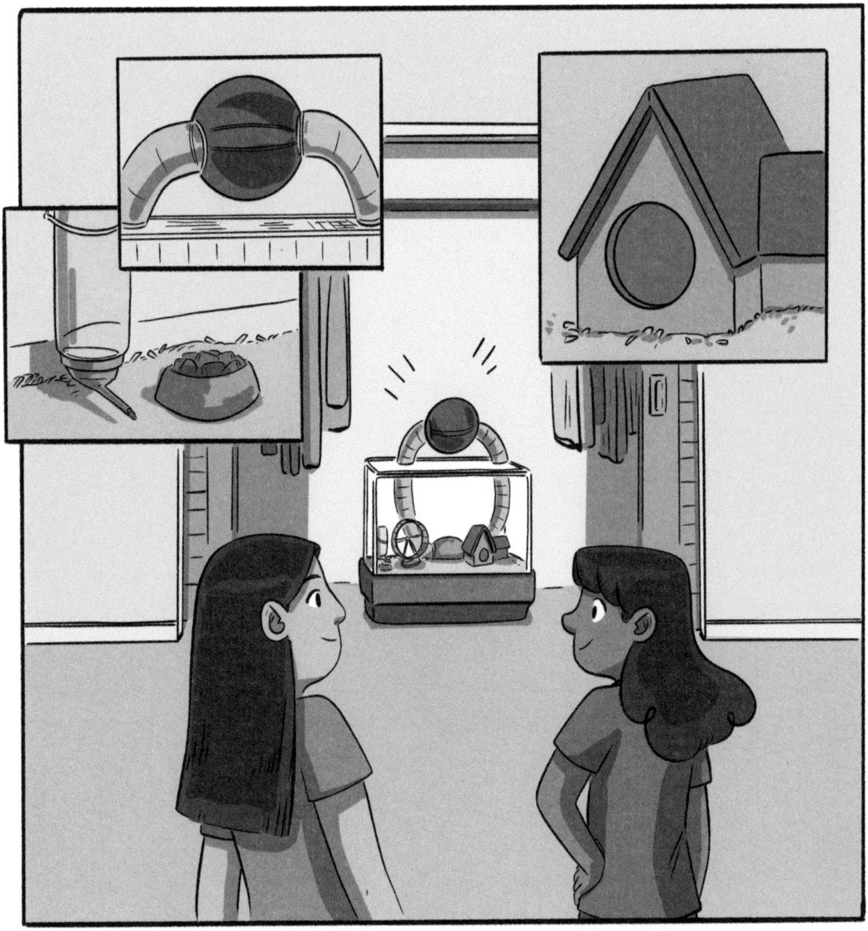

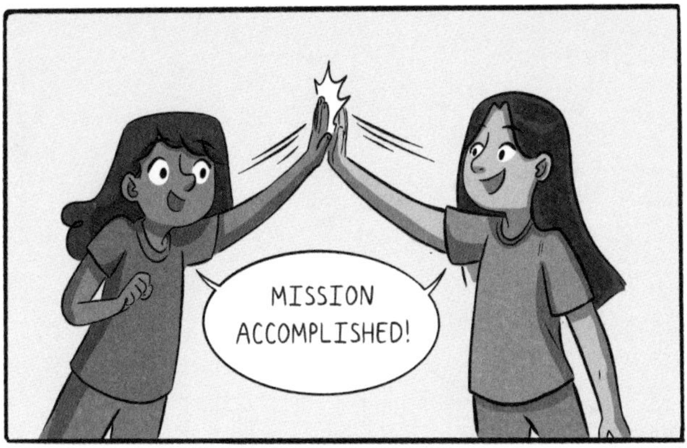
MISSION ACCOMPLISHED!

Chapter Eight

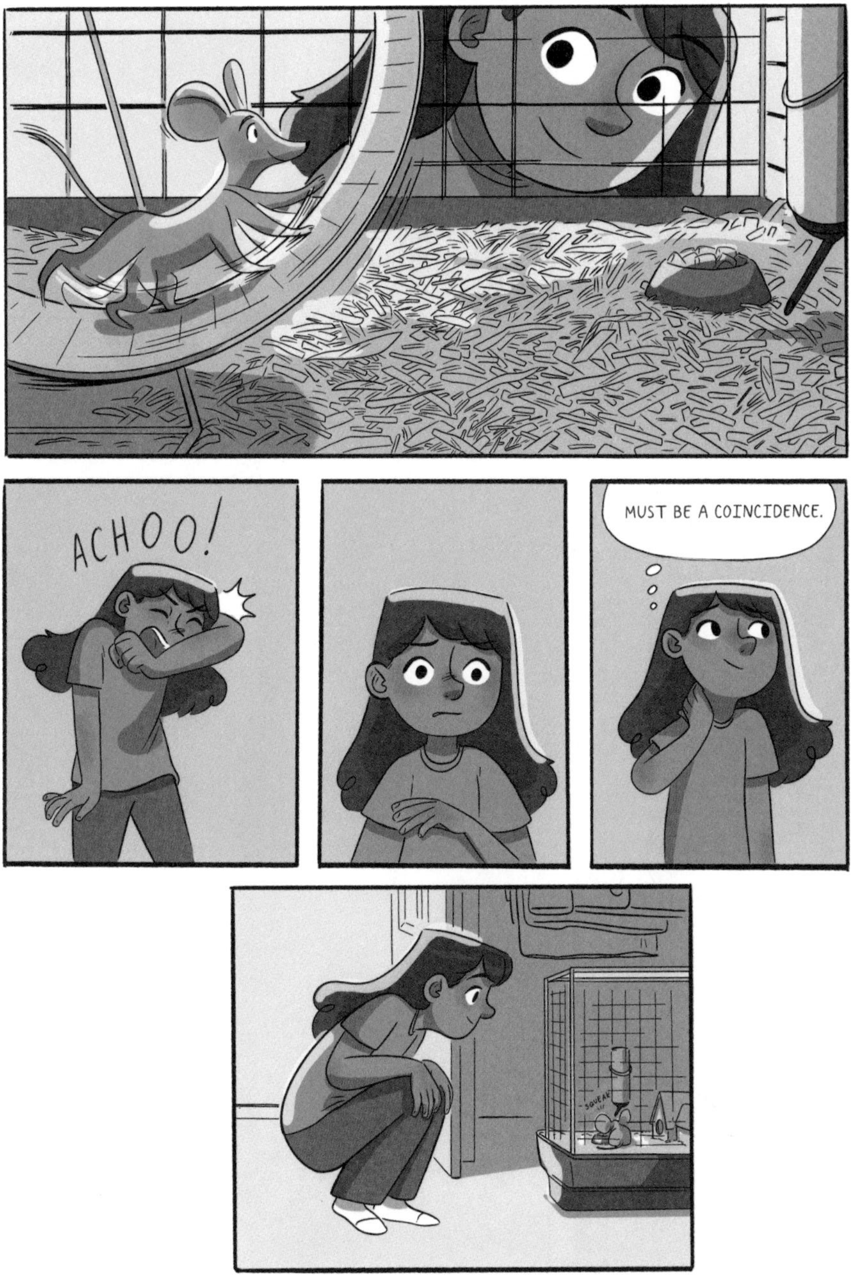
ACHOO!
MUST BE A COINCIDENCE.

TAMING YOUR PET MOUSE

At first, simply sit by your mouse's cage so they can get used to your presence.

I WONDER IF SHE'S USED TO ME BY NOW...

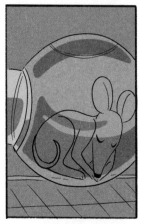

HOW WILL I KNOW WHEN SHE IS?

SNIFF SNIFF

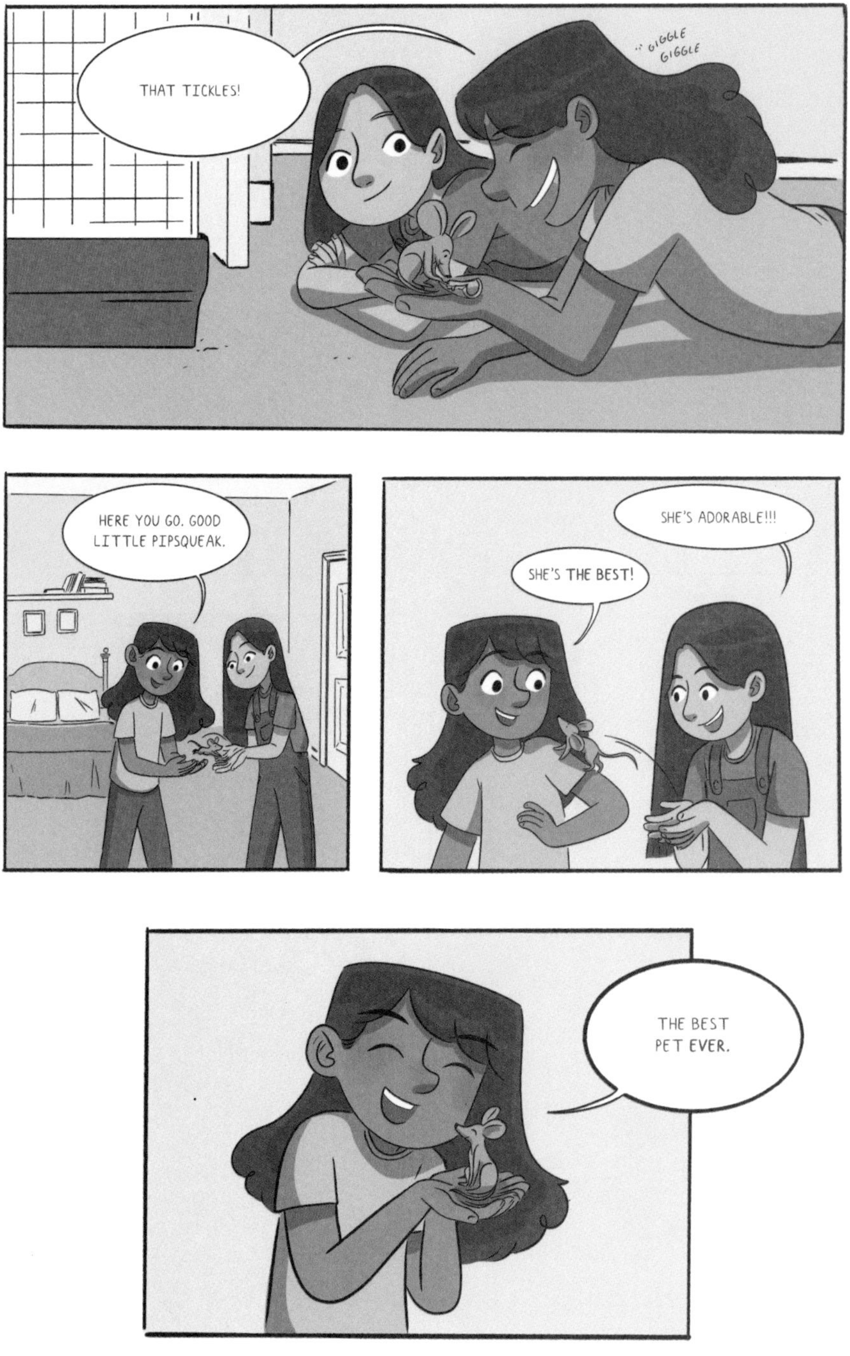
THAT TICKLES!
GIGGLE GIGGLE
HERE YOU GO. GOOD LITTLE PIPSQUEAK.
SHE'S ADORABLE!!!
SHE'S THE BEST!
THE BEST PET EVER.

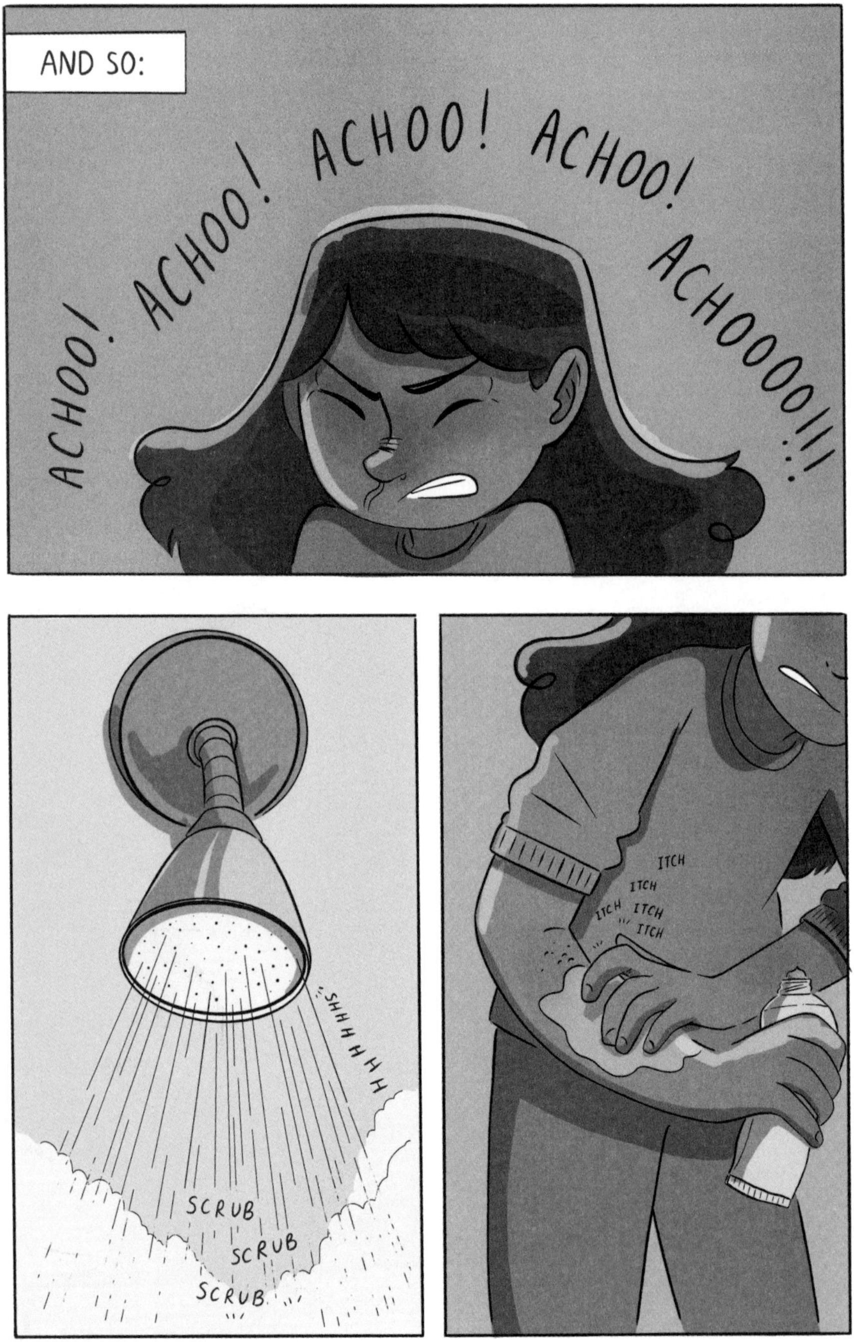
AND SO:
ACHOO! ACHOO! ACHOO! ACHOO! ACHOOOOO!!!!
SHHHHHH
SCRUB
SCRUB
SCRUB
ITCH
ITCH
ITCH ITCH
ITCH

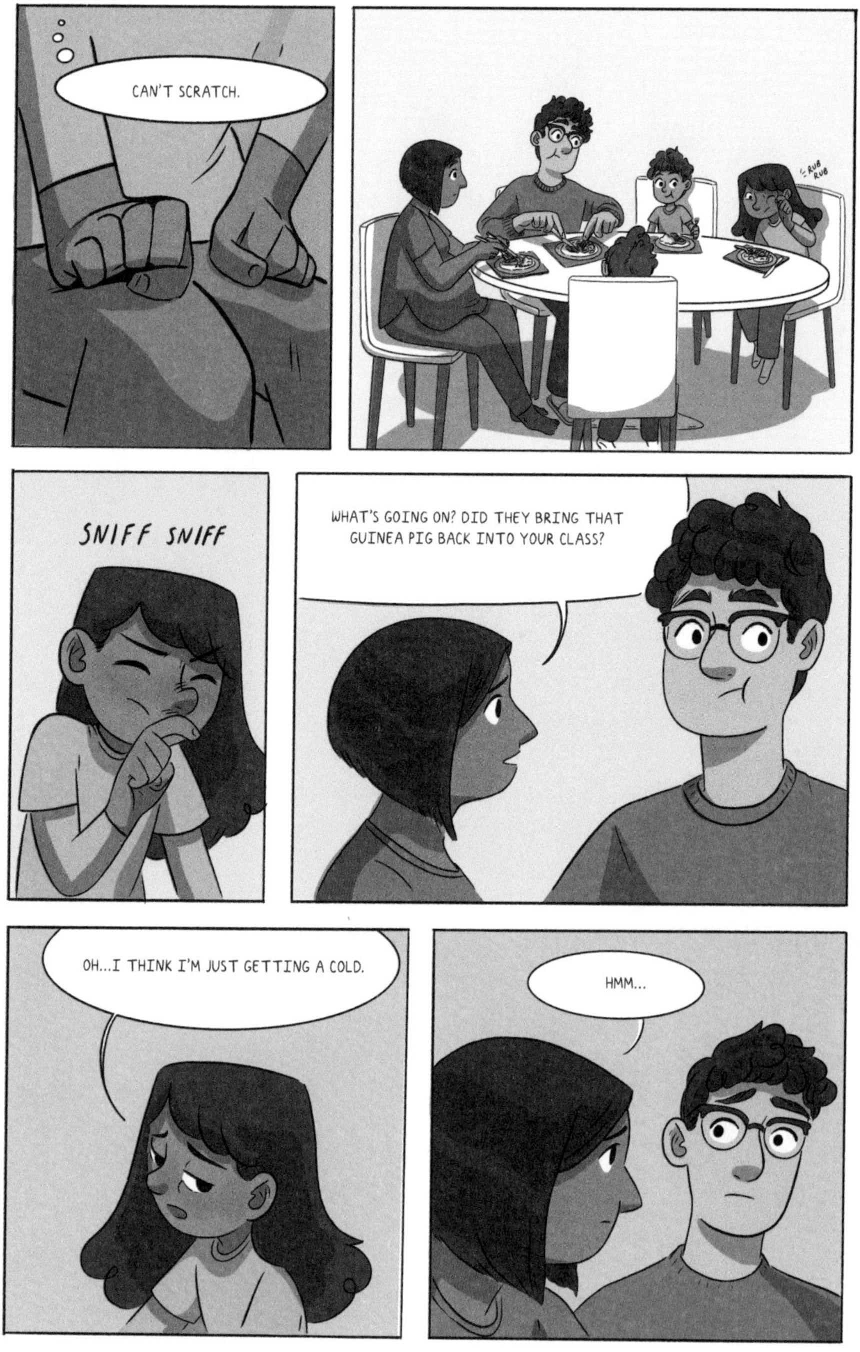
CAN'T SCRATCH.
RUB RUB
SNIFF SNIFF
WHAT'S GOING ON? DID THEY BRING THAT GUINEA PIG BACK INTO YOUR CLASS?
OH...I THINK I'M JUST GETTING A COLD.
HMM...

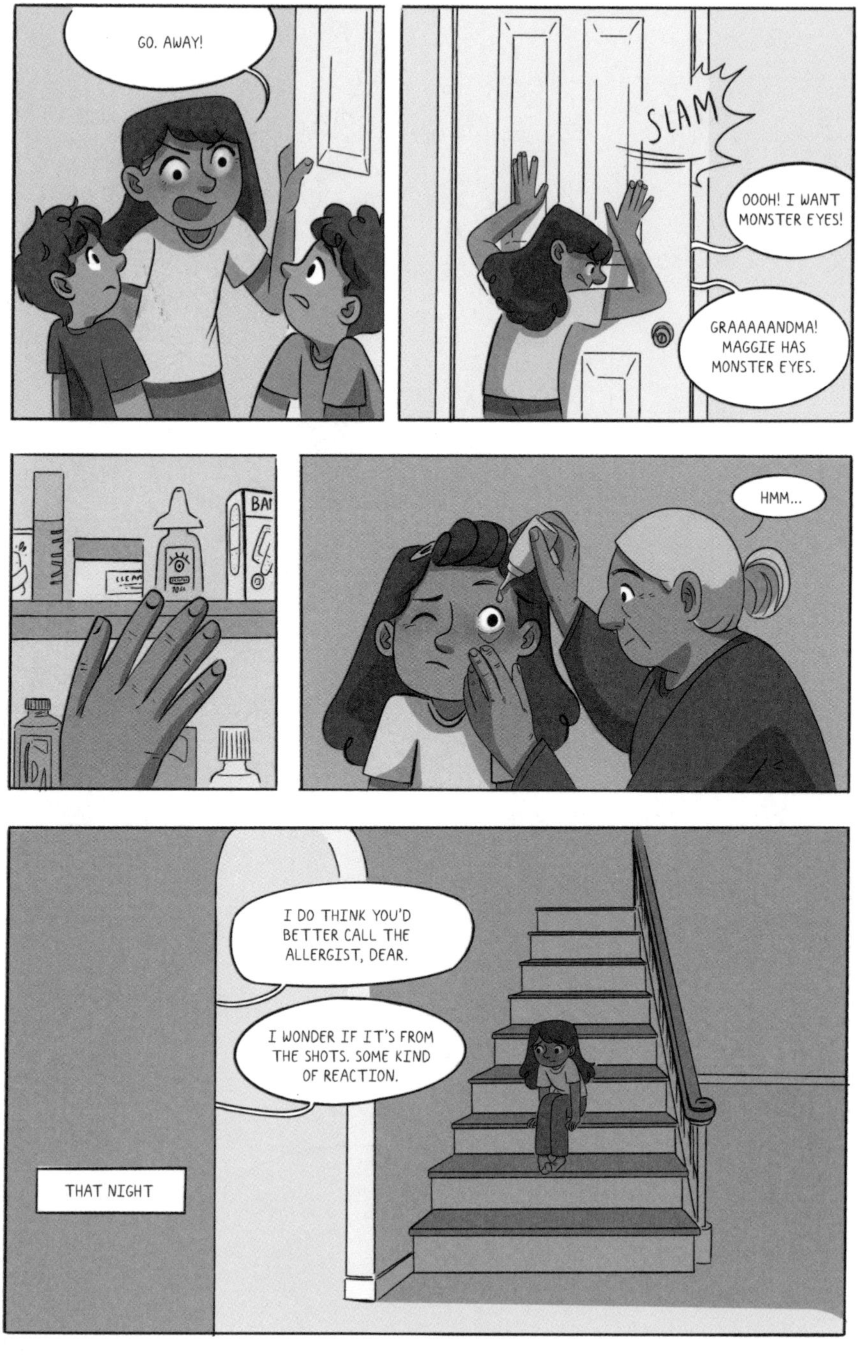
GO. AWAY!
SLAM
OOOH! I WANT MONSTER EYES!
GRAAAAANDMA! MAGGIE HAS MONSTER EYES.
HMM...
I DO THINK YOU'D BETTER CALL THE ALLERGIST, DEAR.
I WONDER IF IT'S FROM THE SHOTS. SOME KIND OF REACTION.
THAT NIGHT

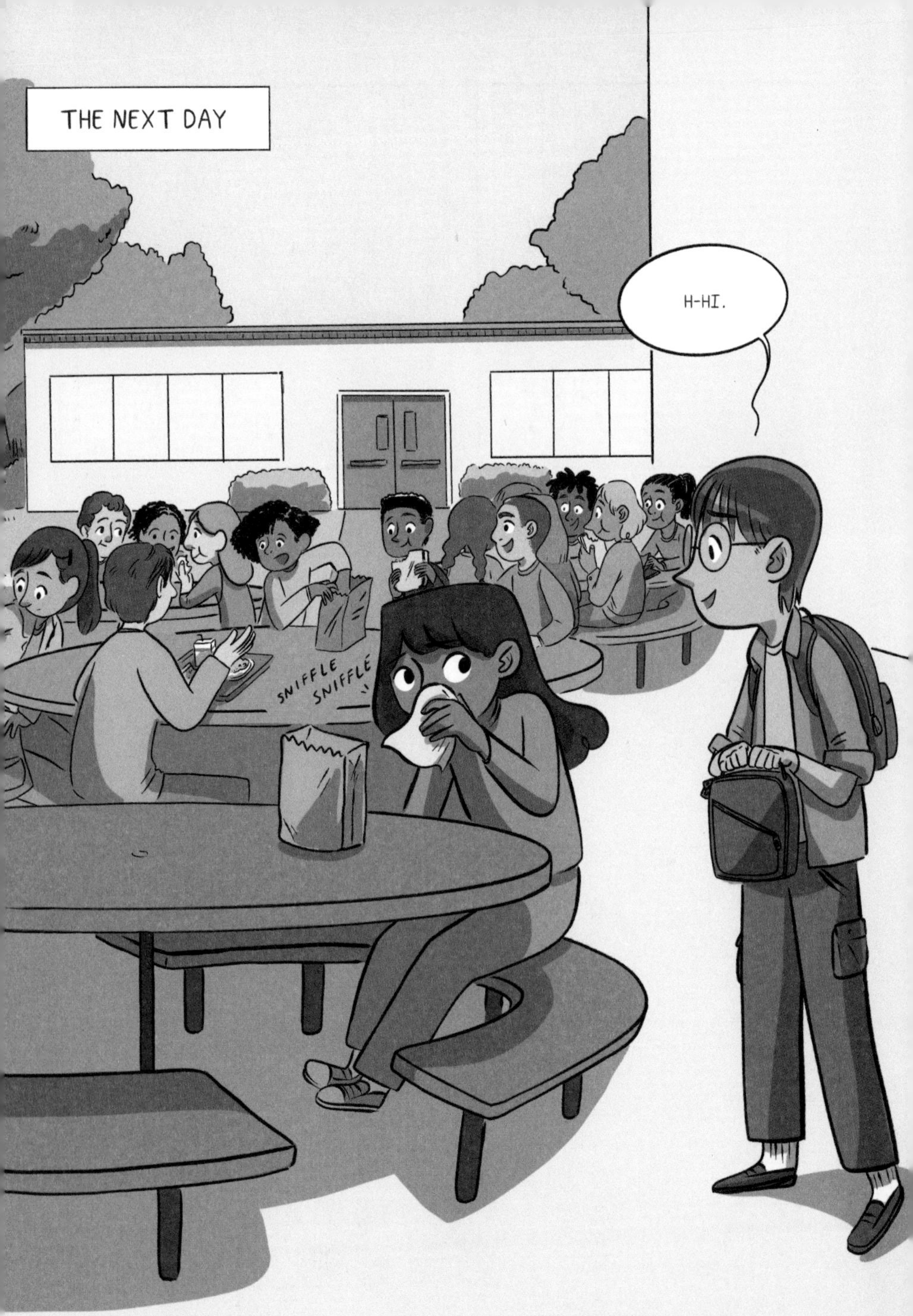
THE NEXT DAY
SNIFFLE
SNIFFLE
H-HI.

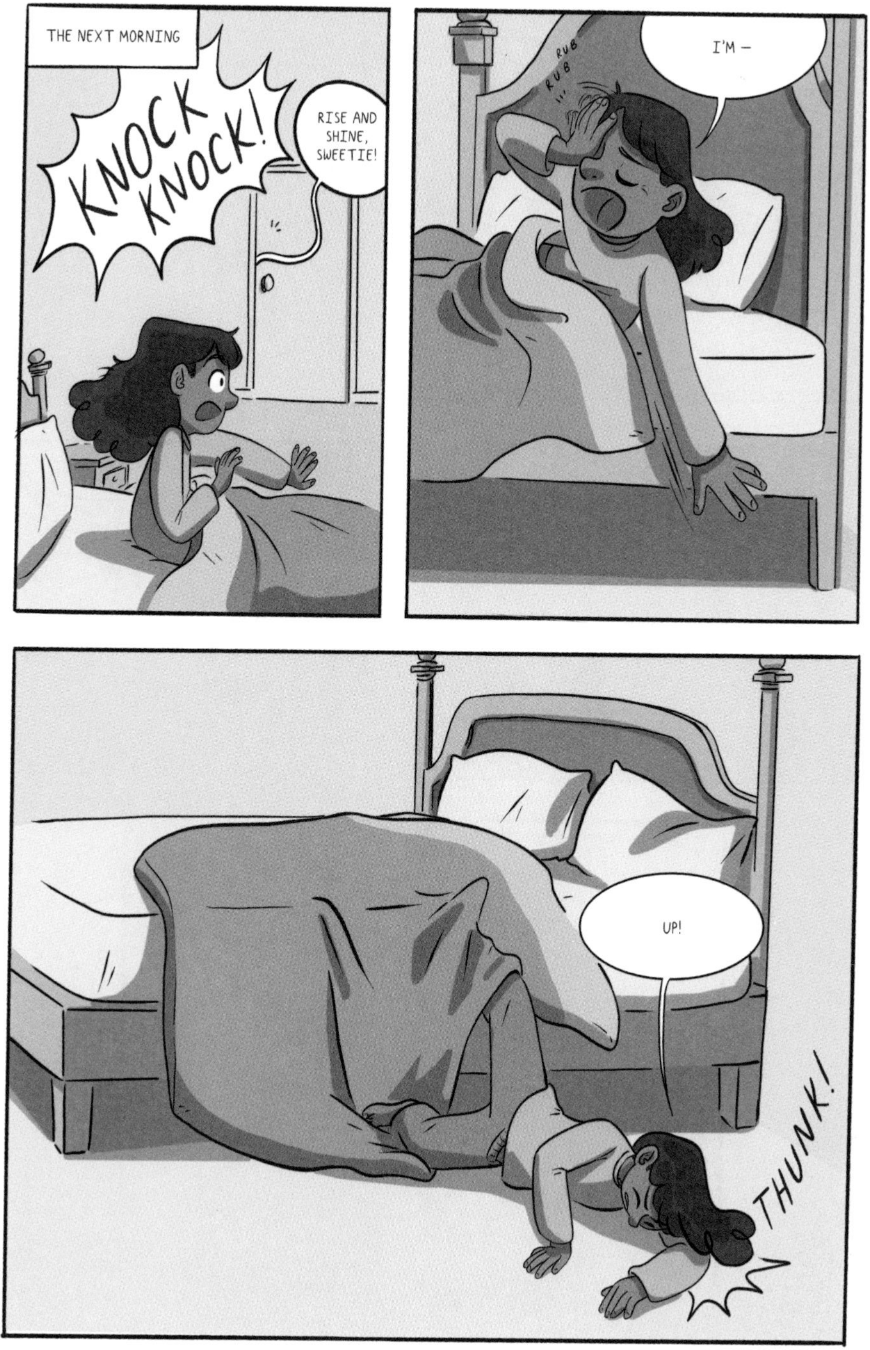
THE NEXT MORNING
KNOCK KNOCK!
RISE AND SHINE, SWEETIE!
RUB RUB
I'M —
UP!
THUNK!

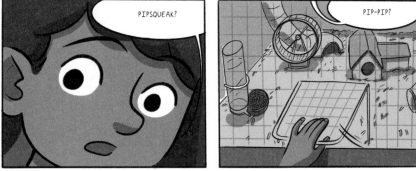

PIPSQUEAK?

PIP-PIP?

WHERE **ARE** YOU?

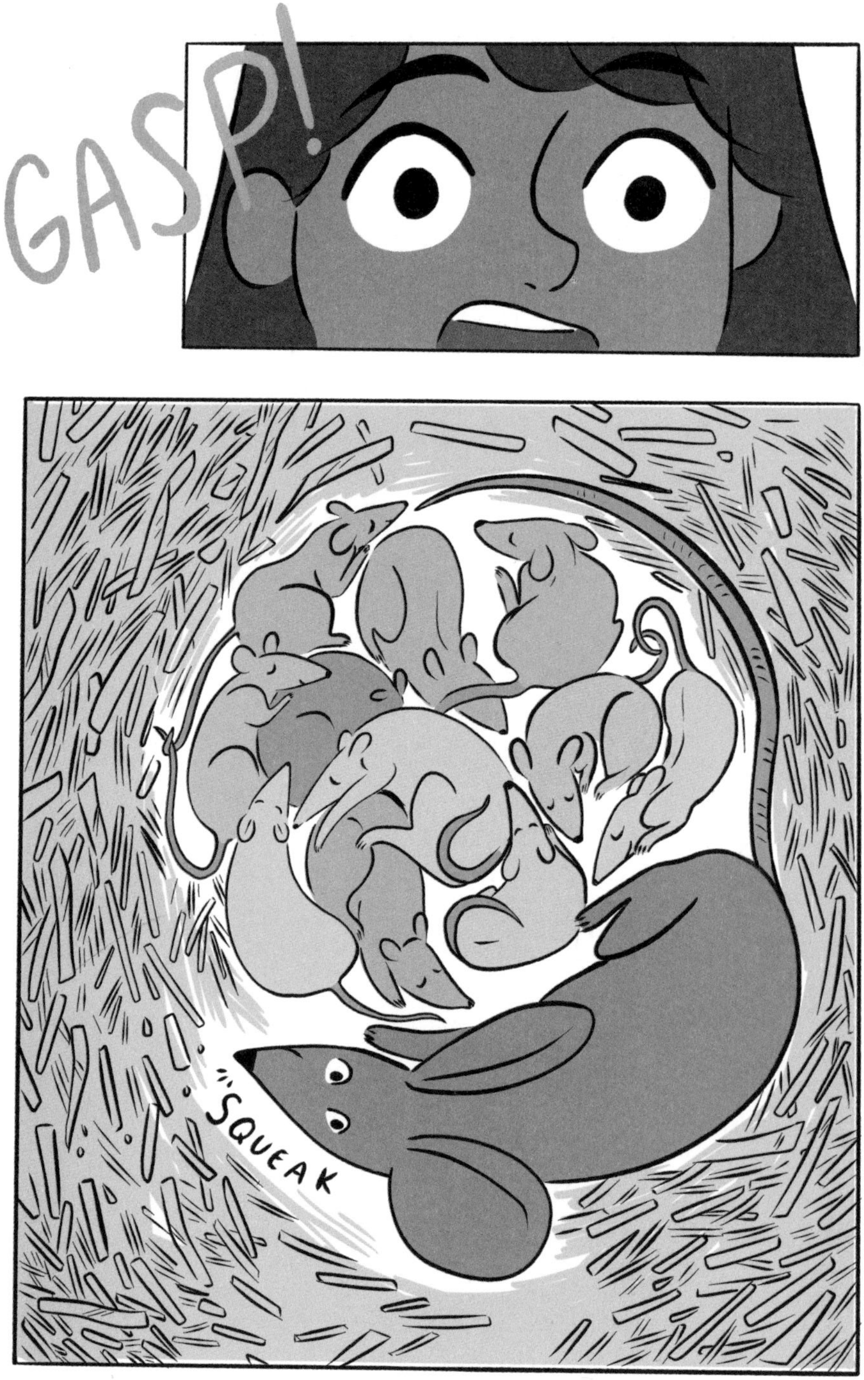
GASP!
SQUEAK

Chapter Nine

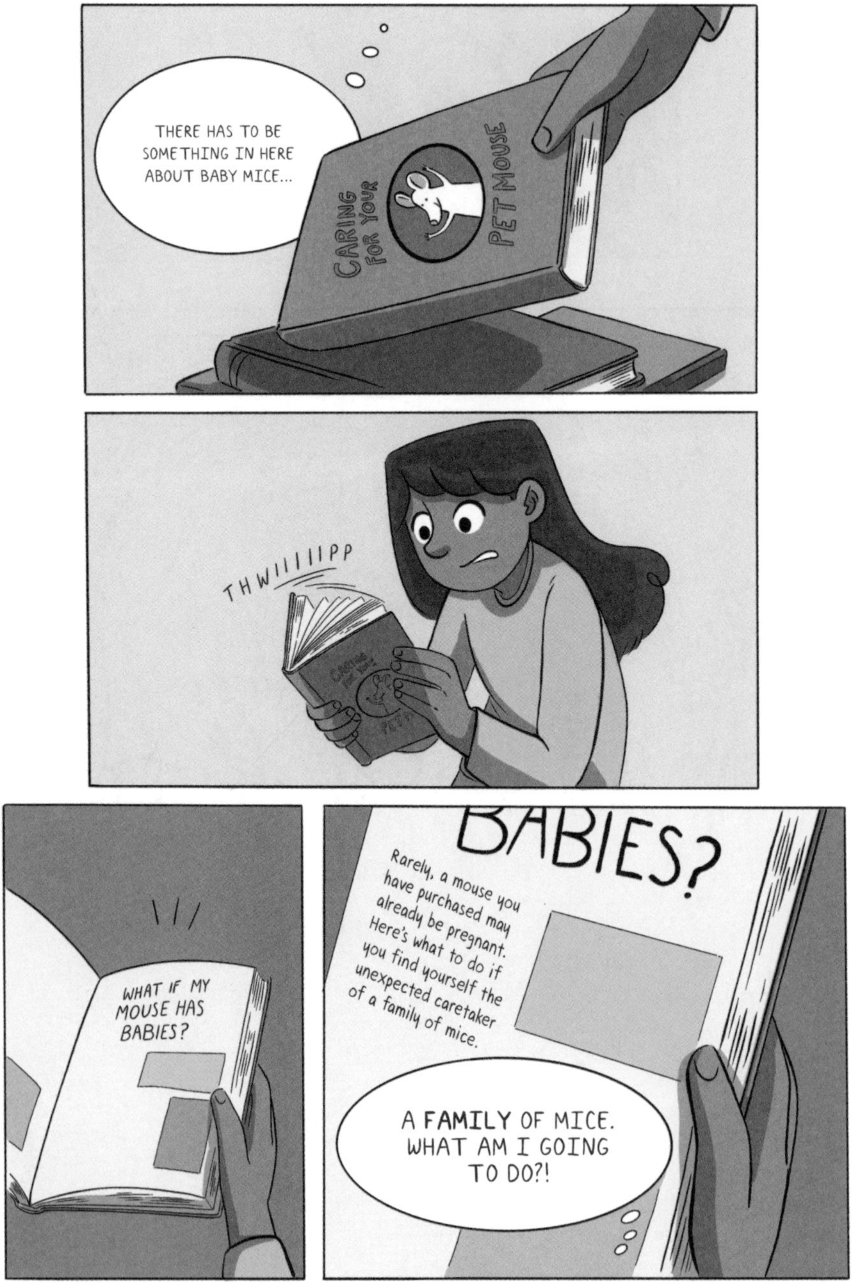
THERE HAS TO BE SOMETHING IN HERE ABOUT BABY MICE...
CARING FOR YOUR PET MOUSE
THWIIIIIPP
WHAT IF MY MOUSE HAS BABIES?
BABIES?
Rarely, a mouse you have purchased may already be pregnant. Here's what to do if you find yourself the unexpected caretaker of a family of mice.
A **FAMILY** OF MICE. WHAT AM I GOING TO DO?!

OCTOBER

SUNDAY	MONDAY	TUESDAY	WEDNESDAY	THURSDAY	FRIDAY	SATURDAY
	1	2	3	4	5	6
7	8	9	10	11	12	13
14	15	16	17	18	19	20
21	22	23	24	25	26	27
28	29	30 BABY DUE DATE	31			

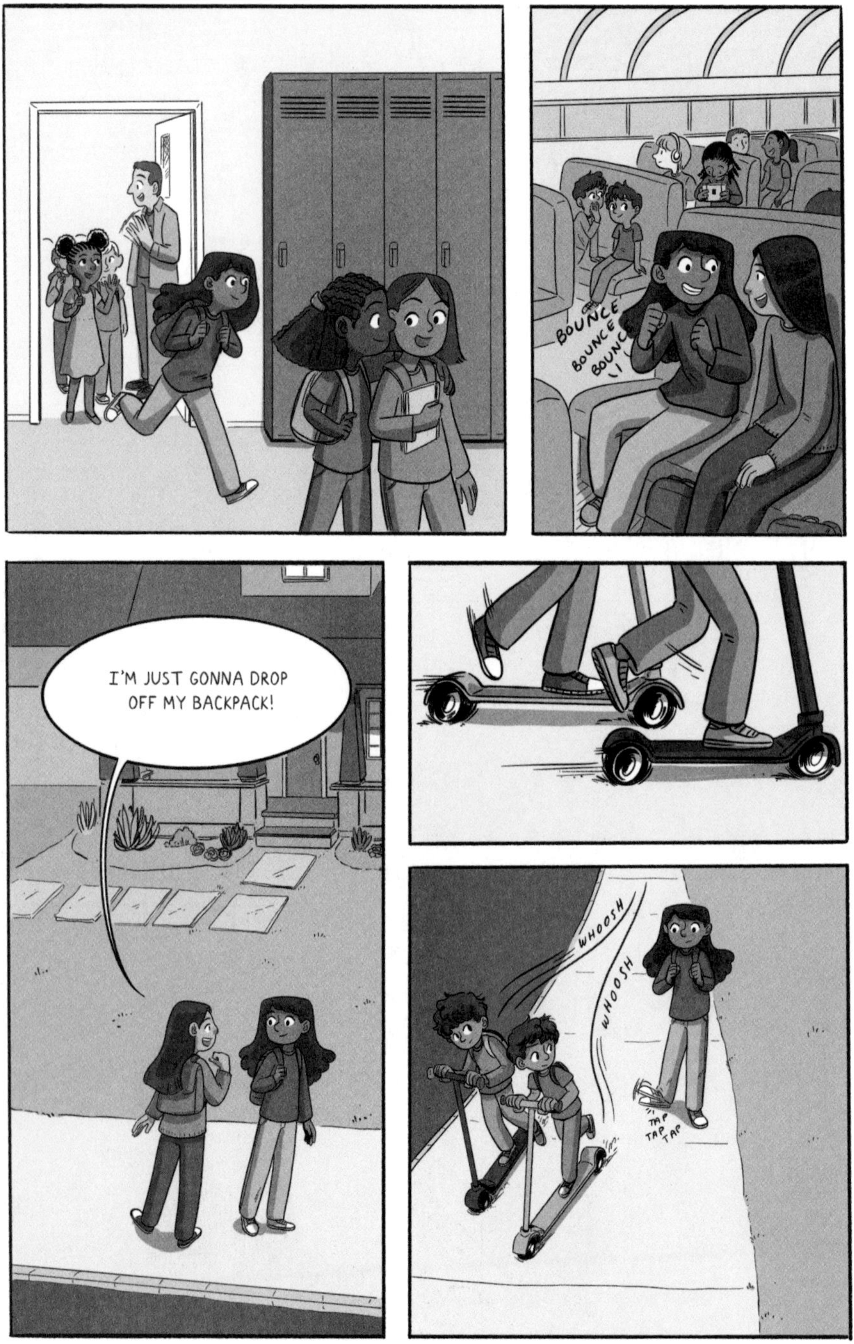
BOUNCE
BOUNCE
BOUNCE
I'M JUST GONNA DROP OFF MY BACKPACK!
WHOOSH
WHOOSH
TAP
TAP
TAP

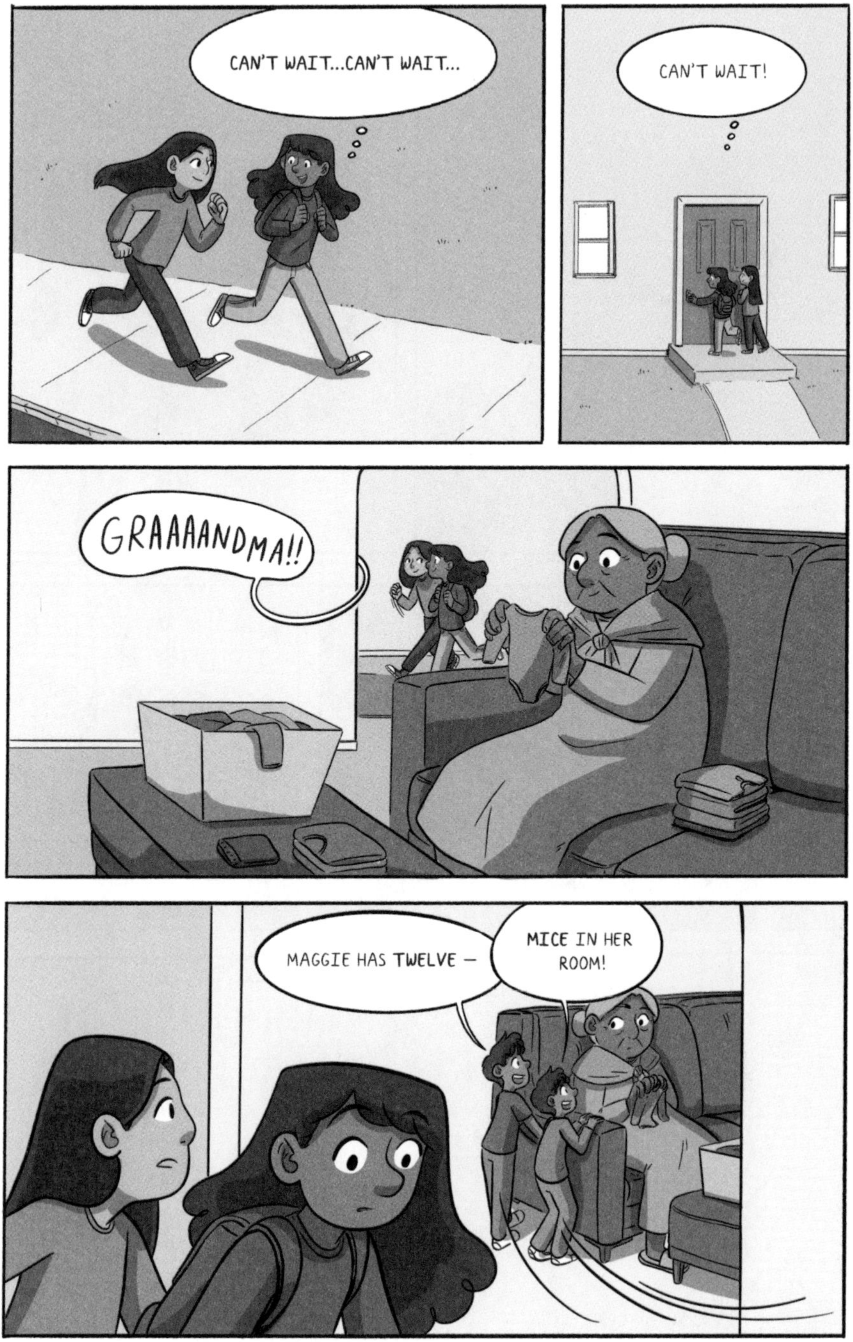

CAN'T WAIT...CAN'T WAIT...
CAN'T WAIT!
GRAAAANDMA!!
MAGGIE HAS TWELVE —
MICE IN HER ROOM!

Chapter Ten

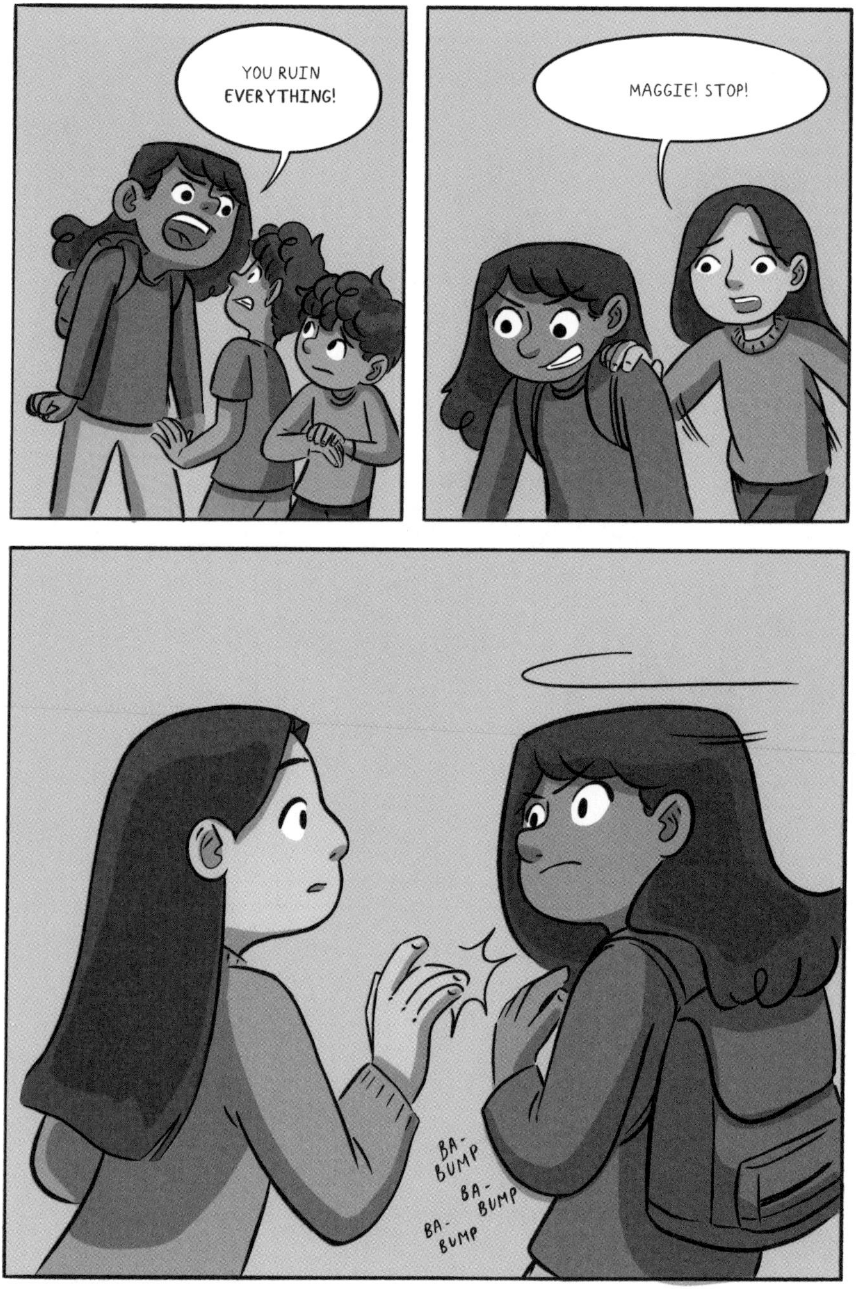
YOU RUIN EVERYTHING!
MAGGIE! STOP!
BA-BUMP
BA-BUMP
BA-BUMP

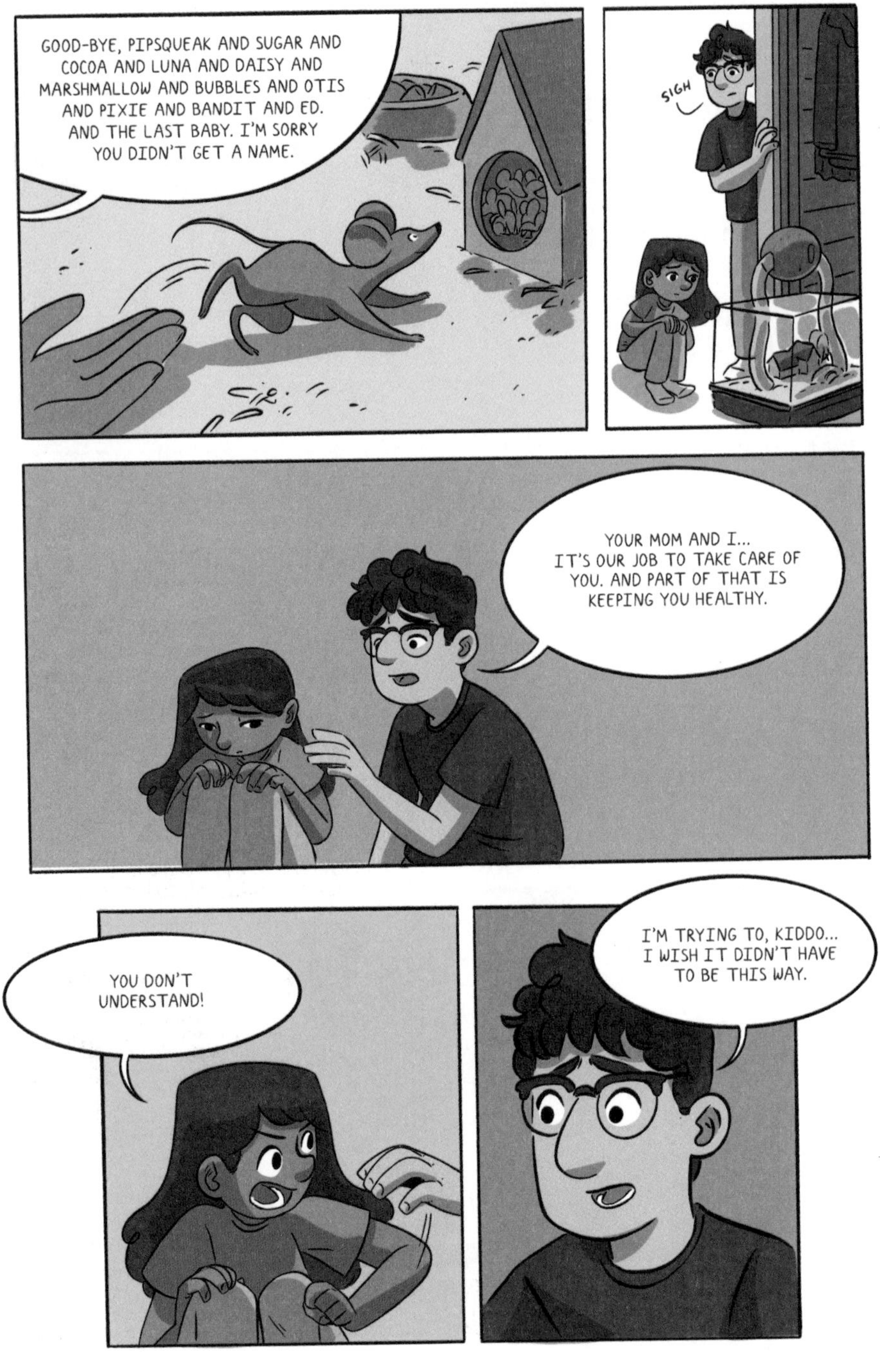
GOOD-BYE, PIPSQUEAK AND SUGAR AND COCOA AND LUNA AND DAISY AND MARSHMALLOW AND BUBBLES AND OTIS AND PIXIE AND BANDIT AND ED. AND THE LAST BABY. I'M SORRY YOU DIDN'T GET A NAME.
SIGH
YOUR MOM AND I... IT'S OUR JOB TO TAKE CARE OF YOU. AND PART OF THAT IS KEEPING YOU HEALTHY.
YOU DON'T UNDERSTAND!
I'M TRYING TO, KIDDO... I WISH IT DIDN'T HAVE TO BE THIS WAY.

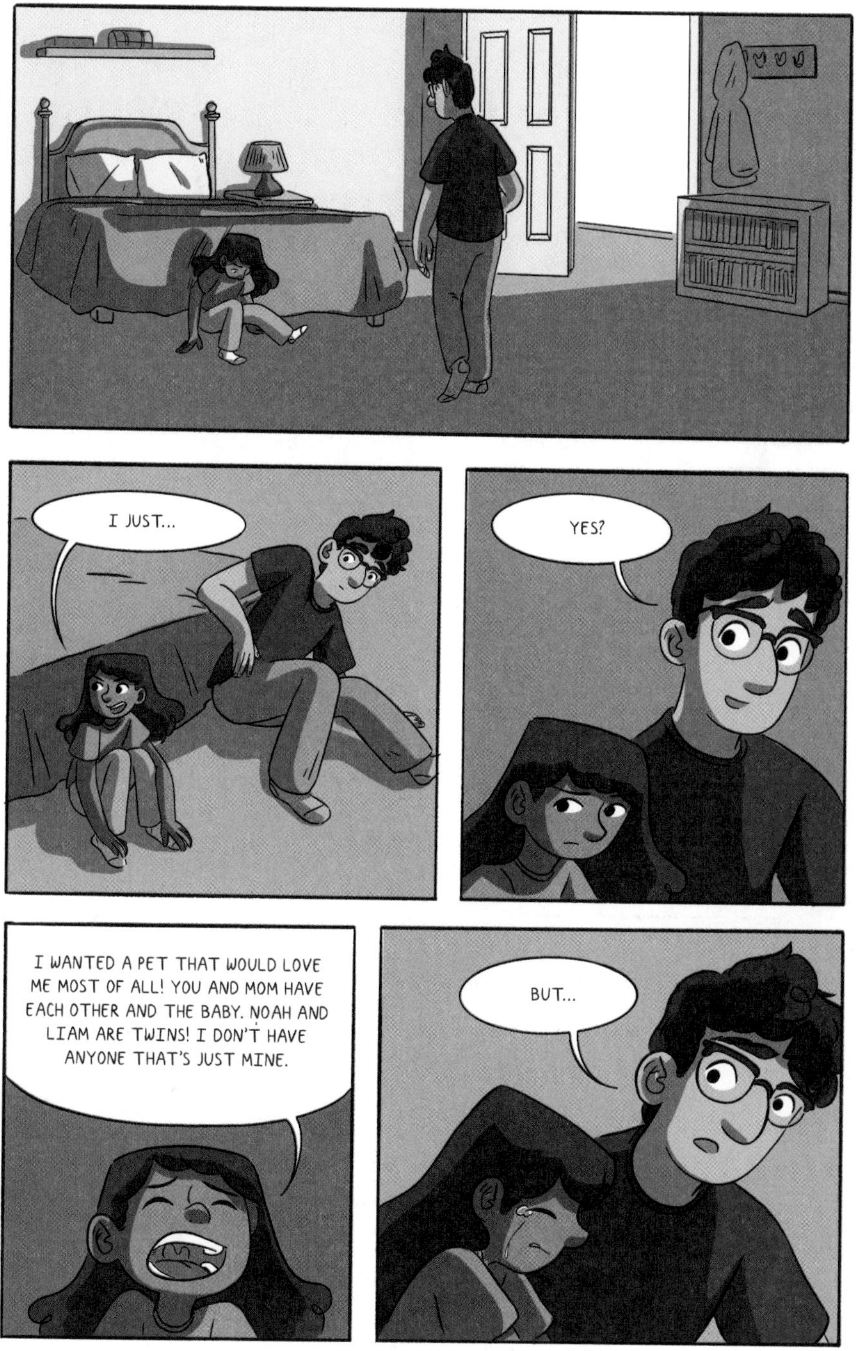
I JUST...
YES?
I WANTED A PET THAT WOULD LOVE ME MOST OF ALL! YOU AND MOM HAVE EACH OTHER AND THE BABY. NOAH AND LIAM ARE TWINS! I DON'T HAVE ANYONE THAT'S JUST MINE.
BUT...

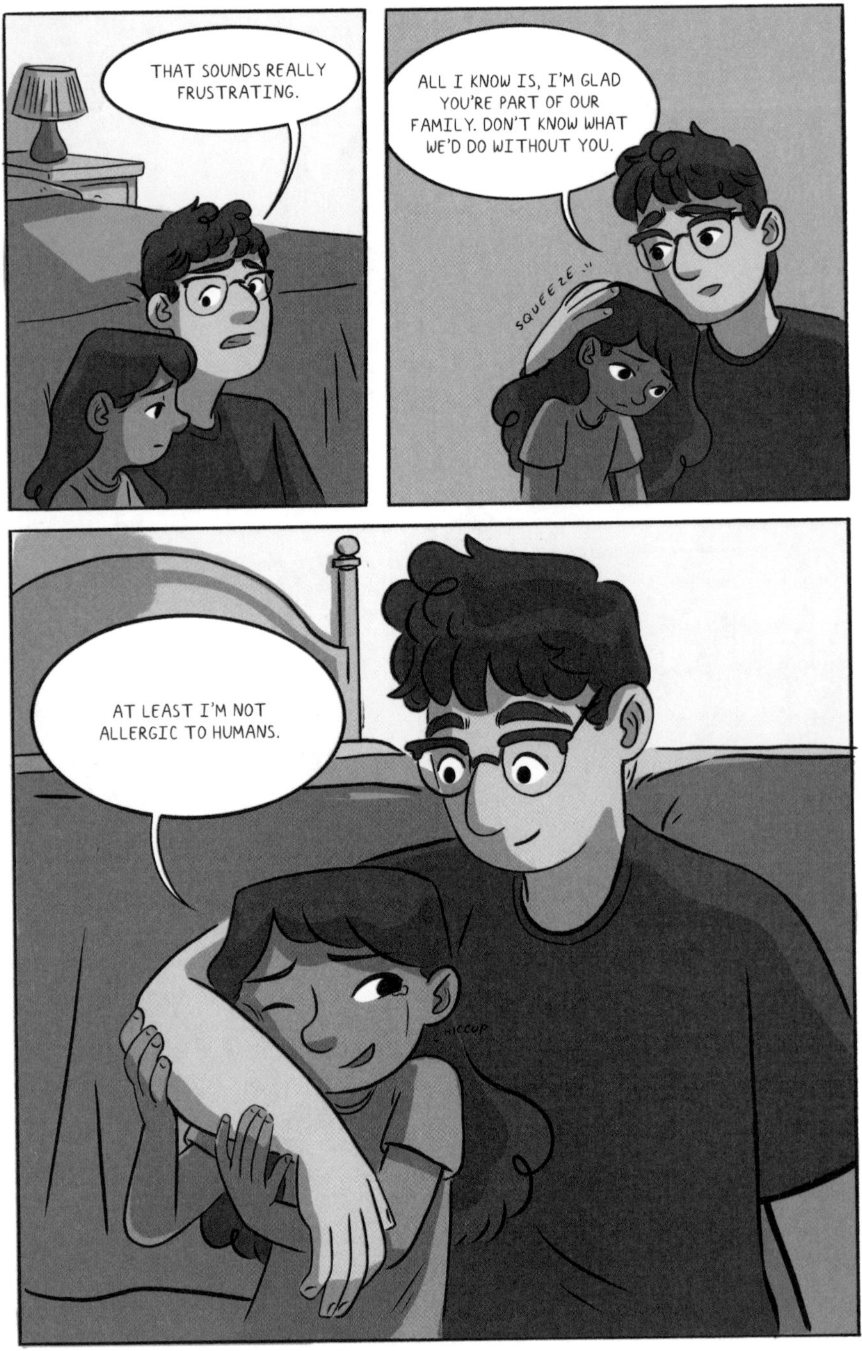
THAT SOUNDS REALLY FRUSTRATING.
ALL I KNOW IS, I'M GLAD YOU'RE PART OF OUR FAMILY. DON'T KNOW WHAT WE'D DO WITHOUT YOU.
SQUEEZE
AT LEAST I'M NOT ALLERGIC TO HUMANS.
HICCUP

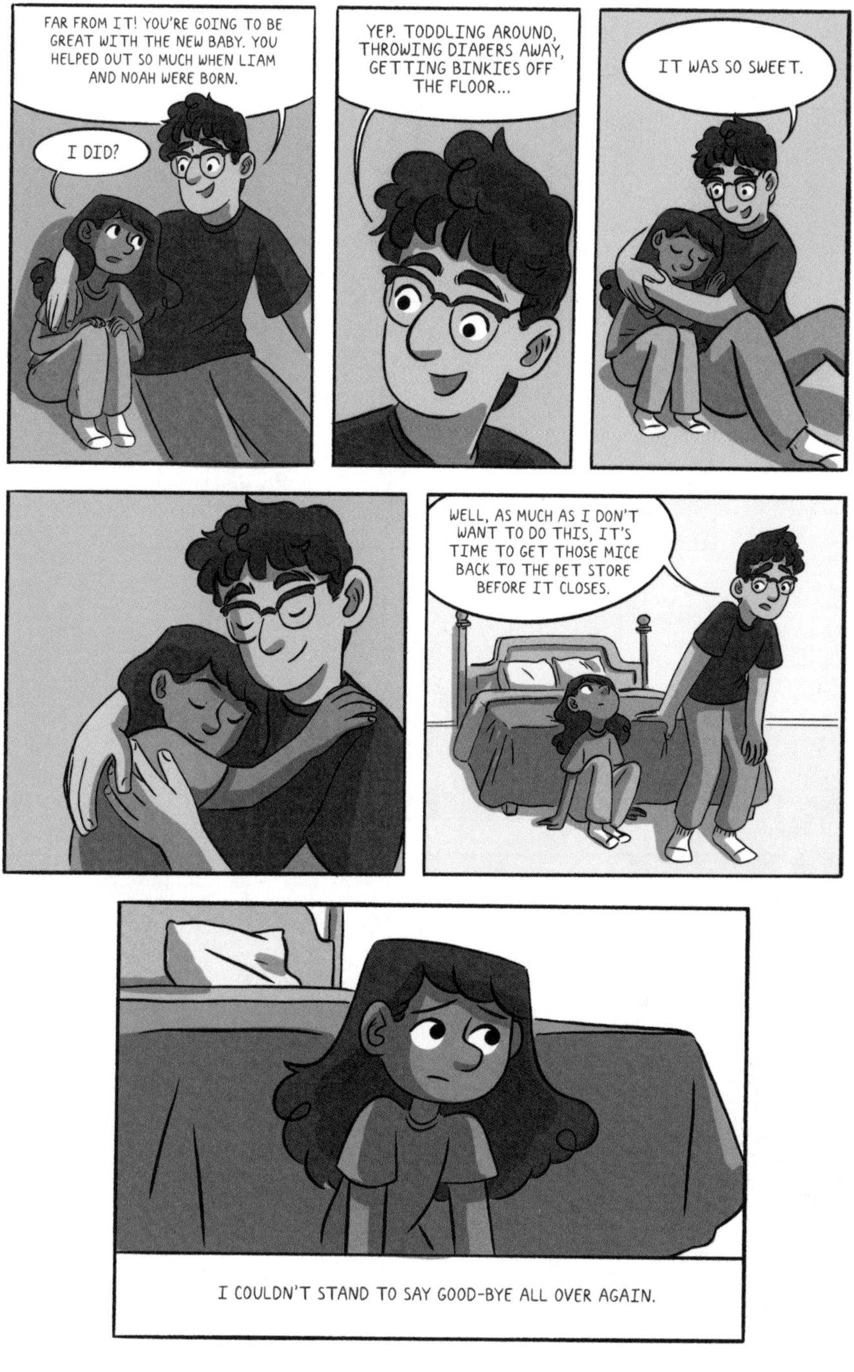
FAR FROM IT! YOU'RE GOING TO BE GREAT WITH THE NEW BABY. YOU HELPED OUT SO MUCH WHEN LIAM AND NOAH WERE BORN.
I DID?
YEP. TODDLING AROUND, THROWING DIAPERS AWAY, GETTING BINKIES OFF THE FLOOR...
IT WAS SO SWEET.
WELL, AS MUCH AS I DON'T WANT TO DO THIS, IT'S TIME TO GET THOSE MICE BACK TO THE PET STORE BEFORE IT CLOSES.
I COULDN'T STAND TO SAY GOOD-BYE ALL OVER AGAIN.

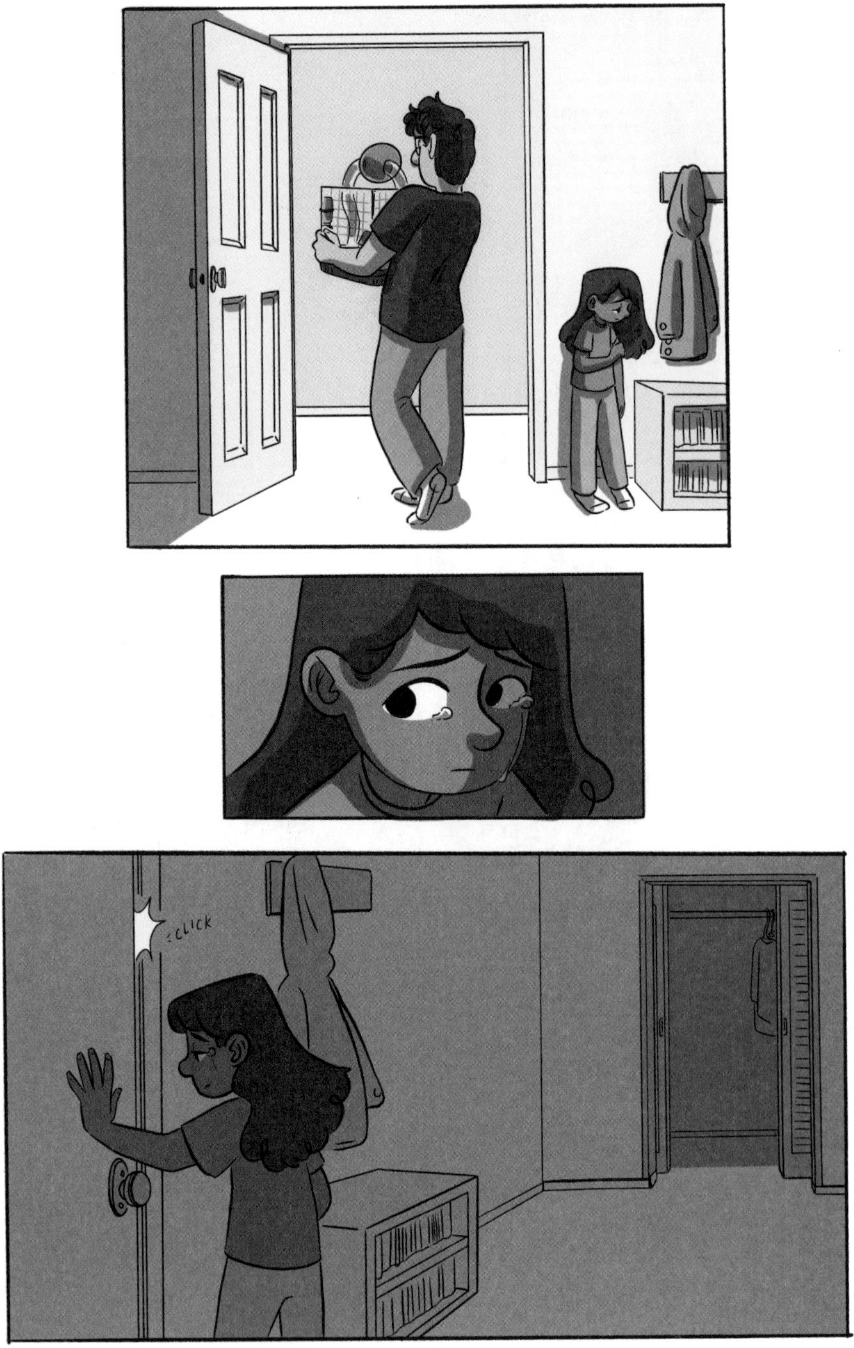
CLICK

HOW COULD SOMETHING THAT MADE
ME SO HAPPY MAKE ME SO SICK?
IT JUST WASN'T RIGHT.

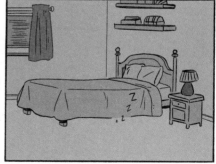

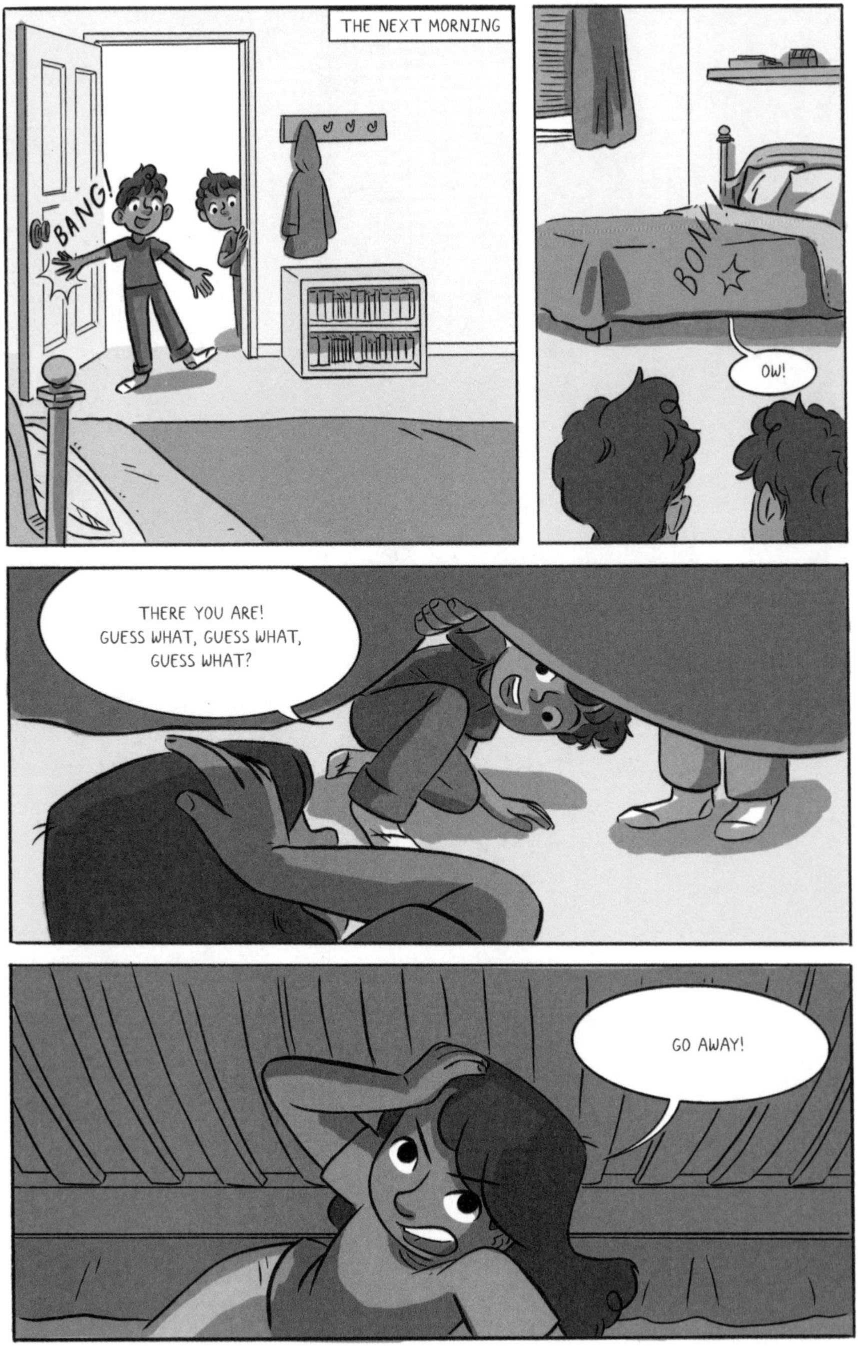
THE NEXT MORNING
BANG!
BONK!
OW!
THERE YOU ARE! GUESS WHAT, GUESS WHAT, GUESS WHAT?
GO AWAY!

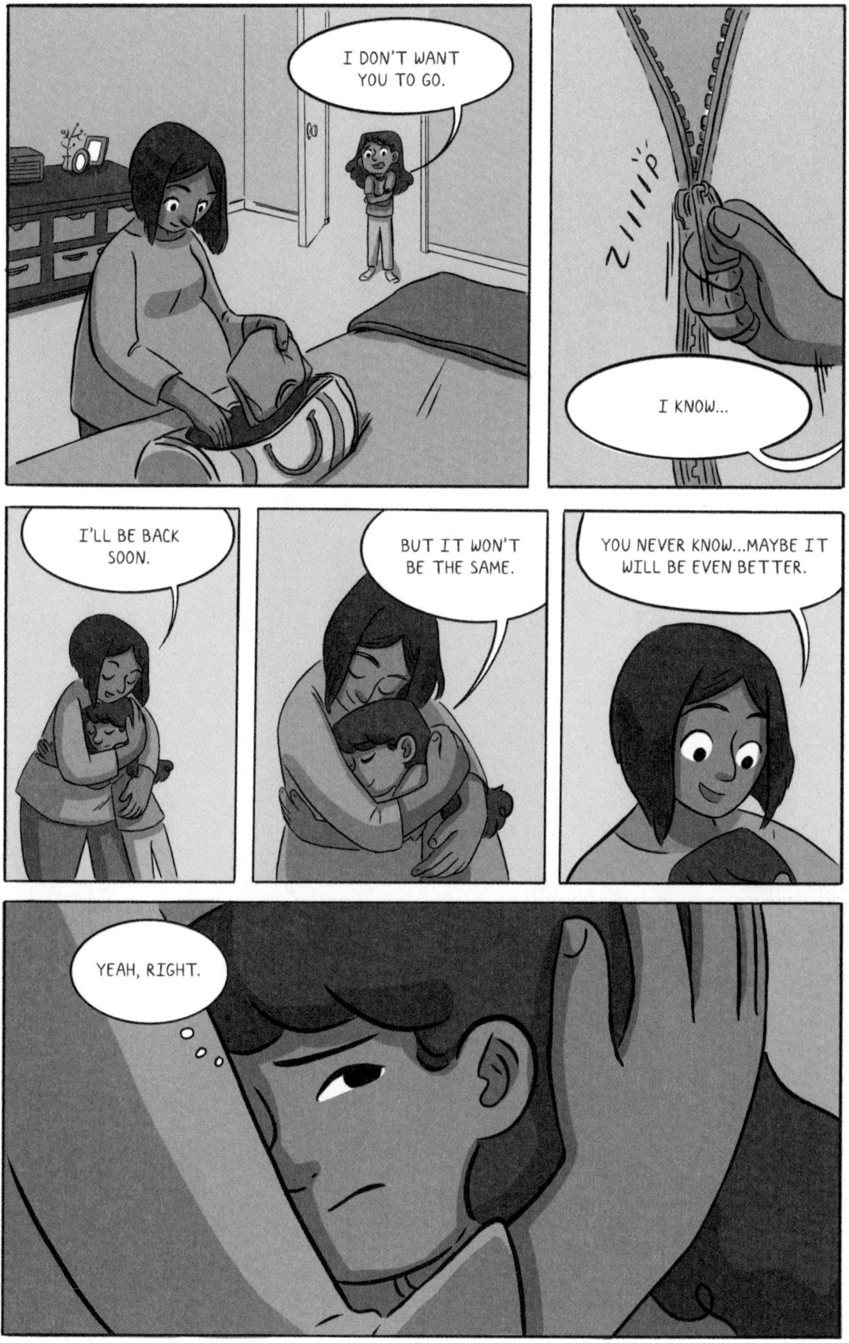
I DON'T WANT YOU TO GO.
ZIIIIP
I KNOW...
I'LL BE BACK SOON.
BUT IT WON'T BE THE SAME.
YOU NEVER KNOW...MAYBE IT WILL BE EVEN BETTER.
YEAH, RIGHT.

Chapter Eleven

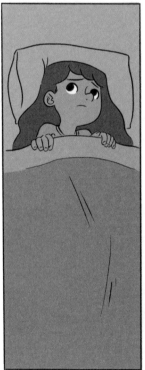

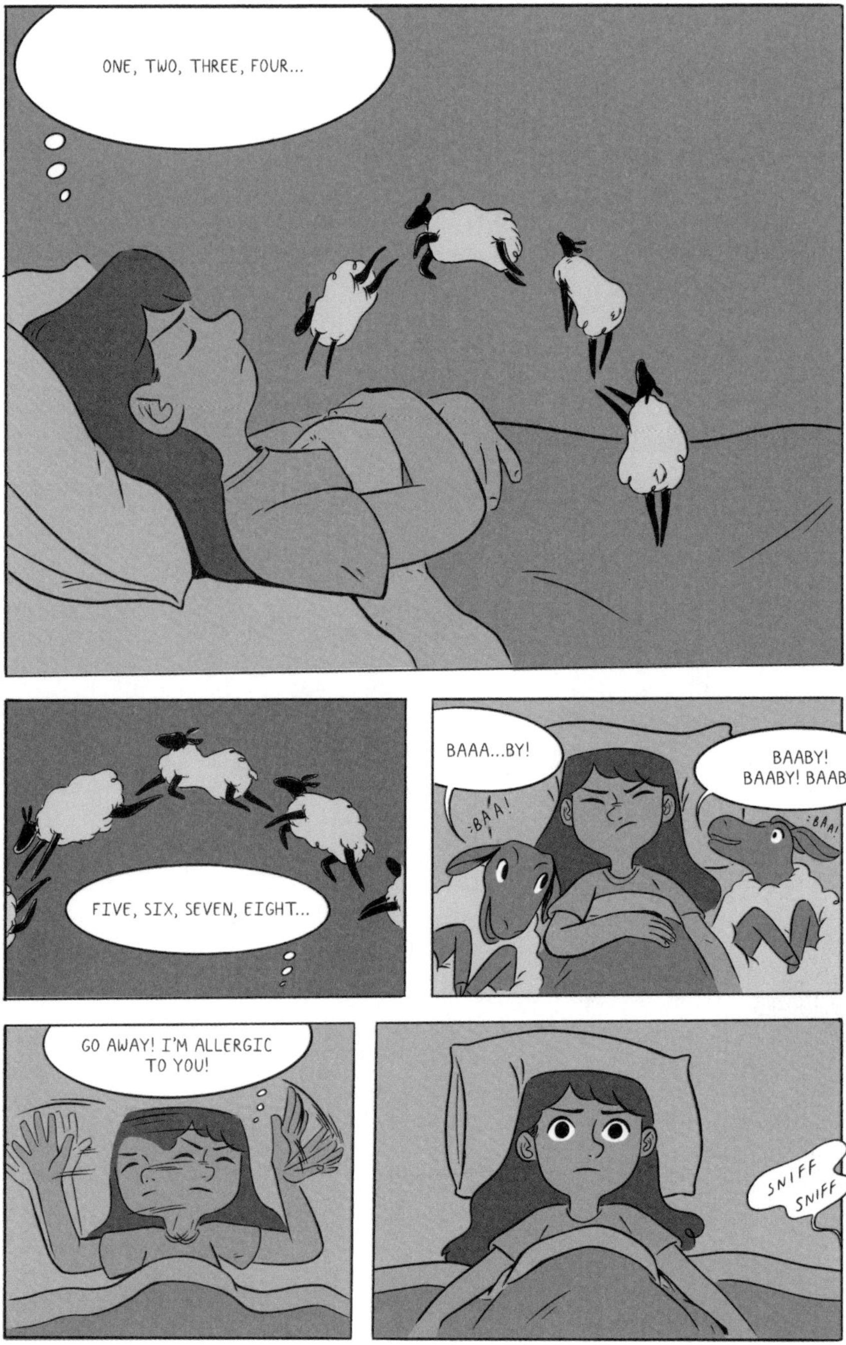
ONE, TWO, THREE, FOUR...
FIVE, SIX, SEVEN, EIGHT...
BAAA...BY!
BAA!
BAABY! BAABY! BAABY
BAA!
GO AWAY! I'M ALLERGIC TO YOU!
SNIFF SNIFF

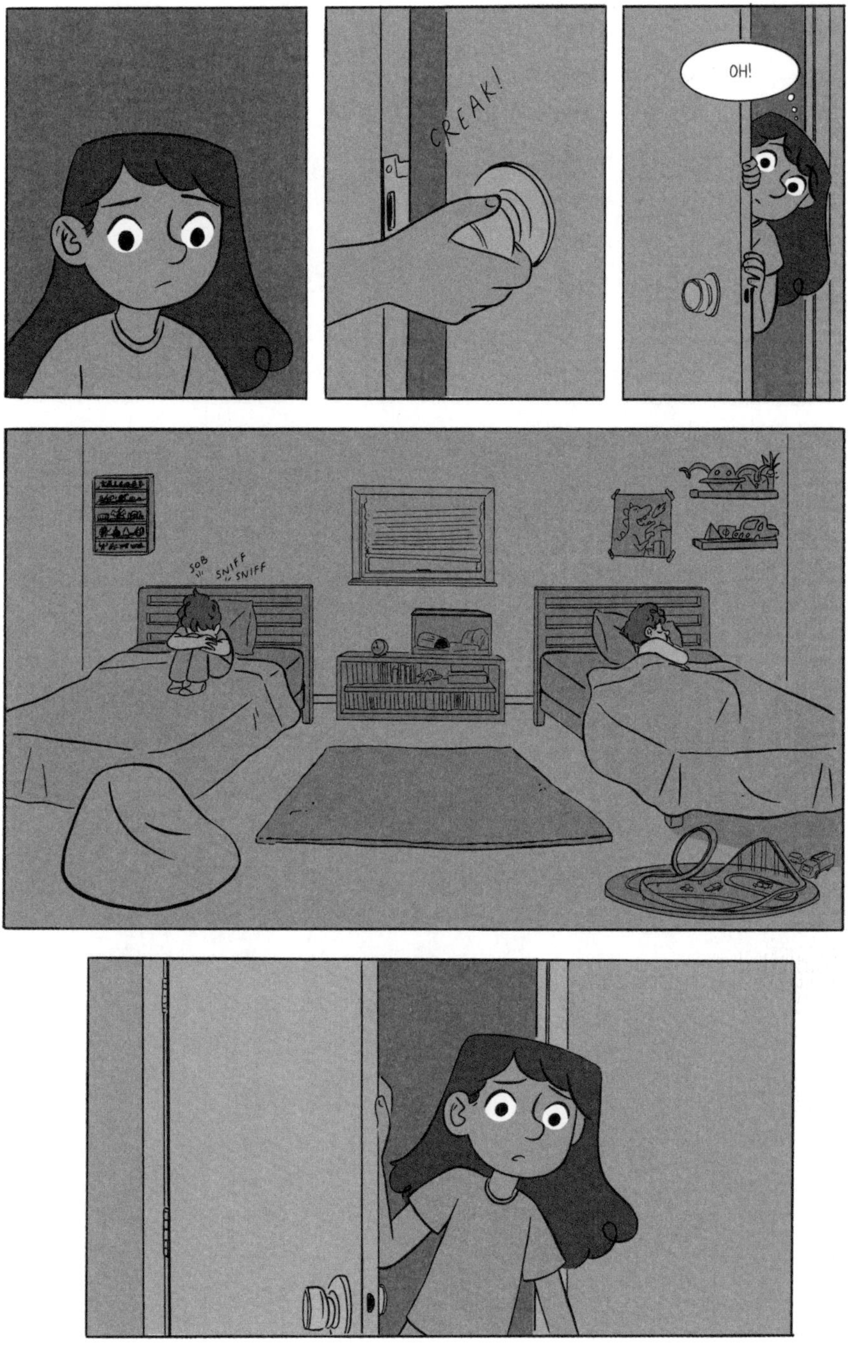
CREAK!
OH!
SOB
SNIFF
SNIFF

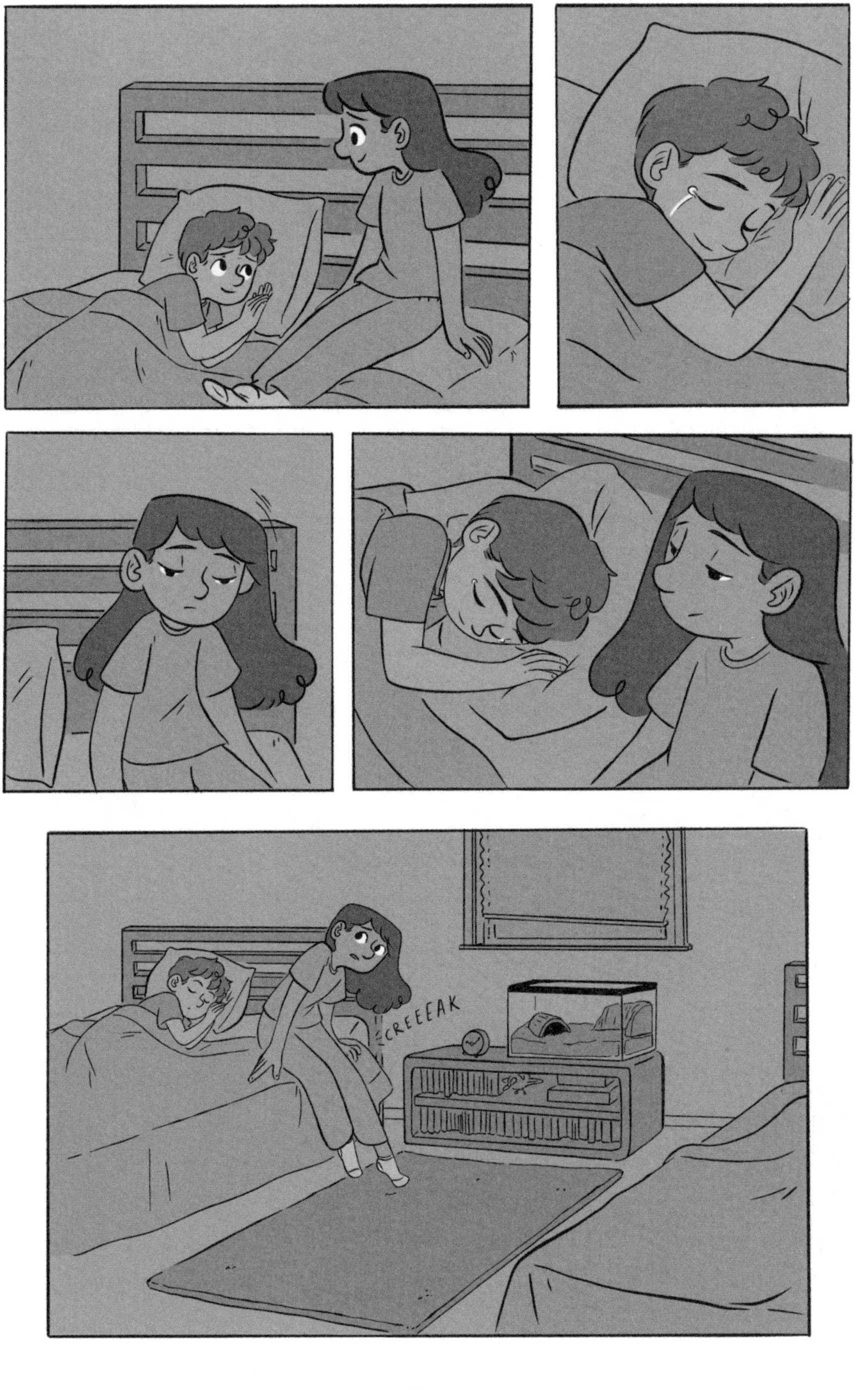
CREEEAK

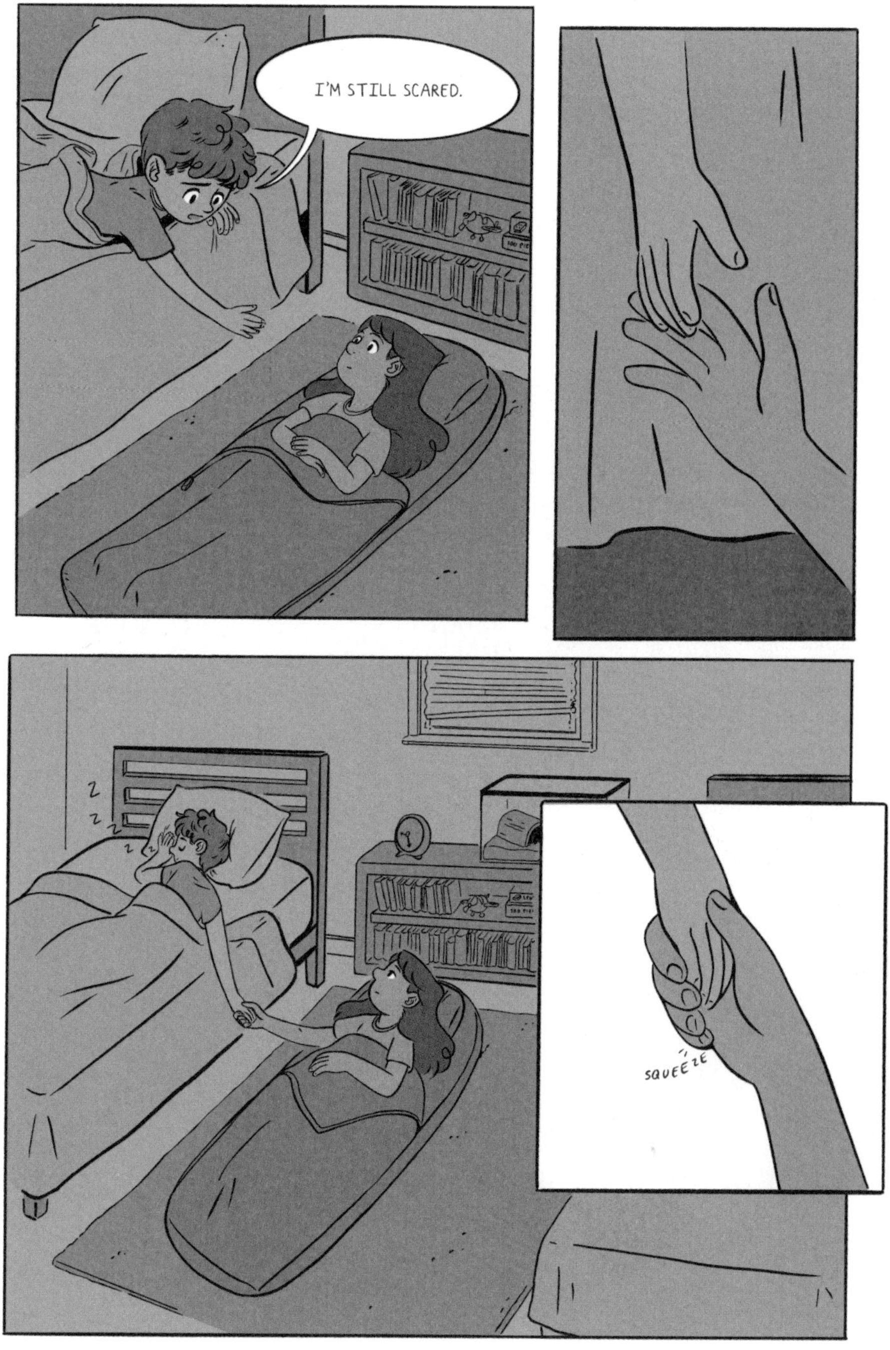
I'M STILL SCARED.
SQUEEZE

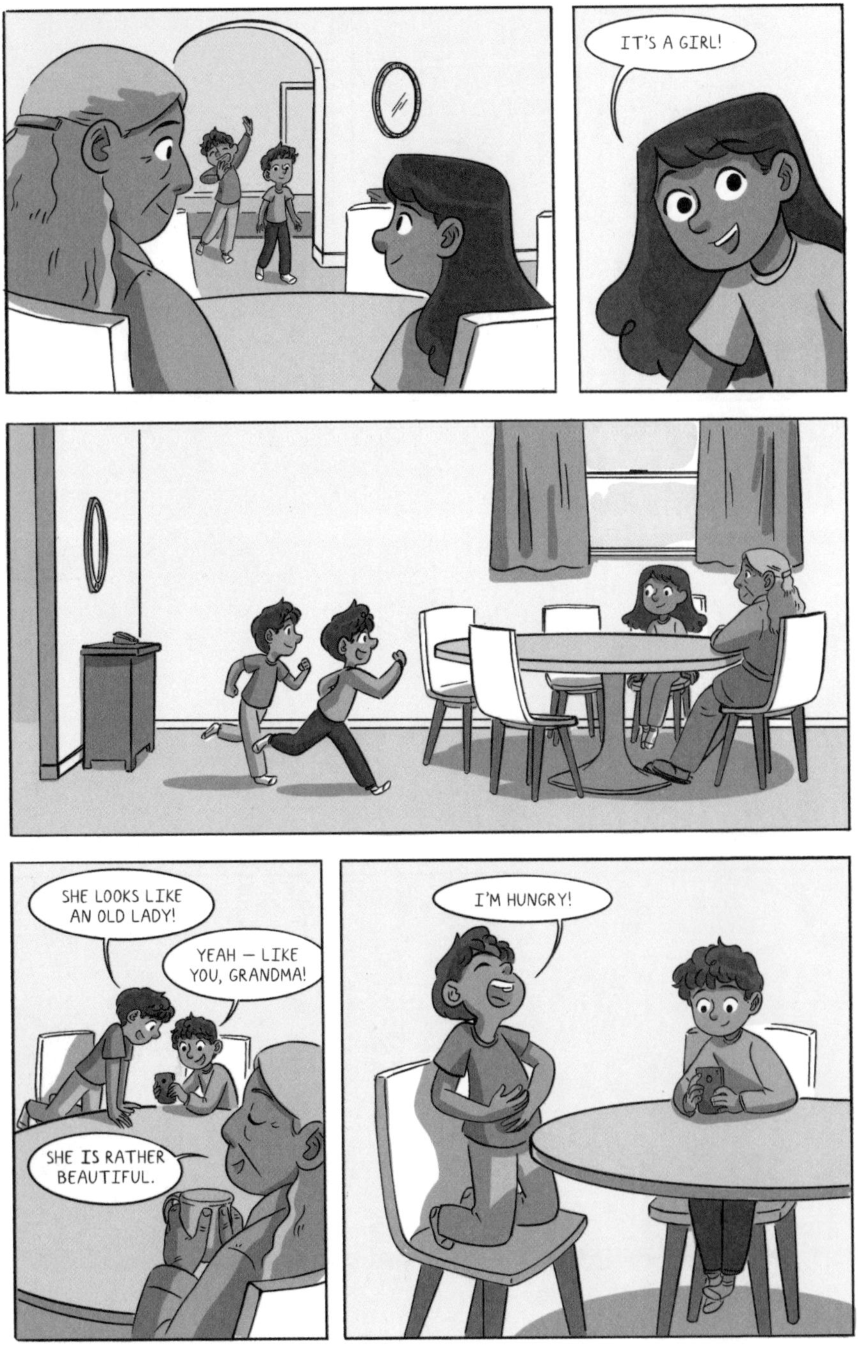
IT'S A GIRL!
SHE LOOKS LIKE AN OLD LADY!
YEAH — LIKE YOU, GRANDMA!
SHE IS RATHER BEAUTIFUL.
I'M HUNGRY!

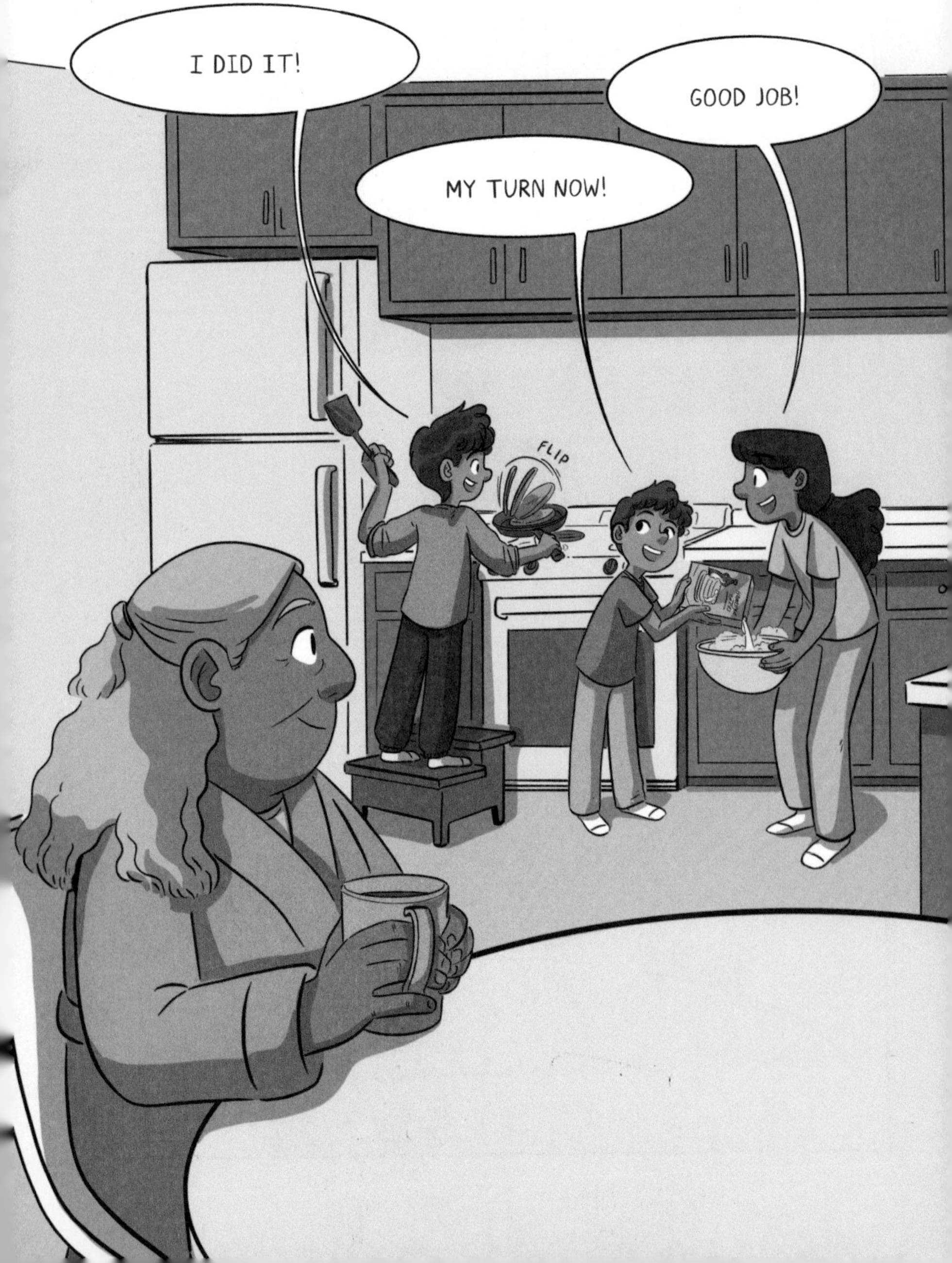
I DID IT!
MY TURN NOW!
GOOD JOB!
FLIP

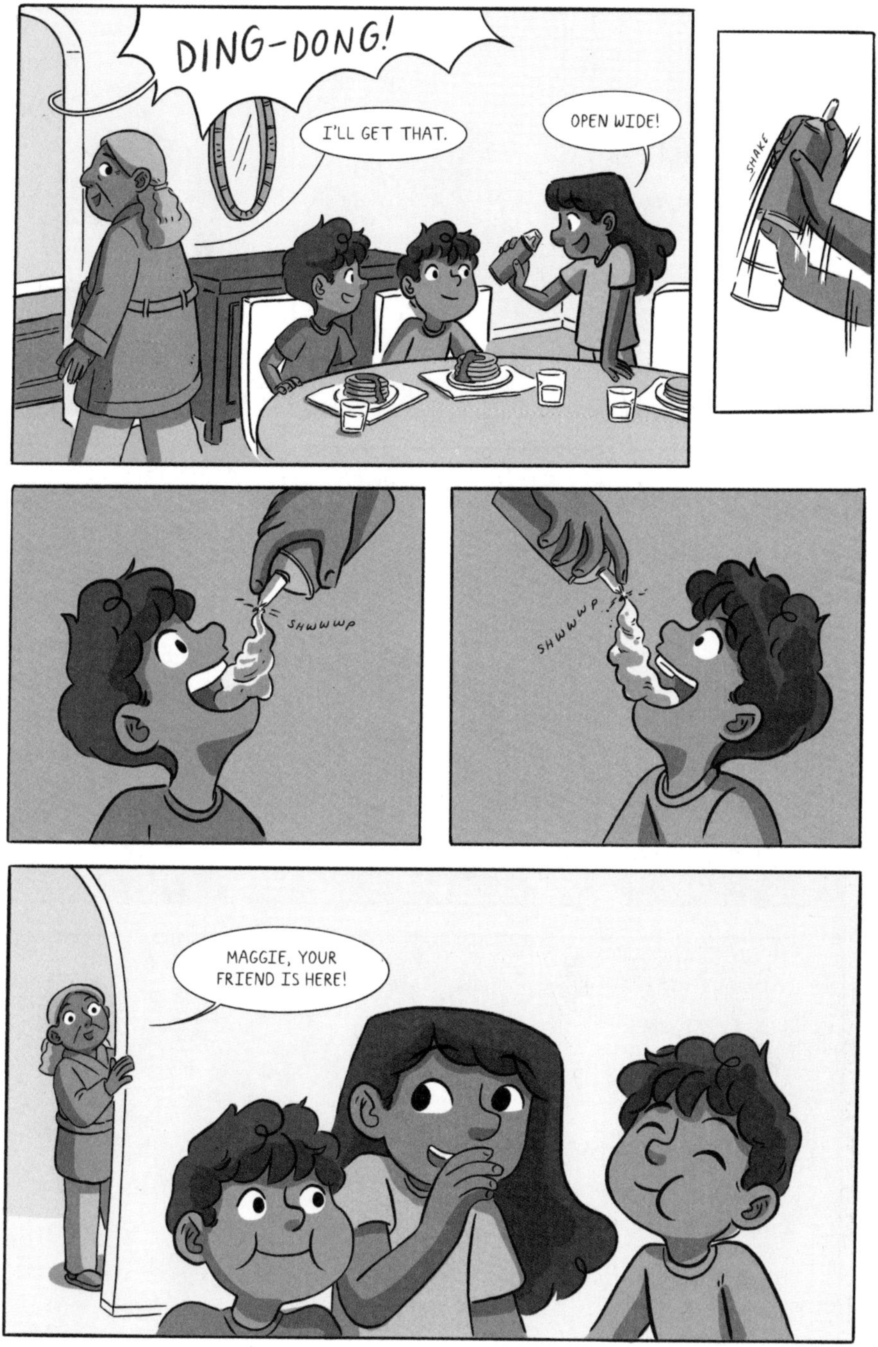
DING-DONG!
I'LL GET THAT.
OPEN WIDE!
SHAKE
SHWWWP
SHWWWP
MAGGIE, YOUR FRIEND IS HERE!

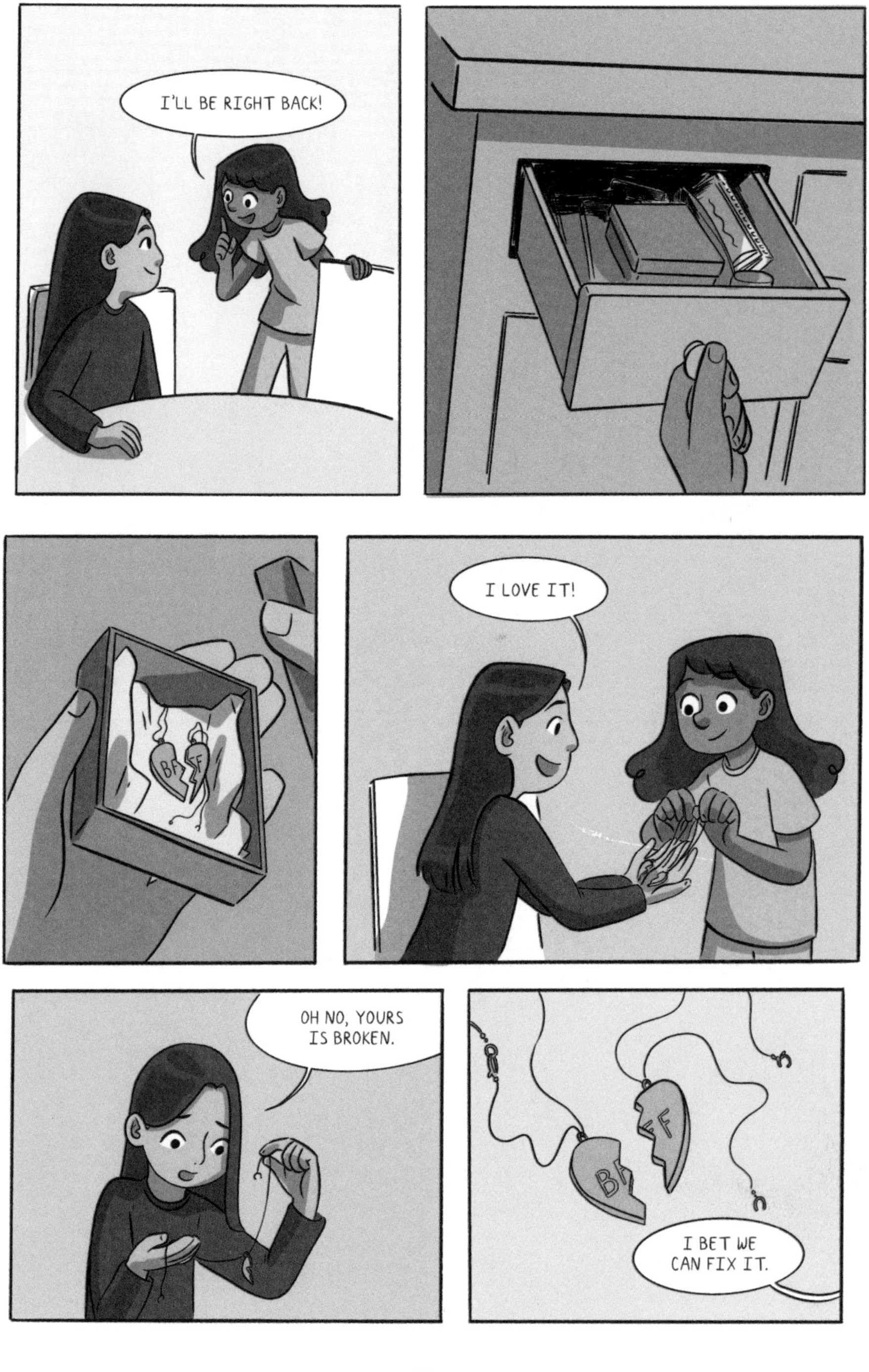
I'LL BE RIGHT BACK!
I LOVE IT!
OH NO, YOURS IS BROKEN.
I BET WE CAN FIX IT.

Chapter Twelve

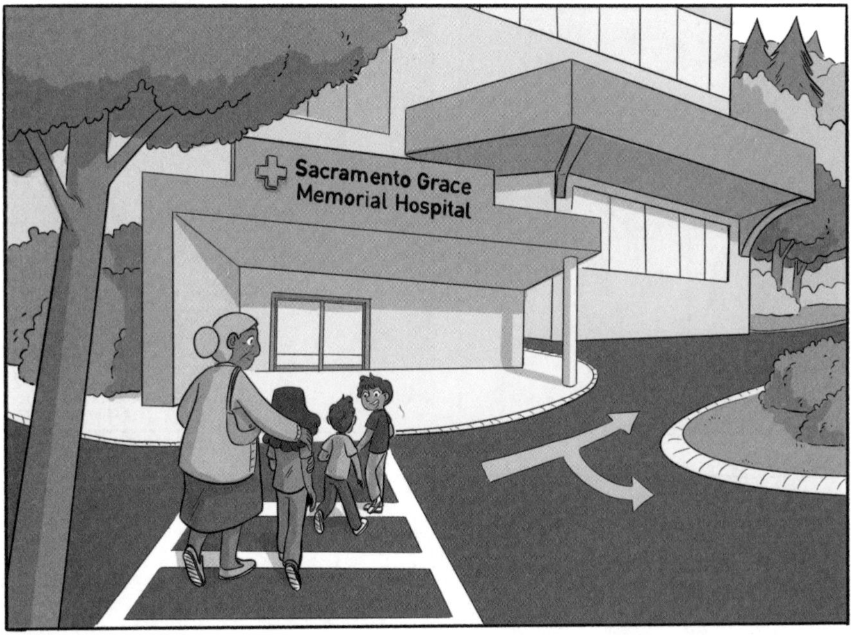
Sacramento Grace
Memorial Hospital

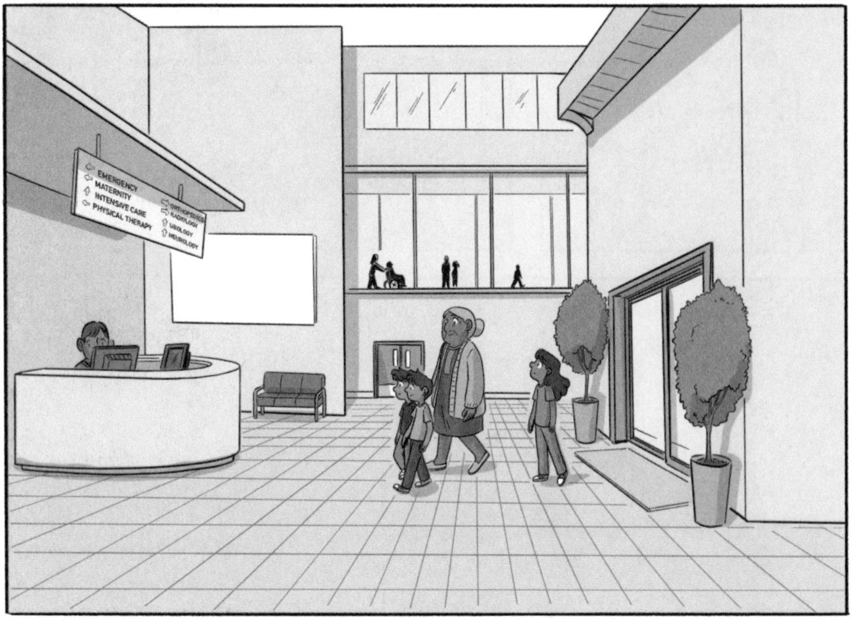
EMERGENCY
MATERNITY
INTENSIVE CARE
PHYSICAL THERAPY
ORTHOPEDICS
RADIOLOGY
UROLOGY
NEUROLOGY

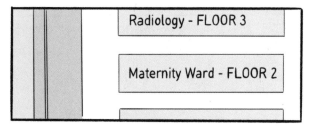

Radiology - FLOOR 3

Maternity Ward - FLOOR 2

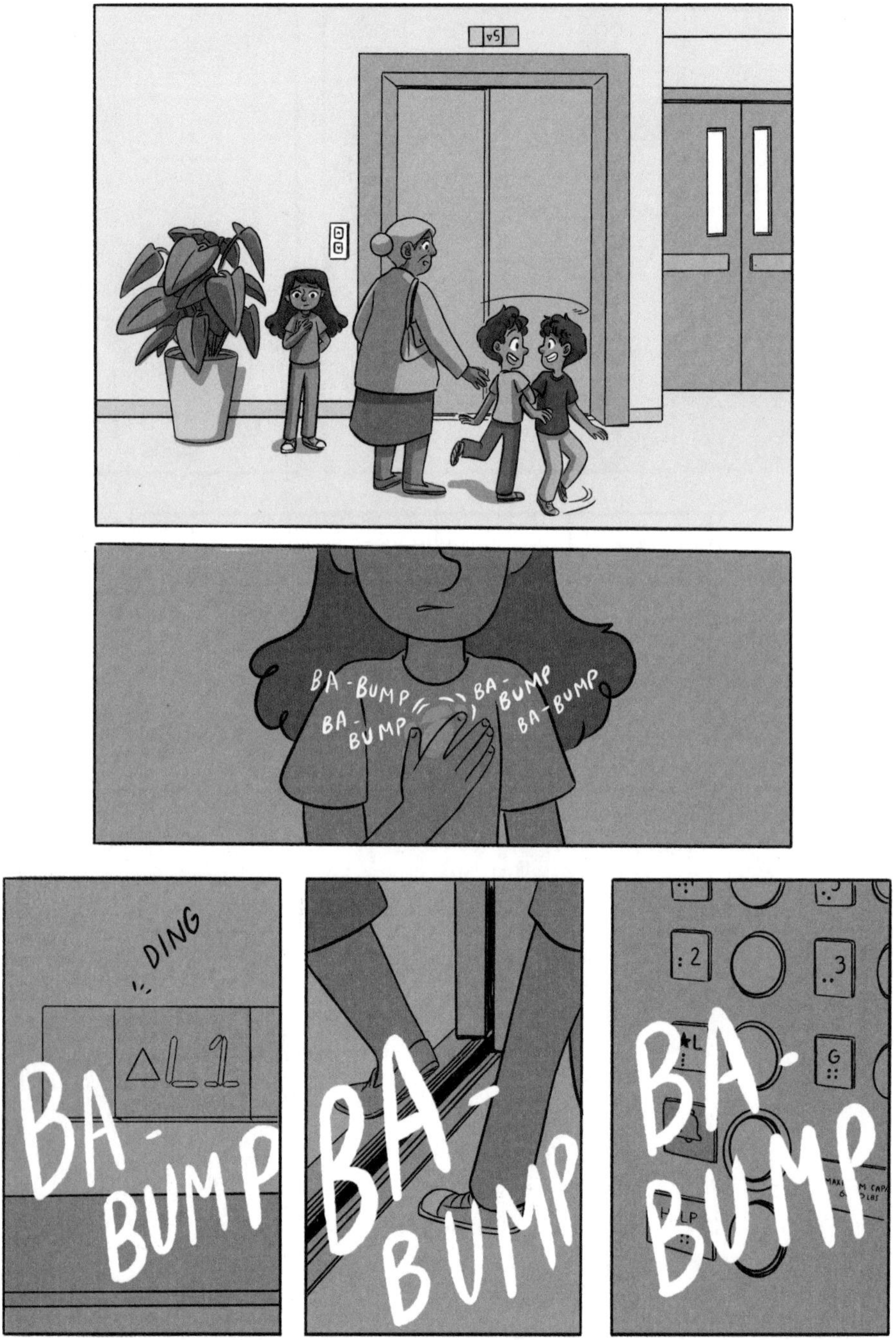
BA-BUMP
BA-BUMP
BA-BUMP
BA-BUMP
DING
L1
BA-BUMP
BA-BUMP
2
3
G
BA-BUMP

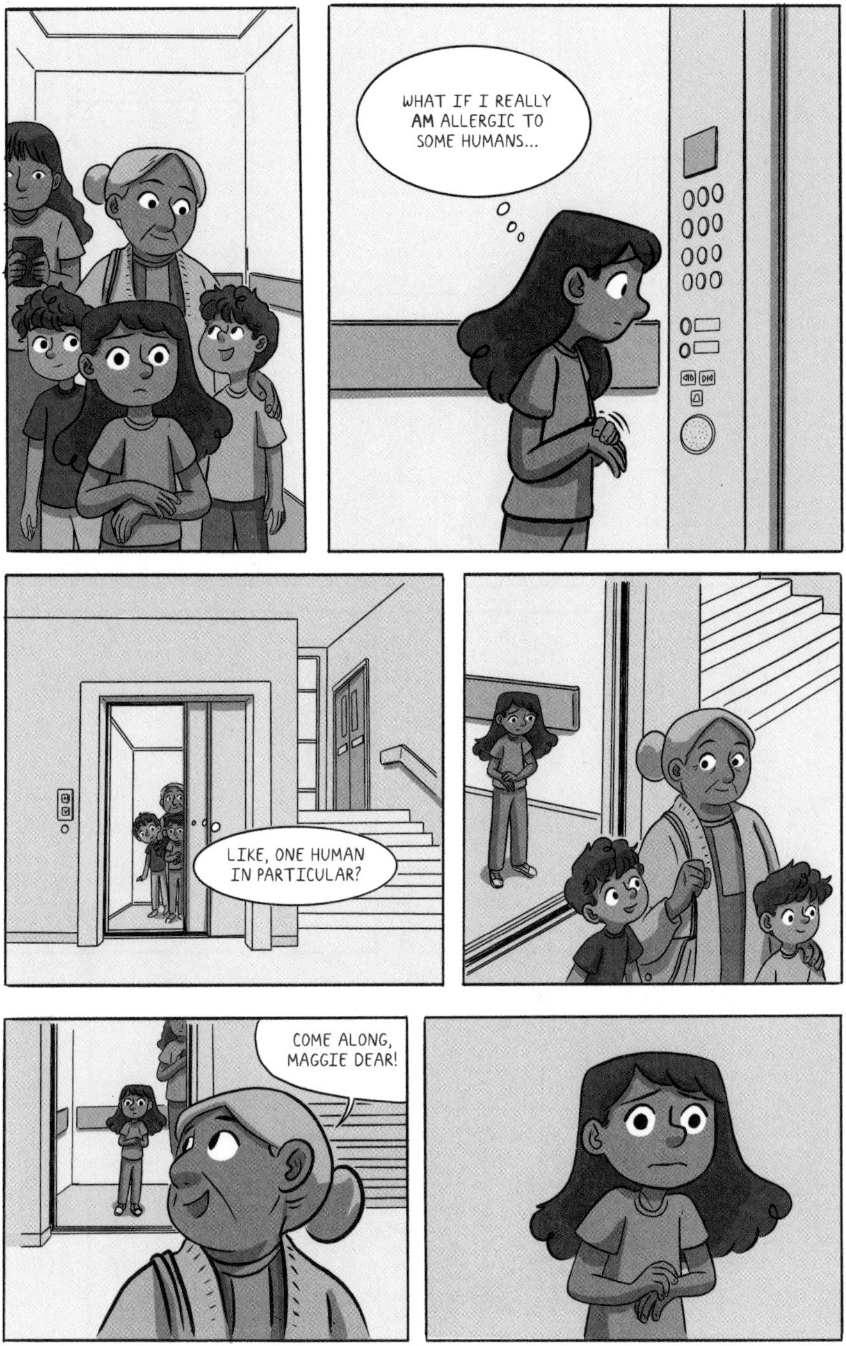
WHAT IF I REALLY AM ALLERGIC TO SOME HUMANS...
LIKE, ONE HUMAN IN PARTICULAR?
COME ALONG, MAGGIE DEAR!

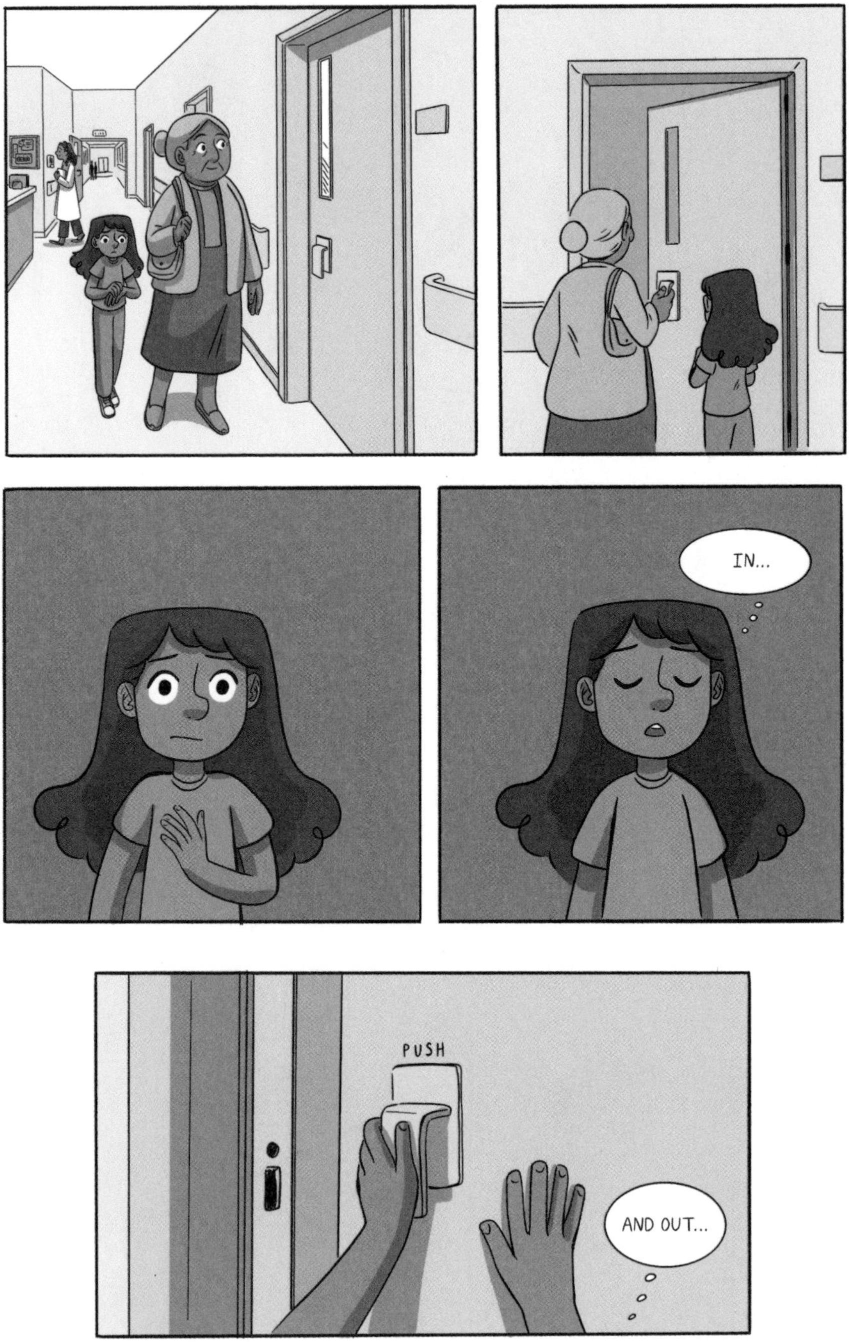
IN...
PUSH
AND OUT...

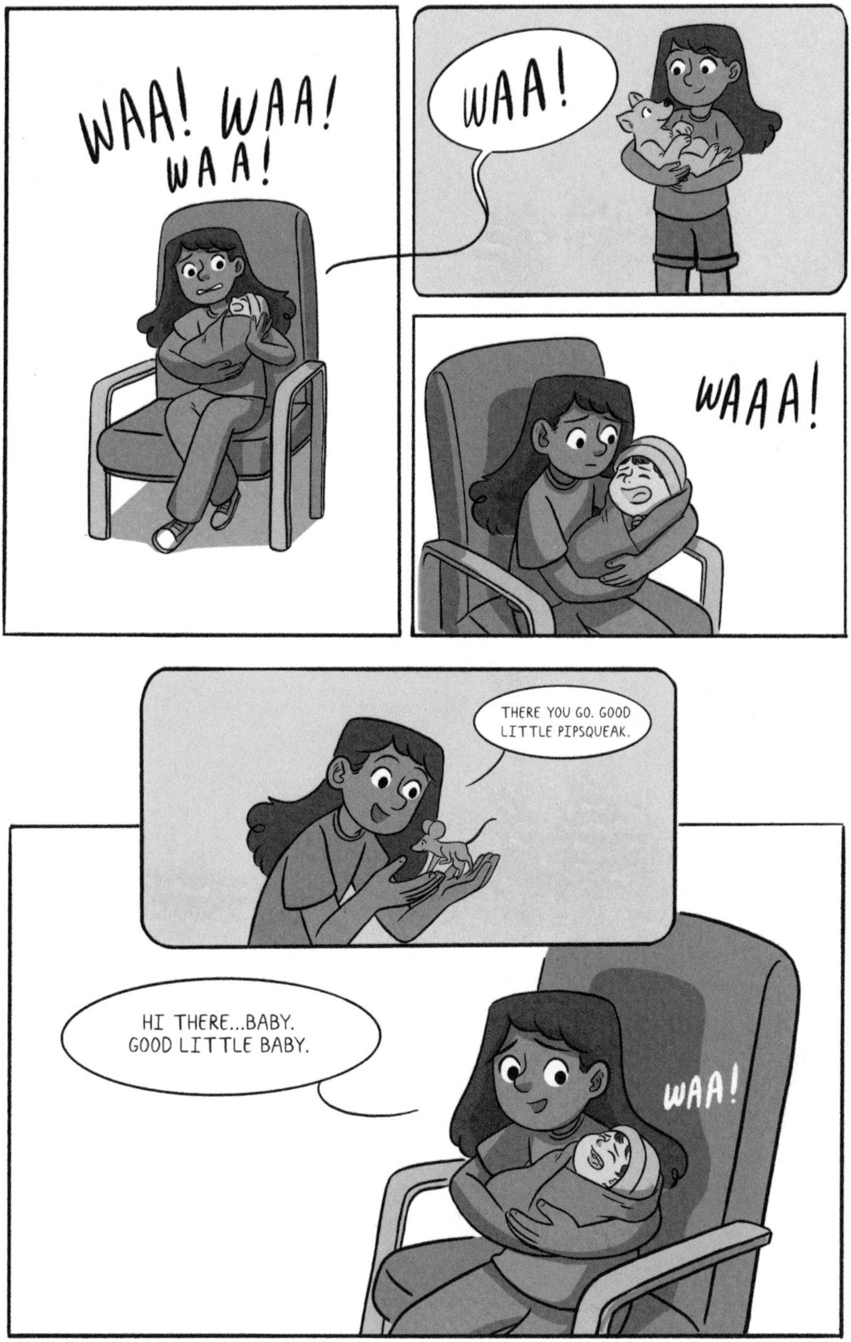
WAA! WAA! WAA!
WAA!
WAAA!
THERE YOU GO. GOOD LITTLE PIPSQUEAK.
HI THERE...BABY. GOOD LITTLE BABY.
WAA!

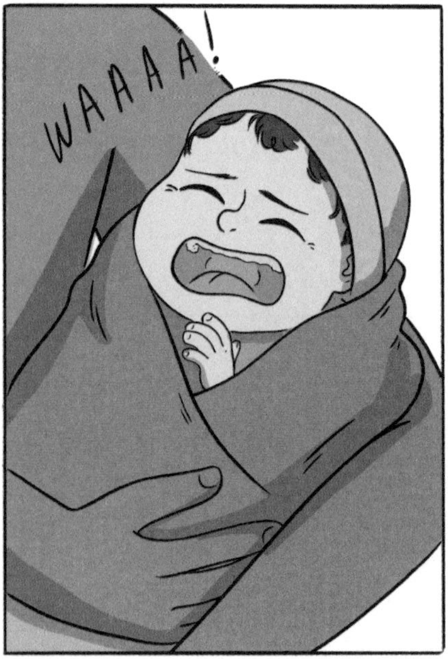
WAAAAA!

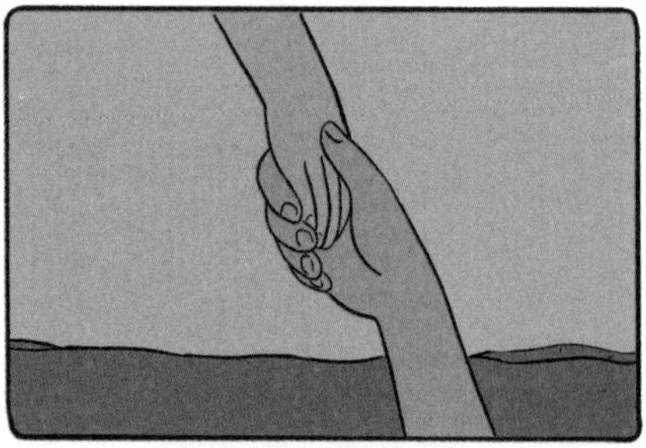

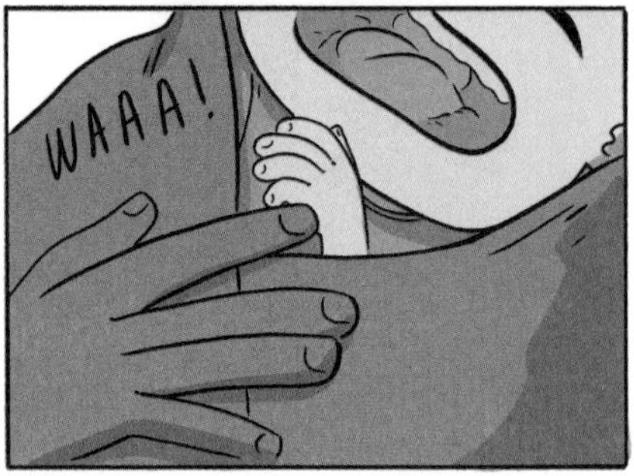
WAAA!

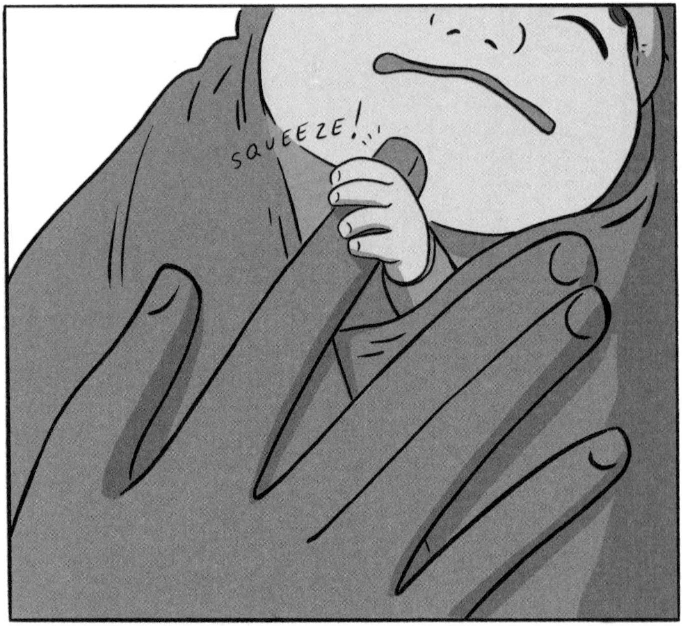
SQUEEZE!

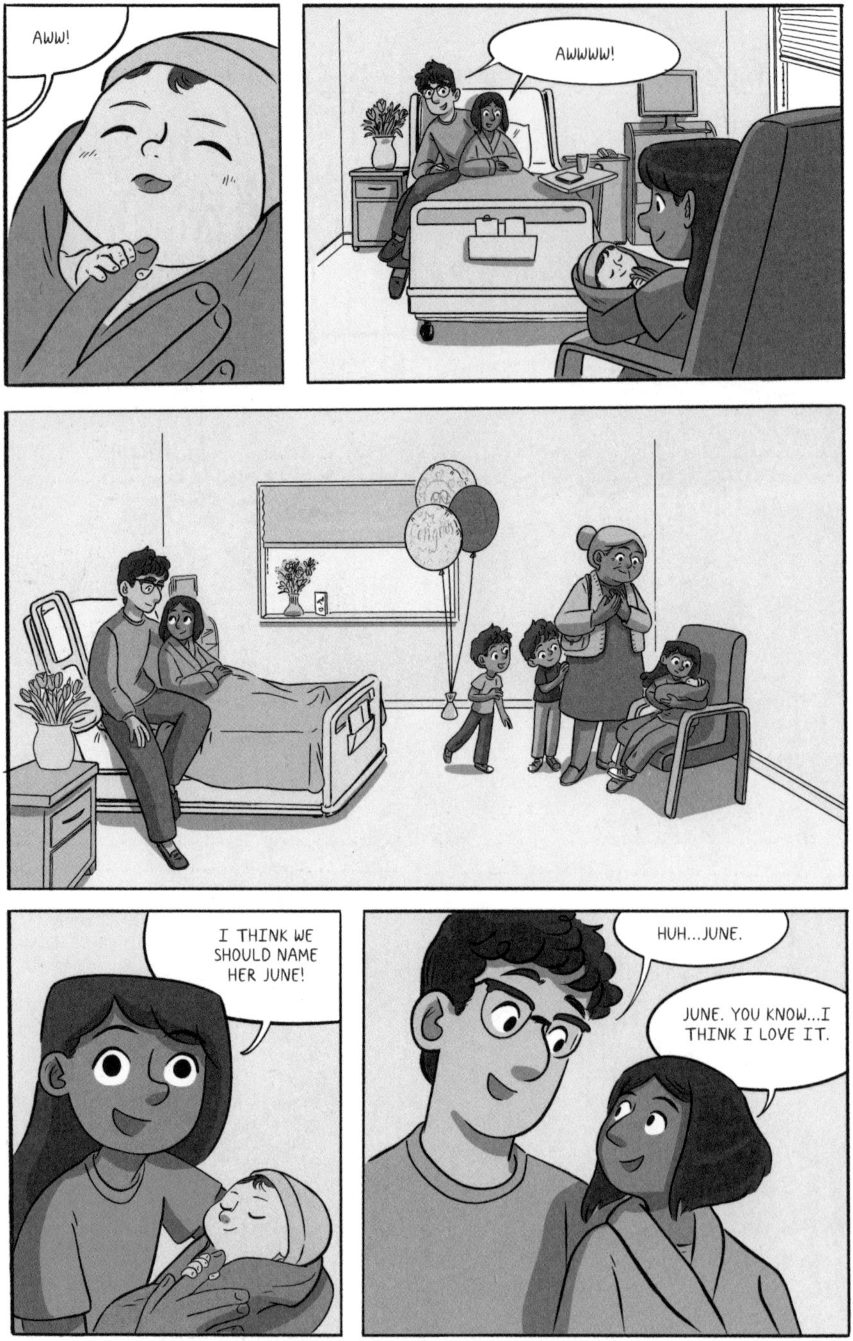
AWW!
AWWWW!
I THINK WE SHOULD NAME HER JUNE!
HUH...JUNE.
JUNE. YOU KNOW...I THINK I LOVE IT.

Chapter Thirteen

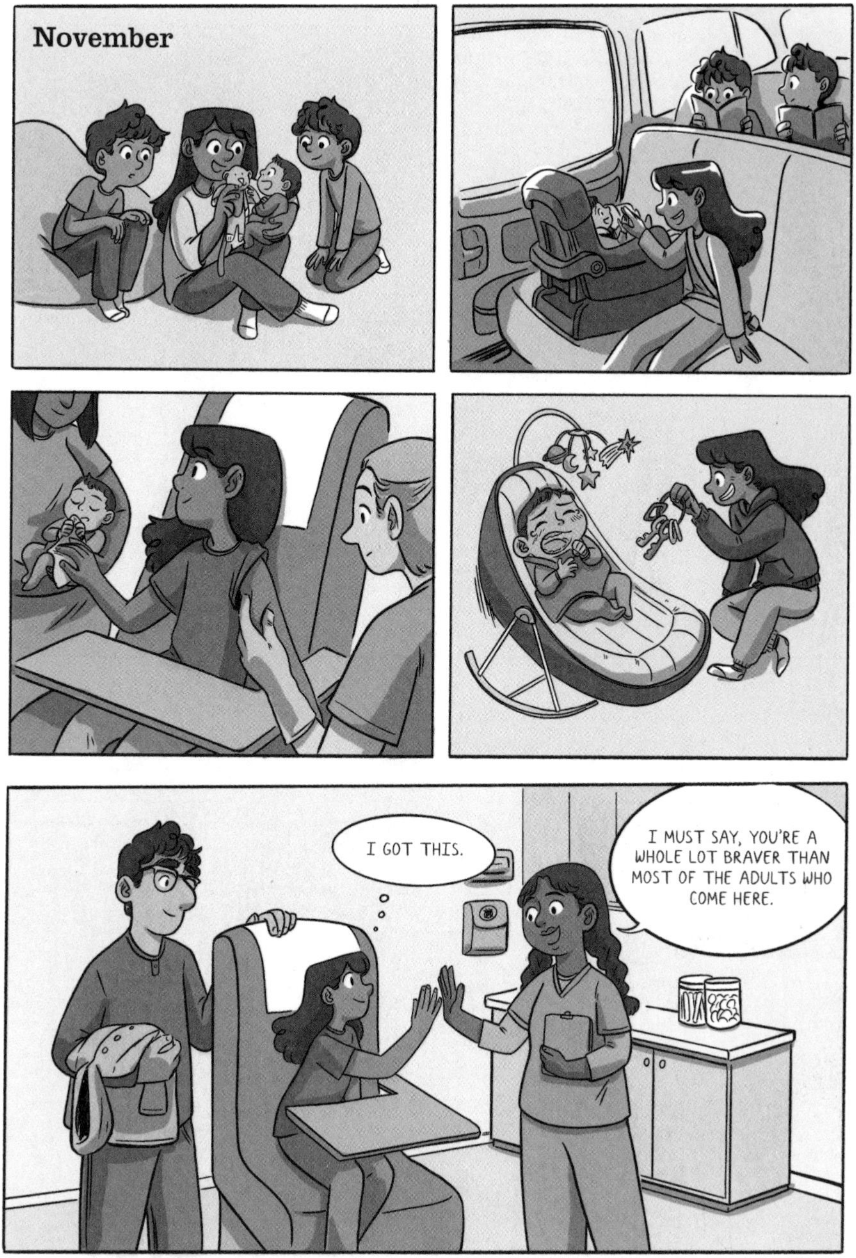
November
I GOT THIS.
I MUST SAY, YOU'RE A WHOLE LOT BRAVER THAN MOST OF THE ADULTS WHO COME HERE.

December

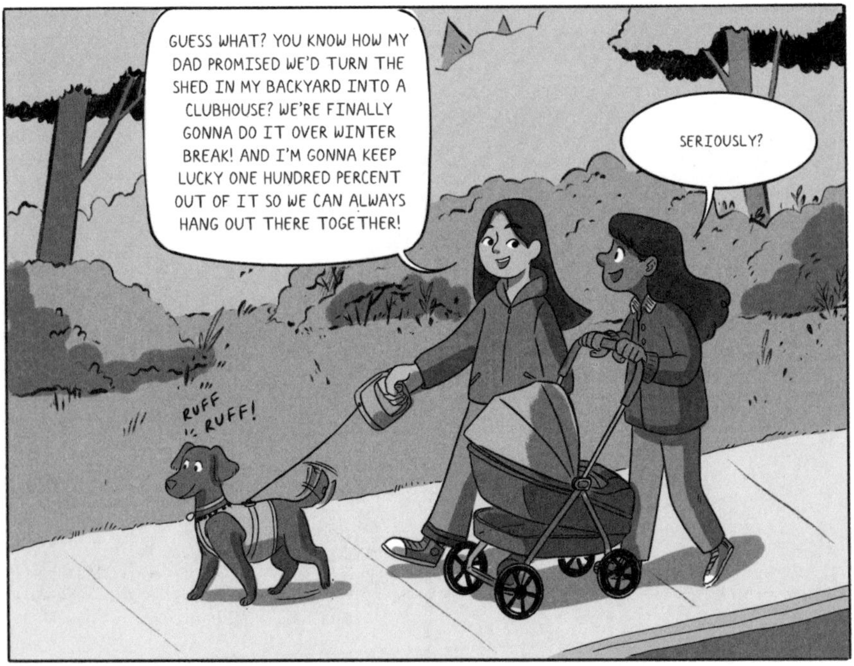
GUESS WHAT? YOU KNOW HOW MY DAD PROMISED WE'D TURN THE SHED IN MY BACKYARD INTO A CLUBHOUSE? WE'RE FINALLY GONNA DO IT OVER WINTER BREAK! AND I'M GONNA KEEP LUCKY ONE HUNDRED PERCENT OUT OF IT SO WE CAN ALWAYS HANG OUT THERE TOGETHER!
SERIOUSLY?
RUFF RUFF!

January

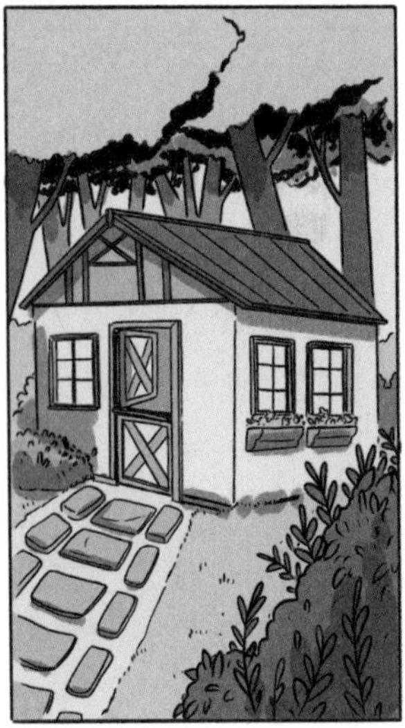

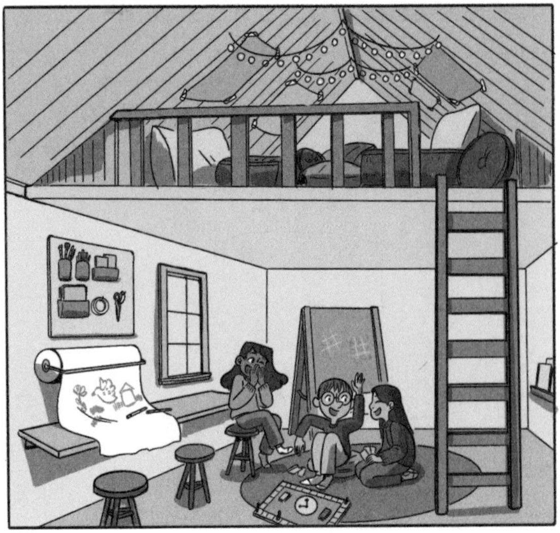

February

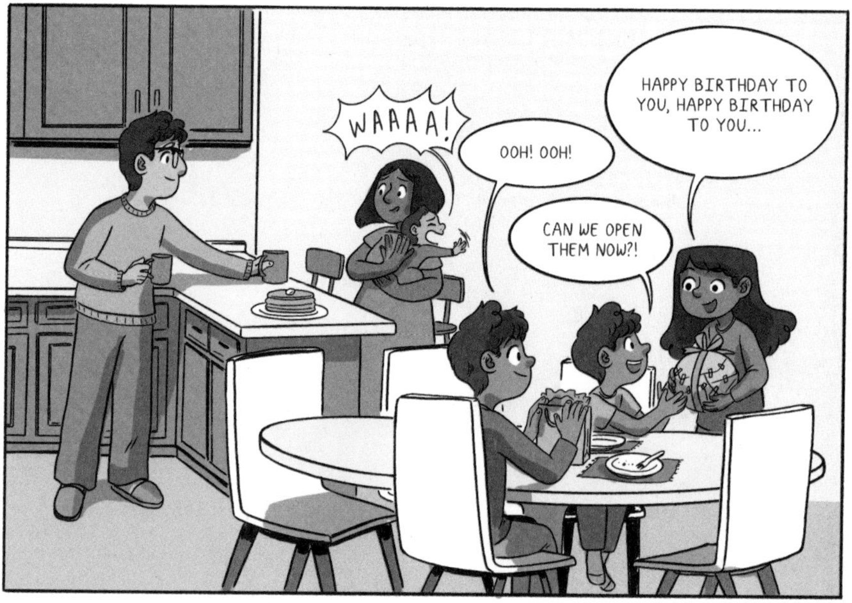
WAAAA!
OOH! OOH!
CAN WE OPEN THEM NOW?!
HAPPY BIRTHDAY TO YOU, HAPPY BIRTHDAY TO YOU...

March

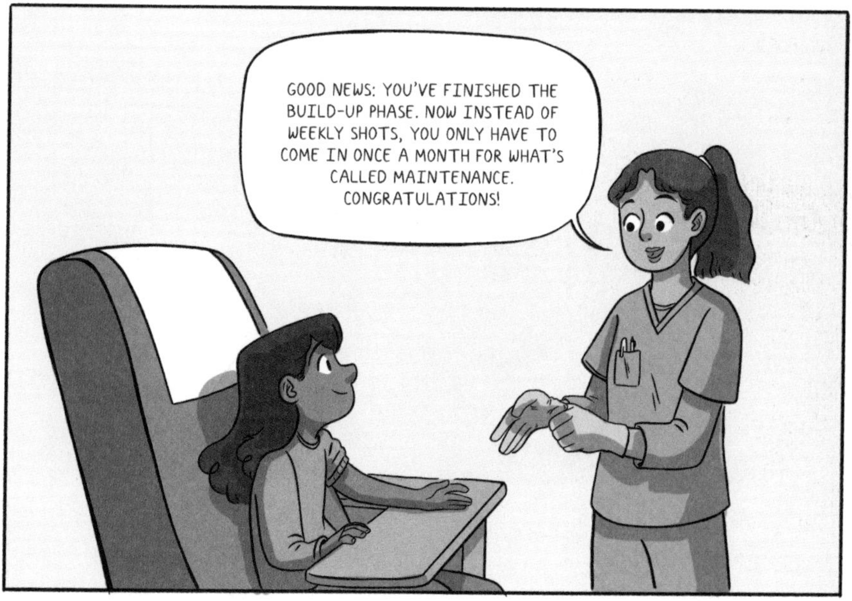
GOOD NEWS: YOU'VE FINISHED THE BUILD-UP PHASE. NOW INSTEAD OF WEEKLY SHOTS, YOU ONLY HAVE TO COME IN ONCE A MONTH FOR WHAT'S CALLED MAINTENANCE. CONGRATULATIONS!

April

May

June

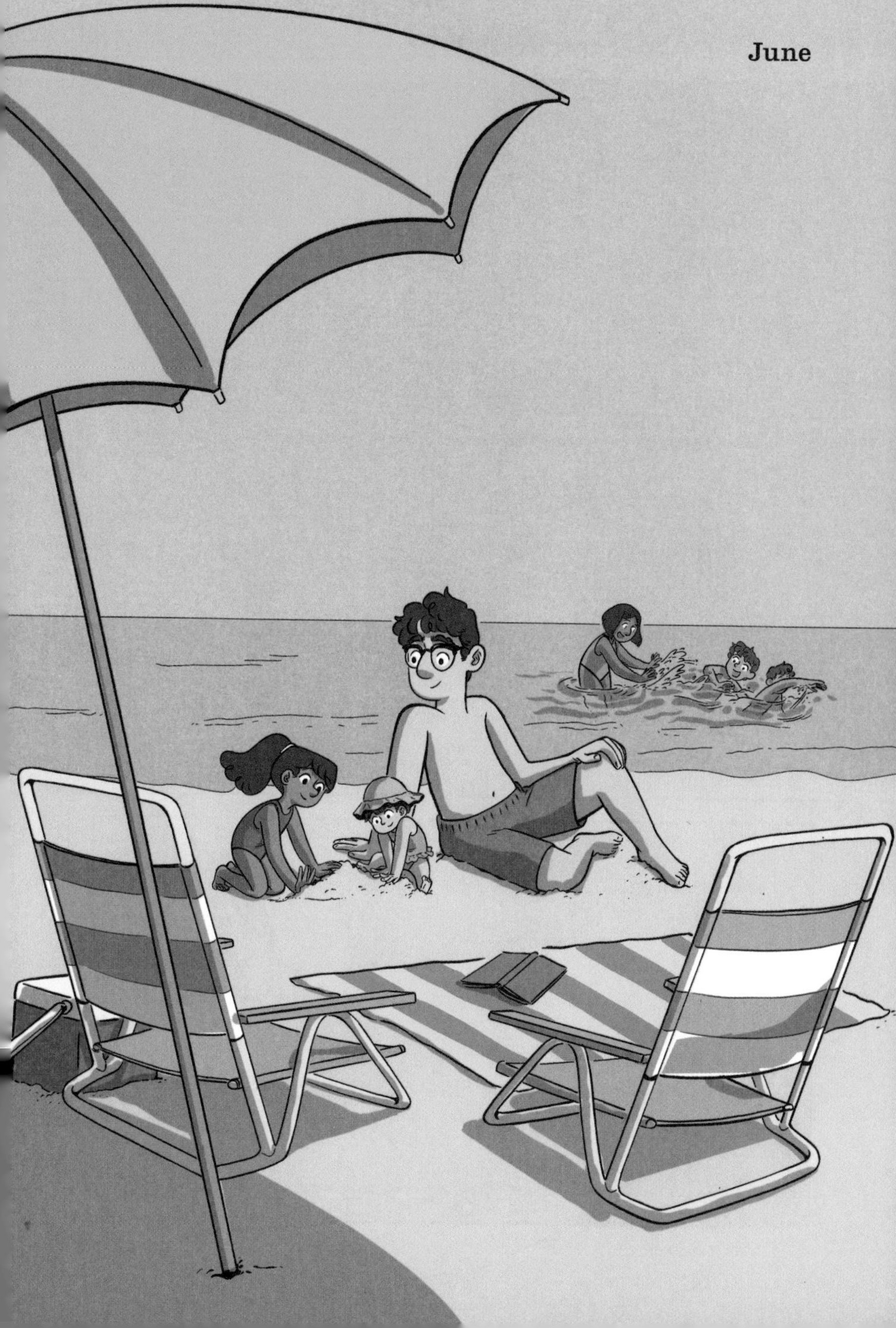

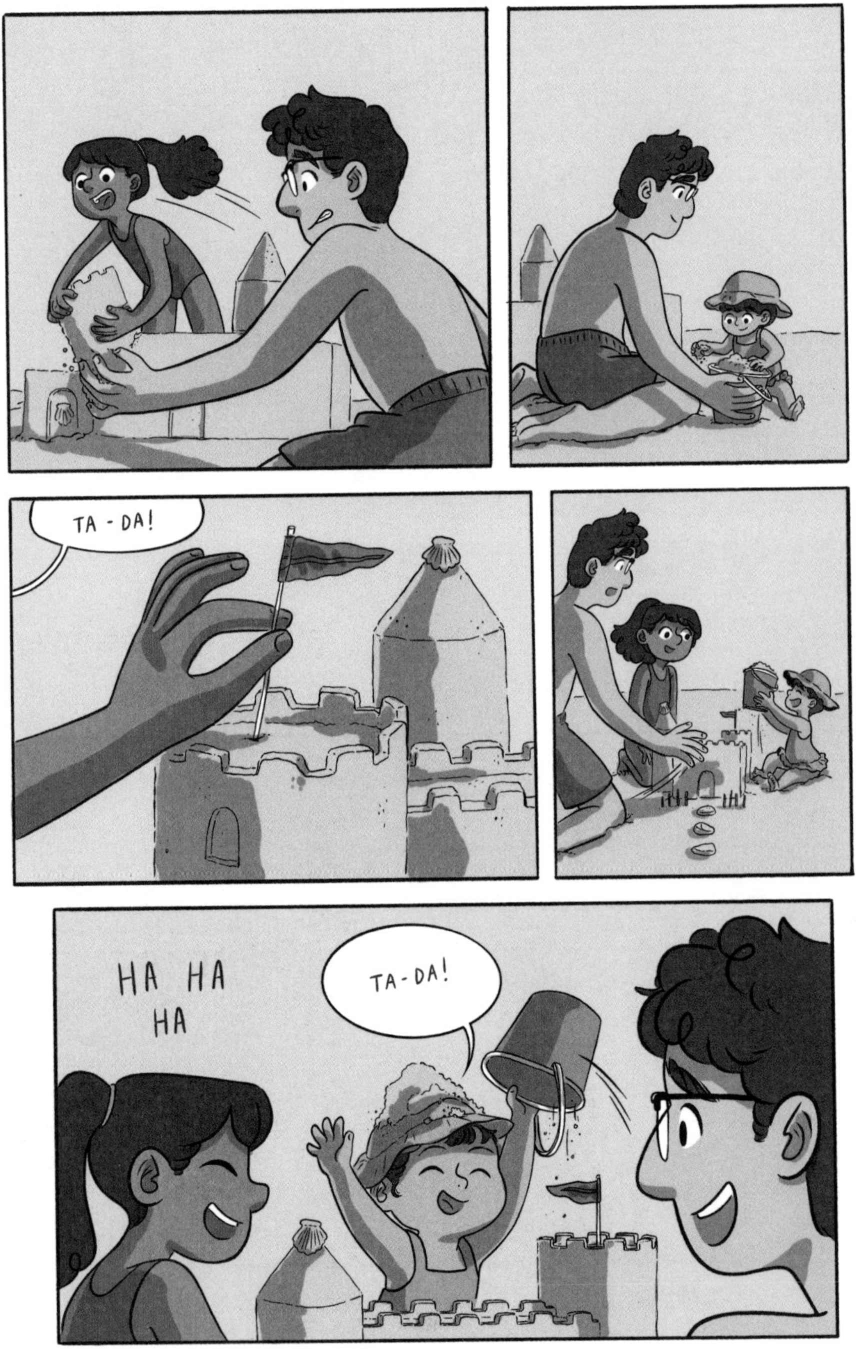
TA - DA!
HA HA HA
TA - DA!

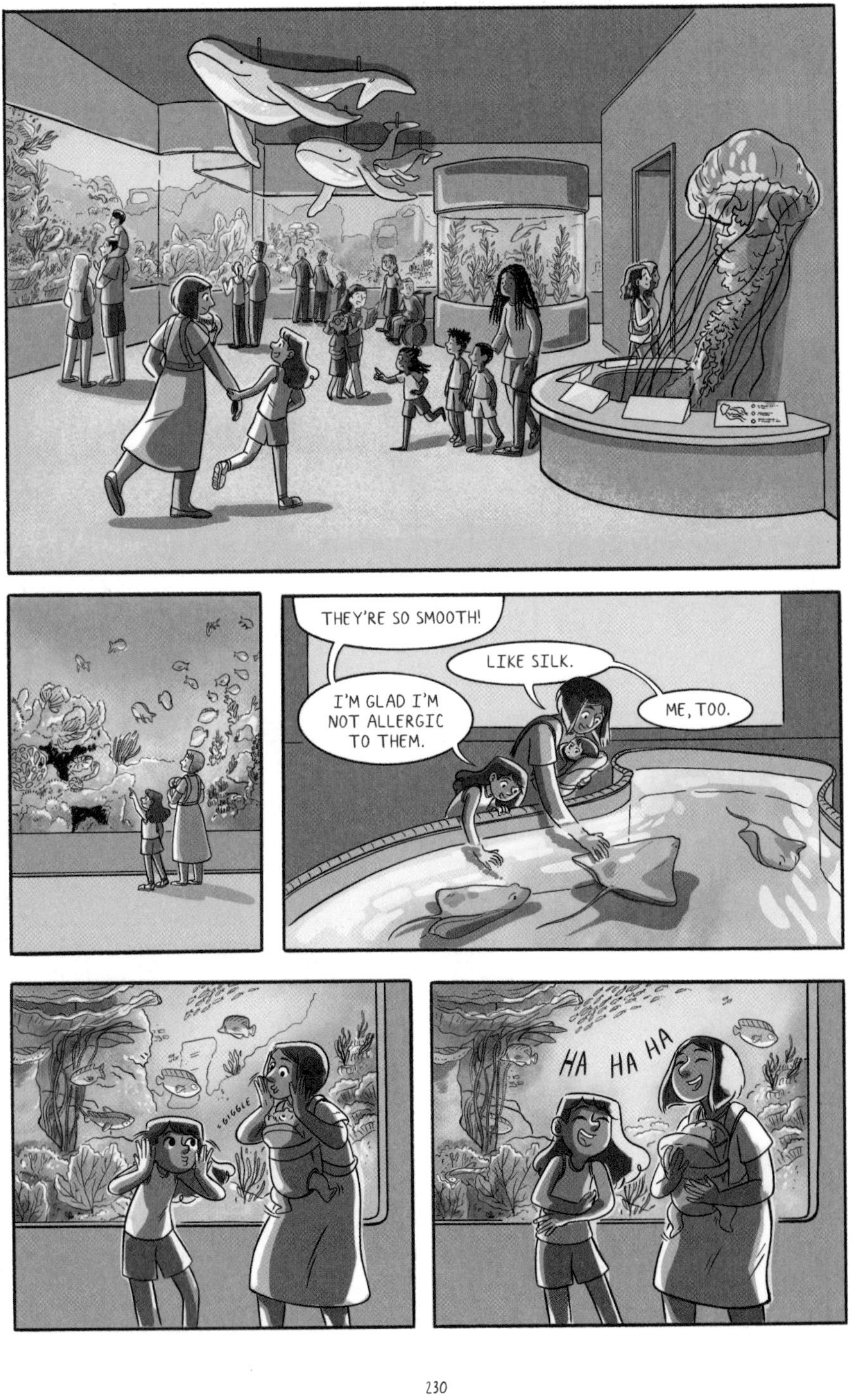
THEY'RE SO SMOOTH!
I'M GLAD I'M NOT ALLERGIC TO THEM.
LIKE SILK.
ME, TOO.
GIGGLE
HA HA HA

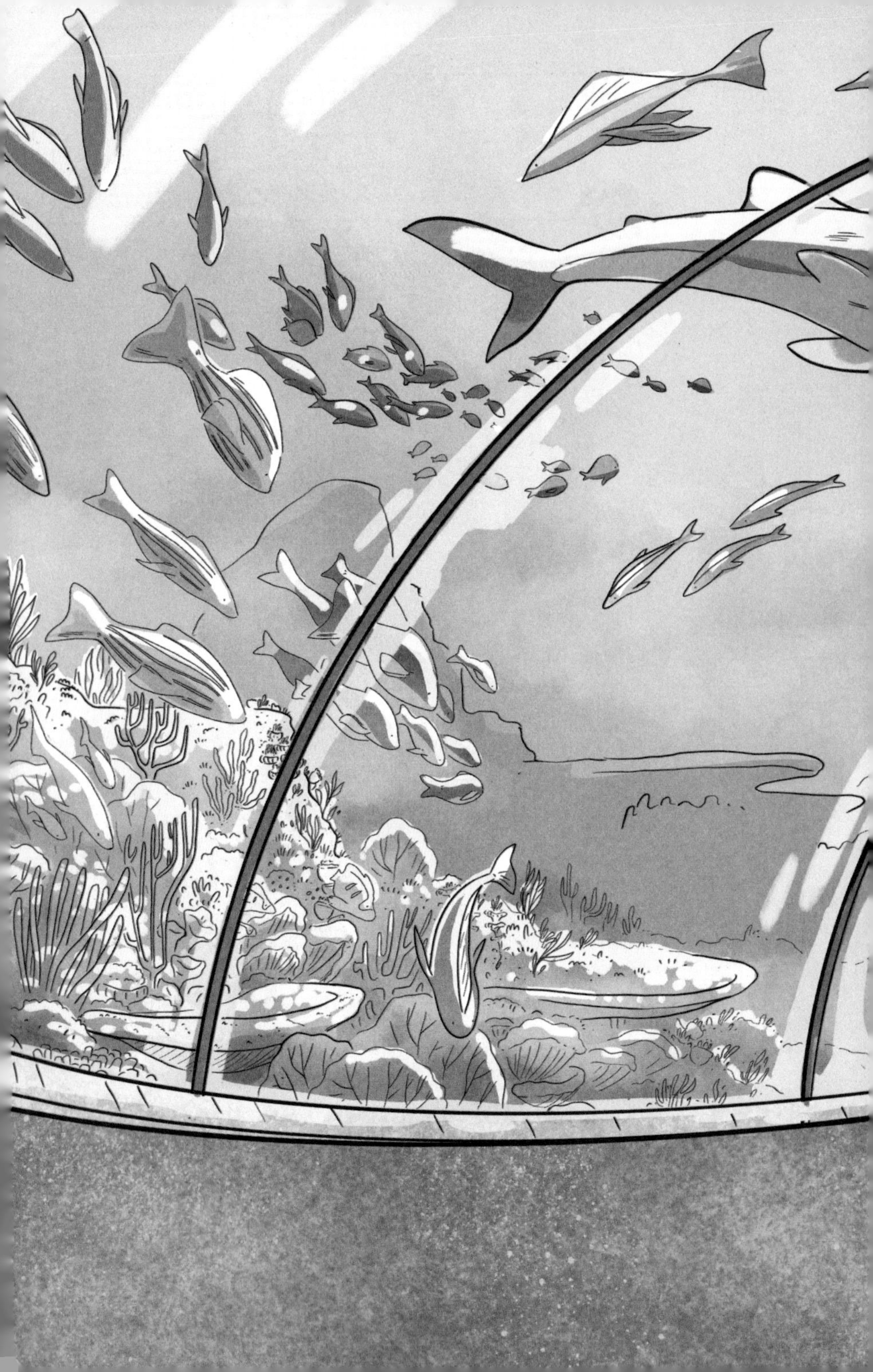

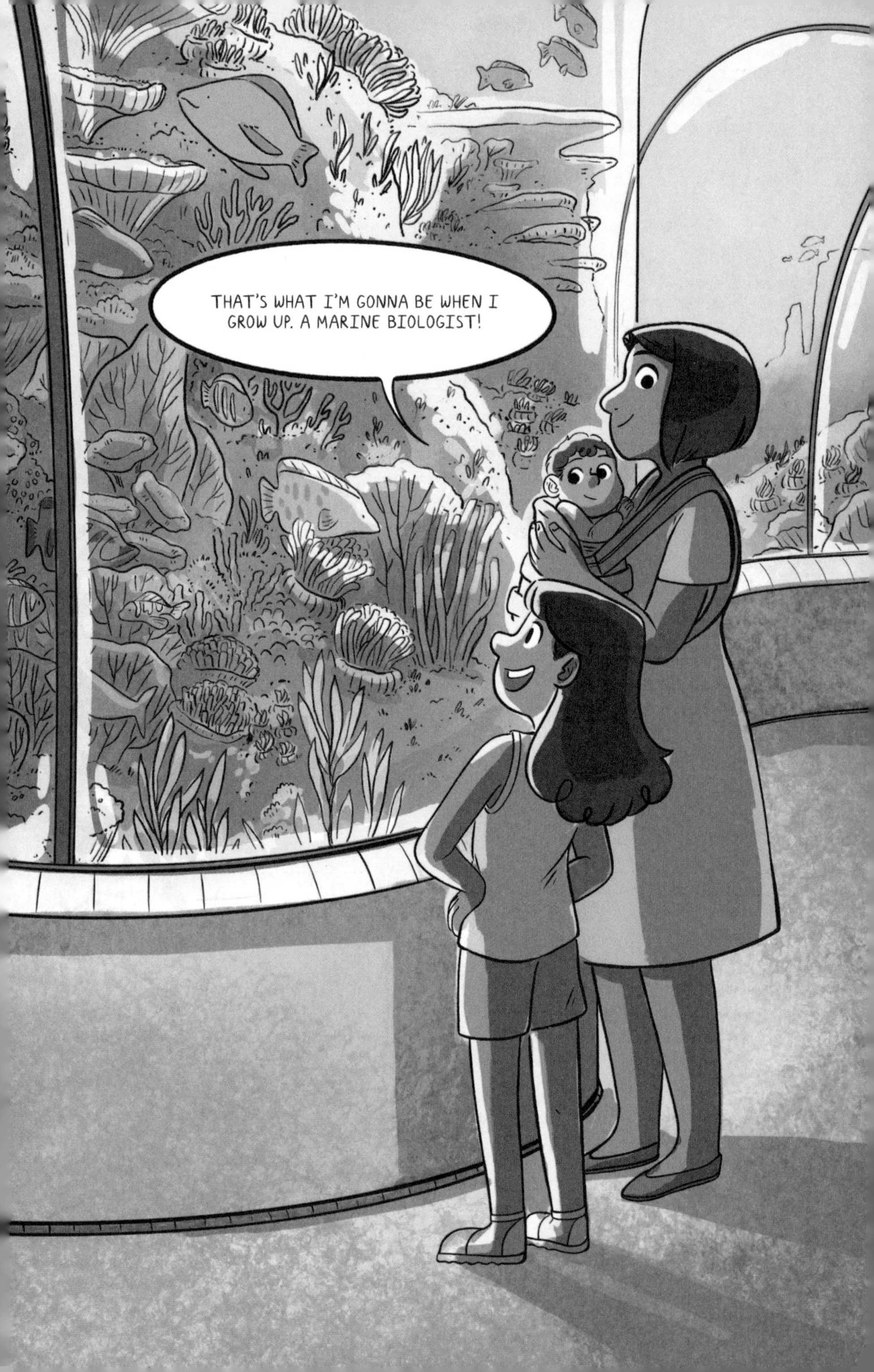
THAT'S WHAT I'M GONNA BE WHEN I GROW UP. A MARINE BIOLOGIST!

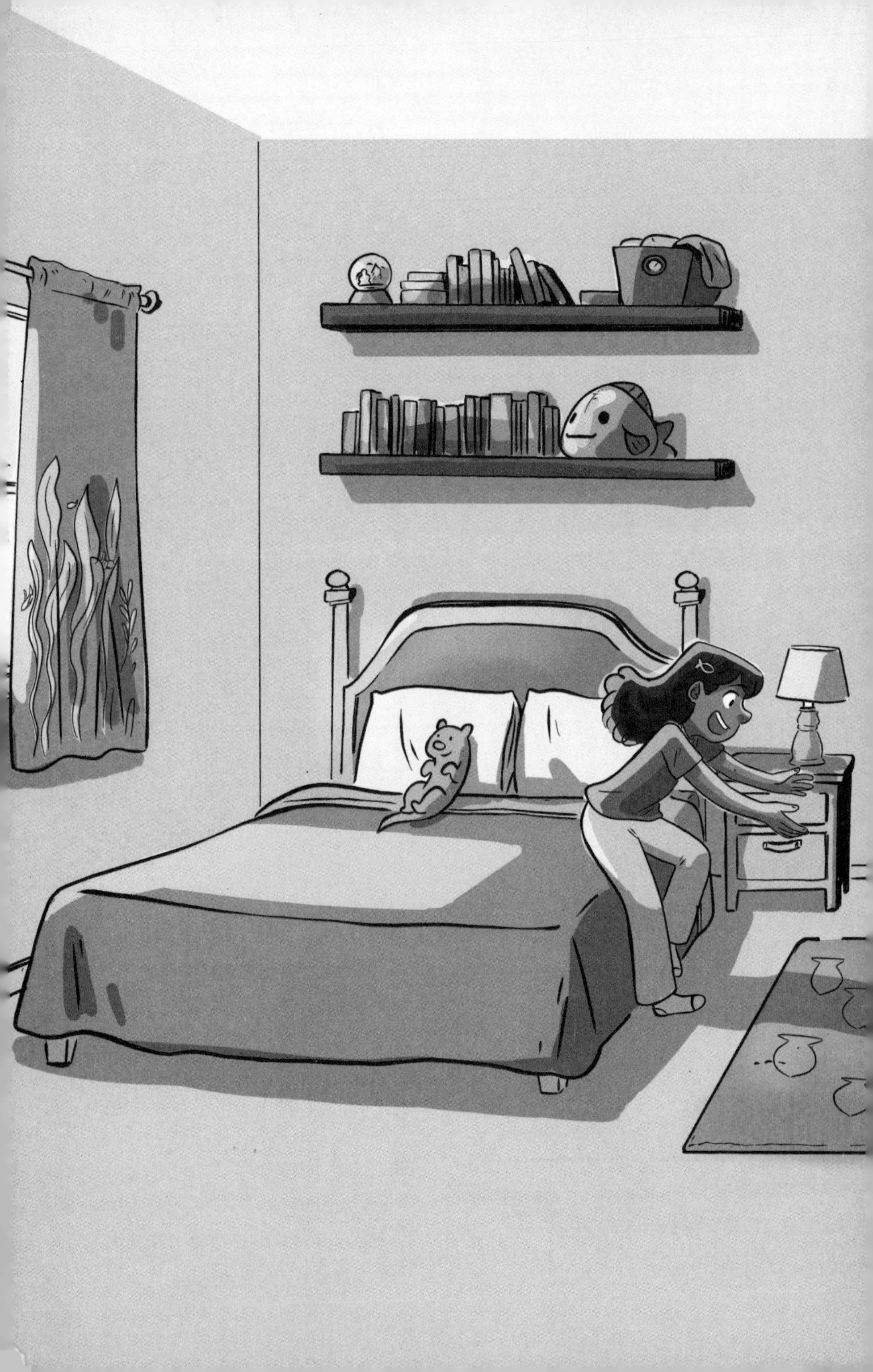

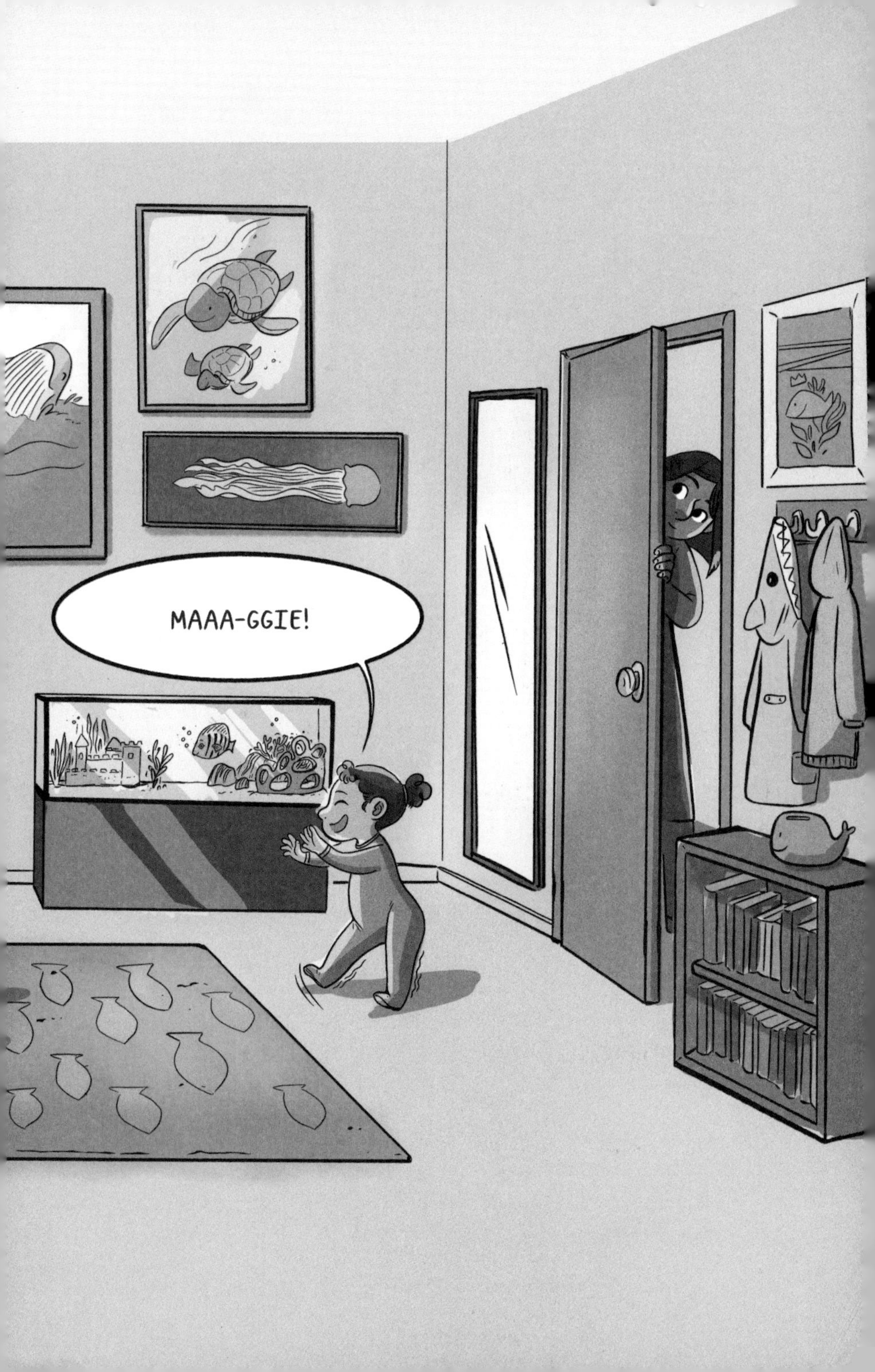
MAAA-GGIE!

Acknowledgments

Thank you to: Ammi-Joan Paquette, for support and enthusiasm from the start. Michelle Mee Nutter, for teaming up, and for incredible, impeccable art. Cassandra Pelham Fulton, for believing in our duo, and for stellar guidance every step of the way. The entire dedicated and creative Scholastic/Graphix team.

Maria Gianferrari and Courtney Pippin-Mathur, for writing lunches and chats. Zara González Hoang, for writing walks and talks. Stacey Donoghue, for helpful early feedback. Anna, the best surprise of my little-kid life. Seth, for never-ending optimism and kindness. And my kids, for believing in *Allergic* from the beginning.

Megan

Thank you to: Megan, for writing such a wonderful story. I couldn't have asked for a better teammate. Kelly Sonnack, for being in my corner as my agent. Ammi-Joan Paquette, for introducing me to *Allergic*. David Saylor and Cassandra Pelham Fulton, for taking a chance on my work. Phil Falco and the whole Graphix team. My amazing flatters, Madison Coyne and Veda Kasireddy.

Mum, Dad, and Joe. Ethan, I love to the moon and back. Thank you for being the reader that inspires me to keep drawing. Greg, for being an amazing partner. Abby, Ryan, Aidan, and Laura. I would truly be lost without all the movie nights, D&D sessions, and hours lying on the floor talking about Ikea furniture.

Finally, thank you for telling me to be open to the possibilities and always reminding me that I could do this. You know who you are, and I will hold that dear to my heart always.

Michelle